ARKANE
THRILLERS
BOOKS 7-9

J.F. PENN

ARKANE Thrillers Books 7-9
Copyright © Joanna Penn 2017. All rights reserved.

One Day in New York. An ARKANE Thriller Book 7
Copyright © J.F. Penn (2015). All rights reserved.

Destroyer of Worlds. An ARKANE Thriller Book 8
Copyright © J.F. Penn (2016). All rights reserved.

End of Days. An ARKANE Thriller Book 9
Copyright © J.F.Penn (2017). All rights reserved.

ISBN: 978-1-912105-90-8

www.JFPenn.com

This book is a work of fiction. The characters, incidents and dialogue are drawn from the author's imagination and are not to be construed as real. Any resemblance to actual events or persons, living or dead, is fictionalized or coincidental.

The right of Joanna Penn to be identified as the author of this work has been asserted by the author in accordance with the Copyright, Designs and Patents Act,1988. All rights reserved. No part of this publication may be reproduced, stored in a retrieval system, or transmitted, in any form, or by any means, electronic,mechanical, photocopying, recording or otherwise, without the prior permission of the publishers.

This book is sold subject to the condition that it shall not, by way of trade or otherwise, be lent, resold, hired out, or otherwise circulated without the author's prior consent in any form of binding or cover other than that in which it is published and without a similar condition being imposed on the subsequent purchaser.

Requests to publish work from this book should be sent to:
joanna@CurlUpPress.com

Cover and Interior Design: JD Smith Design
Printed by Lightning Source UK

www.CurlUpPress.com

CONTENTS

One Day in New York 1

Destroyer of Worlds 99

End of Days 315

ONE DAY IN NEW YORK

AN ARKANE THRILLER
J.F. PENN

"The Nephilim were in the earth in those days, and also after that, when the sons of God came in unto the daughters of men, and they bore children to them; the same were the mighty men that were of old, the men of renown."

Genesis 6:4

"And the angels who did not keep their positions of authority but abandoned their own home – these he has kept in darkness, bound with everlasting chains for judgment on the great Day."

Jude 1:6

CHAPTER 1

FOR ALL THE HYPERVIGILANCE of New Yorkers at the slightest possibility of terrorism, they embrace anything that could be construed as modern art. That's why no one reported the man constructing a strong wooden cross on the High Line that afternoon, next to a section that overlooked the Hudson River to the west. He was young and good looking with an easy smile, his Mediterranean skin burnished by the late sun. He caught the attention of female joggers as they ran past, noting his strong, muscular arms as he sawed the wooden planks. There was a handwritten sign on a cardboard rectangle propped up near his workbench: *Performance art in progress*. That was all the passers-by needed to know, answering any questions that came to mind about his actions.

Later that day, as workers began to stream out of the local offices on the commute home, an older man stopped for a moment. He looked down at the rough wood as the man fixed the cross piece, banging in long nails to hold the planks together.

"You've got that wrong, you know," the man said. "All evidence suggests that the cross Christ died upon would have been more like a T-shape."

The carpenter paused a moment.

"The emphasis of this particular piece is more about emotional resonance than historical truth." He had a slight French accent, but in this city of diversity, that was not markedly unusual. The older man nodded slowly, rubbing his fingers across his beard before he moved on, just another walker enjoying the evening sun.

The High Line was a disused railway track, raised above the streets of Lower West Side Manhattan and transformed into a boulevard of wild grasses, flowerbeds and wooden seating where bees buzzed and birds sang in the heart of the city. The views out across the city landscape and the wide river made it a tourist draw as well as a haunt for local runners and walkers, desperate for a moment of peace above the throng. There were places on the High Line where nature had reclaimed a little corner of the metropolis, and those who craved escape came here to temporarily relieve the itch of the city. Buskers played along these sections, the sound of a jazz saxophone easing the evening into night, and still the carpenter worked on, building a base to hold the cross steady when he raised it into the sky. When that was done, he fixed pieces of rubber tire onto the cross at jaunty angles, the black material lending an urban grittiness to the simple wooden frame, a dark foil for the sunset.

As the night grew darker and the bars began to fill up below the High Line, street food vendors set up stalls to cater to those who wanted dinner with their nature walk. Far more convenient than the wilderness any day and just a stroll from Midtown. The carpenter bought a taco and watched people as they passed. His sign on the ground had gathered a few dollars over the day, perhaps a manifestation of guilt from the city elite for the artlessness of their own lives, briefly assuaged by paying another to be creative on their behalf – like doubting believers paying tithes on a Sunday. Several people had taken photos as he worked, and later those pictures would find their way into the papers. But the carpenter had no fear of discovery, for soon he would be heading back to the monastery – beyond the reach of the tentacles of this sinful city. He understood the necessity of what was to come, but he longed for peace and solitude.

He looked at his watch. Only one more part of the structure remained to be built, a simple pulley mechanism that would help lift its weight so the cross could be drawn upright and seen from the city streets below. The carpenter turned back to his work, clearing his mind of the sounds of the sinners around him. When the relic was recovered, they would be screaming soon enough.

After the final nail was hammered in, the carpenter sat in the dark, waiting, his breathing a calm meditation. As the clock neared two a.m., this area of the city was quieter. Most of the bars were closed but, of course, New York is the city that never sleeps. An audience could be guaranteed for their spectacle at any time.

He heard a car pull up on the street below, the bang of a door and the sound of several pairs of footsteps followed by a dragging sound and the shuffling of feet. The carpenter remained still, every sense heightened. Then a whistle came from the dark in the agreed pattern. He relaxed. The time had come, and now they would need to move fast.

The carpenter pulled a large holdall from beneath the bench he sat on. Unzipping it, he lifted out several cans of gasoline and began to douse the base of the cross. He poured the liquid up around the cross piece, making sure the fragments of tire were coated. The stink of the accelerant made him cough, and he tried to stifle the noise.

Two men ascended from the nearest staircase, half dragging a figure between them wrapped in a voluminous cloak. All three had their heads covered. As they came closer, the men pulled back their cowls. The carpenter looked away from the taller figure, his once handsome face disfigured by rubbled and lumpy skin, dark in places where the pigment had changed. There were rumors of an assassination attempt, a power play gone wrong. Many had tried to kill this man, and all had failed. He wasn't a Confessor, but the carpenter had heard of his relationship with the upper echelons, and knew his orders must be obeyed. The other man was the Monseigneur, the most senior Confessor in New York, with closely cropped white hair and wrinkled skin, but eyes that were as hard as the stone he knelt to pray on. The carpenter crossed himself, bowing towards his superior.

The two men dragged the captive forward. The figure tripped and fell sideways, staggering a little. The cowl slid off and the carpenter stifled a gasp. He hadn't expected a woman, even as he knew the servants of evil came in all forms. The woman's head drooped on her chest, her long grey hair loose about her face. She had been badly beaten, and blood stained the clothes he could see beneath the folds of the cloak. Her face was swollen and mashed, and a stained gag was wrapped around her mouth. She opened her eyes as the stink of gasoline roused her, and the carpenter was hypnotized by the piercing blue. He crossed himself again as the two men dragged the woman to the cross.

"I hope you've prepared well," the Monseigneur grunted. "She would only speak of the ivory artifact. The location of the corpus is still unknown, but it's a step in the quest. For now, she will be a sign to those who know how to look."

He pushed the woman down. She tried to crawl a little way and the Monseigneur grabbed her by the hair and pulled her back to the cross, forcing her to lie upon it.

They used rope to tie her wrists to the cross piece and her feet to the shaft. The carpenter doused a long strip of linen with more gasoline and then wound it around her waist and torso, further binding her to the wood. She didn't make a sound as they worked, and the carpenter avoided her gaze, crossing himself repeatedly. This was for the glory of God, wasn't it? He had been told that this action would help the Confessors with the mission to this city, for if something wasn't done, the fate of Sodom and Gomorrah would take down this island of iniquity. But he hadn't expected that the sign to the world would be this old woman.

A siren came from the road below. The men froze in their work, waiting for it to pass before they continued. When the woman was finally well attached, they hoisted the cross up so she hung there, silhouetted against the backdrop of the city lights.

"God spoke to Moses through a pillar of fire," the Monseigneur said. "Tonight he will speak through this sacrifice."

The scarred man held up a smart phone and activated a camera, focusing it on the crucifix. The carpenter pulled a lighter from his bag along with several tapers. The men each took one and the Monseigneur began to pray aloud in Latin, his voice unwavering. They lit the ends, their faces illuminated by the flaring light. The woman finally seemed to realize what was happening and she began to thrash on the cross, the bonds loosening a little at her wrists as she moaned against the gag.

The Monseigneur leaned forward with his taper, touching the flame to the accelerant on the base of the cross, and the scarred man stretched up to apply his to the end of the cloth wrapped around the woman's torso. His smile spoke of dark desires and the carpenter crossed himself again as he touched his own taper to the base of the cross. He averted his eyes from the woman, who twisted as the flames caught the folds of her gown and billowed around her thin legs. The smell of cooking flesh weaved through the air, mingling with the gasoline. The first of the tires caught and black smoke billowed into the sky.

"Beautiful," the scarred man said with a sigh, zooming his camera in on the woman's tortured face. The whoop of sirens cut through the crackling of flames. "It's a shame we can't stay until the end."

The three men walked away from the burning cross, but the carpenter turned back as they reached the stairs. For a moment, he thought he could hear the beat of huge wings fanning the flames into brightness, but there was nothing behind the sacrifice. The woman writhed in her bonds, her hair on fire, scarlet orange against the black smoke – like the spirit of the elements alighting upon her. She was a human torch with the pitch of Hell and the flames of Satan. The carpenter could hear her screams behind the gag and he hoped that she would succumb to the smoke before the fire consumed her flesh. He crossed himself one last time and followed the others down to the streets below.

CHAPTER 2

Hissing filled his consciousness, the head of the viper bobbing and weaving as it reared to strike. He tried to back away but he was cornered in the tunnel, the rock trapping him. The snake darted forward and sharp pain blossomed on his skin, setting his blood aflame as he felt the fangs sink into his flesh.

Jake Timber woke with a start, heart racing, sweat on his skin, breath coming hard. He ripped the eye mask from his face with a gasp.

"Are you alright, sir?" An air stewardess leaned over him.

Jake shook his head, clearing the vision of the nightmare. "Yes … I'm fine, thank you."

"Then would you please fasten your seatbelt?"

She smiled and walked on to attend to other passengers as the announcement came over the tannoy.

"Cabin crew, prepare for landing."

Jake looked out of the window as the plane descended through the clouds. He craved coffee, but it would have to wait now. He couldn't seem to get enough rest at the moment, and he knew his body still suffered the residual poison from the snake bite he'd suffered in Israel on the last mission. He rubbed at his arm; the puncture marks had faded, but the memory still lingered. The nest of snakes deep in the caves of Sodom appeared in his nightmares now, mingling with his memories of Africa.

His ARKANE partner, Morgan Sierra, was still in Israel, sitting shiva in mourning for a friend who had been lost in their last battle. Jake pushed down the guilt he felt for leaving Morgan alone, for not being the partner she needed. Instead, he had been medically evacuated from Israel as she pursued the Key to the Gates of Hell on her own. But mourning was something she needed to do alone, and Jake had welcomed the chance to come to New York on what was supposed to be a quick mission – a favor for the local office, which was busy at the best of times. He needed the distraction.

Jake pulled the smart phone from his bag and scrolled through the files that Martin Klein had sent. There was a special exhibition later today at the Cloisters, part of the Metropolitan Museum of Art in northern Manhattan. The central item on display was a cross of curious origin and unique carvings, hidden for generations but now on show. The Cloisters Cross, as it was known, had come up in some chatter ARKANE had detected in an extremist forum they monitored on the dark net. The Arcane Religious Knowledge And Numinous Experience Institute was a secret research center for investigating supernatural mysteries across all religions, but recently it was the rise of Christian fundamentalism that had raised red flags. This cross was supposedly connected to a relic, rumored to be the blood of a dark angel, and it had attracted the attention of a number of fringe groups.

The museum of medieval artifacts was not considered a high-risk location, but the New York office had requested a European agent on the ground, someone who could blend into the medieval academic milieu. Jake had happily volunteered, needing something to keep his mind off Morgan, although he was usually more at home in leather than tweed.

If he was honest, this was also about testing himself and getting his confidence back again. A string of injuries had plagued Jake's last few missions, and he found himself questioning his ability in the field. He was even considering whether he should stay with ARKANE; whether Morgan would be better with another partner. He hoped this time away would help him with that decision.

Walking out of the security area a little later, Jake scanned the rows of people for a sign with his name on it. A little boy rushed from behind the barrier, his arms raised high.

"Daddy!" he shouted, leaping into the arms of a man nearby who bent to embrace his son. Jake couldn't help but smile, despite the pang that clenched his heart. Airports were always emotional places for those without family.

He was supposed to be met by one of the local agents, but he didn't know who it was going to be. Jake knew few of them by name, as he'd been focused mainly on Europe and Africa so far in his career. This would be his first time working with ARKANE stateside. Although London was the main ARKANE office, New York was a big local hub for the investigation of religious and supernatural mysteries in North America. The public face of ARKANE was academic, a research institute for religious objects, but the reality was more complicated – a battle waged daily between the forces of good and evil that most would consider myth. There were certainly enough cases here to keep the team occupied.

As Jake scanned the crowd, he caught sight of a stunning mixed-race woman, her black hair long and shiny, her dark skin almost luminous. She smiled at him and he couldn't help but return the greeting. He was surprised when she held his eyes, waving as she weaved between the crowds of people and approached him. She wore a navy blue tailored suit that suggested she worked in the halls of bureaucracy, but still managed to flatter her curves.

"I'm Naomi Locasto," she said, holding out a slim hand. "I'm with the ARKANE team here in New York, and I'll be working with you today."

Jake took her hand, shaking it as he tried to stop himself staring. Her unusual features gave her the look of a supermodel, her full lips African American, her dark eyes and arched eyebrows almost Latino and her straight black hair a shade of Native American. *Welcome to New York*, Jake thought. Perhaps this trip would be more than just a distraction.

"We've had a crazy morning already," Naomi said, as she led Jake towards the pickup area. "A woman was crucified and burned to death on the High Line before dawn. No one has claimed it yet, but the police notified us because of the religious overtones of the murder."

"Who was the victim?" Jake asked as he climbed into the passenger side of the car.

Naomi frowned. "We can't seem to trace her. The body was burned beyond recognition. There's nothing at the scene to identify her and no matching missing persons record. All we know is that she was an older woman who hadn't given birth, and that she died horribly. To be honest, we thought about canceling our attendance at the Cloisters exhibition today, but since you're here …"

"I'm happy to go alone," Jake said. "It's just a monitoring exercise as I understand it, and it's a good chance to brush up on my medieval history."

"You don't really look like an academic," Naomi said, glancing sideways as she pulled out into the freeway traffic headed towards Manhattan. Jake could see she noticed his corkscrew scar, just one of the many that knitted his body together. "Can I ask where you're from? Your accent has a hint of something not quite British."

"I'm from South Africa," Jake said. "But I've lived and worked in England a long time now. Archbishop Desmond Tutu once called my country the Rainbow People of God, but these days it's more of a shattered prism. There are engrained attitudes on so many sides that I struggle to be there … plus, there's no one left to go back for anymore." Jake stared out of the window, surprised to be sharing such intimate details about his homeland with a complete stranger. But something about this woman set him at ease. He looked back at her. "Besides, I prefer a culture of blended people, those whose history has allowed for more intermingling over time, and London gives me that."

Naomi smiled.

"That's why I love New York too," she said. "In this melting pot of cultures, relationships naturally happen between people of all walks of life, like my own blended family. My maternal grandparents are Eastern European Jewish and African American, and on my father's side I have Cherokee and Puerto Rican blood." She smiled with pride. "I rise above definable race categories but in this town, that makes me pretty normal. I love that."

"I think you'd like London, too."

Naomi glanced over, her dark eyes holding a hint of flirtation. "Maybe I'll come visit sometime."

A beat of silence and Jake turned to gaze out the window again as they headed into town. There was a strange sense of the familiar as they drove through the city. New York was one big movie set, where the fire hydrants and yellow taxis immediately made the visitor feel at home, as they had been seen so many times before on screen. The street signs, the accents, the architecture – it was all familiar and oddly comforting.

Jake watched a pedestrian traffic sign shift to WALK and a wave of suits crossed the road, eyes fixed forward in big-city anonymity. *Don't look at me and I won't look at you.* As in London, you could be anyone in New York, and no one would bat an eyelash. The dwellers of this urban jungle were protective of the unusual and extreme, the right to stand out as sacred as that of making cold hard cash.

Naomi looked at her watch as they drove onto Manhattan Island.

"We'll go straight to the museum," she said. "We don't want to miss the tour before the grand unveiling of the cross."

Fifteen minutes later, they pulled into the driveway leading up to the Cloisters museum and gardens. The complex was part of the Metropolitan Museum of Art, but the Central Park location meant that the latter was always packed and busy. In comparison, this was an oasis of calm at Fort Tryon Park in the very north of Manhattan, a collection of medieval art in a rebuilt monastery overlooking the Hudson River. It was a surprising slice of European heritage in the modern city.

The architects had managed a coherence in the structure even though the buildings were made up of several different cloisters, rectangular courtyards for prayer and contemplation. The strong Romanesque style of the eleventh and twelfth centuries was characterized by round arches and barrel vaults, while the Gothic made itself known through pointed arches and freer ornamentation. It was a kind of architectural Frankenstein, constructed out of bits of history from French and Spanish monasteries, the effect one of unusual style elements blended by a passion for the medieval world.

The bright sun cut through Jake's fatigue and he closed his eyes for a second, letting it warm his face as they pulled into the carpark. In these little moments of calm, it was good to just be grateful for a warm day.

"Stay there a moment," Naomi said, getting out of the car. Jake opened his eyes to see her walking towards a silver van selling coffee. He smiled. Some of the places he traveled for ARKANE made it hard to get a good brew, but at least here in New York, it was pretty much guaranteed. Naomi returned with two steaming cups and a couple of pastries in a bag.

"You're a lifesaver," Jake said. He took a bite of the crumbling sweetness and sipped his coffee, starting to feel more human again. "So tell me why you're babysitting me for this little trip?"

"I'm a linguist," Naomi said, her dark eyes fixed on Jake. "There are over 800 languages spoken in New York, and many of the religious and supernatural occurrences require language expertise. Of course, I don't speak them all, but I love a challenge so I tend to get assigned to most cases in one way or another. The cross we're here to see has an unknown script on it that can't be translated. Some say it's a form of corrupted Hebrew, a mistake from the Middle Ages, but I want to see it for myself. To be honest, I'm not usually in the field – I'm office bound, but none of the other agents were up for this assignment."

"The notes I was sent imply the cross was originally British. Is that right?" Jake said. He took a bite of the second pastry.

Naomi nodded. "The provenance has never been proved, and the British government didn't buy it originally because the art dealer wouldn't reveal his source. But one scholar suggests it was originally from the Abbey of Bury St Edmunds, one of the wealthiest monasteries in England."

"Until Henry VIII dissolved them all, of course," Jake said, wiping the crumbs on a napkin. "Let's go see this marvel."

CHAPTER 3

JAKE AND NAOMI WALKED into the Cloisters main entrance, and an usher directed them towards a small group of specially invited scholars milling about as they waited for the tour prior to the unveiling of the cross. There was a muted excitement in the air, a level appropriate for academics whose passion remained of the more intellectual kind. The group congregated in one of the main Cloisters, a rectangular court constructed from fragments of the Benedictine monastery of San Miguel de Cuixà near the Pyrenees. Columns of Languedoc marble in shades of coral surrounded a garden with a fountain in the center, the sound of the water a peaceful refrain. Jake had a peculiar sense of being transplanted in time and space, the European architecture making it seem as if he had flown across the ocean for hours, only to arrive in nearby France.

A man stepped up into one of the Gothic arches so he was framed by the dark stone. He brushed his thinning grey hair to one side, pushed his glasses up his nose and coughed slightly to get the attention of the group. He waited for a hush before starting, his voice reedy and slightly high pitched with nerves.

"Welcome, esteemed colleagues from around the

world. I'm the curator of artifacts and today we're so excited to share the Cloisters Cross with you, revealed for the first time in its entirety. Well, almost." The curator smiled. "We have hunted down the base of the artifact but the figure of Christ, the corpus, continues to evade us. Still, it is truly a marvel to see this impeccable and unique medieval artifact. It is one of only three almost complete medieval crosses in the world." He paused for dramatic effect. "Follow me."

The curator turned and walked through the archway, followed by the group of academics – mostly men and a few older women. Naomi certainly stood out in the crowd and Jake noticed a few appreciative glances in her direction.

It was cool as they walked through the stone corridors, surrounded by the glories of medieval Europe. One door was flanked by a pair of sculpted figures that guarded the entryway, while around them on the walls was a bestiary of animals. Jake found his pace slowing as he looked from side to side, noticing a dragon curling its tail around a tree portrayed in sepia fresco.

"It's an amazing place," he whispered to Naomi. "It feels so familiar and yet, the way it's arranged jars somehow, like something is just out of place."

Naomi shook her head with a smile. "I know, and I can't believe I haven't visited before. Living in New York for so long and yet I still don't know all its treasures."

They emerged into another courtyard open to the sky above. The curator paused. The scent of lavender and rosemary filled the air, overlaying a more complex aroma.

"We have a medieval garden here at the Cloisters," he said. "We grow the herbs, fruits and flowers that the monks would have had in those far-off times. Tending of the gardens was considered a holy duty, as much as prayer, and we like to think we continue to praise the Creator with our efforts. In celebration, we would like to offer you all some tea made from our garden of medieval herbs before we proceed into the main event."

The curator waved a hand and a group of servers carried trays forward, handing out steaming cups of hot liquid, the smell an enticing mixture of flower petals and a medicinal tinge of peppermint.

Jake handed a cup to Naomi and took one for himself, blowing on it a little before taking a sip. There was an aniseed note, a floral edge, and the overall taste was refreshing – perfect for jet lag. Around them, the academics drank enthusiastically, discussing the vintage as if it were a rare wine. Then they followed the curator onwards into a large room, with stone blockwork like the walls of a castle turret. It had a low ceiling held up by arched spines and columns topped by carvings of plants. Windows on one side let in a blueish light from outside. In the center of the room, a cross stood mounted on a stone plinth, starkly illuminated from above to highlight the elaborate carvings. It was delicate, slightly bowed in shape, and a warm golden color. A hush fell over the group as they gathered around the sacred object.

The curator held his hands together, fingertips touching as if he was about to pray. His voice was sonorous, the acoustics resonating his words as he spoke with gravitas.

"It has been said that the symbolism on the Cloisters Cross is akin to that of the Sistine Chapel compressed into an object you can hold in your hands. It's made of morse ivory, the traditional term for walrus tusk, carbon dated to the end of the seventh century. It was perhaps 500 years old when it was carved, so it was already an object of antiquity."

The curator walked around the cross, reveling in his chance to impress a captive audience with his knowledge. "You need to examine it from all angles to appreciate the master craftsmanship as the carvings emerge from all surfaces. It was originally decorated with color, and traces of ultramarine blue, malachite and vermilion have been found on the surface, all pigments used by Romanesque artists." The curator tilted his head to one side, gazing at the cross. "Personally, I prefer the unadorned simplicity. Come, you may gather closer to examine it."

The center of the cross was a round engraved medallion. Each of the top three arms ended in a square terminal, where other tiny carvings could be seen. The long shaft of the cross held the pattern of a pruned tree trunk. Jake bent to look more closely at two tiny figures, Adam and Eve, clinging to the bottom of the Tree of Life, their faces upturned to Heaven in desperation. Moses was portrayed with the Brazen Serpent lifted high on a forked stick, and each individual figure on the cross had a different face, turned to show an aspect of their biblical character. It was truly a masterpiece.

As they stepped closer to examine it, Naomi stumbled a little, and Jake reached out to help her. She frowned and looked at the ground, confusion in her eyes.

"Are you okay?" Jake whispered, taking her arm.

"I'm … um … yes, the floor seems a little uneven, that's all."

Her eyes were unfocused for a moment, but then she shook her head and bent to the cross.

"The earth trembles, Death defeated groans with the buried one rising," Naomi said quietly. "That's one of the Latin couplets on the shaft." She pointed at the top. "But it's the titulus I came to see especially. Look, where the hand of God is portrayed within a stylized cloud. The Gospels use the phrase, *Jesus of Nazareth, King of the Jews*, but this has *Jesus of Nazareth, King of the Confessors*. It's a very unusual phrase." She bent even closer. "And there, you can just see the line of corrupted Hebrew." She squinted at it.

"That's strange, it looks like –"

The curator clapped his hands together, a little gesture of scholarly excitement as he prepared to share more of the story of the artifact.

"It's important to understand the great journey that the cross has traveled to reach us here. It came to the Met from a Yugoslavian art collector, Ante Topic Mimara, who recovered works of art at the end of the Second World War. He withheld the provenance of the cross, dying with its secrets intact, but there are reports from a Hungarian immigrant that the *crucifixus maledictus* had been seen in the Cistercian monastery of Zirc in the Bakony Mountains in Hungary. It was known as the *crucifixus maledictus* because of one of the carvings, *Maledictus omnis qui pendet in ligno.* Cursed is everyone who hangs on a tree. This refers to the traditional method of crucifixion, and of course Jesus reversed this curse with his sacrifice for us."

Jake bent forward as the curator's voice faded in volume, as if the sound came from beneath a swimming pool. It wasn't unusual to have blocked ears after a flight and he shook his head a little as he tried to catch the words.

"It's thought that the cross was sent to Hungary as part of a ransom for Richard the Lionheart in 1194, when he was captured on his way home from the Crusades. The Abbot of Bury St Edmunds was instrumental in the exchange, with many of the riches of the monastery given in ransom. It's thought that the cross was amongst that treasure."

Light-headed now, Jake swayed slightly. Naomi reached out a hand to steady him, and Jake noticed a few of the academics had moved back to lean against the thick walls.

"The carvings on the cross portray the story of the Passion of Christ," the curator continued, "expressed through the testimony of the evangelists while the Tree of Life winds up the front of the cross. It's stunning even without the missing corpus. The back of the cross … features the individual prophets holding texts from their holy books. They …"

The curator rubbed at his temples as his words trailed off, a confused look crossing his face as he lost track of what he was saying. He clutched the edge of the plinth, turning towards the arched doorway before sinking down to sit on the floor.

Jake felt a lifting sensation, a weightlessness, almost as if he could fly. He wanted to climb up to the top of the Cloisters and jump into the air, sure of his ability to soar like the birds. At the same time, he lost control of his limbs and he sank to his knees, realizing that around him, others were doing the same.

"The tea," Naomi whispered, her voice faint as she dropped to the floor next to him. "They grow *Datura metel* here, downy thorn apple, a powerful hallucinogenic plant used in medieval magic as well as medicine." She looked around at the other academics lying prone on the stone floor, their movements sluggish. "We've been poisoned."

Jake's tongue was thick in his mouth and he couldn't shape a reply as footsteps echoed on the stone floor, two sets deliberately walking towards the room. Jake saw them emerge from the archway in a haze of vision, their features morphing in and out of focus, first lizard like and then shining like angels. He couldn't move his limbs even as his mind seemed to soar above them into the vault of the ceiling. He tried to focus on them, tried to capture aspects of their faces, but he couldn't see properly. They both wore dark cassocks like priests, a uniform that attracted deference and little suspicion in a place like the Cloisters, but they walked like military men.

One of the men carried a suitcase. He laid it on the floor in front of the cross, opening it to reveal a padded interior. He lifted the Cloisters Cross from its stand, reverence in his eyes and in the way he handled it. He pulled it gently, the pieces sliding apart, and he laid each ivory element gently in the case before closing the lid carefully. Ignoring the prone academics on the floor, the pair walked out again, their actions taking only a few minutes. The stone plinth stood empty, the spotlight only serving to emphasize the negative space where one of the great treasures of Christendom had stood so briefly.

CHAPTER 4

THE UPPER BAY SPARKLED and rays of bright sun illuminated the magnificence of the city below. His city. Gilles Noiret never tired of this view, never grew weary of the myriad possibilities that New York could offer those who grabbed for them.

He ran his company from this towering pinnacle, the seventy-second floor of the Chrysler Building. Officially, the escalator finished at the seventy-first floor, but after purchasing the highest levels for his exclusive investment company, Gilles had constructed this sanctuary in the tangle of concrete supports and electrical equipment under the chrome-plated cap of the building. He loved staring out from the Art Deco turret, its silver starburst pattern pointing towards the spire above, with the knowledge that millions of eyes turned towards it every day, orientating themselves by its height and beauty.

Gilles took a tentative breath and felt it catch, sweat prickling as he dreaded the attack to come. He began to cough, a hacking sound that shook his whole body for several minutes.

Clutching his desk, Gilles retched, gasping for air until his lungs released the phlegm that clogged them. He hawked up a glob of bloody mess and spat it carefully into a handkerchief, the warm softness of it in his hand making his stomach clench. It was a piece of him, evidence of his disease. Every time he suffered an attack, he feared it would be his last.

It offended him to be so physically degraded, so broken, and the thought of dying here, choking to death on his own rotting flesh, set his resolve. He had not lived at the pinnacle of wealth to die in the same way as any poor man living rough on the streets. That was not how the American dream was meant to end.

He flipped open his laptop and played the video of the dying nun, her face contorted as she burned. He felt a rising excitement as he watched, the only physical pleasure he could summon as his body rotted from within.

As the video ended, a cloud passed overhead and Gilles caught a reflection of himself in the glass, bent double like an old man. His face was disfigured by the poison he had imbibed just a few years ago at a dinner held by his own brother, meant to kill him so he wouldn't have to share their inheritance. The immigrant sons of Russian and French ancestors, they had taken competition to extremes, both in business and their personal life. But it was Gaspard who had ended that night in the morgue and Gilles had never regretted finishing the brother who had only ever been a rival. There would always be more to compete with in this city of alphas: those with an edge of the blade in their ambition.

Gaspard had left his mark nonetheless, and the dioxin had caused rapid hyperpigmentation. Gilles' once handsome face was marred with patches of darker skin as well as hyperkeratosis, where the skin thickened and became scaly and bumpy. It itched and ached, but the surface ruin was nothing to what the poison had done internally.

In recent months, even the most advanced medicine had failed, so Gilles had sought alternative remedies from the fringes of health and spirituality. He had tried injections made from the tinctures of plants from the deepest Amazon and potions made from endangered animals. He had hired healers of all stripes, from those who chanted and gave him herbs to smoke, to those who told him to look inside and cleanse his soul. He had even paid for *muti*, traditional medicine from South Africa made from body parts. Nothing had worked yet, but he wouldn't give up until his dying breath.

During nights of pain-wracked insomnia, he had ventured into the margins of society, obscure message boards on the dark web – that part of the internet hidden from search engines and accessed via proxy servers. Gilles found things there that turned even his stomach, but he'd also found a glimmer of hope on a religious conspiracy message board that talked of a powerful relic with healing properties.

The group called themselves the Confessors, a word used in the Eastern Orthodox Church to signify a saint who had suffered persecution and torture for their faith, but had not been martyred: someone who suffered in the world but was not yet dead. Gilles understood what those words meant, and that day had begun his quest for the relic. He had pretended piety with the Monseigneur, assuring the Confessors that he only wanted to cleanse his soul and that they would have the relic for their Order. But that blood would be his … and so soon now. It was almost within his grasp. His men had sent word they were on their way from the Cloisters with the cross, and Gilles had not notified the Monseigneur. He would see what they had first.

The intercom buzzed.

Gilles smiled and pressed the button to let the men in, counting the seconds as they ascended in his private elevator.

A knock came on the door and two men dressed in cassocks walked in, their bearing proud in fulfillment of the mission and expectation of reward.

"Any problems?" Gilles said, staying behind his desk to save his energy even though he was desperate to see inside the case.

"None at all," the man carrying the case said. He set it on Gilles' desk and turned it to face his employer.

Gilles pulled the case towards him. A smile dawned on his face as he beheld the stunning Cloisters Cross, the sunlight making the ivory gleam. He ran a fingertip over the surface, tracing the lines of the Tree of Life, signifying his own resurrection. This time he was close … He had to be.

The Confessors believed that the blood was held within a vial inside the cross. Gilles' heart beat faster as he reached for the shaft with a shaking hand, tipping it over as he lifted it up so he could see within.

The ivory was indeed hollow, but there was nothing inside.

"Where is it?" Gilles whispered. He shook the shaft, coughing with the effort, but nothing fell out. "It's not here!"

His eyes blazed and the two men backed away from his anger, hands raised in supplication.

"Get down to the Sisters of the Guardian Angel," he rasped. "No subtlety this time. I want that vial, whatever it takes."

CHAPTER 5

JAKE ROLLED SIDEWAYS, MUMBLING as he tried to call for help but only succeeding in banging his head on the flagstones. Naomi lay next to him, her dark eyes meeting his, and Jake sensed a calmness in her, a silent message of hope. She had known the name of the herb and if she wasn't concerned, then he was willing to trust her judgement. He breathed more deeply, trying to recall the details of the men who had taken the cross as he waited for the effects to wear off.

It was ten more agonizing minutes before someone came to see why the scholars were so quiet and raised the alarm. The room was soon crowded with medical staff checking the group and the hubbub of gossip. Half an hour later, the victims began to move more freely, the paralysis released as the drug wore off.

Naomi sat up, rubbing her head where she had knocked it against the stone. She turned to look down at Jake and her long dark hair brushed against his hand. The sensation was magnified by his inability to move, and he willed her to lean in closer. Right now, he would be content to lie here all day, and leave the cross for the police. ARKANE didn't deal with theft or even murder, only with the supernatural, and he had seen nothing of that here today, only a very physical crime. There was concern in Naomi's eyes as she bent over him.

"I guess you drank more tea than I did, but you'll feel alright in a minute." She smiled with encouragement. "Clearly the dosage was meant to render us semi-conscious but not do any permanent damage."

She stood up and walked away to speak with one of the doctors as Jake's strength returned and he pulled himself up to a seated position. A heaviness still pervaded his limbs and his mind was dulled, his hearing still slightly wavering, but the fog was starting to lift now.

"We're cleared to leave," Naomi said, as she returned and crouched next to him. "The museum authorities called the police about the theft and the poisoning. There was a targeted hack on the security cameras just before the cross was taken, so there's no footage of the men."

"Could they be art thieves?" Jake said, rolling his neck until it clicked. With the combination of jet lag and soporific drugs, he seriously needed some more caffeine. "Don't they steal to hire these days?"

"Hmm," Naomi mused as she helped him up, her hand soft on his arm. "I'm not so sure. The chatter we had on the dark web was linked to a group called the Confessors, and given the wording on the cross, it would make sense if they were involved. We should at least look into it a little more back at the office. After all, what else are you doing today?"

She smiled, her eyes flashing with renewed energy, and Jake thought of a few things that might be more fun than tracking down the medieval cross. But he was here for work, and she was a colleague ... as was Morgan, he thought with a trace of guilt. ARKANE didn't make it easy for a relationship to form, that was for sure. Jake followed Naomi back to the car, grabbing another coffee for the ride back downtown.

After negotiating the heavy Manhattan traffic, the car pulled up at the entrance to the United Nations Plaza between First Avenue and the East River, a bastion of international peace and diplomacy in the heart of capitalist individualism. This was a city where such extremes could coexist in a myriad of dimensions. The plot of land was owned by the United Nations, technically extra-territorial although under agreement to follow local, state and federal laws. Jake wondered how many people around here knew of what lay beneath the official buildings, the hidden world of ARKANE.

Security guards verified their IDs at the gate and checked under the car for any devices, pulling open the doors for the sniffer dogs. Like security guards in sensitive places all over the world, these men were professional but unsmiling. Even though they must see Naomi regularly, there was no banter or casual conversation. As they checked the vehicle, Jake looked over at the huge sculpture of a .357 revolver, its barrel knotted in a symbol of non-violence that represented one of the aims of the UN. It was an idealism that Jake appreciated, but he was pretty sure that humanity would never shrug off its destructive side. Nature itself was murderous and every species struggled to survive another day – mankind was just a reflection of that struggle.

He looked further across the plaza to the row of colorful national flags, fluttering in the breeze in front of the main UN building. Jake recognized some of the more obscure countries – Armenia and Belize, Nauru and Uruguay – remembering how his father used to test him years ago. *It's a big world, son*, he would say as they matched countries on a world map to the capital cities and flags of the nations. *You need to know that there's more than this*, *where the color of someone's skin isn't so important.* As a farmer who had worked the land, his father never ventured out of South

Africa, planning to travel on retirement when he expected to hand the farm to his son. A flash of memory and Jake saw the world map on the wall spattered with blood: his father, mother and two sisters butchered by a drug-fueled gang years ago. He took a deep breath, tearing his gaze away from the flags, pushing the grief down as they drove into the underground carpark. He had left those memories behind a long time ago and hadn't expected a resurgence in this distant city.

Naomi drove down several levels, finally pulling into a bay painted with silver lines. At the other end of the floor, the parking bays were marked in blue. Naomi caught Jake's glance at the color coding.

"I know it seems petty," she said, "but a parking space is worth killing over in Manhattan. The UN crowd don't really know what we do on this end, but boy are they precious about their turf. Come on, I'll show you the office."

They entered an elevator, swiped their ID cards and waited for verification of their bio-information before it moved further down. Jake's ears finally cleared in the swift descent. The doors opened a minute later onto the New York office of ARKANE.

It was noisier than the London labs under Trafalgar Square, with the bustle of the city spilling over into the enthusiasm of those who worked here. But the lab areas were set up in a similar way, with glass-walled, temperature-controlled rooms where artifacts were investigated for their supernatural properties.

"I guess you work with objects like this in London?" Naomi paused in front of one of the research bays, where an unusual necklace was strung across a metal stand. A man in a lab coat scraped at it, pushing tiny samples into a test tube.

"I'm usually out in the field, to be honest." Jake squinted at the object. It was made up of animal teeth, beads and shells. "What is this?"

"It's a shaman's necklace originally from Borneo but recovered from a cache in a Queens apartment. What's particularly interesting is the teeth – they don't come from any known species. When boiled they produce the ability to see into other realms. Local legends say the teeth are from dragons in that other universe."

Jake raised an eyebrow, his corkscrew scar twisting.

"Just another day at ARKANE." He grinned. "Gotta love the variety."

"Exactly." Naomi smiled. "Let's get to my office and see what we can find on the cross."

Naomi led Jake past the rows of glass-walled labs and all the way down another corridor, until they reached a little section tucked away from the main area. The word *Linguistics* was displayed on a sign on the door.

"Because I work across so many cases, I get my own room," Naomi said, opening the door to a messy space not much bigger than a cupboard. "Sorry for the chaos – I do know where everything is, honest."

Looking around the room, Jake had a sense that Naomi spent a lot of time here. There was a kettle and toaster on a little fridge and what looked like a rolled-up sleeping bag and travel mat in the corner. Books were stuffed into floor-to-ceiling shelving on one side of the room, their spines showing all kinds of languages, many he didn't even recognize. Did she live for her work, as he did?

Naomi grabbed her laptop and whipped it open. Jake caught a glimpse of her screensaver – an older Native American man's face in profile, looking out over the ocean. Her father perhaps, as she had mentioned Cherokee blood. She opened the ARKANE systems, typing quickly and pulling up some documents for Jake to look at.

"As we were lying there after the cross was taken," she said, "I was thinking about the strange script on the titulus. I think it might be Enochian."

"The language of the angels?"

Naomi nodded. "Supposedly. It was recorded in the occult journals of John Dee in late sixteenth-century England. It was meant to be the language that Adam spoke with God, and that was used to name all the animals. I guess you could call it a language of creation. Dee was a mathematician and astrologer, advisor to Queen Elizabeth I, with one foot in science and the other in magic."

"But the dates don't match," Jake said. "It's odd that it should be on the cross, considering the age of the carving is way before Dee's time."

Naomi frowned. "I seem to remember something …" She tapped on the laptop, bringing up a copy of the Hermetic work *Monas Hieroglyphica*. "Here, this is one of Dee's great works and he took a copy to Hungary to present to Maximilian, the Holy Roman Emperor. If the cross was in Hungary at the time, it's likely that Dee would have seen such an unusual piece, and that could have been the basis for his own Enochian language."

As she flicked through the virtual book, Jake spotted an image on the edge of one heavily illustrated page. It depicted a glass flask full of ruby liquid.

"Stop there," he said, and Naomi zoomed in, expanding the image. "The chatter that ARKANE picked up mentioned something about the blood of an angel," Jake said. "Can you read the text around it?"

Naomi's lips moved silently as she read the strange text, her dark eyes fixed on the screen. Jake could almost see the workings of her mind as she turned over the words, her body taut as she concentrated.

"It's retelling a legend from the mouth of an angel," she said after a few minutes. "The one who drinks the blood will see into the supernatural realm, and may bargain the drops for whatever they desire. Time and space are nothing for those who stand beyond." She shook her head slowly, a smile dawning on her lips. "That's pretty cool, actually. Do you think that the Cloisters Cross holds this relic?"

"It certainly explains the interest in it," Jake said. "And makes me more concerned about getting it back. What else is significant about the cross?"

"As well as the angelic aspects, the cross is about resurrection, which isn't surprising, but it's done in an unusual way." Naomi retrieved some close-up pictures of the cross. Jake bent closer to the screen, feeling the warmth of her skin near his arm. She smelled of coconut and jasmine, and he couldn't help but lean closer.

"You can see the pruned tree on the shaft," she said. "It's a date palm, the Latin name is *Phoenix dactylifera*. It dies and comes to life again in a similar manner to the phoenix, the bird that rises from the flames."

"So the Tree of Life portrayed as the seat of immortality, like the Fountain of Youth," Jake said.

Naomi nodded, and then pointed at something else on the screen.

"This Tree of Life is mentioned in Genesis, chapter three, *And the Lord God said, 'The man has now become like one of us, knowing good and evil. He must not be allowed to reach out his hand and take also from the tree of life and eat, and live forever.'* But the book of Enoch, which is in the biblical Apocrypha, has a verse which states that in the time of judgement, God will give all those whose names are in the Book of Life fruit to eat from the Tree of Life. The book isn't canonical, so most aren't aware of it, but its only extant copy is in Ge'ez, the language of Ethiopian holy writing, one of the earliest parts of the church."

Jake remembered visiting the Ethiopian Coptic church on the roof of the church of the Holy Sepulchre in Jerusalem in the hunt for the Pentecost stones. Momentarily, he wondered if Morgan was somewhere near there right now, thinking of him on the other side of the world.

A bell chimed, announcing an incoming message. Naomi leaned in to read it.

"There's been a woman reported missing who fits the profile of the crucified victim. A Sister from the Order of the Guardian Angel." Naomi met Jake's eyes.

"Let's head up there," Jake said, grabbing his coat. "And stop by the weapons locker on the way out."

CHAPTER 6

SISTER ROSALIE REACHED UP to light the candles at the back of the chapel, her concentration focused on the depth of the flames as they caught. The main door to the street swung open with a creak, the sound echoing through the church. It was a little early for any worshippers to be arriving for the service, but the church was always open as a place of contemplation. In her forty years of service, the city had been a backdrop to her own daily devotions and she welcomed those who worshipped at any time. Sister Rosalie liked to try and guess what people did when they came in, wondering what troubled them and why they sought out the Lord in the middle of their day. She crossed herself and sent up a prayer of thanks that she could serve the community here, then turned and walked to the chapel archway to see who had entered.

Three men strode down the center of the aisle carrying holdall bags, their long dark coats disguising what might be beneath. They walked towards the altar, menace in their echoing footsteps. Sister Rosalie glimpsed one of the men as he passed, his eyes narrowed with a determined expression, his features pinched with a hunger that wasn't of the corporeal kind. She quickly ducked behind a column, hoping she hadn't been seen. Her breath came fast and she stifled it with one hand. These were not penitents seeking the Lord's grace – these were men bent on violence.

After the disappearance of the Reverend Mother, the Sisters of the Order of the Guardian Angel had been reminded of what to do if they were ever under attack. As citizens of New York City, they weren't alone in preparing for invasion, but the nuns were also trained in spiritual warfare. The prayer of the breastplate of Saint Patrick came to Sister Rosalie's lips now. *I armor myself today with the power of the Most Holy Trinity*, she said under her breath.

She peeked out again from behind the column, watching as the men strode towards the doorway that led into the convent area behind the church. The long coat of the man at the back fluttered open and she spotted a handgun in his waistband. As the men stepped through the archway out of sight, Sister Rosalie scurried to the opposite side of the church, where another door led into the convent rooms. Her heart thumped in her chest as she considered how she could help the Sisters within, as well as safeguarding the secret at the heart of the convent. The Reverend Mother had protected it, and now that task fell to her. She pushed open the door carefully and stepped inside, her footsteps almost silent on the marble floors.

A scream came from the rooms beyond, followed by the shouts of the men rounding up the Sisters. A banging noise resounded, as if something had been knocked over. Then, all was quiet. Sister Rosalie pushed away her feelings of guilt as she navigated the hallways towards the inner rooms of the convent. The Sisters would be safe for now. Most of them knew nothing of the relic and the old ones would hold their tongues against the invaders.

The truth behind the name of their order was obscured by over-engineered religious metaphor, but a chosen few were aware of what lay beneath. This great city was protected by the relic of a Guardian Angel, and it was held here in the convent, passed down over the years by women of faith who were able to resist the temptations of what it might offer.

Sister Rosalie reached the tiny chapel on the edge of the private quarters. It was here that the Reverend Mother had visited daily, saying prayers that she reserved for this sacred place. The altar was simple, a rectangular block of stone covered with a white cloth; a carved wooden crucifix on top, the figure of Christ twisted in agony as his eyes beseeched Heaven for release. Two heavy copper candlesticks flanked the figurine.

On the wall behind the crucifix was a wooden cabinet, the real focal point of the room. It was painted with the figures of angels, binding another of their kind in the center. Its face was stricken with guilt and pain, and from its pale flesh, blood flowed onto the earth. Shoots of new life sprang from the dark stain, with tendrils of leaves and buds that bloomed into flowers.

It was faintly blasphemous to think that an angel could supercede the worship of Christ, but legend told of the power of the relic and perhaps that made it more real than the figure of Christ crucified. Sister Rosalie edged around the altar and reached for the cabinet.

"Stop there, Sister." The gruff voice came from behind her, and Sister Rosalie instinctively put her hands in the air, turning around to see who spoke.

It was the first man who had walked into the church, his eyes scanning the chapel around her. Thank the Lord she hadn't yet opened the cabinet. There was still a chance he would move on from this place.

"You're welcome in the Lord's house," she said softly. "But we don't allow laymen in this area. It is reserved for the nuns. Shall we go out into the public area of the main church?"

The man snorted with laughter.

"I don't think so, Sister. It seems you have something here that my boss wants badly. I don't think that would be out in the public area, do you?" He walked towards her, eyes narrowing. "I think it might be in here. If you just stay quiet now, I won't have to hurt you."

Sister Rosalie dropped her head in the very aspect of a devout nun, assuming the mantle of the downtrodden woman of God this man would expect. But her soul burned with the passion of her Lord, her dedication to protecting the heart of the convent, and with the righteous anger of the saints.

The man stepped closer and bent to lift the altarcloth, checking underneath. Sister Rosalie grabbed one of the metal candlesticks and with all her strength, slammed it down on the back of the man's neck. The thud of metal against flesh shocked her but before he could recover from the first blow, Sister Rosalie raised the candlestick again. She couldn't let him up or he would finish her. Grunting with effort, she smashed it down again, her breath mingled with sobs.

The man slumped to the floor, and Sister Rosalie stood over him, her fists tight on the metal raised high above her head. As blood trickled from his unmoving mouth, she dropped the candlestick as if it burned her. It clanged to the floor and rolled to the side of the room. She fell to her knees in front of the altar.

"Oh Lord Jesus, forgive me," she whispered as she crossed herself repeatedly, fearing that she was now tainted with the blood that she had shed.

A scream rang out from the rooms beyond and Sister Rosalie looked up at the sound. It wouldn't be long until the other men came to look for this one. She had to get out of here. Rising again, she went around to the wooden cabinet and opened it, her fingers shaking.

Inside was a glass vial, its clear sides revealing a viscous dark red substance. Was this really the blood of a Guardian Angel, Sister Rosalie wondered, or was it all just a myth?

Another scream and then a moan from the gathered nuns.

"No, please!" The voice was Sister Mary Clare's.

Sister Rosalie froze, the vial in her shaking hands. The young girl was one of the most attractive of the novitiates and her violation would not be difficult for the men. She looked down at the vial. Was this really worth the sanctity of the Sisters? Surely the Lord would desire the protection of his daughters first, the real treasures of the convent?

She glanced down at the prone man. She had already sinned enough today, and her vow to keep the relic safe seemed worthless in the face of real suffering. Her Sisters needed her. She stepped out of the chapel and walked towards the main convent room, the vial clutched in her hand.

She pushed open the door and almost wept at what she saw. Sister Mary Clare was bound, her habit pulled up and one of the men had his hand between her legs, pulling aside her underclothes as he unbuckled his belt. The look of lust on his face was like the fiends of Hell that Brunelleschi had painted on the dome of Florence. The other nuns were herded into a corner, while another man stood with a gun in each hand.

"Tell me where it is," he said, his quiet tone all the more menacing. "Otherwise she'll only be the first to be violated."

"Stop." Sister Rosalie spoke from the doorway, her voice calm with authority. She held the vial up. "This is what you want. Take it and leave us in peace."

The armed man kept his guns trained on the Sisters.

"Check it," he said to the other man, who hesitated a moment, disappointment in his eyes as he left Sister Mary Clare bound on the floor.

Sister Rosalie held the vial out as the man approached.

"This is the blood of the Guardian Angel," she said.

He took it from her hand, holding the vial to the light and tipping it slightly so the contents swirled inside.

"How do we know it's real?"

Sister Rosalie smiled coldly. "Faith of course, something perhaps your master lacks. This relic has been the heart of the Order for as long as records have been kept." Her eyes flicked to the cowering Sisters, to the weeping Sister Mary Clare on the floor. "But the real heart of the Order is the Sisterhood."

She pushed past the man and knelt next to Sister Mary Clare, pulling the weeping nun into her arms and rocking her back and forth. Sister Rosalie's eyes blazed as she looked up at the invaders. "You have what you came for. Now get out."

The man backed away from the group of nuns, his guns still trained on them.

"If this is some kind of trick, we will be back, Sister."

The other man spoke, his eyes on Sister Mary Clare. "And I'll enjoy finishing what we started."

They turned to leave, but a roar of anger stopped them. Sister Rosalie paled as she realized that she should have carried on beating the man in the chapel. He stumbled along the corridor, his colleagues rushing to help him back into the room.

"You bitch." He pointed the gun at Sister Rosalie with a wavering hand, clicked off the safety and took aim.

CHAPTER 7

"Please." Sister Rosalie stood, moving away from the rest of the Sisters. "Just take the vial and leave us now."

The man's eyes were manic, pain turning him into a wounded animal, desperate to lash out. For a second, it seemed like he might relent … but then, the sound of a gunshot echoed through the room.

A surprised sigh escaped Sister Rosalie's lips. She saw the panic on the faces of the nuns as they looked at her and a coldness spread through her body. She looked down to see the hole in her habit, the blood on her side. She dropped to her knees, hands clutched at her ribs as the pain blossomed. She gasped, her breath ragged.

The man stepped forward, pressing the muzzle of the gun to her head. Sister Rosalie looked up at him, but she couldn't hate him. The love of the Lord pervaded her now and she whispered a prayer of forgiveness. *They know not what they do, Lord.* The man's eyes flickered, as if he saw beyond her physical form. He hesitated and then turned away.

"She's finished," he growled, looking around at the rest of the nuns. "If the vial is fake, we'll be back for the rest of you."

The men backed out of the room, and then turned to run towards the rear of the building, taking the vial with them. Some of the nuns crowded round Sister Rosalie, taking her hands and praying as one ran to call an ambulance and others tended to the shocked Sister Mary Clare.

Jake and Naomi stepped into the Church of the Guardian Angel just as a gunshot rang out in the rooms beyond. They both pulled their weapons and ran towards the sound. Jake hesitated at the arched doorway, listening for an indication of what was within. Several pairs of footsteps rushed away from them, and they heard the sound of voices raised in prayer and weeping. Jake pushed open the door and ran down the corridor with Naomi behind him. She pulled her phone from her jacket, calling for backup from the local police.

He glanced into one of the rooms, seeing the group of nuns crowded around one of their own, several on their knees swaying in prayer. They looked up at him in alarm, instinctively bunching together.

"It's okay," he said. "We're friends. Which way did they go?"

Naomi stepped forward into the room, and the nuns relaxed as they saw another woman.

"Out the back," one of the nuns said. "They've taken something. Please – help us."

Jake turned and sprinted towards the back of the convent, his weapon held low in front of him. Ahead, he heard the revving of a vehicle and men's voices. He peered around the corner of the back door as two men pulled a wounded third man into a minivan.

He shot at them, firing twice, hitting one man in the shoulder while the other bullet pierced the side of the vehicle. The men returned fire and Jake ducked back behind the doorway, hearing the chip of bullets into stone. The van accelerated away and Jake ran out after them, firing at the van, hitting it a couple more times before it pulled away, screeching around a corner and out of sight. Police sirens wailed in the distance but it was too late to follow now. There were no plates, but there were enough cameras downtown that they should be able to track it.

Jake turned and headed back into the convent, pausing at the doorway to the room within. Naomi knelt with the nuns in the center of the room, where one woman lay in a pool of blood. Naomi looked up, her eyes filled with tears.

"This is Sister Rosalie," she said. "They shot her and took the relic of the Guardian Angel."

Jake knelt next to the woman as the prayers of the gathered nuns rang loud around them. The wound in Sister Rosalie's side pulsed blood onto the marble floor of the chapel, despite the wad of bandaging that one of the other nuns held against it. She gasped for breath, her eyes unfocused.

"It's OK," Jake whispered, tears pricking his eyes at her suffering. So often he survived the aftermath of violence, arriving too late to stop it. "We've got you now. You're going to be alright. The ambulance is almost here."

Naomi reached forward and stroked the hair from the nun's forehead.

"God is with you," she whispered softly to the nun, with a faith in her voice that Jake didn't have. He felt a pang of something like envy that Naomi could believe and find comfort in something beyond this earthly life.

The nun lifted her hand towards the light above her, reaching for the coffered ceiling. Her eyes were fixed on a point beyond the physical realm and Jake hoped she could see a better life ahead. Then she turned her head, her eyes clear as a summer sky after rain, a realization dawning in her eyes.

"Follow the angel," she whispered.

Her eyes closed and Jake felt her body sag, the life leaving it even as her physical remains lay still in his arms. He laid the nun gently on the ground, putting a prayer cushion under her head as the other Sisters gathered around to mourn.

Jake and Naomi rose to let them tend to her body, walking to the doorway.

"At least she wasn't afraid of death," Naomi said. "Her faith gave her strength and a hope for the afterlife."

Jake wanted to voice his lack of belief, his surety that there was only the void after this. This minute was all they had, this day the only one they could live and there was nothing beyond. But he just nodded, feeling a sense of isolation at his unbelief in this house of God.

"They took the relic," Naomi said, turning to look back at the nuns. "And the people who did this must also have the Cloisters Cross."

Jake nodded. "I'm going after them …" He left the opening for her, unsure as to whether a deskbound agent with little field experience would want to dive further into this mission. Morgan would have jumped at the chance, but she was halfway across the world.

Naomi crossed herself, ducking her head towards the altar and then turned. There was fire in her eyes and Jake saw echoes of an ancestry riven with conflict. This woman wouldn't run from a fight.

"This is my patch, Jake, but you're welcome to join me on the hunt." She walked towards the convent door, Jake following as their footsteps echoed in the nave. "I know where to start. Here in New York, there's only one famous angel that springs to mind."

***

Across the city, in a lab buried deep under the Chrysler Building, Gilles Noiret paced back and forth. The men had brought the vial straight to the underground carpark, and he had rushed it to his private lab. They had been trying to find a cure for his illness for years, and now the equipment would be used to test what was in the vial.

The Monseigneur would hear of the theft all too soon and would demand access. Gilles had to be quick. He had wanted to drink the liquid then and there, take the risk on what it might do. But his fear of poison was so great that everything had to be tested before it reached his lips. This vial was no different.

A scientist in a lab coat used a pipette to extract several samples of the dark red liquid, putting it into test tubes and one on a slide to examine under the microscope.

"How long will this take?" Gilles barked at the scientist. "I must know what it is."

"Of course," the scientist whispered, his concentration fixed on the liquid. "The preliminary tests won't take long."

He loaded the test tubes into various machines, starting the processes to test the blood. Then he bent to the microscope, putting the slide under the lens.

"Hmm," the scientist said, standing up straight again.

"What? What is it?" Gilles demanded.

"It's definitely blood. It looks to be from some type of animal though. I don't see any obvious anomalies that would make it anything special."

One of the machines beeped and the scientist went to check the computer screen next to it for the results.

"As I thought. The DNA shows that the blood is from a type of goat that is only found natively in France. It's certainly old, several centuries in fact. But I'm sorry sir, I can't see what efficacy this would have if drunk."

Gilles spun around, fists clenched. He felt the tightness in his chest begin to spasm at the onset of a coughing fit. Desperation rose within him, a faith born of a belief that he could cheat death – that he would not be subject to the laws of humanity. His wealth ruled this city and he would not go out with a last rotting breath.

He snatched up the vial on the bench, ripping the glass top from it. He lifted it to his lips and drank the contents, gulping the coppery taste down, forcing himself to swallow the thick liquid.

The scientist gasped, his eyes crinkling with disgust.

Gilles turned to grab a tissue and caught sight of his own face in a mirrored flask on the bench, a hideously scarred and puckered visage with a mouth painted in the blood of a long-dead animal. He pulled a tissue from a pack and wiped his mouth, the crimson stain all that was left of the so-called relic.

There was still hope that the blood had some power. He would not let this be the end. Gilles sat down heavily, waiting for some kind of reaction, hoping for some kind of miracle. The threatening cough subsided but the blood sat heavy in his stomach. Nausea made him want to retch it up, but he kept swallowing to keep it down, breathing deeply to calm himself.

"Water," he barked. The scientist grabbed a bottle from the fridge and handed it over wordlessly. Gilles chugged the liquid down, washing the metallic taste from his throat. There was no feeling other than his own revulsion at drinking the blood. After several minutes passed with nothing, not even light-headedness, Gilles put his head in his hands. He massaged his temples, willing his rising rage to subside.

"What else are you working on?" he asked the scientist, his voice tightly controlled. "Do we have any other options?"

The scientist walked briskly to his desk and pulled out a few printed pages.

"There's an experimental therapy that we can look at. It shows a muted but still positive response in some subjects."

Gilles stood. "Get it, whatever it costs."

He went to his private lift and headed back up to the penthouse, disappointment flooding him, anger at his own stupid hopes of a miraculous cure. He would send the Monseigneur and his pathetic Confessors packing, their myth turned to ashes in his mouth.

But as he walked into the apartment, a ray of sun peeked through the clouds, illuminating the Cloisters Cross. The sunlight hit the empty shaft, where the corpus of Christ should hang. The legends told that the corpus was the true home of the relic, and the vial had been found alone, with no ivory body of Christ as its resting place. Perhaps the nuns had lied or perhaps they didn't even know that what they'd had was the blood of an old goat. But the corpus was still out there – as long as that was true, there was still hope.

Gilles took his phone out of his pocket, dialing quickly.

"Follow whoever leaves the convent. This isn't over yet."

CHAPTER 8

THE SOUND OF GOSPEL music came from the passage that led under Bethesda Terrace. The voices of a young black choir soared in glory and the acoustics of the space resonated with harmonies. Jake noticed one young woman, her dreadlocks tied back with a red scarf and her arms lifted to the ornate ceiling above. As she sang, she stepped in time with the choir, their simple choreography a way to bring the body into worship. For a moment, Jake was taken back to the townships in South Africa, when as a child he had always been jealous of the way the black community sang with such abandon, such joy. His own white church had been a place of dull song with no passion, a controlled droning that seemed intent on crushing the lively spirit.

Naomi sang a few lines of the tune as they walked past and danced a little, joining the choir in a moment that transcended the pain they had just witnessed at the convent.

"You have a lovely voice," Jake said, noting how her face lit up and her body relaxed as she moved, a glimpse of the woman behind the agent's facade.

"Years of Pentecostal worship," Naomi said, with a smile that spoke of deep contentment. "I'm not exactly a committed believer these days, but boy, do I love the music. I think that many people just go to church to sing and experience the bliss of communal voice. Whether the Lord gave us music, or whether we found it ourselves, it surely is one of the best ways to open the mind to something more than the mundane."

They walked out onto the stone terrace in front of the most famous angel in New York, the Angel of the Waters, standing tall over the large fountain. The bronze figure looked as if she had just touched down from a heavenly descent, one arm out to bless those who came here seeking help. Her wings were outstretched and currently a roost for a number of pigeons that sat atop the sculpture, preening their feathers in the sun. Groups of tourists snapped pictures of the scene as a clamor of bike bells filled the air. A group of tour riders arrived, their guide gesticulating as he explained the fountain's origin within Central Park.

"She's meant to be the angel from the gospel of John, chapter five," Naomi said. "An angel would come down and stir the waters of the pool of Bethesda. Any who entered after the blessing would emerge healed. I think that many come to New York wanting the same miracle in their lives – a resurrection of sorts, or a rebirth."

"What do you expect to find here?" Jake asked, looking around.

Naomi shrugged. "I'm not so sure, to be honest, but this is the most well-known angel in the city. With the Enochian language on the cross and so many angelic references, I have to think that this is connected somehow. Let's at least check it out."

They walked around the perimeter of the fountain, navigating the throngs of tourists taking photos and lovers kissing on the edge, fingers entwined in the water. There were coins in the fountain, thrown in for wishes perhaps. Jake fumbled in his pocket for a quarter and leaned over the water. He let it slip under, sending out a thought for Morgan, hoping that she was safe. Perhaps she was even thinking of him too.

Applause rippled out from the passage and the choir emerged for a break between sets. A couple of members from the group lit cigarettes and turned their faces to the beaming sun as they reveled in the beautiful day. Another sold CDs to the appreciative tourists who had gathered to listen. Jake noticed the young woman with dreadlocks and the red scarf emerge with a backpack. She looked around at the fountain and scanned the crowd. She caught Jake's eye and walked towards them, waving a little.

"Hi," she said. "Don't worry, I'm not asking for anything."

Jake laughed. "I thought your performance was excellent. I'd be happy to put some money in the hat."

"Can we help you with anything?" Naomi said, stepping closer.

The young woman smiled and pulled out her cell phone.

"Actually, I think I'm here to help you. I'm Regina – I just got a text message. I can't say from who, but she says you did something to help the Order of the Guardian Angel this morning."

Naomi's face was serious. "We've just come from the convent. How do you know about them?"

"The Order has lay sisters like me all over the city who serve the community any way we can. I mostly work on the streets – I was a homeless junkie when one of the Sisters found me five years ago. I thought she was an angel, actually." Regina pointed up at the fountain statue. "Just like our angel here, the Sister held out a hand and saved me. Now, I try and help others."

"That sounds fantastic," Jake said. "But we're not looking for salvation."

Regina nodded. "The relic – I know about it. We all do. It's one of those 'matter-of-faith' things to most associated with the Order, but maybe it's based on historical truth way back. Anyhow, my contact has asked me to take you to a place that might help you figure out where the relic is."

"Sounds like a plan," said Jake. "Let's grab a cab."

Regina shook her head. "Actually, it's a little more complicated than that. Where we're going isn't exactly open to the public – and you won't find this route on any GPS."

Naomi raised an eyebrow. "That sounds intriguing."

Regina looked her up and down, eyeing the tailored trousers and jacket. "It is. But girl, how much do you love that suit?"

***

After winding through Central Park, Regina led Jake and Naomi down a zigzag of side streets until they reached an area that even Jake wouldn't want to visit at night.

"Where are we going?" Naomi asked as they walked.

"It's more about how we're getting there," Regina replied with a smile. "I dated a sandhog once. He showed me a lot of the tunnels under the city."

"Sandhog?" Jake asked.

"I guess you could call them urban miners, construction workers who spend their lives underground – boring tunnels, building ducts for new projects, excavation, making sure the water pipes are OK. There's a lot that goes on under this city." She paused by a grate on the sidewalk, pulling a tire iron from her backpack. "Of course, if we're found, we'll get arrested. But just act like this is normal and no one will even notice." She grinned, a feral look coming into her eyes, and Jake caught a glimpse of the girl who had once survived on these streets.

Regina glanced around quickly. There were no cop cars in sight. With one smooth movement, she wedged the end of the tire iron into the grating and heaved it up. She pulled it sideways to reveal a metal ladder leading down into darkness.

"Quickly now," she said. "Wait for me at the bottom."

Jake looked at Naomi and shrugged, then stepped on the ladder and descended. The light dimmed as he went down, his footsteps echoing on the rungs. The sound of dripping water intensified as he reached the bottom. He pulled out his phone and used the torch function to look around. The tunnel was six feet at the tallest point so he would have to crouch to walk through it, and there was shallow water running along the concrete bottom. It smelled earthy with a metallic tang, but underneath there was a hint of the rotting decay and sewage that flowed through these tunnels somewhere.

Naomi stepped down from above and Jake resisted an urge to help her descend the last few rungs. His South African upbringing could sometimes be misconstrued as sexism and he had a suspicion that both these women were more than capable of looking after themselves.

"This is so cool," Naomi said as she looked around, wiping her hands on her tailored suit, oblivious to the dirt. Her eyes were bright in the torchlight. "I've always wanted to come down here, but all the official tours are waaaay too boring."

A clang came from above as Regina pulled the grating back over the hole and then came down to join them. She pulled a pair of gloves and a powerful headtorch from her backpack and put them both on.

"Sorry I don't have more gear for you, but this was a short-notice thing. We don't have too far to go anyway, so your phone batteries should last as torchlight. This way."

Regina stepped into the side tunnel, staying on one side

to avoid the water channel. Her left hand touched the wall lightly with sure fingertips, as if the brickwork were braille and its message only for those of the underground world. The walls were brick blocks, like a prison or an institution, but Regina's body became more relaxed down here, and she exuded a sense of freedom. *Perhaps she was more free down here*, Jake thought as he walked hunched over. It was simple to follow the law when you had money and security, but when life was more extreme, when survival was on a toppling edge, it was sometimes easier to live away from prying eyes.

They walked in silence for a few minutes, the sounds of the tunnel becoming more intense: dripping water from the roof above, the burble of the water channel at their feet, the scurrying and scratching of the rats that made their home down here. Then, suddenly a clang from behind them.

Regina stopped, her head whipping round to look back behind Jake. He saw terror in her eyes, residual fear from her previous life.

"That's strange," she whispered after a moment. "I've never known anyone else use that entrance and there's no scheduled maintenance in this part of the tunnels this month. I know the rotation." She frowned. "I'm sure it's nothing. Let's keep moving."

Jake felt the familiar prickle of hair rising on the back of his neck as his senses heightened. Naomi had a hand on her gun and he pulled his own weapon silently, holding it next to his phone. Had they been followed from the convent down here?

They continued down the tunnel, emerging into a wider shaft with ledges that were high enough above water to remain dry most of the year. On one of the ledges, a lounge chair with an ashtray on the arm sat next to a few boxes – a makeshift living room in this strange oasis of dark calm. Above the chair, unreadable bulbous letters in faded paint proclaimed existence below the skin of the street. Mankind has always marked its place upon the earth, from the earliest cave dwellers to these more modern troglodytes.

"I knew the man who based himself here," Regina said. "He was already old when I met him, and older still when someone turned him in to the authorities because he was sick. He cried when they took him away to hospital. I think he wanted to die down here, where he felt free. Up above, people tell you what to do, how to behave. I know it's hard to believe, but some people prefer this to the shelters." She paused, looking around. "Down here used to be my home. I knew all the ways to escape in the dark, but most of the predators are up top anyway."

Regina took another small tunnel that led off from the large one, twisting and turning until Jake was sure he would never be able to find his way back. In his younger days, he could track through dense bush where all the trees looked the same and still navigate to a water hole. But here … he shivered. How many skeletons lay forgotten in this warren of tunnels under the city? How many had become lost and died alone, clawing at the walls?

They stopped by a manhole with a small square grating on the top.

"We've got to go down quite a long way now," Regina said, shining her torch down into the hole below. "The entrance is off this access shaft, which as far as I can tell hasn't been used since they built the lower tiers of the place."

She pulled the tire iron out again and hooked the cover to pull it away. Naomi bent to help.

"You still haven't told us where we're going," she said.

Regina grinned. "I think you're gonna like it when we get there."

CHAPTER 9

Jake found the access shaft a little too tight for comfort. It was a square chimney just wider than a man's shoulders – a small man's shoulders – and he was over six feet and broad with it. He concentrated on breathing deeply, focusing on the brickwork in front of him as he mechanically stepped down the ladder after the two women.

He could hear Naomi and Regina chatting below, the echoes of their laughter filtering up to him. Naomi seemed to find these dark places a natural habitat, her smart suit forgotten as she had enthusiastically followed Regina down the shaft. If they were being followed, it would be easy to find them with this level of noise. He paused for a moment to reach around his back and check the gun was still safely tucked there before he continued down. After a few more minutes, he found Naomi and Regina standing in an alcove off the main shaft in front of a metal access hatch.

"Welcome to the New York Public Library," Regina said with a broad grin. "It has seven floors of stacks but the official plans don't show the sub-basement where some of the city's most politically sensitive documents are kept. The treasures and rare manuscripts are above, but down here are the secrets. We'll be entering directly into that area."

Jake's mind flashed to the ARKANE vaults, buried deep under Trafalgar Square in central London, way below the transport level and the pipework necessary to run the city. Could those levels be accessed in the same way? It was something to talk to Director Marietti about when he got back to London.

"Oh, wow!" Naomi said, her eyes shining with excitement. "I've heard rumors of this level but I've never been able to get in, even with ARKANE access."

"What are we looking for here?" Jake asked. "And how does it relate to the relic?"

Regina began to turn the wheel on the hatch, opening the lock that held it shut.

"The Mother Superior of the Order of the Guardian Angel has always been a prominent figure in the city," she said. "In the background, for sure, but influential in her own way. Those who held the position have always written diaries and those records are locked here in the vault because of the secrets that the Mother Superiors have always kept. My source at the convent said that the last recorded sighting of the original relic was around 1890, so we'll be trying to find the diary from that time."

Regina pulled the door and it swung silently open on oiled hinges. She put her finger on her lips as they stepped inside, motioning them into silence. Directly in front of the door was a huge wooden slab, the back of a giant bookcase or storage unit. Regina inched into the space behind it while Naomi easily followed and Jake squeezed along after them. Regina peeked her head around the end. After a moment, she stepped into the room, beckoning for them to emerge.

"It's OK," she said. "There's no one here. There never is, actually, and I've been coming here for years. It's always this awesome temperature, keeps you warm in the winter and there doesn't seem to be any security to worry about. I think they've forgotten about this place. The last documents deposited down here are dated 1972."

The vault had a low ceiling and rolling shelves that stretched into darkness ahead of them, creating a sense of intimacy. The sound of their voices was muted by the stacks of paper, books and documents that lay filed on the shelving. The place smelled of age and knowledge, crumbling into dust, for life was a constant fight against entropy, the degeneration of all things. It looked like some of the archives here had already succumbed. Jake thought of Martin Klein's database back in London, and how much his friend would love to get hold of what was in this vault. It could be a possibility later, but for now Jake walked to the first shelf and scanned the contents, written in spidery handwriting on an index card taped to the end.

"Do you have any sense where the diaries might be?" Jake asked. "We don't have time to go through the whole vault."

"Of course," Regina said. "I searched for them after I became part of the Sisterhood." She walked down the narrow aisle, Naomi and Jake following behind until they reached a particular aisle. Regina pulled a cord to turn on the light in the stack. The illumination was dim but it was better than their torches. She turned the handle to open up the rolling stack, revealing a row of identical black books standing upon the shelves, each one with a date etched in gold on the spine. Year upon year of diaries, each one an inch thick.

Jake raised an eyebrow. "This could be a problem."

"We just need to narrow down the date range," Naomi said, trailing her fingers along the spines as she scanned the dates. "As much as I'd love to sit and read these earlier tomes, we should start with the year the relic was seen and go from there. We'll scan for mentions of it and hope the

Mother Superior wrote about it." She pulled the book from 1890 off the shelf and a cloud of dust lifted into the air. "You take this one, Jake." She handed it to him, coughing as the dust settled on her skin and clothes.

Regina pulled down the next one in the series. "I'll look at this one."

Naomi took the following year and they all sat on the floor, books on their laps. The sound of pages turning was soon the only thing that could be heard, their breathing more rhythmic as they settled into the search.

Jake's diary was a monotonous account of life in the convent, with lists of ailments amongst the nuns, accounting notes and snippets of information on visitors. Page after page of this made his attention wander as the minutes ticked by. He glanced up at Naomi, who leaned against the stack behind her, dark eyes fixed on the page, her slim fingers gently laid on the ivory paper. She was attractive above ground in her bureaucrat's suit and perfect hair, but she was stunning down here covered in the dust and dirt of adventure. She looked up and caught his gaze, a smile playing around her full lips.

"Found anything?" she said, her voice soft.

"Convent admin mainly," Jake replied. "You?"

"This could be interesting. The Mother Superior has started to visit an asylum and she speaks of women there needing divine protection. It's located –"

Her words were cut off as a dull clang came from the end of the vault, back where the access hatch led to the shaft.

"Get back," Jake whispered, rising quickly and pulling his weapon. Pushing Regina to the back of the rolling stack, he peered around the end of the row, Naomi right next to him, her weapon drawn. Jake's pulse raced as he considered their options. This was the worst environment for a gun fight. There was no other exit they could use and from what Regina had said, they would not be heard even if the place was burning down. He glanced around at the paper surrounding them. And this place would burn indeed.

For a moment, there was silence.

Then, the unmistakeable noise of a heavy object landing in the aisle near them, and a grenade rolled into view. There was no smell and no visible smoke, but a hissing noise betrayed the leaking gas.

Jake didn't hesitate. He yanked off his jacket and threw it over the grenade, dampening the gas down, but he knew it wouldn't hold the chemical for long. "Get to the end, as far away as you can," he said. "Run, now."

He sprinted in the opposite direction, back towards the hatch they had come through, where whoever had thrown the grenade must surely be. As he reached the back of the bookcase, he looked round the corner quickly. He saw the back of a man's blue jacket and one leg as he stepped into the hatch.

Jake drew his gun and took a shot, knowing he wouldn't be able to get through fast enough. The man grunted but pulled through, the shot catching only his jacket. Jake squeezed into the space, fighting to get to the door, but as he reached it, he heard the unmistakeable sound of the wheel lock being spun into place.

He pounded on the metal.

"You coward," he shouted. "Come in here and face me in person."

He banged the door one last time and then swore, a torrent of Afrikaans that wasn't fit for translation. He squeezed back through the gap and into the vault again. Covering his mouth with his shirt sleeve, he crouched low to the floor and crawled back towards the stacks, beginning to feel the edges of his vision go dim. It made Jake angry to think he might die like a librarian instead of a warrior – not the way he had planned to go at all.

"Back here, Jake," Naomi called. The two women had crawled right to the back of the corridor, as far as they could get from the source of the smoke. Regina lay with her head in Naomi's lap, her eyes closed, her breathing shallow. The Mother Superior's diary was next to them.

"She succumbed quickly," Naomi said, coughing as she spoke. "We should never have brought her into this. There's been too much death already today."

Jake sat down next to her and she leaned her head on his shoulder. He reached one hand up to stroke her hair.

"Well, passing out twice in one day next to you isn't so bad," he said.

Her laugh was soft and she lifted her head. He turned to look into her dark eyes.

"I hope we can manage it again sometime."

Moments later, the world shifted and Jake slipped away into darkness.

CHAPTER 10

JAKE OPENED HIS EYES to a hazy view of the stacks, illuminated by a nimbus around the light next to them. His head pounded and nausea rose within him, but as he came fully alert, he realized that the gas had been merely to knock them out. The Mother Superior's diary was gone, as were both his and Naomi's guns, but it looked like nothing else had been touched. Maybe whoever did this didn't want to leave bodies as evidence that would point to the stolen diary. This way, no one would be any the wiser about the incursion.

Naomi's head rested on Jake's shoulder and he was acutely aware of her soft body against his. Her breathing was natural and she stirred a little. Her dark hair smelled of coconut shampoo and he closed his eyes for a moment, inhaling her scent. Regina's head still lay in Naomi's lap and she looked like she was breathing more easily, her skin a normal color. Jake reached down to check her pulse, relieved to find it steady and strong. He shook Naomi's shoulder gently.

"Hey ... wake up," he said, softly. "You OK?"

She sighed and lifted her head, taking a deep breath as she focused on the vault and rubbed her eyes.

"Regina," she said, bending to the young woman in concern.

"She'll be alright in a minute," Jake said. "It looks like we were only drugged for the short term while they took the diary. We'll make sure she gets some help when we get out of here."

Naomi looked up at him with a dawning smile.

"That must mean that the book really does hold the location of the relic, and I think I read about it before the gas attack. I know where we need to go next."

***

"You can take the boat out into the Sound but just don't land on any of the islands," the skipper said as Jake signed the paperwork. "It's illegal and they're really strict about it. You do not want to cross the Corrections Department, believe me."

"We just want to do a little sightseeing," Jake said. "Maybe some night fishing later on."

The skipper frowned.

"Not really the weather for it but hey, it's your call. The insurance is all in order." He stamped the documents and filed them quickly, locking away the cash Jake had provided. There were a couple of extra hundred-dollar notes in the pile after his questioning glances at their dusty and dirty clothes, evidence of the underground excursion.

After Regina had roused from the drugged sleep, they'd traced their way back through the tunnels and left her at the ER, where she assured them she would be fine. Then, Jake and Naomi continued the hunt alone. They had two backpacks now, delivered at short notice by an ARKANE agent from the central office. Their weapons and torches had been replaced, just in case, but they still wore the clothes from the day's adventure.

Together, they headed out for the dock, the skipper leading the way. He showed Jake the controls of the boat, explained the safety features and wished them a good evening. Naomi helped cast off and they set out north from City Island towards Chimney Sweeps and the Blauzes, where there was apparently some good fishing.

As soon as they were far enough away, Jake turned the boat east towards Hart Island. The throb of the engine through his feet and the movement of the ocean made him smile. Being out here in the wind was far preferable to the dark tunnels beneath the city. He took a deep breath of the salty air. Naomi sat at the bow, her dark hair tied back with a few strands caught by the breeze.

"Some call it the island of the outcasts," she said, her voice wistful as they caught sight of the shoreline ahead. "It was originally a prisoner of war camp for Confederate soldiers – it's functioned as a juvenile prison workhouse, a quarantine camp for yellow fever, a missile base, a hospital for tuberculosis patients, and of course, a lunatic asylum."

"And now?" Jake asked, steering the boat across the bay, his hand steady on the wheel.

"It's a mass burial ground for those unclaimed and unknown. Those without a name, or those with a name but no one to bury them. Those too poor to afford a proper grave. Babies who died in hospital or were abandoned. There are over 800,000 people buried here. The graves are dug by the inmates of Rikers Island who come by ferry every day."

Jake thought of Morgan and their visit to the mummy crypt of Palermo, where the baby room had been the most disturbing place. He shook his head with a sigh.

"Mass graves aren't exactly my idea of a fun tourist day out, you know."

"Sorry." Naomi smiled. "But the Mother Superior's diary specifically mentioned this place. She used to minister to the women here at the asylum. Her words were something like, *the relic will protect those who suffer here. They deserve it more than the rich languishing in the towers built from the bodies of those they exploit.*"

"Ouch," Jake said. "She sounds like a firebrand."

"Just the type to buck tradition and bring the relic here perhaps. The diary must be important or it wouldn't have been taken."

Jake scanned the waters around them.

"Indeed, but it does mean that we might have some company soon."

"It's near impossible to get permission to come onto the island," Naomi said. "Even those who find relatives buried here have to go through the prison administration system. Then if you get permission, you're restricted to the ferry dock gazebo where the burial records are held."

"So we have no choice but to trespass, right?"

"Absolutely none." Naomi turned and her eyes were bright, her smile alive with enthusiasm. "Besides, where would the fun be in going through the usual channels? I'm having a pretty exciting time with you, Jake Timber. Trespassing twice in one day. I really have to get out of the office more often."

As they neared the shore, they looked for a place to land the boat, avoiding the official pier where there would likely be cameras. The island was low with sparse cover. Just a few trees, scrub and patches of dust. It was unkempt, as if those who came here couldn't leave fast enough. Buildings dotted the landscape but all were rundown, used as storehouses while they still stood, but they looked as if they would be left to crumble or soon be leveled to make room for new graves. There was a sense of abandonment, a place only inhabited by ghosts and the dead.

Jake slowed the engine as they scanned the shoreline, avoiding the treacherous reefs. Signs dotted the perimeter on the rocks above the shallow beaches. *New York City Corrections Department. Restricted area. No trespassing. No docking. No anchoring. Violators will be prosecuted.*

"I'm not intending to violate anything," Jake said. "How 'bout you?"

"Certainly not," Naomi said. "How about landing over there?"

She pointed out a cobbled beach under the shadow of an imposing building with a tall chimney, the ruins of the island's power plant. Jake steered the boat in, revving slightly before pulling up the motor so they could coast up the stones a little. Naomi jumped gracefully out onto the shore, holding the boat steady so Jake could disembark. They dragged the boat further away from the water line, the sound of metal on stone loud in the still air.

"No point in trying to hide the boat," Jake said. "If we get caught, it's better to be clueless tourists than clandestine operatives."

Naomi pulled a map from her backpack and peered closely at it, turning it around until she got her bearings.

"OK, the asylum isn't too far. This way."

They walked up from the beach through the trees, stepping quietly with an instinctive respect. It was a place that demanded silence, as if to wake what slumbered here would be abomination. The ground was covered in patchy mist and Jake fancied that the souls of the unloved clung to the earth, seeking solace. What is heaven if you have no hope of seeing those who made life on earth so happy? He thought of his parents, his sisters, murdered too young. He didn't really believe in an afterlife, but in quiet moments, he could sense their presence and there was still hope that he might be together with them in the end.

A red brick building loomed from the trees, with tall window spaces that gaped black inside. The map named it as the Pavilion Building, which had once housed the Hart

Island Lunatic Asylum, a women-only residence that held the overflow from Blackwell Island Insane Asylum.

"They only brought chronic cases here," Naomi said. "Perhaps the ones who couldn't be treated, so they kept them somewhere their screams wouldn't disturb the public."

"And where the so-called civilized didn't have to deal with them," Jake said.

The forest floor grew right to the doorstep of the building, green shoots withering as they touched the brick as if afraid to cross the threshold. It was quiet and still, with no sound of birdsong or rustle of animals in the overgrown foliage. The ambient noise was only the far-off city and the ocean waves that washed all the way to the Atlantic. The air was damp, clinging to their skin, and the smell of the forest had crept in here, nature slowly reclaiming that which man had left behind. Jake willed the encroachment on faster, for perhaps only when this place was a crumble of ruins would the shades of these women be at peace.

He stepped inside with Naomi following close behind. The structure was falling apart, the inner layers of the original building showing through. The years of weathering had stripped the paint and paper from the walls, revealing the struts and planks. The floor was cracked through repeated floods and winter cold. Piles of dead leaves had blown in through glassless windows. The place was clad in decaying shades of brown and green, natural colors that dominated as the traces of human touch were slowly, but inevitably, erased.

They walked onwards. In one room, four metal beds stood against a wall regulation-distance apart, rusted and surrounded by fallen masonry. In another, three plain wooden caskets sat next to planks and plastic gloves, waiting for the bodies that would be laid inside. What kind of a life would it have been, incarcerated here and then buried in these crowded graves? Jake shivered and turned away.

"Maybe there are some records upstairs?" he said.

They walked up to the second floor, their footsteps eerie in the quiet place, and turned into the first room on the left.

"Oh." Naomi let out a soft gasp at what she saw.

CHAPTER 11

JAKE PUT OUT A hand to grip the doorframe as a distinct memory came to him. In his younger days in the military, he had been part of a peacekeeping force sent to Rwanda in the aftermath of the genocide. The piles of clothing and shoes on the edge of mass graves were all that was left of the Tutsi people, butchered with machetes and farm tools. Those piles in turn had echoes of Auschwitz and the Nazi death camps ... and this room, the floor deep with shoes that seemed to have no owner. Whatever the color of a person's skin, it seemed that humanity would always seek to destroy those viewed as Other.

"Are you OK?" Naomi's voice broke through Jake's reverie.

He let out a deep breath. "Yes ... sorry. I was just remembering something that happened a long time ago."

"I know this looks like the aftermath of atrocity," she said. "But actually the inmates used to make shoes as some kind of occupational therapy. They left all this here when they closed the asylum."

Jake shook his head, his smile hiding the turmoil inside. "I can't help but jump to the wrong conclusion. You've got to admit – it's a pretty awful sight. Somehow more disturbing than a load of bodies. But it looks like there's nothing up here. Let's check outside before it gets too dark."

They walked around the perimeter between the wards to the west and came upon a burial pit lying open like a dark maw in the earth.

"Some bodies have apparently been disinterred," Naomi said. "If they can be identified by relatives, they can be reburied somewhere easier to visit."

Jake peered down into the hole, the edges of plain wooden coffins visible under a thin layer of earth, each marked with a scrawled number in black ink.

"Burn me," he said. "I want none of this lying beneath the earth business. The idea of bodily resurrection has always freaked me out."

Naomi giggled. "A little too much like the *Living Dead* for my liking, too. I wouldn't want to be over here for the zombie apocalypse, that's for sure."

There was a sound in the distance and Jake put his hand out, motioning for Naomi to be silent. It was a car engine coming their way.

The pair ran swiftly to cover at the side of the building, ducking behind a ruined wall so they still had a view of the overgrown road. A battered truck pulled up and two men got out. One was younger, good looking. The other was a grim-faced boxer type in a blue jacket, who slung a shovel over his shoulder as they emerged from the vehicle. They spoke in fast French and Jake was only able to make out one word: *tombe* – the French for grave.

Jake pulled Naomi down behind the wall.

"The guy on the right," he whispered. "I think he was in the vault. I didn't see his face, but that jacket looks familiar."

"We should follow them," Naomi said quietly. "They look like they know more than we do at this point."

Jake nodded. They checked their weapons and left the bulky packs by the wall. With Naomi following close behind, Jake slipped around the side of the building, staying far enough back not to be seen as he peeked through cracks in the structure to keep the men in sight. Soon the men stopped and put their tools down, with the young man checking a GPS location on his phone.

Near where the men stood was a verdant patch of green distinct from the brown surrounds, evidence of life blooming from those buried beneath. The man in the blue jacket tugged a map from his pocket and then bent to examine some small white markers. He grunted with a nod and the pair began to dig.

"We need to get into those trees," Jake whispered, nodding at the copse near the men. "We can't stay here or we won't see what they find."

Naomi turned and stepped quietly away, careful as she walked around the masonry and debris on the ground near the buildings. There was no hesitation in her gait and Jake noticed that she was more confident now, as if she had grown into her agent self during their day together. Still, Jake missed having a partner he could read like a book, whose every action he could anticipate because it would be his own. He missed Morgan, but he still had doubts that she would want him back as a partner, damaged as he was in body and mind. He followed Naomi quietly, resolve rising within him. He wouldn't let her down today – he was still a soldier, an ARKANE agent, a man she could rely on. He straightened his back and inhaled slowly, filling his lungs with the air of the forest and easing the tension from his limbs. He was ready, whatever might come.

The pair slipped through the trees, navigating a wide circle within hearing distance of the men, who spoke softly as they dug. It seemed like the older man was complaining, even as the younger man did most of the work. When the voices were directly in front of them, Jake and Naomi crept forward through the copse until they were within sight of the grave but still hidden in the trees.

The spade made a dull sound as it hit wood under the dirt. The young man bent to brush the earth from a coffin.

"Soixante-dix-sept," he said, reading a number from the tattooed wood.

"C'est ici," the older man replied with a half smile. "Bon travail, Marc."

He pulled out a smartphone and dialed a number, spoke a few words, then held the phone up to witness the find.

"Creusez," the man said. *Dig.*

Jake turned to Naomi and signaled for her to wait. Her eyes were shining, her weapon held in unwavering hands. He could see her chest rise and fall quickly, her breathing elevated. He would need to depend on her, but ideally he didn't want blood shed again today. Not here on this island of so many dead.

The younger man, Marc, shoveled the earth off the top of the coffin and stood looking down at it, his features disturbed.

"Ouvrez," the older man said, holding the phone up at an angle so the view was down into the grave.

Marc let out a torrent of French, clearly unwilling to open the coffin beneath. The older man leaned forward and cuffed him hard round the back of the head, a blow that was a promise of more. Marc raised the spade he held in a moment of rage, but stopped as he looked at the smart phone in the man's hand, his eyes darting to the older man.

After a moment, he lowered the spade and took a deep breath. He crossed himself and bent again to the coffin, levering the plywood slats from the top, breaking them open. His face contorted with disgust at his own actions.

"Regardez," Marc said, straightening, his eyes wide.

Jake held his hand up to Naomi, signaling her to be ready to move.

The older man bent forward to look into the grave, his

attention fully fixed on what was below, his arm held out straight with the smart phone.

Jake burst from the bushes, his gun trained on the older man.

"Don't move," he said, his tone ice cold with quiet authority.

The two men looked up. Jake saw the older man's eyes narrow, his body twist a little as he threw the phone at Jake and reached for his gun. Jake didn't hesitate. He shot the man in the leg. The man grunted and his body spun round. Naomi stepped quickly from the trees near the wounded man, her gun held out. She kicked his weapon away, her gun trained on his head.

"Let's all just keep calm," Jake said, a little amazed that they had managed this with so little bloodshed.

Then it all went to hell.

CHAPTER 12

Naomi stepped too close to the grave's edge, her inexperience in the field making her underestimate the young man's threat. Jake opened his mouth to shout a warning, but it was too late.

Marc spun with the spade and thrust the sharp edge into her calf, chopping into her flesh – once, twice, his face contorted with violence. She went down onto her knees with a cry. Jake reacted immediately, shooting the young man's shoulder, spinning him around. As he reared back up, spade raised for another blow, Jake shot him again in the chest. His body dropped into the grave.

The older man took advantage of the diversion and grabbed for Naomi's gun, bellowing in French, his growls those of a rabid animal. As she dodged his reach, he swung the other meaty fist, connecting with her jaw. She fell back onto the ground, collapsing with a cry as he wrestled with her for the gun.

As Jake swung his own weapon on the pair, Naomi bucked her hips and rolled into his line of fire, her back momentarily obscuring the man. Jake swore and ran closer, trying to get a better angle.

Then, a gunshot rang out and the pair were still. The metallic smell of gunfire and blood pervaded the clearing.

For a second, Jake thought Naomi must have been hit. With no field experience, she would only have fired on the range before. But then she rolled away from the older man, her face and hands and clothes splattered with gore from the close-range headshot.

Naomi clutched at her gun, her hands shaking as she held the weapon out towards the dead man as if waiting for him to rise. She moaned a little, her eyes open and staring as shock held her rigid. The wounds in her leg were bleeding, crimson jagged slices through her trouser suit and skin.

"It's OK now," Jake said, jumping quickly into the grave to check Marc's body for a pulse. The last thing they needed was retribution from the grave. But the man was dead. "You're OK now. Just breathe."

He climbed back out and went to Naomi, taking the gun from her hand and laying it beside them. He pulled her into his arms and held her shaking body.

"Sssh," he whispered, remembering his own first kill – a rebel militia gunman. It was a long time ago now, back in South Africa when he had first joined the military. There had been so many since then, but he still felt the stain of every one, even if he never knew their names. If it was death by a thousand cuts to his soul, he still had time to pay.

After a moment, Naomi wrenched her body from his, turning onto her knees beside him. She vomited, retching as she heaved up everything inside. Jake stroked her hair gently.

"I know how it feels," he said. "The first kill changes things. But your reaction means you're completely normal, believe me."

Naomi spat and wiped her mouth on her sleeve.

"They told us about this in the ARKANE academy," she said, "but we all laughed it off. You think somehow you won't ever need to fire a weapon, or to kill with one. Especially as a linguist." She exhaled and leaned her head back to look at the sky. "But I could see from his eyes that he would have finished me if he got the gun, Jake. It was him or me."

"I know, and you need to remember that if you wake in the night thinking about it." He bent to examine her leg. "Right now, you need medical attention and a tetanus shot."

"It'll be fine," Naomi said, but she flinched as he touched her.

"No, it won't be," Jake said. "Take it from me. I know about injury and this is the only body you have. We also need someone to come and deal with the dead here. What's the protocol for your office on cleanup?"

"I just have to make a call," Naomi said. "I haven't had to make this particular one before. It's a day of firsts, for sure."

"Gunshots carry across water, so chances are we'll have the Corrections Department here to arrest us in no time." He looked over at the grave. "But let's check this out first. Are you OK? Can you walk?"

Naomi nodded, rising to her feet, weight on her good leg. "I'll survive." She walked to the edge of the grave. "We need to get him out first."

Jake smiled. She was tougher than he gave her credit for.

Together they bent and grabbed the younger man under his arms, lifting the body from the grave and laying it by the side. The man had levered open the top section before they emerged from the trees, and the upper half of a skeleton lay revealed against the cheap wood. There were two things in the grave with it: a large metal cross lay around the bones of the neck, and an oilskin packet rested between its ribs – as if it had once settled on top of the body but had sunk as the corpse rotted away.

Jake stepped down carefully onto the half of the coffin that was still covered, reached down and lifted the package away from the remains. Despite the bones, the grave smelled only of earth. For a moment, Jake felt a sense of peace. This woman had died fulfilling her mission in life, helping those in true need and giving them a protection she believed worthy of them. He only hoped they could honor her memory now. He handed the package up to Naomi and climbed back out of the grave.

She unwrapped the oilskin to reveal an ivory figurine of Christ crucified, the patina similar to the Cloisters Cross they had seen this morning.

"The corpus," Naomi said. "It's beautiful." She looked up at Jake. "But should we take it from the island if she believed it would protect those here?"

"The dead don't need a relic to save them," Jake replied. "The Mother Superior brought it here for the mad, but they aren't here anymore. I think the Sisters of the Guardian Angel carry on her work, so they should have it back."

Naomi nodded and handed the figurine to him. He bent closer to look at the finely carved detail, the etching of agony on the face of the savior.

"You need to make that call now," he said. "And we need a helicopter back to Manhattan. I also think we should take the corpus back to ARKANE before we return it to the convent."

Naomi nodded and pulled a phone from her jacket pocket. She turned away as she spoke to the central ARKANE dispatch. Jake smiled at the new confidence in her voice. It had been quite a day.

He weighed the corpus in his hand as Naomi turned back, her phone call over.

"It feels heavier than I would expect for something so fragile," he said.

Naomi bent closer. "The museum exhibition suggested that some corpus icons had a cavity for a relic inside. Some piece of a saint's body, a sliver of bone, a nail from the cross or a holy thorn."

Jake turned the corpus and looked on the end of the carving, where Christ's feet were hammered together on a block. He could just make out the edges of a plug in a slightly different shade of ivory.

"Do you have a nail file, by any chance?" he asked.

"Seriously?" Naomi's look was daggers. "Just because I'm a girl, I get to carry the nail file?" Jake blushed a little and she laughed. "Actually, I do have one in my pack."

Jake jogged away and returned quickly with their two packs. Naomi pulled out a small metal nail file and Jake used it to prise the plug off. He handed it to Naomi.

"Don't lose that." He grinned. "We'll have to pretend we didn't touch it."

He looked inside and tipped the corpus, jogging it a little and shaking it gently. A small glass vial slid out wrapped in a hand-scrawled note. The paper was ivory colored and although thick, it was clearly fragile.

"Careful," Naomi whispered, but her eyes urged Jake on. He unrolled the paper and removed the vial, its dark ruby contents sticking to the sides. He read from the note.

"New Amsterdam was built on the bones of slaves but its wealth was guaranteed by the dark angel who lies bound in darkness. This blood was given for the Buttonwood men who promised to honor its release. The one who drinks must choose its fate."

"Hmmm," Naomi said. "Not particularly helpful, is it? New Amsterdam was a seventeenth-century colony on the tip of Manhattan Island, and the Dutch West Indies Company began the import of slaves to this area as laborers. I'm not sure about the rest of it."

Jake held the vial up to the fading light.

"At least we know what's in here ... but I wonder whose blood it really is."

The *whup-whup* sound of a helicopter came to them across the ocean.

"Let's get back to the open area near the asylum," Naomi said. "They can touch down there."

Jake slipped the vial and note into his pocket, plugged the end of the now-empty corpus, and wrapped it back in the oilskin. He carefully put it in his backpack and then helped Naomi back through the trees, leaving the open grave and the bodies behind them. She limped forward, hissing a little when she stumbled and put weight on her wounded leg, but she didn't complain.

As Jake clutched the vial in his pocket, he felt a strange sensation. The world seemed to shift and he thought he saw movement in the trees. He glanced back, heart thumping, and the shadows altered. There were shades of people there, but he sensed that they weren't in this time. Perhaps not even of this place. He heard the rustle of great wings and turned quickly, expecting a figure to drop from the sky. Then the beating of helicopter blades drowned the sound out and he helped Naomi to get into the ARKANE chopper, where a medic started to dress her wounds.

As the helicopter rose into the sky, Jake looked back down at the island. Sunset tinged its contours with russet and gold, the earth absorbing the rays as it had done the blood and flesh of so many. The vial throbbed warm in his hand and Jake felt a rising need inside him, as if he was drawn to something in the city below, the feeling intensifying as they drew closer. As they swept down the edge of Manhattan Island, the sun blazed and it was as if the skyscrapers were painted in blood. Jake sensed a dark omen rise within him, something he had not felt since the crypt of the demon in Sedlec – something not of this earth.

***

Gilles Noiret slammed his fist down on the desk in front of him. The camera feed had been shut off as a tall man emerged from the trees with a gun. Gilles only got a glimpse of this man before the feed was lost.

A wracking cough shook Gilles as he screamed his frustration, and he sat back down heavily, waiting for the fit to subside, clutching a handkerchief to his mouth. When he pulled the cloth away, it was speckled with black blood. He didn't have much time, and that bastard held his last hope in the real corpus.

Once he was in control of his body again, Gilles called his team.

"I'm sending a photo of the man who now has the corpus. Find him and get me that vial."

CHAPTER 13

THE HELICOPTER LANDED AT the downtown Manhattan heliport on Pier 6 in the East River. Naomi was looking increasingly pale and the temporary dressing on her leg was sodden with blood.

"You need to get to a hospital," Jake said. "I'll take the corpus back to ARKANE myself."

She hesitated and he could see how torn she was, desperate to finish what they had started together. But after a moment she nodded, wincing as Jake helped her away from the helicopter towards a waiting car.

"The Buttonwood men," she said as they walked across the tarmac. "I was thinking about it as we flew over – anything to keep my mind off the pain. It was the Buttonwood agreement in the late eighteenth century that began the New York Stock Exchange."

The words set off a thrum within Jake, as if finally the correct chords had been struck. His whole body resonated and the vial burned in his pocket. He was overwhelmed with the need to get to the Stock Exchange building, only a few blocks away on Wall Street. He tried to control his voice, not wanting to betray the turmoil inside.

"I'll check it out," he said.

"Call me when you know anything." Naomi climbed

into the ARKANE car waiting at the curb. Jake nodded as she pulled the door shut, waving as she turned to look behind, her eyes betraying a mixture of frustration and relief.

Jake began the walk up to Wall Street, the throb of the vial in his pocket getting stronger as he strode away from the heliport towards the ferry terminal and then up Broadway. If he had been a new agent, perhaps he would have taken the vial straight to the lab, spooked by its unusual properties. But in his time at ARKANE he had seen some strange things, and curiosity now overcame doubt. After the demon in the Sedlec crypt and his days in the darkness of coma, the edges of the world had blurred and he was more willing to consider the supernatural.

He had learned that what many saw as fantasy was sometimes more real than the physical world, and truth often wore a veil. There were depths to the world that few perceived because humanity primarily trusted in the physical senses. But now that he knew there was more, Jake trusted that whatever was in the vial would lead him on. He clutched it in his hand and felt a craving, a taste in his mouth like hunger. He didn't know what for, but he felt drawn forward, north towards Wall Street.

The streets were crowded and Jake dodged the slow-moving tourists as he walked at the fast pace of native New Yorkers. As he traveled, he became aware of unusual figures on the sidewalk around him, shades of the past weaving with the present. Figures dressed in clothing from another era, vehicles that were long past vintage, and in a brief glimpse around the corner of a building, he saw ancient forest encroaching on the city streets. A realm with no people, a past too far back even for this great city. Jake experienced a sense of vertigo as he witnessed these things, his mind unsure how to process them. He pulled his hand away from the vial in his pocket and for a moment, the world was normal again. Yet he craved to touch it again, like the edges of an addiction he knew could destroy him.

Then ahead, Jake saw a face in the crowd, a man with rough features staring at him. The man's eyes narrowed as he spotted his prey, and he spoke quickly into a cell phone. Jake ducked into a side street, ran down a block and zigzagged northeast, away from the main Broadway drag.

He should have known that those who wanted the corpus would be after him. He felt for the vial in his pocket. Did they know about the blood inside? He should run for ARKANE, get in a cab, and hide in the labs beneath the UN. The technicians there could work out what was in the vial and the mystery would be solved – he could go home to London. But he felt drawn onwards, unable to resist the sensation. It was like a clock ticking down to a climax, the timer seconds away from detonation. Urgency spurred him onwards.

Jake continued north, walking swiftly, eyes forward like a local. At the back of Trinity Church, he cut along Rector Street, emerged again on Broadway and then crossed over to Wall Street and then Broad Street. Tourists lined up near the security rails to gaze up at the grand entrance to the New York Stock Exchange. He joined the back of a tour group from the Wall Street Experience as the guide launched into his spiel.

"The classical facade of the building is topped with a triangular pediment." The guide pointed up to the top of the building before them. "It may surprise you to know that the sculpted figure in the middle represents Integrity. She stretches her arms out to protect the works of man beside her – science, industry and agriculture." He gave a wry smile. "Of course, we've all lived through the financial crisis of 2008, so I'm sure you all understand what integrity means these days."

Jake tuned out the man's spiel and clutched the vial in his pocket, trying to understand what he should do next. He was drawn to this building, but there was no way of getting inside the Stock Exchange without immense security protocols. ARKANE could arrange access, but he felt sure there was no time now. These barriers were the closest he could get.

Suddenly, he felt a prickle on the back of his neck, a heightened sense of being watched. Jake turned to survey the area, picking out one, two … no, three watchers, their eyes fixed on him. They began to walk toward him, fanning out to prevent his escape in any direction. He was hemmed in.

Jake calculated the distance to the doors of the Stock Exchange building. If he jumped the barrier and ran for it, chances are he would be shot by security wary of a terrorist attack. If he waited here, these men would surround him within a minute.

He clutched the vial in his hand, feeling it pulse in time with his heartbeat. He could taste blood in his mouth. The thought electrified him.

These men didn't want the corpus.

They wanted what was inside.

Time and space are nothing for those who stand beyond. The strange words from the book of John Dee rang through his mind. Was this truly a relic that could reveal the supernatural realm? That could give a bargaining power to the one who drank.

Jake's rational mind chastised the ridiculous idea as the ravings of a man who had finally broken and should leave behind this agent life. But part of him thrilled at the thought, the audacity of faith that there might be more than this.

He looked around at the faces of the tourists who had come to worship at the temple of Mammon, their disapproval of what went on in these hallowed halls hiding a desire to be just like those within. Behind them he could see more figures, as the moment flicked in and out of history before his eyes. Above the hubbub of the street, he thought he could hear the beat of giant wings.

The men stepped closer, hands in their jacket pockets, clearly concealing weapons. Jake had seconds before they were on him.

He pulled the vial from his pocket and took the stopper from the lid. Jake had expected the metallic scent of blood, but all he could smell was the chill stone of a cave beneath the earth.

His heart beat faster, a hammering in his chest as he approached a fulcrum of time, a tipping point that would take him into the unknown. He was sure of one thing – this blood, whatever it was, could not fall into the hands of these Confessors.

But what would drinking it do to him?

Jake felt reckless in that moment. He remembered lying in a coma, the warmth of a black blanket over his mind, a detachment from the world. He was no longer afraid of dying – in truth, part of him longed for the end of it all.

As the men closed in around him, the vial pulsed in his hand. Jake lifted it to his lips, tipping his head back to gulp the warm liquid, his throat burning as it went down.

CHAPTER 14

THE LIQUID SEEMED TO set his body on fire and for a moment, Jake thought he would be consumed by an inner flame.

Then the world shifted and shimmered. The people around him faded and the noise of the world dulled. It was as if he stepped through a waterfall into a world beyond, into the cave he had smelled in the vial.

No, not a cave. It was a crypt, somewhere hewn deep in the rock under Manhattan. And in the darkness, he could feel … something.

Jake heard the whisper of wings and the flutter of breath before he saw it.

The chamber was vast and dark, his footsteps a faint echo as he walked towards the sound. As his eyes adjusted to the dark, he realized that the whole place was crisscrossed with shining lines, ropes of spun silver and precious metal that held the captive in place and gave the place an eerie light.

An angel, if that's what it was, hung suspended in the center of the crypt, its pale skin hooked through with barbs, its arms outstretched and pulled apart by the shining cords in a parody of crucifixion. Its shape was as a man, its torso rippled with muscle, with a loincloth of sorts wrapped around its slim hips. There was a sheen to its skin, a translucence like alabaster. Its wings looked to be over six feet in length, densely feathered and beautiful, but they were pinioned to its body by loops of silver chain.

The angel lifted its head, its perfect features set in an expression of sorrow. Jake met its dark eyes and fell to his knees as vertigo shot through him, a sense of shifting in time and space to a place apart, somehow separate – as if the world had begun to spin around this underground prison.

Its eyes were the green of the depths of the ocean and the sparkle of a thousand stars, and it saw right through him. Jake wanted to look away but the angel wouldn't shift its gaze, studying him as a man might study a nest of ants before he burns it down, uncaring of mass slaughter. Jake sensed the angel scanning his memory, reading his past, noting the scars on his body and his psyche. He felt violated in that moment and yet, when it relaxed its gaze, the emptiness was a kind of freedom.

It has been long years since men came here. It is past time you released me.

Jake heard the words in his head but nothing was said aloud. The angel spoke directly into his mind.

I know you, Jake Timber. I see your past. Release me and I will give you what you desire most.

Images of his murdered family surfaced in Jake's mind, his father and mother holding out their hands to him, smiling as they welcomed him home. His youngest sister, lying in the porch swing, reading a book, her young body no longer broken and violated. The house at Walkerville was bright, lit by the sun. There was no blood on the walls, no stink of rotten, flyblown flesh in the air.

"You can bring them back?" Jake said in wonder, wanting to hold onto the glimpses of a life he had lost.

I can take you back and you can stop it. Kill before they do.

Jake saw the faces of the gang who had carried out the atrocity, each one a hated countenance. He had hunted them down afterwards and killed them, revenging his family before fleeing the country. But the grief was with him every day.

If he could go back, he could be at home the day before the gang came. He would be ready for them and his sisters, his parents, would still be alive. Tears welled up within him and he gulped them back. For so many years, he had lived with the guilt of their deaths. Was this the answer?

The angel's face flinched suddenly, as if it was being forced to speak further by some unseen power.

I can give you the peace you seek. I can bring your family to life again. But I – must – also show you what will happen to this city if you release me.

Jake's mind was filled with flame and he reeled back at the stink of smoke. The haze cleared, and he looked out at Manhattan Island as if he was back in the helicopter, looking down as it swooped over the city.

The downtown area was now a mass of burning buildings, the screams of people below a cacophony of pain and death. There were riots on the streets and the police were overwhelmed by brutality, driven back by hordes of rampaging men. People plunged into the waters around the island to escape the violence, only to be consumed by dark shapes that dragged them under, leaving dark patches of blood on the surface as their bodies were ripped apart. Creatures leapt across the chasms between buildings, dragging bodies for feasting and violation. It was a scene of Hell from a Hieronymus Bosch painting, something that could only spring from the mind of madness. Jake tried to shut out the sight but the images were forced into his head, a tableau of slaughter.

I am a hostage for the city, a shield against its destruction, for while I am here, this island cannot fall to the dark powers. But if I am released, then vengeance will fall for its years of corruption.

The images faded and Jake breathed deeply, inhaling the cold of the crypt, his mind whirling at all he had seen. He pointed at the ties that bound the angel.

"You don't look like a willing hostage."

The angel's face twisted, hate rippling over its features.

I was hung here to pay for my own sins.

"What did you do?" Jake asked.

You might have called it love.

The angel's voice in his head was faint as Jake had a vision of a beautiful woman, laughing as she splashed in a stream, her naked body dripping and glistening in the sun. Jake felt the angel's lust for her, but there was something beneath it, a jealousy and a need to possess that which he could never attain himself. As the woman turned, he saw that she was pregnant, her breasts full and heavy. She giggled as the angel stroked her with its wings but the sense of transgression of natural law weighed heavily upon the scene.

"Nephilim," Jake whispered and the vision dissolved.

The angel bowed its head.

For my sins, I am bound here. Only after seventy times seventy years will I be released from this earthly prison by He who imprisoned me here. But your kind are curious, Jake Timber.

The early men of New York found this place, and promised me release if I helped them establish the city, giving them insight and knowledge that would bestow wealth and power upon them. They promised to free me when they had achieved their goals – I gave them my blood so they would return. Ever since, I have awaited that day. Now you are here.

"Those men are long dead," Jake said. He closed his eyes for a moment and took a deep breath. "And I cannot release you if it means the city will fall under some dark destruction. There is already much suffering above, but there are people who bring light."

Jake thought of Naomi and her desire to help the people of the city. Regina and the Sisters of the Guardian Angel. His time with ARKANE and how he would never have been recruited by Marietti if he hadn't fled South Africa in the aftermath of his family's tragedy. He thought of Morgan.

"As much as I want my family back," he said. "That time is passed. I cannot take your exchange, even for them."

Time is nothing.

The angel's features twisted in anguish.

"Then your many years in chains should pass quickly," Jake said in a soft voice.

Then you must return above. I will let you go if you take another vial of my blood. For then another can make a choice as you have done, for the next generation.

Jake hesitated, knowing that others would choose differently – that to take the vial back up would put the city under threat.

You have no choice if you want to return to your life. Approach and bring the vial.

Jake stepped through the maze of silver cords, twisting and turning to avoid touching them. As he drew closer, he could see the muscle tone under its skin, a deeply masculine beauty of sculpted marble. This angel was a warrior and surely no man could stand against it, or others like it, if it was free.

Yes, there are more of my kind, but we are not so concerned with your lives. Don't worry, Jake Timber. You have enough of your own troubles ahead.

Jake inched closer until he was standing directly before the angel, looking up into its terrible beauty.

"You see my future?"

Of course, time is nothing. Release me and I will tell you. Use the knife below and cut the ties that bind me.

Its green eyes burned like a fire of emerald and for a moment, Jake was hypnotized by their promise. He bent and picked up the silver knife that lay on the ground beneath the angel. Its handle was bright, reflecting the light from the cords and the glow of the angel's body.

He shook his head, breaking the gaze.

"I'm sorry. I can't."

The angel nodded.

Then use the knife and catch my blood in the vial. Then I will release you.

Jake held the vial up and used the knife to cut into the angel's side, where the lance that pierced Christ would have slipped in. Blood welled from the wound and Jake caught the first few drops in the vial before stoppering the lid once more. As he watched, the cut closed and the angel's skin was whole and unblemished again.

There was a pitcher with water on the floor next to a wooden drinking cup. A simple torture, since it would be forever out of the angel's reach. Jake poured some water out and lifted it to the angel's lips. Its green eyes softened and for a second, he saw a glimpse of the beyond in its gaze. A stab of hope rose within Jake as the angel drank deeply until the cup was drained.

Thank you.

Jake heard a rushing sound fill the crypt and the angel faded into a shimmering silver mist. He dropped the cup and clutched at his ears, trying to equalize the pressure by gulping. As the mist cleared, he found himself back in front of the New York Stock Exchange, the moment frozen as he had left it.

But there was something different in his body. He sensed the change. There was no throb of pain from his old injuries, no hesitation in his muscle memory. He felt revived. Had the angel's blood healed him?

Time began again, but slowly at first. He slipped past one of the men who came for him and walked away as time sped up and life resumed. From a safe distance, Jake looked back to see the men milling about in confusion as they searched for him and he ducked into a side street heading back to ARKANE. The vial of angel's blood in his pocket was cold now, with no sense of power. The corpus would go back to the nuns, but this would go down into the ARKANE vaults away from those who might be tempted to use it.

CHAPTER 15

JAKE STOOD ON THE back of the Staten Island commuter ferry watching the sunset turn the sky orange behind the Statue of Liberty. He had wanted to see this view before he left New York, and knew he had enough time before his evening flight home. Naomi was recovering in hospital and was enthusiastic about turning her skills to being a field agent. The Cloisters Cross had been recovered from the penthouse flat of reclusive billionaire Gilles Noiret, who had been found dead, his body rotted by poison. The Sisters of the Guardian Angel had chosen to give the corpus to the museum to be displayed on the shaft of the cross. It had been a big day, and for once Jake thought that his sleep might be without nightmares.

Wisps of cloud painted the horizon with shades of pink and burnt umber and he remembered the visions of the angel, the glimpse into a realm that seemed just a hallucination now. Jake took a deep breath, inhaling the ocean air, his lungs expanding. His body definitely felt stronger now, and there was no pain from the wounds he had suffered over the last ARKANE missions. He would need to get scans to confirm it when he got home, but he was sure the angel's blood had healed him.

But there was something more.

The cracks in his mind, the guilt over his murdered family – they were still there but they were softer now, as if the edges had been rubbed off. The scars were no longer raw and angry, but part of his body. He would always be aware of them, but they didn't own him anymore. Had the angel given him this gift after a moment of compassion in the crypt? He would never know.

Jake wondered how much of the day's events to write in his official report, and what he would label the vial for the ARKANE crypt. What would he tell Morgan? Maybe nothing. Maybe only that he was able to recover the relic and return it to the convent, that the Cloisters Cross had been retrieved, that the vial needed to be kept safe.

He smiled and looked back at the famous skyline. New York had its problems but it was a vibrant city that would survive another generation, unknowing of what lay chained beneath.

The ferry horn honked. A lone seagull rode the wind on the wake of the boat and as he gazed into the froth of the water, Jake knew his future was with ARKANE. He was strong again now and once he flew home, he would be back on duty alongside Morgan, as the partner she deserved.

AUTHOR'S NOTE

As ever, my books are based on real historical places with truth twisted into fiction and this one is no different! You can see the visual inspiration for the book at: www.pinterest.com/jfpenn/new-york/

New York

It's difficult to write about New York without resorting to cliché movie locations, but in the Cloisters, I found a little slice of medieval England.

The chapters about the Cloisters are based on *The Cloisters Cross: Its Art and Meaning*, and *A Walk through the Cloisters*. Both publications are available from the Met in free PDF format here:

http://www.metmuseum.org/visit/visit-the-cloisters

The Cloisters Cross is as described except for the Enochian script, which is actually considered to be Hebrew written backwards.

I've walked the fantastic High Line in Manhattan and I highly recommend it to anyone wanting a little escape from the New York city streets. There is a church of the

Guardian Angel in Manhattan, but everything about the nuns is fictionalized.

The scene in the subway tunnels was based on the video of *Undercity* featuring urban historian Steve Duncan. You can watch it here: www.vimeo.com/18280328

Also, check out www.undercity.org for more underground adventures.

You can find out about the vaults under the New York Public Library here:

http://gothamist.com/2008/10/24/underneath_the_new_york_public_libr.php#photo-1

Hart Island is indeed a mass burial ground, and I have tried to honor the location, although I haven't been there. There was an asylum and they did manufacture shoes.

www.untappedcities.com/2013/07/22/abandoned-hart-island-new-york-citys-mass-burial-ground/

Angels

The idea for the angel chained under the city came from a sculpture I saw while walking in London – an angel's wing rising from the streets near the Bank of England. I had a vision of this huge supernatural being trapped under the heavy buildings. Then I saw the bound fallen angel by Paul Fryer in his art installation Morning Star, and the two ideas fused in this book.

DESTROYER OF WORLDS

AN ARKANE THRILLER
J.F. PENN

"I am become Death, destroyer of worlds."

Bhagavad Gita

CHAPTER 1

London, England. 5.13am

TENDRILS OF CRIMSON DAWN touched the Thames and turned the river to blood as it heralded a new day. The city was quiet, a magical place at this time when millions of people lay still in their beds. The ancient buildings rested before another crazy morning in the maelstrom that was London.

A ray of light caught the face of Big Ben as its hands ticked each second past, marking another cycle in the city. A block away, between Westminster and Soho, pigeons picked at the remnants of last night's revelry in Trafalgar Square, overlooked by the grand facade of the National Gallery. A black cab curved past St Martin-in-the-Fields church, heading towards the Mall and down towards Buckingham Palace. It swooshed through a puddle and muddy water sprayed up onto the pavement as it passed.

The air was chill, the night had not yet left. The square was still in shadow as a squeak of wheels pierced the air. A man in a high-visibility orange jacket pushed his rubbish cart between the fountains under the shadow of Nelson's Column. As he wheeled the cart through the square, he picked up litter with a slow stoop and glide: sandwich wrappings, a lost teddy bear, flyers for the next activist march, the discarded flotsam of the city. He had seen it all over the years since immigrating here, but the treasures people threw away still surprised him. Back in India, most of this would be reused and even sold on.

But he would never see his homeland again now.

Sweat beaded on the man's brow, dripping down into the deep lines around his eyes. He whispered a mantra, over and over, as he took those final steps, his lips forming and reforming the sacred words.

Security cameras, ever watchful, tracked his progress across the square. But his cart had a Westminster City Council logo on the side and he wore the uniform of a street cleaner, so he remained unseen. This was the city of many faces and his brown features were nothing special here in London, a place he called home. No matter now though – the gods called for blood and he had been chosen.

He inhaled the cool air and looked up at the bronze lions guarding Nelson's Column, their regal faces composed as they stared back. A skeletal horse stood high above him on the Fourth Plinth of the square, the modern sculpture on this spot changing over time to reflect the shifting city allegiances. A jaunty bow tied around the horse's front leg displayed the electric lights of the stock exchange ticker tape that ran around it. Its sparse rib cage reminded the man of home, the dried bones that washed up on the shore after floods. At least his family would never go hungry again after this.

He wheeled his cart closer to one of the fountains and looked at his watch.

One more minute.

The man bent and put his hands into the water. The coolness on his skin calmed his mind and he splashed some on his face as he whispered a final prayer. He looked up to the sky to see the last stars of night fading into the dawn and smiled. It was still a beautiful world. Perhaps in his next life, he would return to this great city in a different guise.

The man turned back to his cart, lifted the lid of the bin, reached in and pressed a button. There was a moment of stillness, when a shimmer seemed to hang in the air.

Then, the light exploded.

The bomb blast echoed around Westminster, the impact immediately destroying both fountains and blasting a hole in Trafalgar Square. The giant marble column topped with Nelson's statue shattered. The proud bronze lions melted in the blast and the memorial plaques made from enemy cannon tumbled into the crater.

As the echo from the blast died, the shrill sound of sirens broke the air. Alarm bells went off in every building in central London as Buckingham Palace and the Houses of Parliament went into lockdown.

Above the sound of panic, the *chop chop chop* of a helicopter drew closer. It flew from the south, low along the Thames, emerging over the central city like a wraith. It was black with no markings, and those who saw it thought it was a military response to the bomb.

Seconds after the blast, it hovered over Trafalgar Square, directly above the crater. Dust from the blast swirled about it like fog, cloaking it from the cameras. The side doors opened and three men rappelled down thick ropes that snaked into the hole beneath them.

The bomb had laid open hidden levels beneath Trafalgar Square. These levels were not on any official maps, and few were aware of them. They had never been breached.

Until today.

Inside the crater, the men unhooked themselves from their lines, turned head-torches on, and quickly made their way through the smoking rubble to the door of a vault. It was made of thick metal, overlaid with ancient wood and inscribed with occult patterns. It was also criss-crossed with modern steel bars and protected by a high-level electronic security system.

But the lights on the door were flashing orange, blinking from the blast damage.

One of the men attached a magnetic device to the vault control panel. He pressed a key on the pad, his foot tapping as they waited. It wouldn't be long before the scene crawled with military and police. They had to get out of here quickly.

A whirr and a click.

The door opened.

For a moment the men stood at the entrance, their hesitation betraying a moment's doubt about their mission.

Then the leader stepped inside.

He pulled a Geiger counter from his bag and walked into the vault. It stretched into the distance with separate opaque rooms for books, religious artifacts and unknown objects hidden inside, a cornucopia of hidden knowledge.

But they were only here for one thing.

The device beeped and the man turned towards one of the rooms.

"Quickly now!"

The other two men rammed the door with a short metal post, the grating thump echoing through the vault. Once, twice, and then the door crumpled, shuddering on its hinges as they pushed it open.

The leader stepped inside, the light from his head-torch piercing the gloom.

There was a box on a low shelf painted with scenes from the Mahabharata, one of the great Sanskrit epics of ancient India. The man smiled with relief. He picked it up and placed it in his bag.

Together, the men ran from the vault, clipped themselves back onto the lines and were hauled up into the helicopter. They flew off over the city, leaving destruction in their wake.

CHAPTER 2

Mumbai, India. 10.35am

THE MASSIVE STATUE OF the god dominated the room. Its golden surface glinted, reflecting the light of the candles before it as Shiva Nataraja, Lord of the Dance, ushered in the next cycle of destruction and renewal. A wreath of bright orange marigolds, their petals still wet with dew, lay around his neck and the thick smell of them permeated the room, hemmed in by heavy curtains that kept the city out. The calm gaze of the god rested on the dying man in the bed before him. The room was luxurious, a fitting place for the final hours of one of the richest men in Mumbai. But death came for the rich in their towers as well as the poor crouched in the slums down the road, and Vishal Kapoor couldn't buy any more time.

Asha Kapoor stood by the bed, watching her father. She counted his breaths as his chest rose and fell in slow motion. Her fingers lightly stroked the aquamarine silk sari wrapped around her slim body. She had dressed as a good Hindu daughter to please him but his eyes hadn't even opened today.

She walked with soft footsteps to the shrine and looked up at Shiva, his features serene as he gazed into eternity. Mankind was nothing to the divine and yet she had a plan that would cause a ripple in history.

Even the gods would take notice.

The candlelight flickered and she trailed her fingers through the flame, the edge of pain sharpening her senses. Fire represented the end and a new beginning. Her father's body would soon be on the pyre and she would see a new world created after he was gone.

A rattle came from the bed and her father's breath caught in his throat. Asha's fingers tightened until her nails dug into her skin. Could this be the end? Her heart beat faster and a smile played at her lips in anticipation. He had lingered long enough.

The handle rattled on the locked door behind her, then a brisk knock on the wood.

"Asha, are you in there?"

Her brother's voice held a note of concern. Asha took a deep breath. Mahesh had hired the best doctors in Mumbai, but none held out any hope for their father's survival. Vishal had given up on life in the last days, choosing to succumb to his disease. *It's karma*, he had whispered one night as she had read to him from the Mahabharata of the battles of ancient India. His lungs were riddled with cancer caused by chemicals he had inhaled in his years of digging up the earth, first on archaeological digs and later in the mines as he had expanded his business empire.

But Asha was still angry at him for giving in. Despite her ambition to take the business further, her Papa was still the only man she loved. She brushed tears from her cheeks.

Once he was dead, she would take over and make the company greater than he ever had. He would be proud.

She composed her face into that of the concerned daughter. Her long dark hair hung about perfect features, her light coffee skin inherited from her mother, Rani, a Bollywood actress her father had wooed and won. Mahesh had both the looks and the weakness of their mother but

Asha had inherited her mind and ambition from her father, and for that she was glad. She opened the door.

"It won't be long now," she whispered, as her brother strode inside the room. "I couldn't bear to have the doctors poking him with needles anymore. He never shied from death and now he will go to the gods peacefully, without all those tubes."

Mahesh reached for her hand and squeezed it.

"You're right. It's how he would want the end to be."

Together they walked to the bedside and looked down on their father. His head faced east according to Hindu custom and, above it, a lamp flickered soft light across his features. Vishal's expression was composed and there was no suffering on it even as he wheezed his final breaths. The Hindu priest had placed a mark of ash on his forehead and his arms lay on top of a simple white sheet. Asha knew that her father would be pleased. Despite his wealth, he preferred the simpler things from the days of his youth.

She leaned down and kissed him on the cheek. His skin was dry and cool against her lips. The prick of tears stung her eyes again but she brushed them away. He would want her to be strong.

Mahesh bent to his father's right ear and whispered a mantra. If his party-boy friends on the Mumbai circuit could see him now, Asha thought. Suddenly the religious good son. Mahesh's movie-star looks and endless money had made him popular before his marriage and many of his friends had tried their chances with Asha. Of course, there had been dalliances in the dark, but none of those men understood her ambition and she had shunned their marriage proposals, much to her father's chagrin. He had tolerated her choice of independence, wanting her to have a love match as he had. There was one man she respected, one whose company she sought. He awaited her now, but she couldn't go to him empty-handed and she shivered a little at the thought of his displeasure.

Asha walked to the window and pulled back the curtain to let some light in. The wall of glass overlooked Back Bay and the Girgaon Chaupati beach on one side, while the other looked out towards the Arabian Sea. From up here in the Malabar Hills, she could see the ocean and endless horizon. The tower was testament to what her father had achieved, working his way up from a young laborer on archaeological digs to one of the richest men in India. His wealth stretched from the ship-breaking yards of Bangladesh to the mines of Karnataka and West Bengal and into the digital age. This very building contained cutting-edge scientific labs and the hub of their e-commerce division.

As Mahesh whispered his mantra, Asha turned back to the statue of Shiva, the god's golden face promising something even more remarkable than what they had already achieved with the company. There had always been rumors about the discovery that propelled her father from obscurity to extreme wealth. Of course, there would always be those who spoke ill of success, but she had seen a look in her father's eyes that told of a darker truth. When he had fallen sick, she had pored through his old diaries from the time before and discovered what he had given up in exchange for money and power.

But that secret was worth much more than everything they had now, and Asha wanted it back.

A gasp came from the bedside.

She turned quickly and strode to the bed, her sari brushing the floor. Vishal Kapoor opened his eyes and stared at the statue of the god as he breathed his last. Asha saw wonder in her father's gaze as Shiva Nataraja began his dance of death, and he slipped into the beyond.

Mahesh wept, silent tears running down his cheeks as he mourned his father.

Asha took a deep breath and as she stepped back towards the window, her cell phone vibrated in her pocket. She pulled it out to see the text she had been waiting for.

It is done. The package is on its way.

CHAPTER 3

DR MORGAN SIERRA STOOD on the edge of the bomb crater at the center of Trafalgar Square. The air was still thick with dust and she coughed a little, trying not to inhale too much. She ran her fingers through her dark curls and shook her head as she looked down at the destruction below.

The red alert code had beeped on her phone just after dawn and it had taken her less than two hours to get here from her home in Oxford. In that short time, an enormous tarpaulin had been erected over the scene, protecting what lay beneath from the prying eyes of the media. The military guarded the perimeter of the crime scene and the central city was in lockdown. After all, Buckingham Palace and the government buildings of Westminster were only a block away.

The sound of helicopters buzzed overhead with the incessant desire for more news. The media reported a terrorist attack, but Morgan knew it was more than that.

This was a raid on a place that few knew existed, hidden in plain sight although it wasn't on any official plans. Even the Prime Minister wasn't privy to its secrets. Below Trafalgar Square, wound between the foundations of ancient buildings and the modern Tube lines, lay the labyrinthine global headquarters of ARKANE, the Arcane Religious Knowledge And Numinous Experience Institute. The public-facing side consisted of academic papers on religious artifacts and dry conferences in dusty universities, but in reality, ARKANE was a secret agency investigating supernatural mysteries around the world. There were secrets held here that the world wasn't ready for and the vault below the city protected artifacts that could destroy civilization itself. The secrets ARKANE kept below were more than just a threat to a single nation, they could be used for power on a grander scale.

Now the vault had been breached.

Morgan felt the scar on her side throb, and she rubbed at it through her shirt. It pulsed sometimes when she drew close to the darkness, reminding her of the battle with the demon in the Bone Church of Sedlec. The Devil's Bible was down in the vault. Could that have been what was stolen? What else was down there? Part of her desperately wanted to know, while another part wanted to delay that moment of truth just a little longer.

Her stomach churned at the possibilities. Agents had died to bring items here for safekeeping, to hide them from the world and prevent them being used for evil deeds. She had personally added items to the vault, expecting never to see them again, and she still had nightmares of what she had seen in Houska Castle, unleashed from the Gates of Hell. But it seemed that her short leave for recovery was over. As a specialist in the psychology of extremist religion, and with military experience from the Israeli Defense Force, Morgan knew that she would be back in the field as soon as they could get a lead on the bombing.

"Coffee?"

Morgan turned to see her ARKANE partner, agent Jake Timber, holding two steaming cups.

"I think we're going to need a lot more of this today," he said as he offered her one. Jake gave a rueful smile, the corkscrew scar over his left eye crinkling a little, but his dark eyes remained hard as he surveyed the damage to the iconic square.

Morgan lifted the cup to her lips, taking a sip of the bitter black before sighing deeply.

"I can't believe it," she said, shaking her head. "Who did this? Do we know any details yet?"

"Not much," Jake said. "There's bad news, though. Marietti's in hospital. The Director's tough, but he's unconscious and badly injured. Apparently he was working in the lab nearest the vault."

Jake leaned over the edge of the crater. From their vantage point, they could see the top of the vault and the sliced-open spaces that the ARKANE researchers worked in every day. Construction workers in hard hats scurried around the levels, securing metal pipes, beams and other broken parts of the complex below the surface.

"What was he doing down there?" Morgan asked. The Director's office was above ground in a building to the side of the square, part of the public-facing side of ARKANE. He should have been safe.

"He's been increasingly worried about something," Jake said. "I know he's had migraines for months now. Apparently he's been working late every night in the lab, but we don't know what on. At least no one else was here and he's the only one injured. The bombers did a targeted smash and grab."

"Surely Martin can find out what Marietti has been up to?" Morgan said.

Martin Klein was ARKANE's official librarian and data archivist, nicknamed Spooky because of his ability to find patterns in the chaos of information that streamed into the databases every day.

"Apparently Marietti wiped the logs every night after he finished. He really didn't want people to know what he was doing." Jake pointed down into the hole. "Martin's down there right now trying to fix the defenses. The security system was hacked directly after the bombing and that wasn't meant to be possible. He's also checking the vault's inventory to see what's been taken."

"We should get down there," Morgan said.

Together they walked away from the center of the square and down Duncannon Street to a nondescript doorway next to the Halfway to Heaven pub, an appropriate name for one of the hidden entrances to the ARKANE lower levels.

Security was tight and they had to pass automatic biometric checks as well as human defense protocols before being admitted into the lab-level corridors. This end of the building was undamaged and there were technicians working on decoding artifacts, business as usual despite the bombing. Marietti would be pleased, Morgan thought. He hated anyone to waste time and there was always so much more to do to hold back the dark.

They emerged into the exploded section of the complex and dodged around the scaffolding being erected to reinforce the lower levels. The door of the vault was open and Martin Klein peered into the innards of the electronic keypad. He muttered to himself, shaking his head and tapping away on a tablet as he bobbed up and down on the balls of his feet.

"How can we help, Spooky?" Jake said as they approached.

Martin turned with a start, his concentration broken. His shock of blond hair stood up in clumps, a sure sign that he had been tugging at it as he worked.

"Morgan, Jake. Glad you're here." Martin pushed his thin wire-framed glasses up his nose. "I need to show you something."

His fingers danced over the surface of the tablet computer.

"My office is buried," he said, "but I can still access the databases from here." He pulled up video footage of the vault and played a short clip of the attack. He froze the image as one of the intruders lifted a box from the vault, a military balaclava obscuring his face. "They knew what they were looking for. They went directly to this box and then left quickly."

"What's inside?" Morgan asked.

Martin swiped the screen and quickly brought up an inventory of treasures from the vault. Morgan wanted to read the whole list, the researcher in her desperate to know what else was hidden down here. Before joining ARKANE, she had worked at the University of Oxford, specializing in the unexplained between science and faith, that which fell through the gap of psychology and religion. This vault was one of the reasons she had joined ARKANE in the first place. The knowledge and secrets down here haunted her dreams, yet she had been out in the field on missions since arriving, with no time to lose herself in study.

Martin pulled up an image of a bronze statue, a dancing god surrounded by flames.

"Shiva Nataraja," he said. "One of the primary Hindu gods portrayed as the cosmic dancer who is both destroyer and creator. It's a common enough statue in India." Martin pointed out aspects of the figure. "He dances within the flames of the universe and his left hand holds fire, signifying destruction. His left leg is raised and he stands on a demon of ignorance."

"Lord of the Dance," Morgan whispered, bending closer to look at the image. "It's said that Shiva's long dreadlocks come loose as he dances and they smash the stars into each other, destroying the universe. The snake around his waist is Vasuki, one of the *nagas* or snake gods."

"This attack is a lot of effort for just a statue," Jake said as he gestured at the destruction around them.

"It's not even a whole statue," Martin said. "It's only one

piece. The notes indicate that the sculpture was broken into four. The dancing Shiva, the flames that surround him, and then the base in two pieces. The ARKANE vault only contained the fire segment." He tapped on the screen again to reveal the history of the piece. "Marietti lodged it here back in the late 1980s, just after he joined ARKANE from the Vatican. But there are no notes as to its provenance, where it was found or why it was in the vault. As you said, Morgan, these statues are common enough in India. There's no indication as to what is so special about this one."

"Go back to the video," Morgan said. There was a detail about it that bothered her. Martin flicked back to the video and they watched it again. Morgan tapped the screen, freezing it as the men entered the vault. The leader used a device to scan the area.

"That looks like a Geiger counter," Morgan said. "Was the statue radioactive?"

Martin nodded. "A little, but there are plenty of other radioactive artifacts down here so it must have a distinctive signature." Jake raised an eyebrow. "Oh, don't worry. That's why the walls are so thick and we discourage people from spending much time inside. But there's nothing in the records as to why the statue was radioactive. Another mystery."

"We need Marietti," Jake said. "How's he doing?"

Martin tapped the screen again and it shifted to display a hospital room. A figure lay on the bed under white sheets, wires from his body attached to machines and the steady beep of monitors pulsed rhythmically from the screen. Graphs showing Marietti's vital signs popped up under the video feed. Martin shook his head.

"He's still unconscious and has been since the military first on scene found him under the rubble. But the doctors have said they could wake him under extreme necessity."

Morgan looked at Jake and saw indecision in his eyes. She knew that he had a history with Marietti and the Director's injuries were severe. Waking him would be dangerous. But she and Jake had both lain in hospital, injured after their battles with demonic forces and human foes. Marietti knew the risks of their job and he would have ordered the same if the circumstances were reversed. Jake turned to Martin.

"Tell the hospital we're coming," he said.

Martin nodded. But as they turned to go, he called them back.

"Wait. Can you … come inside the vault for a minute?"

Morgan frowned at his words and Jake looked as confused as she did, but they followed him into the vault.

"The cameras are down right now," Martin whispered. "It's safer to talk here, but we must hurry."

"What's going on?" Jake asked.

Martin exhaled sharply, steeling himself. "There's no way a breach like this could happen without someone inside leaking specific details. I've also found evidence that someone was monitoring Marietti's movements."

"They knew he was down here?" Morgan said.

"Yes, definitely," Martin said. "I don't think he was meant to survive."

Jake shook his head. "There have been rumors of a power struggle within ARKANE and some are concerned it's been infiltrated by those who would see darkness triumph. It's hard to believe but …"

"'Better to reign in Hell than serve in Heaven?'" Morgan said, quoting *Paradise Lost*.

"Indeed." Martin tapped at his screen. "If you go after this sculpture, you need to proceed carefully and I think we should keep it off-books as much as possible. I'll sort out funds and logistics from here, but keep a low profile if you can."

An hour later, Morgan and Jake walked into the private wing of an exclusive London hospital. Despite the luxury, the smell of antiseptic made Morgan's skin crawl. She and Jake had both spent enough time in hospital after ARKANE missions, albeit not quite as plush as this. Hospitals were not her favorite place.

After clearing security, they found the Director's room. It had a large picture window with reinforced glass looking out over London, stylish furniture and artwork on the walls. But the view didn't matter to this patient. Marietti lay on his back, his eyes closed, his skin sallow. His chest moved up and down as he breathed and the machines around him beeped softly, the rhythm a welcome sign of stability.

Morgan walked to the bed and stood looking down upon him. The Director had lied to her at the beginning of her time with ARKANE, but she had grown to trust him anyway. There were things that he knew, things that would make even the strongest turn away, and yet he had made it his life's work to protect the world's secrets and keep them all safe. But what had he been doing down in the labs last night – and what was the significance of the statue? Why had it been stolen now, after it had been in the vault for years?

It was clear that they knew little about the Director. Even Jake, who had known him the longest, recruited back when he had been in the military in Africa, still knew little of the Director's past. Morgan laid her hand on Marietti's unmoving arm and willed him to wake up. They needed to know what to do next, and usually it was the Director who sent them on a mission. He was stalwart and strong and his shoulders were broad enough to carry all of them.

But now he was reduced to this.

We are so fragile, Morgan thought. *This human frame that seems so strong is easily broken.* Now Marietti was brought low, there was only a thin line between the people of London and the supernatural that crouched in the shadows waiting for darkness to fall so they could claim dominion.

There was a sudden long beep and a line spiked on one of the machines.

Marietti coughed, his body wracked with shudders. Jake pressed the emergency call button by the bedside as Morgan leaned forward and put her hand on the Director's forehead, trying to calm him.

"It's OK," she said, stroking his brow as he shook under her hand. "We're here. You're going to be OK."

Marietti's eyes flew open.

"Don't let the pieces of the statue come together," he whispered, his voice hoarse and cracked. "The weapon is–"

His words were cut off by a gurgle as blood spewed from his mouth. He clutched at Morgan's arm and his fingers tightened around her as a doctor and attendant nurses rushed into the room. Then his body stiffened and he seized, collapsing in convulsions on the bed.

CHAPTER 4

Asha heard the beating blades of the helicopter on its approach to the towers and walked to the window to watch as it hovered and then landed on the helipad. From London, the box had been taken to a private jet and flown immediately back to Mumbai, and then brought here from the airport in the fastest time possible. She smiled to think of what had arrived with it. In the midst of the mourning rituals, she was still playing the compliant sister and devoted daughter. Mahesh wouldn't know what she planned until it was too late.

Minutes later, there was a knock at her office door.

"Come in," she said, turning to face the entrance. She wore a white trouser suit today, the Hindu color of mourning. The curves flattered her lithe figure, and she found that being underestimated as a mere desirable woman helped her.

The door opened and the scarred man, one of her favorite bodyguards, stood in the doorway with a bag in his hand. Asha wanted to run across the room and grab it from him, so desperate was she for what was inside. But such eagerness did not become her position.

"Put it on the desk," she said abruptly, her voice giving no sense of her anticipation.

The man walked across the carpeted floor, his boots leaving dirty marks on the plush rug. His face was staunch but she felt his eyes flick over her.

He placed the bag on her desk and pulled the top flap open so she could see the box inside. Her fingers itched to touch it, to finally hold the sacred statue that her father had prohibited her from searching for. She remembered his cautionary words even now. *It's too dangerous, Asha. We're not ready for the power it can command.*

But she had searched in secret for the last year, tracing her father's history. In his younger years, he had worked on archaeological digs around the world. He had not been religious back then, choosing to call himself Christian or Muslim, Hindu or Buddhist depending on what dig he worked on. He had once been part of a Vatican team excavating in the caves of Ellora. They had found something there, an object of great power.

Now, finally, it was within her grasp.

Asha walked to the desk, her breathing shallow. She rested her hands on top of the bag and looked up at the man.

"Did you look inside?" Her voice was honey soft and smooth. She smiled and let the tip of her tongue touch her lips, wetting them slightly. The man's pupils dilated and he shifted uncomfortably in place. He shook his head, dragging his eyes away from her mouth.

"Of course not, your orders were clear."

She nodded. "Good. Then you may stay and watch."

As Asha pulled the box from the bag, her fingers shook with anticipation. The energy vibrating from it made her heart race. It was painted with bright colors, displaying images of the god Shiva in his various incarnations. In one he was seated cross-legged on a tiger skin, his body painted blue with a snake around his neck. His right hand was raised in blessing and his dreadlocks flowed down to create the River Ganges. The box itself was a priceless work of art, but it wasn't what she sought.

She took a deep breath and lifted the lid.

Her eyes widened. She slammed the lid back down again, the sharp sound echoing in the room. Her eyes blazed and narrowed as she looked at the man.

"There's only one piece in here. Where's the rest?" Her voice was ice cold, sharp as a dagger.

Fear flickered across the man's face, confusion in his eyes.

"I swear it. This was the only box in the vault with that radioactive signature. We didn't look in it, we didn't take anything. I promise."

Asha pressed the call button on her desk. The door opened and two bodyguards entered the room, their meaty hands resting on their guns as their huge bodies blocked the exit.

"No, please," the man cried. "I'll find the other pieces."

He fell to his knees, his hands reaching towards her in supplication.

Asha ignored him. "Take him to the Kali temple."

The two bodyguards grabbed the man by the arms and dragged him out, still screaming his protest.

As his cries faded, she opened the box again and looked down at the single piece of the statue, the semi-circle of fire that was meant to surround the god. The bronze edges had been filed into flames that would burn the world to dust and herald a new age. She could see how it would fit into the base, but she needed the other pieces to complete the weapon. She had pored through the diaries and journals and there had been nothing about this. Her father and the man he had found it with must have broken it apart and hidden the pieces separately. It was too late to discover the truth from her father, but perhaps the team he had discovered it with were still alive. She would find them and they would speak when faced with the chamber of the goddess.

But first, she had to face her own reckoning.

Asha clenched her fists and pounded on the table in frustration. She was so close.

In the corner of her office was a private lift. She walked to it with heavy footsteps and pressed the button. She didn't want to face him now, but she had to.

The lift took only seconds to get to the roof garden and Asha walked out into the verdant space beyond. The smell of tropical flowers and the patter of a waterfall filled the air. Up here it was possible to forget that the slums of Mumbai jostled below, crammed full of those millions who eked out a living on the edge of abundance. It was said of India that you could throw away a mango stone and a tree would grow, and up here, that was true. Vishal had planted the garden many years ago when he had first made his fortune and now Asha tended it in his memory.

Palm trees overhead created dappled shade on a stone path made from rocks gathered from all corners of the Kapoor empire. Pebbles from the beaches in Bangladesh where ships were broken up and sold. Glass from the south of Kerala and even precious stones from the forts of Rajasthan.

Huge glass panels high above could be opened and shut electronically, regulating the atmosphere and heat levels. Solar energy gathered from the roof was used throughout the building. The garden was a fusion of modern technology and the inherent natural power of the gods harnessed together, a fitting metaphor for what Asha intended.

But the statue was the key, and she had failed to get it.

She walked on.

A space had been cleared in the corner of the verdant garden in recent months. As her father lay dying, his position weakened, Asha had taken control of the area, making the changes necessary so her guru would come here. She took tentative steps towards the place now.

She stepped out of the greenery into a bare sandy area strewn with sharp stones and ash from cremation grounds. The smell of flowers dissipated, replaced by the stink of human waste and the tang of blood. The trees had been cleared so he sat under direct sunlight, cross-legged, eyes closed, fingers resting on his knees in the *chin mudra* position, thumb and forefinger touching.

He was naked except for a tiny loincloth, his matted dreadlocks hung to his waist, his bushy beard untrimmed. His dark skin was covered in ash dotted with beads of sweat. In front of him was a human skull fashioned into a *kapala* bowl, its interior stained with red and black from blood and rotten flesh.

Asha slipped off her shoes on the edge of the sand and walked barefoot towards him, each step soft and silent even as the sharp stones pricked her feet. Pain and blood only brought her closer to the goddess. She barely breathed and her heart pounded, as it always did when she approached him. She sank to her knees with no regard for her fine clothes. They meant nothing here. She was no longer a desirable woman, heiress to one of the biggest companies in India. Here she was just an acolyte in front of her guru. She rested her hands upon her knees and bowed her head.

"You do not have it."

His voice was rough and guttural and it grated across her skin. There was disappointment in his tone and Asha felt his judgement like the stripe of the whip. She shivered a little even under the hot sun. This man had a direct line to the gods. He was a sadhu, a holy man, an Aghori, considered the most extreme of their kind and renounced by other sects for their use of the dead in ritual.

The Aghori believed that by transcending social taboo, they could pierce the illusion of reality. If Shiva was perfect and created everything, even those things considered disgusting and rotten must also be perfect and therefore brought the devotee closer to God. Being near the dead allowed the living to understand what really mattered.

Asha had met the Aghori a year ago, when she had

attended a Hindu pilgrimage with her father. But they had brought a luxurious tent, fine linen and ample food with them. As Asha had watched the beggars calling out to the gods, she realized that they were closer to the divine than she could ever be in her rich lifestyle.

She had found him while wandering the pilgrim's camp one day, wearing only a simple cotton sari, no makeup, her hair loose about her face, disguised as a woman of simple means. His rejection of material things drew her to him and his devotion to the goddess Kali made her his disciple. Her father had hated the Aghori and while he was alive, her guru was banned, but now she kept him close.

"I have one piece," she said softly. "And I will find the others."

He opened his eyes, the dark pupils ringed with ash, flakes of blood dusting his eyelashes. Asha felt convicted in his gaze.

"You must hurry," he whispered. "The ritual must be performed on the most auspicious day, when the sacrifice will be the greatest, and the power of the weapon will demonstrate the might of Shiva."

"I will have the pieces in time." Asha's voice was strong and she met his gaze with an unblinking stare. "The statue will be whole. I promise."

The Aghori reached for the *kapala* skull and turned it over. He pulled out a sharp knife, then held his hand out and sliced his palm. He drew the blade slowly across his flesh so the blood welled and dripped into the skull.

Asha could hardly breathe as he clenched his palm and let the drops fall. The sight of blood excited her, reminded her of what awaited in the temple of Kali.

But that would have to wait.

The Aghori dipped his finger in the blood and then leaned forward. He pressed it against Asha's forehead, marking her with the crimson liquid. She smelled the coppery tang over the sweat of his body and she closed her eyes as he touched her. He was the only one who anchored her to what was real, and through him she would see God.

CHAPTER 5

"He's coding! Get the crash cart!"

As the high-pitched whine of the machines sounded the alarm, Morgan and Jake stepped back to let the medical team do their work. The doctor injected something into the line in Marietti's arm and a moment later, his body relaxed. He sank back on the bed, still once again.

The doctor turned.

"He's in a bad way so I've sedated him." He shook his head. "His body just needs time to rest and heal."

"How much time?" Jake asked.

The doctor frowned. "It's hard to say. His wounds are extensive. The blast shook his brain as well as his body. You'd better go. There's nothing you can do here."

At the door, Jake turned to look back at Marietti, now prone on the bed. His face creased with concern for the Director.

"We have to find out more about that statue," he said. "And why Marietti put that piece in the vault."

"We could go to his house," Morgan suggested. "See if there's anything we can find there about his past. If there's nothing in the databases, I can't see any other way."

Jake nodded. "Good idea. I visited once years back, the only time he ever had a party, apparently. It was an interesting gathering. Politicians, priests, and people whose names were definitely not their real ones. But then, he mostly kept his life private."

"It's our only option," Morgan said. "Marietti said that the pieces shouldn't come together again, and something about a weapon. We can't wait for him to recover."

"Let's go."

Marietti's house was in a quiet street north of Hampstead Heath. It was a simple two-up, two-down in a terrace and didn't look like much from the outside. It wasn't what Morgan would have expected from the Director, but then she hadn't really considered where he lived before. She associated him with his office overlooking Trafalgar Square, where the only personal touch was the fine art he borrowed from the various art galleries of London. Every time she went in there, he had a new one on the wall.

Spring was just beginning to show on the Heath, with the tips of daffodils starting to protrude from the renewed earth, and the white bells of snowdrops peeking out from under the hedgerows. This part of London had an edge of wildness and people came from all over the city for a glimpse of nature. Morgan could see how Marietti would find some kind of peace here, and she imagined him walking across the Heath in his quiet time, looking up at the trees, maybe smiling at the squirrels as they foraged. The Heath teemed with Londoners at the weekend, and perhaps it reminded him of why he worked for ARKANE. Why they all took the risks they did.

Jake took a set of keys from his pocket. They jangled as he searched through for the right one.

"He gave me a key a while back," he said, noting the inquisitive look on Morgan's face. He raised an eyebrow with a cheeky grin. "You can give me one of yours if you like. Just in case."

Morgan elbowed him in the ribs, smiling a little as they pushed inside. The reality was that they all knew so little about each other beyond the ARKANE missions. She and

Jake had come close a number of times to taking things into the more personal realm, but their missions had gotten in the way.

And perhaps that was for the best.

Marietti's house looked like it hadn't been redecorated since the 1970s. The man was clearly more concerned with his work, and he certainly spent most of his waking hours at the ARKANE offices. It smelled musty, as if the windows hadn't been opened in a long time. There was a picture by the door, a young Marietti with a broad smile on his face, standing next to an archaeological dig. Morgan didn't recognize that smile, for the Director was known for being staunch, unsmiling, serious in the face of almost constant threat.

"So what exactly are we actually looking for?" Jake asked as they walked inside.

"Martin said that Marietti put the sculpture in the vaults in the 1980s," Morgan replied, walking softly down the hall. Every step felt like a trespass, even though she knew the Director would want them to pursue every lead. "We should look for something about his history back then. He said he didn't want the pieces to be put back together again, but where *are* the other pieces?"

Jake frowned. "Because whoever wanted the piece in the vault must surely want the others."

"Exactly," Morgan said. "So we need to get to them first."

They entered the main living area, evidently the room of a bachelor. A wingback chair sat near the window with a view out over the Heath. There was another chair near the door, but the place was not set up for conversation. A pile of books lay near the leather chair and Morgan crouched down to look at them. The history of nuclear war. The physics of nuclear weapons. An introduction to Hindu mythology.

"How do these relate to each other?" Morgan opened the book on nuclear weapons. "I would expect Hindu mythology, but why this interest in nuclear tech? It doesn't seem like something ARKANE would usually be involved in."

ARKANE investigated mysteries of the supernatural, those outside the auspices of other agencies and the police. They were called in when things weren't quite normal, when the explanation for an event couldn't be found in the rational world.

"Marietti was involved in so many things." Jake poked his head into the kitchen, adjoining the living room. "I don't think there was a limit to his curiosity, so this could have just been personal interest."

"But apart from the saber rattling over Iran and North Korea, the world is much safer in terms of the nuclear threat these days," Morgan said.

She picked up another book, a pop-science paperback on particle physics. She leafed through it, the words pretty much meaningless since her own speciality was psychology and religion and the impact of war on both. This leafy suburb of Hampstead was so far from the war zone of Israel, where she had grown up and begun her studies, but she felt the echoes of conflict here. The book had a few color images in the middle and she flicked through the pages to them. One immediately caught her eye.

"Jake, look at this." She held out the page. It showed a massive sculpture of Shiva Nataraja outside the headquarters of CERN, the largest particle physics laboratory in the world, based outside Geneva in Switzerland.

"What is a Shiva statue representing the end of the world doing at a nuclear research lab?" Morgan said. "We need to check that out."

Jake nodded. "It's a start, but I think there's more to be found here."

He circled back to a shelf near the kitchen containing an eclectic range of books as well as a number of photo albums. They were old, from the time when photos were more precious, when film was expensive and people would take a roll and only one of the photos would be worth printing. Jake pulled an album down and leafed through it.

Morgan came to stand at his shoulder. She was so close that she could smell his aftershave and feel the warmth coming from his body. She was glad they were working together again. In their last mission together, he had been critically injured and she had finished the Gates of Hell mission alone. Then he'd gone to New York. He hadn't told her much of what had occurred there but he had certainly returned a stronger man, with no indication of the injuries he had sustained only a few months ago. Just another secret they kept from each other.

The photos in the album showed Marietti as a priest, standing stiffly in front of various famous world monuments. They were trophy photos, markers of his travels but nothing that could help them in particular. Jake picked up another album and flicked through. Then he stopped on a page.

"That certainly brings back memories," he said softly.

The photo showed a group of soldiers, both black and white, standing before a mud hut in a clearing. Marietti stood on the end of the line and Morgan could just make out the Vatican cross sewn on his uniform. Next to him was a younger Jake.

"When was that?" Morgan couldn't help but reach out to touch the photo. Jake's face had fewer lines and there was no corkscrew scar above his eye. But there was still a sense of the wild animal in the way he stood, a young lion holding his power in check, desperate for the hunt. These days, he was still lithe and muscular but he had learned to use that power more effectively.

"Early '90s," Jake said. "I met Marietti in the Sudan. The war was brutal but we were told not to intervene. Marietti was sent as a representative from the Vatican because the Islamic Front was slaughtering Catholics. He understood powerlessness at a time when I still believed that we could solve every problem the world had. I probably would have died fighting there without his counsel."

"Was he ever your friend?" Morgan whispered.

"It was never a two-way relationship, to be honest. He was more like my father back then but since he was made Director, we haven't shared so much personally." Jake turned to Morgan, his eyes bright. She could see his determination. "He will recover, I know he will. He's a fighter. And if he wants to stop the pieces of the statue being brought together again, we'll do that for him."

Morgan nodded. "Then we need to track down those pieces before whoever blew the vault finds them. We should look at the photos from the 1980s, before you met him."

Jake pulled all the albums from the shelf and together they searched through, trying to order them by year. There were no labels on the photos, no text describing the images. Either Marietti had a perfect memory of all these people in all these places, or he was trying to protect his past even as he held onto these tokens of what had once been. Morgan reckoned it was probably the latter.

A page fell open to show Marietti standing with a group at the edge of a mass grave, the outline of individual bodies blurred by the sheer number of them. Jake's face darkened.

"Rwanda," he said, his eyes clouding over. "Those were dark times."

"Why would he keep a picture like that?" Morgan asked.

"It's the most recent genocide in living memory," Jake

whispered. "A testament to man's ability to destroy himself. Marietti believed that we all have within us the ability to create or destroy, and that battle can be individual or borne out at this tribal level. He told me once that it was a lesson he wished to remember always."

He turned the page to happier times.

"The Taj Mahal," Jake said, holding out the album to Morgan. "That smile suggests he knew the person taking the photo well. We need to find out what he was doing in India back then."

Jake took out his smart phone and took some pictures of the images. Then he closed the album gently and placed everything back on the shelf as they had found it.

"It's strange being in here without an invitation," he said.

"I know how you feel," Morgan replied. "But none of us share our personal space with each other right now. I've never even been to your place."

Jake stepped closer, his face only inches from hers. The chemistry between them had been building for so long now, and Morgan wanted to lean into him.

"Are you angling for an invitation?" he said softly.

Morgan's phone rang, the shrill tone breaking the moment between them.

CHAPTER 6

Asha changed into a simple yellow sari and cleaned off her expensive makeup. By adopting the posture and attitude of a lower-class woman and taking off the trappings of wealth, she could roam the streets of Mumbai without notice. Just another solitary figure in a city of millions trying to scrape a living.

Her father forbade such excursions into the city streets alone, but she had been doing it since she was a teenager, determined to learn about the city she lived in and not just from the side of the rich. Over the years, she had developed her own network and her own projects.

She emerged from the basement of Kapoor Towers to a blast of hot air from the street outside. The sound of tooting horns, ringing bells and vendors hawking their goods welcomed her into the bustling city. Mumbai was on a peninsula and so the city had stretched far north and across the bay as it grew. But here, in the oldest part, the only way to grow was to build up.

Asha adjusted her headscarf, pulling it over her face to obscure her fine features from anyone who looked too closely, and walked a few streets before hailing a taxi.

"Dharavi," she said. "Sion-Mahim entrance."

Soon, they pulled in next to the Dharavi slum, founded in 1882 during the British era and home to nearly a million people. Many workers ended up here when they arrived in the city from the rural areas seeking work, and like the rest of Mumbai, Dharavi was full of enterprising entrepreneurs. Pottery, textiles and tanning works crammed into the space along with other production sites and a growing waste and recycling enterprise.

The urban poor in Mumbai worked hard and Asha always found the people here to be an inspiration. She preferred their grafting attitude to that of the entitled young people she had grown up with, obsessed only with fashion and practicing the latest Bollywood dance instead of working. And while she could hold her own at the pinnacle of the Mumbai socialite scene, she actually preferred to walk the streets here in the slum.

She splashed through a puddle, lifting the hem of her sari to avoid getting it wet. The dank water smelled of chemicals used in the tanning process and the air reeked of rubbish and sewers, overlaid with the constant smell of cooking.

Asha weaved her way through the streets, head down in the manner of a good wife hurrying home to her family. She liked to walk unseen, and she had perfected the look of a downtrodden lower-caste woman since she had first started coming here years ago.

She turned a sharp corner and entered the health clinic. She was known here only as the go-between for a rich benefactor who provided funds for the clinic and the shelter for unwanted children and young mothers fallen upon hard times.

"Ms Shah." The receptionist looked surprised as she walked in. "We weren't expecting you today. I'll let the doctor know you're here."

Asha nodded. "Tell her to take her time. I'll be in the day room."

She walked through into a large open area where groups of young women sat, some with babies on their laps, others obviously pregnant. The sound of chatter filled the room as they wove baskets and gossiped as they worked.

The clinic was open to all religions and although the slum was mostly Hindu, it also had a large Muslim population. The girls here were often victims of abuse who had run from home fearing retribution in a culture that still blamed women for sexual attack.

Asha understood the feeling of being marginalized, but these women were part of her bigger plan – even if they weren't aware of it. Every woman and child had blood samples taken when they asked for help, and anything interesting was sent to her lab for testing. The slum was a melting pot and as Asha looked around the room, she saw myriad genetic codes in their faces. She smiled at the thought.

"I'm sorry. I didn't know you were coming." The doctor looked worried as she approached, a brown paper bag clutched in her hand. "I'm about to start surgery."

"I just came to see whether you needed anything."

The doctor looked at her more closely. "And presumably for the latest batch."

Sometimes Asha considered removing the woman, silencing her unspoken questions. But the doctor worked for a pittance and helped more girls here than seemed possible with the number of hours in one day. Asha admired her. In her softer moments, she wondered if she could have been this doctor in another life.

But she was meant for bigger things. The goddess had far more in store for her.

"Come," the doctor said, looking around at the room full of young mothers. "We can't talk in here."

They walked into an adjoining examination room and the doctor pushed the door shut. She handed Asha the bag. There was a jar inside filled with an opaque liquid and something meaty that touched the sides with its bulk.

"Miscarriage," the doctor said. "A child of incest, as you requested."

There was a hint of disgust in her voice, perhaps at her own betrayal of those she served.

Asha pulled a thick wad of rupees from her bag and gave it to the doctor. "There's more when you need it. Make sure you notify me of any new specimens like this."

The doctor folded the money into the pocket of her coat and walked out, slamming the door behind her. Asha didn't mind the doctor's moral concern. The tissue would be used for a greater good.

She headed back to Kapoor Towers, the specimen jar hidden in her bag.

With her Masters degree in Biochemistry, she had taken her interest in genetics even further in the last few years and, with company funding, she had expanded the lab, driven by her own history. Her mother had died of a rare tropical disease that she had caught on one of Vishal's business trips. She'd had some kind of genetic inability to recover from it and had been dead within a day of getting sick. That discovery had fueled Asha's own passion for genetics, in the hope that somehow she could go back in time and save her mother, or at least those who suffered in the same way.

Even as Mahesh had taken responsibility for the mining side of the company, Asha had developed Kapoor Labs, focusing on gene editing. There were several floors dedicated to science, and she oversaw most of them, with each department reporting in weekly on progress. But she had a side project going, something at the intersection of faith and science. She grabbed her white coat and tied back her hair into a neat bun as she entered the lab area.

She pushed open the glass door to the inner labs, where a small team reported directly to her. Nico had his back to her as she entered, bent over a microscope to look at the finer detail of a slide. The door whooshed closed behind her and he turned at the sound.

"I wasn't expecting you until later, Miss Kapoor," he said. "I haven't quite finished the assessment of the latest round."

"I have a new sample with possible mutation to add to the mix," Asha said. She put the paper bag in one of the medical fridges.

"I'll get to it next," Nico said.

He was tall, his dark hair cut close to his skull. His lanky frame was evidence that he cared more for the experiments in the lab than he did for his own health. He had studied molecular biology and genetic engineering at Harvard, before a stint in China working on CRISPR technology, altering the genetic makeup of crops. He had been part of the team that worked on the first editing of human genomes, although he had avoided the ethical debate that sprang up after the release of their findings.

Asha had found him then and offered him so much money that he had agreed to come back to India for her special project. This lab was not listed as part of the official company assets and much of what they did here was off-books. But along with her search for the weapon, this was Asha's passion.

"Another new specimen arrived today," Nico said. "I haven't even opened the box yet, but it's marked for the Naga project."

He gestured at a polystyrene specimen box sitting on the lab benchtop, marked as bio-hazardous genetic material. Asha grinned.

"I love presents."

She walked over and grabbed a scalpel. She cut the string and pulled open the top of the box. A small snake lay inside, some kind of cobra by the look of it. It had three heads and a lump where a fourth had been growing, but it was a juvenile and couldn't have lived very long.

"That's fantastic," Asha said. She looked at the label and checked the laboratory that sent it. "Is this from the same group that sent the fetus with the extra arm buds?"

Nico nodded. "They're doing good work. Not sure where they're getting the specimens from, though."

Asha held up a hand. "It doesn't matter, as long as they send them to us."

She had long desired to create a living version of one of the many-armed deities of Hindu mythology. Nico had wanted to try Ganesha because of his popularity and the fact that he only had four arms, although he also had an elephant head. But Asha doubted that they would be able to graft such an animal onto a human body as well as grow the extra arms.

Her own fixation was the goddess Kali, one of the aspects of Durga. Depicted with four arms, Kali would be an eminently more practical choice for a hybrid. They were also progressing well with the *naga*, the seven-headed king cobra. The snake represented eternity, eating its own tail in the *ouroboros*, creation into destruction, an echo of the Shiva Nataraja.

While Mahesh focused on earthly power and the wealth they could dig up from the ground, Asha understood the power of inspiration and how the people would follow miracles and wonders. The faithful would rise up at the signs she would bring forth and this would bring even more to pilgrimage on that great day. The more who came to worship, the greater the sacrifice and the more powerful the weapon. It didn't matter that these signs and wonders were built in the lab rather than occurring naturally.

India was on the forefront of technology in the finest scientific tradition, but it was also still mired in myth and daily ritual. Asha wanted to fire a revival of devotion to Kali, for the people to flock back to the gods. That would make the sacrifice so much sweeter.

"Show me where we are on the Kali project," she asked.

Nico walked to the back of the lab and entered a code on a panel. A door slid open.

It was dark inside and as they entered the lights flickered on, revealing a row of tanks. Each one held a specimen, a human fetus at various stages of growth, all attached to tubes, simulating artificial wombs. Some had two arms and extra buds where other limbs had begun to grow. Others had multiple fully-formed limbs and one even had two heads.

Asha smiled at what they had achieved and walked over to one of the tanks to gaze down at their creation. Nico came to stand next to her.

"You know they will never breathe," he whispered. "They will never grow up into the mature deities that people could actually worship."

"It doesn't matter," Asha said. "A dead child with the aspect of a goddess will still inspire millions to pilgrimage. We're so close now."

CHAPTER 7

MARIETTI COULDN'T OPEN HIS eyes but he knew where he was by the antiseptic smell, a vain attempt to banish the stench of the sick and the dying. There was a heaviness in his limbs and the pain of his injuries throbbed in time with his heartbeat even as the sedatives kept him in a semi-aware state.

Dark shadows hovered around the edge of his consciousness and he sensed the beating of black leathery wings about him. There were many who would relish his end, but Marietti was not ready to give up yet. Not with so much at stake.

A sound outside the door drew his attention.

But it was only the voices of the nursing staff as they passed, chattering about the latest episode of some TV program.

He was safe, for now at least, and Marietti found himself slipping into the past, back when he was still a priest – to the time before they had even found the statue, .

Vatican City, Rome. March 16, 1981

Elias Marietti stepped out of his tiny flat in the back streets of Vatican City. He walked to the corner shop for his daily espresso and knocked it back with enthusiasm, a welcome wakeup jolt of energy to start the day.

The sounds of the city wound about him as he walked along the street: the distinctive exhaust from a Vespa motorbike, the shout from an angry driver trying to navigate the crowded streets, the call of a street vendor selling fresh vegetables brought in from the countryside this morning. Marietti loved Rome – not just the sense of power and history that lay under the streets, but also for how close real life was here. The Church was the beating heart of Rome, whereas in other places, it was only peripheral. When he was here he understood his purpose and his place in the world, but the further he traveled from it, the more the ties loosened and doubts crept in.

Now his step was jaunty and a smile played about his lips as he walked. Today could be momentous because late last night, he had found a hint of something buried in the archives, something that had been covered up as part of a larger purpose. It might be the key to what he sought.

Marietti worked within the Vatican Secret Archives, or the Archivum Secretum Apostolicum Vaticanum in the proper Latin. It officially contained the historical records of great world events spanning twelve centuries. Of course, there were famous documents held there that all knew about: Pope Leo X's 1521 decree excommunicating Martin Luther that sparked the Protestant Reformation; the 1493 papal bull that split the New World between Spain and Portugal after Columbus landed in North America. Even the transcripts of Vatican trials against the Knights Templar and later, Galileo.

That official part of the archives had been opened up to scholars in 1881 and were hardly secret. No doubt there were still treasures to be found in the eighty-five kilometers of shelving and over 35,000 volumes, but those public documents were not what excited Marietti today. He worked in the part that still remained behind closed doors in a section that few knew about, let alone were allowed access to.

He smoked a Nazionali cigarette as he walked, enjoying the warm sun on his face and the smoky taste in his mouth. He could just about live without women and possessions as his vows dictated, but he would struggle to give up his twin addictions of cigarettes and coffee. Thankfully, Vatican City ran on both substances so it was unlikely that he would ever have to choose. He reflected on the document that he had found last night as he walked through the streets towards the Archives. Officially, no materials dated after 1939 were available to scholars because the Vatican still protected Pope Pius XII's involvement with the Nazis in the Second World War. There were many who did not want the truth of that time to be made known. But Marietti was part of a task force dedicated to delving into the occult layer beneath that history.

He had led an expedition to Antarctica in 1979 in the expectation of finding a treasure trove of artifacts, but instead they had only found more papers. These had been taken back to the Vatican and they were still going through the millions of pages. At least his German had improved and he had become adept at understanding the doublespeak of the Reich.

It had been hard at first to ignore the casual comments about the Final Solution and racist rhetoric, but he had learned to skim over much of it. That part was not his focus. The Nazis had taken art and treasures from the people they murdered, and Heinrich Himmler in particular had been obsessed with discovering items of ancient power that would help them win against the Allies.

Marietti had been going through a diary of Himmler's last night and he had found a comment that intrigued him. But it had been late, and his eyes had been tired.

Today he would look anew at the document and his heart beat a little faster at what he might find.

Marietti walked along the Via di Porta Angelica

through the Porta di Santa Anna to the entrance of the Archives, adjacent to the Vatican Library. He showed his pass to the guard on the gate and the man nodded him through.

The courtyard beyond was busy as scholars arrived for their designated entry times. Swiss Guards in their colorful uniforms manned the security post at the gate from the Cortile del Belvedere. The blue and mustard striped uniform with Renaissance-style puffed sleeves did nothing to disguise the swift professionalism of the Swiss Guard, highly trained soldiers responsible for the security of the Pope and the Holy See.

Marietti showed his credentials again. One of the soldiers took it and looked more closely at him, matching his features to the photo. Despite his daily entry, security was on high alert as there had been threats against Pope John Paul II and every care was being taken to minimize risk.

After a minute, Marietti was waved through. The high ceilinged corridors smelled of an antique store overlaid with lavender furniture polish, as the cleaning of the Vatican never stopped. It echoed with the footsteps of those hurrying to the various parts of the archive and he strode along with them, a grin on his face as he considered what he might find today.

After navigating the twisted corridors, Marietti finally entered the room that his small team were using to examine the Nazi papers. There was a huge wooden desk of dark wood in the middle, surrounded by towering shelves of old books behind glass.

One of the task force's research assistants, Joseph Manfredi, was there already. The younger man leaned over the desk, examining the document that Marietti had left open late last night. Manfredi turned as the door creaked and his cheeks flushed a little under the light down of his blond facial hair.

"You're here early," Joseph stammered. "I didn't expect you so soon. You were still here when I left last night." He pointed at the document on the desk. "Is this what it looks like?"

Marietti pulled on a pair of thin white gloves used to handle fragile documents. He pointed at the document.

"Look at the notes on the edge of the page." There were doodles and scribbled phrases, streams of consciousness documenting the author's train of thought. "These match Himmler's handwriting." Marietti turned the page. "But this is what I'm really interested in."

It was a hand-drawn map of the Indian sub-continent, rough lines representing the world as it was back in the early 1940s. There were marks on the map and a large black swastika drawn with thick lines in the corner. The swastika had been corrupted by the Reich, although it originally came from ancient India and was used by many world civilizations. It represented the principle of creation, the four swirling arms representing the four directions or the four faces of Brahman, God. Hindus drew swastika symbols on doorposts to welcome the goddess Lakshmi to bring good luck and it was associated with the sun, a positive symbol that had been perverted by the Nazis for their dark purposes.

"The Nazis believed in a pure Aryan race," Marietti said. "This ancient tribe supposedly invaded India thousands of years ago and started the hierarchy of castes, where some individuals were worth more than others. As a young man in the SS, Himmler considered the Kshatriya warrior caste as a model for the Nazi forces. He even carried a copy of the Bhagavad Gita and referred to Krishna's instructions that one should satisfy duty on the battlefield. He required his men to have a pure conscience around killing for a higher purpose."

"Of course, I've heard these rumors of Himmler's obsession with India," Joseph said.

"But this is the first time we've found a map, albeit a rough one." Marietti grinned. "This is what we've been looking for." He pointed at one of Himmler's comments in the margin of the document. "It sounds as if they found the potential location of a fabled treasure, buried in an Indian cave system."

"Could it be one of the books of the Nine Unknown Men?" Joseph's eyes glittered at the possibility. The Nine Unknown had sworn to protect the most dangerous knowledge of ancient India and many sought their hidden books of power.

"Perhaps," Marietti said. "We just have to figure out what these dots represent." He pulled an old atlas from the shelf. As he turned the pages to a map of India, the smell of spices drifted out.

"The largest mark is here, and I think I know where that is."

CHAPTER 8

As she paced the office in front of the glass window, Asha stopped at every turn to look out over the city. She could just about make out the tiffin-wallahs delivering hot lunches to the downtown offices. Time ticked past and she wasn't any closer to getting the other pieces of the sculpture. Everything had to be ready in time and she could not fail the Aghori. But where were the other pieces?

Her father had looked at this view every day, and yet she didn't know his mind well enough to decipher where he might have hidden them. She thought back over her father's life. The key to their hiding place would be to understand what had meant the most to him.

She turned and looked around the office.

There were pictures on the wall: Vishal with the Prime Minister after the last election and with a Bollywood star at a glitzy launch, another of him wearing a hard hat in front of the ship-breaking yard, and still another in front of one of the mine entrances. She stopped for a moment in front of a picture of the three of them, Mahesh on his lap and Asha herself leaning against her father's knee, looking up with a smile. It had been soon after their mother's death, yet he had made sure they were cared for and never felt alone. She touched her father's face through the glass with a gentle fingertip.

He had certainly doted on his children when he had time to spend with them, which hadn't been often, but Asha knew that he had been proud of both her and Mahesh. Despite that pride, she guessed that Vishal had really seen his legacy as the company and the hundreds of thousands of lives he was responsible for. Perhaps that meant the sculpture fragment was somewhere in this building, within the pinnacle of what he had created, as a representative piece of his empire?

But no, she thought.

The flower garden on the rooftop was a better representation of what he truly valued. When Vishal had found out he was dying, all he had wanted was the sun on his face and the refreshment of a simple glass of water in the heat of the day. He had shed all worldly desires. In the evenings, when his pain was at its worst, he would muse on mortality. He even laughed about it, because all his wealth and power could not prevent the end coming when the gods decided it was time.

He died well, Asha thought. She intended to go with such dignity when it was her time and face her goddess with open eyes.

In those last days, Vishal had gone every day to the Towers of Silence, tall circular structures used to expose the dead according to the Zoroastrian religion. The bodies of the dead were left for scavenging birds to consume the flesh and pick the bones until nothing was left. In this way, the unclean body, considered by some to be possessed by the Corpse Demon, could not pollute the sacred earth.

Asha turned to the wall of glass, looking north towards where the Towers of Silence lay not far from here. She narrowed her eyes. Could a piece be there?

She pressed the intercom button on her desk.

"I need a car out front," she said. "And get me the driver who used to take my father in his last months."

After a moment, the receptionist buzzed back.

"The driver will be downstairs in ten minutes," she said.

Her father's preferred driver was an older man and he snapped to attention as Asha walked towards the sedan car. He didn't meet her eyes but stood looking forward, his back ramrod straight. He wore a dark suit with a white shirt and blue tie with the Kapoor ship logo on it. His shoes were perfectly shined. It was as if he had been waiting for the call to drive even though his master had passed on. Her father had always fostered this kind of dedication in people and Asha smiled at the man.

"I need you to take me to where you used to take my father in those last days."

"Yes ma'am." He nodded. "And I'm so sorry for your loss. Your father was a great man."

His dark eyes were full of sorrow and Asha made a mental note to ensure the man was looked after. Her father would have wanted that.

They drove slowly through the streets of Mumbai and Asha stared out at the crowds through the dark tinted window, a centimeter of glass shielding her from the pollution of the roads, muting the noise of horns. Driving in Mumbai was barely worth it, but she relished the time to think on the short trip.

"Mr Kapoor had special permission to visit from the Parsi community," the driver said, after a few minutes. "Only people of faith can enter the holy grounds."

"But you know someone there, don't you?" Asha said, her voice sweet as honey, her smile open and honest. "I just need to know what my father was thinking in those last days." She let the tears well up and one perfect drop slid down her cheek. She brushed it away. "I miss him so much."

The driver looked stricken at her frailty and Asha turned her head so he couldn't see through her artifice. "Of course. I can try, ma'am."

They soon pulled up next to a locked gate with signs on it prohibiting access to the Towers of Silence. A dense tangle of trees and flowers could be seen behind, barely contained by the walls, and behind it, they could just see the top of the tower.

"Please wait here," the driver said. "I'll ring my contact."

"Here," Asha said, handing the driver a wad of rupees. "This may help."

The driver got out of the car and made a call. A few minutes later, a thin man came to the gate and unlocked it. The two men spoke together in hushed tones and money changed hands before the driver beckoned. Asha pulled a headscarf on, covering her face in modesty, and stepped out of the car.

"This man will take you to the tower," the driver said. "He knew your father in those last days."

The thin man led Asha through the garden. The sound of Mumbai retreated as the dense foliage created a fecund barrier to the encroaching city. They emerged from the verdant green at the side of the tower and walked up two flights of stairs to a small platform overlooking the inner chambers.

"Your father would sit here for hours," the thin man said. "I would share my chai with him sometimes if the wind blew up and he began to shiver. But he wouldn't move until his prayers were done." The man shook his head. "Funny really, because he wasn't even Parsi. He didn't really understand our faith, but he certainly understood death. I'll leave you for a time."

From where she stood, Asha couldn't see what lay at the base of the tower. She waited until the man's footsteps faded before she stepped forward to look down.

There were three concentric walls: the bodies of men lay in the outer ring, women in the second, and children in the middle. There were several corpses in various stages of decomposition lying in the pit. A man, little more than a skeleton with tufts of flesh like growths upon his bones. Two tiny bodies of children curled around each other. Asha wondered how they had died and whether they found comfort together in death.

There was an ossuary pit at the center of the tower for the collection of bones once they had been bleached by the sun and scoured by the wind and rain. Lime was added to help the disintegration and the matter filtered through multiple levels of coal and sand until eventually nothing was left.

It was simple and stark and Asha understood why they did this, for what is human life but the world incarnate, made flesh for a time. Then we must all return to dust, our bodies subsiding back into nature. It wasn't shocking. There was no real sense of anything human left here.

The cry of a vulture broke the air and a huge bird flapped down to peck at what remained of the man's corpse. Asha had read that the vultures here were under threat. Their numbers were dropping and there were not enough of the carrion birds to devour the bodies from the Parsi community. Even the ancient rituals of death were under threat in the march to modernity that transformed India day by day.

She gazed down at the bodies and tried to find a way into her father's mind. What had he thought about when he sat here? Had he considered the sculpture? Had he even thought of it at all? She had to believe that he had, and if so, what impact would this place have on where he might have hidden it?

A ray of sun burst through the clouds above and lighted on the innermost ring where the bodies of the children lay. The shadows shifted and Asha suddenly saw the outline of a trapdoor.

There was something underneath.

She ran down the stairs, lifting her sari out of the way

so she didn't trip in her haste. Her headscarf fell onto her shoulders, but she was beyond caring about modesty.

"Excuse me," she called. The thin man emerged from a stone arch holding a cup of chai.

"Are you OK, ma'am?"

"There's a trapdoor in the middle of the tower," Asha said. "I need to know what's down there."

"The sacred area of the ritual precinct can only be entered by the *nusessalars*, the pallbearers," he said. "They look after the bodies and that's their way to the circles of the dead."

"I need to see it." There was a hard edge to Asha's voice. She no longer played the submissive woman. She was Asha Kapoor, one of the richest and most powerful women in India.

The man hesitated. "I'm sorry, but I can't let you in there."

"You let my father in."

The man sighed and nodded slowly.

"But he was dying, and you are not."

"We're all dying," Asha said softly. "The question is when and how much pain we suffer … and whether our families go with us."

The man paled at the clear threat in her voice.

"Come."

He led her through the stone arch and down some stairs. The smell of rotting flesh and the almost sweet stench of decomposition filled the air, but the corridors were swept clean. The bodies were outside, up above, and strangely these underground passages were for the living. Asha had no sense of dread here, only anticipation at what she might find.

Their footsteps echoed in the narrow passageway as they walked towards the center of the tower and the man stopped in a circular antechamber.

"I can go no further," he said. "My faith forbids it. But if you must, then step that way." He pointed at one of the archways from the narrow room.

Asha walked onwards alone.

The passageway opened up into a round chamber where a spiral staircase wound its way up to the trapdoor in the ceiling. There were two stone slabs, evidently for washing bodies before they were taken above. There were niches in the walls where bodies could be laid in waiting but all were empty now.

It was still and quiet and Asha felt at peace. She didn't flinch before death, and this was death's waiting room. She believed the physical body was nothing but a vessel and that the true self would be reincarnated. She wondered what her father would come back as, or if he had escaped the cycle of Samsara. She intended to earn such great karma with her deeds that she would escape the cycle this time around. But for such a sacrifice that would gain the attention of the gods, she needed the complete statue. She walked around the stone chamber, wondering what her father had thought when he was down here.

Then, something caught her eye.

There was a carving on the wall, a tiny ship etched into the stone. She walked closer and bent down. The stone had been recently replaced, the mortar around it crumbled and the edges more polished than adjacent stones. The ship was a crude rendition of the Kapoor company logo, a nod to Vishal's first billion from the ship-breaking industry. Strange to see it in this place. It had to mean something.

Asha pulled a nail file from her bag and used it to chip away at the mortar around the stone. It fell away quickly and she levered the rock from its place. Behind it was a box. As she moved to let the light fall upon it, she gasped aloud, her inhalation echoing around the room.

How could this be?

She reached in with trembling fingers and pulled the box out.

It was made from cedar wood and decorated with dots and swirls from the paintbrush of a child. She hugged it close as she remembered painting it alongside Mahesh when they were young. Vishal had said that it would honor their mother if they painted it with love. He had kept her ashes in it and Asha had thought it safe in the family vault, so why was it here?

The box was heavy – heavier than it should be if it only contained ash, but she resisted opening it. She didn't want to see the physical remains of the mother who had loved her. But her father had clearly come here in his last days, desperate to hide something precious in a place guarded by death.

Asha opened the box.

It was filled with grey dust, like sand from a forgotten beach. There was nothing here of her mother and Asha steeled herself. She poked the ashes with the nail file, swirling it around until she heard a chink of metal against metal.

She levered the file and a corner of bronze emerged from the dust. She pulled it from the box, uncaring now of the grains that clung to her fingertips. It was one half of the base of the Shiva Nataraja statue.

A triumphant glow flushed over her body. The Aghori would be pleased and he would bless her. The day of sacrifice ticked closer, but she still had time to find the other two pieces.

Asha closed the lid, hiding the sculpture again, and laid the box gently in her bag. She replaced the stone and smoothed the mortar back into place, then she ran her fingers over the carving of the ship. Perhaps it was a clue to where her father had hidden the next piece?

CHAPTER 9

THE ENERGY BETWEEN MORGAN and Jake crackled before she stepped away.

"Another time," she whispered. She answered the phone. "What is it, Martin?"

She put the phone on speaker and his tinny voice filled the room.

"I've looked back through the ARKANE database at Marietti's official history. It's patchy and I'm still trying to get more details from the Vatican Secret Archives. He was working closely with them back in the 1980s. But when he was in India he worked with a man called Vishal Kapoor, who became one of India's richest billionaires. There are, as yet unconfirmed, reports that he died yesterday. It's not public knowledge yet because of the potential effect on his company's share price, but we'll confirm it later today."

"He couldn't have ordered the raid, then," Morgan said.

"But the timing is too coincidental," Jake added.

"I'll keep digging," Martin said. "But in the meantime, there's something you should look at right away. Vishal Kapoor was one of the team who donated the statue of Shiva Nataraja to the CERN laboratory in Switzerland. He went with the statue to deliver it and his company was heavily involved in the nuclear program in India." The sound of tapping came from the phone. "I've booked you both on a flight to Geneva. By the time you get there, I should know more about the background between Vishal and Marietti."

* * *

The plane banked over Lake Geneva towards the airport near the border of Switzerland and France. The lake sparkled in the sun and Morgan leaned closer to the window, resting her head on the glass to get a better look. The water below was calm and deep blue and she longed to dive into the depths. It had been too long since she'd had time to lie back and relax in the waves. Growing up with her father in Israel, they had often gone swimming in the Mediterranean. His favorite place on the coast was Caesarea beach where they could swim next to an ancient Roman aqueduct, built by King Herod in the first century. There were never any lifeguards there and she could clamber on the ancient rocks, poking into crevices to see what she could find. Not something that would be allowed here in Switzerland, of course. No clambering on monuments here, ancient or otherwise.

"Do you ski?" Jake asked, breaking her thoughts as he leaned over to look out the window. "It's not too far to Chamonix from here."

"Not very well." Morgan grinned. "But I could probably beat you at surfing a sand dune."

Jake laughed. "I might have to take you up on that sometime." He pulled out his smart phone, opening the notes on the CERN laboratory that Martin had sent through. "So this place is basically trying to explain the universe?"

"They study the nature of matter," Morgan said. "Most people have only heard of the Large Hadron Collider, the huge twenty-seven kilometer ring built underground beneath the border between France and Switzerland. They accelerate particles and then slam them together and see what happens." She tilted her head. "Well, that's the basic explanation anyway."

Jake grinned. "Sounds like a fun place."

"There are a ton of conspiracy theories, of course," Morgan continued. "Some think that the Collider is some kind of alien portal, like a stargate. Or that the particle accelerator could destroy the world with antimatter."

Jake raised an eyebrow, his corkscrew scar crinkling. "You and I have seen enough to know that there is often some truth behind the conspiracy theories."

Morgan nodded. "But I think it's more likely that people just don't understand the physics – I certainly don't. But CERN has been at the cutting edge of scientific discovery since 1954. This is where Tim Berners-Lee invented the World Wide Web back in 1989. Get a load of scientists together and see what they come up with. It's a great idea."

"Maybe we need to do something like that for the supernatural world?" Jake mused. "Imagine how much fun we'd have."

The plane descended for landing and Morgan and Jake soon emerged into the arrivals hall. A young Indian man stood holding a sign with their names on it, his eyes scanning the crowd. They walked over and he greeted them.

"Welcome to Geneva," he said, with a faint Indian accent. "I'll be taking you on your tour today. I'm Amit, a research scientist on secondment here, so I can answer all your questions. This way."

He led them to a black sedan and they got in.

"It's not far," he said. "I'll take you to the visitor center first."

They soon pulled up in front of a huge golfball-shaped structure, the high dome evoking the circular shape of the Large Hadron Collider. Morgan wondered what secrets they kept here, deep under the earth, away from the prying eyes of interested tourists.

"I understand that you want to see the statue of Shiva?" Amit said, as they climbed out of the car and stretched their legs. "I can take you there straightaway. As a Hindu, I'm proud that my country donated the statue to the lab."

They followed Amit down a winding path beyond the visitor center towards more lab buildings, all labelled to help tell them apart. It was a huge campus and Morgan looked around in interest as they walked, wondering what really went on here. Perhaps like ARKANE it had a public-facing side, publishing the findings that were understandable to people in some way. But she was sure that they found things here that were unexplainable, indistinguishable from magic as Arthur C. Clarke said of any sufficiently advanced technology. Once she would have laughed at the idea of conspiracy, but she had seen things with ARKANE that made anything possible.

"What does the statue represent to you as a Hindu and a scientist?" Jake asked.

Amit paused, his face serious.

"Lord Shiva danced the universe into existence. He sustains it and eventually, he will destroy it. Whether you see this as a metaphor or an ancient truth, it's a powerful symbol for what we study here: the very building blocks of the universe. I believe that even if we find the answer to every scientific question, beyond that will still be God, the great unknowable. The American cosmologist Carl Sagan spoke of the parallel between Shiva Nataraja and subatomic physics. He understood the Hindu idea of cycles of time, an infinite number of deaths and rebirths. To understand this is to realize our own insignificant place in the universe." Amit paused and then pointed onwards. "This way."

They rounded a corner between buildings 39 and 40, a

short distance from the main building, and suddenly there it was. A two-meter-high copper statue of Shiva Nataraja. Morgan walked closer, drawn to the smooth skin of the god as his almond-shaped eyes stared implacably down at her.

"It was made using an ancient technique of bronze casting," Amit explained. "The original sculpture was made from wax, each perfect detail carved according to the exact image of Shiva, for each statue must be perfect in homage to God. A clay cast was made and then the wax melted from inside before metal was poured into the space left behind. The clay was chipped away, leaving the bronze statue, which was then filed and polished to create the final piece. This is an art that we continue to use in India for many sacred statues."

Jake bent down to read the plaque at the base.

"It's meant to symbolize the marriage of technology and mythology," he said. "Presented by representatives of the Indian Department of Atomic Energy back in 2004."

Morgan walked slowly around the statue, examining it for any other markings. The bronze fire surrounding the god shone in the sun and it seemed as if he could step down from his pedestal at any moment and pound the earth with his heels. She could almost hear the ringing of the hollow bronze and feel the shaking of the ground beneath. The demon under Shiva's feet had an expression of horror as he was crushed, but the god remained calm and expressionless as he renewed creation.

On the back side of the sculpture, behind Shiva's right knee, Morgan noticed scratches in the metal. They were unusual, as the rest of it was so perfectly polished. She bent closer.

"Look at this," she called to Jake. "It looks like a row of numbers, a code of some kind: 2717389178042068."

Amit came closer and as he bent to look at the code, his face paled.

"It can't be," he whispered. "It's just … It must be the artist's mark, some kind of number representing the workshop where it was made." He turned away and Morgan could see that he was shaking. The code was certainly more than an artist's mark. She took a picture with her smart phone and sent it off to Martin Klein back at ARKANE.

"Perhaps you could tell us about the men who donated the statue," Jake said. "We're particularly interested in Vishal Kapoor."

Amit turned, his face still pale from the discovery.

"There's something–"

A gunshot split the air, cutting off his words. A metallic ping echoed from the statue as a bullet hit the bronze.

"Down!" Jake shouted, pulling Amit to the ground.

Morgan crouched low and scooted around the statue away from the direction of the gunfire. They had come unarmed to the research facility, but now she regretted the assumption of a purely academic visit.

She poked her head out quickly and then pulled back as more shots peppered the statue.

"We have to get inside," she said. "They'll be on us soon enough. Before security can get here, at least."

Amit was shaking and his hands clutched at Jake as he whispered desperate prayers.

"The numbers," he said, his voice shaking. "It can't be …"

He stood suddenly and ran towards the main building, stumbling as he pushed himself up. Jake lunged at him, his fingers brushing Amit's coat, but he couldn't get a grasp.

A single shot rang out.

The young scientist fell to the ground, clutching his leg as blood spurted out on the pathway. He screamed in pain.

Alarm bells began to ring and security guards emerged from the building, but Morgan knew that they wouldn't find the shooter. Whoever it was would be long gone, their warning delivered.

As security swarmed towards them. Martin's comments about a leak at ARKANE troubled her. Was this a warning to stop them proceeding any further with the search? Was Marietti in danger?

Jake put his hands on his head and Morgan followed suit. No point in making a scene. They'd be out of here soon enough once Martin got on the case.

"Amit was about to tell us something about Vishal Kapoor," Jake said. "We need to know more about his business and how it relates to nuclear energy."

"And what the hell does that code mean?" Morgan replied. "Hopefully Martin will be able to get something from it so we know where to go next."

Two hours later, after being questioned and searched and ultimately having Martin plead their case remotely to have them set free, Jake and Morgan walked out of CERN and caught a taxi back to the airport. A text came in on Jake's phone and he held it up for Morgan to see.

"It's from Martin," he said. "The code on the statue contained the latitude and longitude references for the Taj Mahal. He's just sorting out flights for Agra."

"I haven't been there for a long time," Morgan whispered, her voice trailing off as she looked out the window at the mountains in the distance.

She closed her eyes for a minute with her head turned away so Jake wouldn't see her expression. She had been to the Taj Mahal on honeymoon with her husband Elian, only months before he had been killed fighting on the Golan Heights. They had both been in the Israeli Defense Force and knew the risks, but their time together had been so brief. Sometimes she could barely summon Elian's face to her mind, let alone recall the touch of his skin on hers.

But the Taj ... Morgan sighed softly. She remembered the romance of gazing up at the perfect dome under the full moon as they sailed along the Yamuna River, and later, the opulent hotel in Agra where they had lain entwined for the night. *I will love you forever*, Elian had whispered, *like Shah Jahan loved his queen*. But that great love had ended in tragedy too, and like Shah Jahan, she was the one left behind.

"Martin's arranged a military transport," Jake said, tapping on his phone and interrupting her memories. "We should just be able to make it to the airport in time."

Morgan brushed the hint of tears from her cheek and turned back to Jake. He looked over and grinned, his excitement at the thrill of the chase clear in his expression. Morgan couldn't help but smile back because she knew exactly how he felt. Despite all she had lost, ARKANE gave her more than adventure. It gave her a purpose.

It suddenly struck Morgan that she could summon Jake's face in her sleep now. They had worked together on enough missions and been through so much danger, seen so many unexplainable things. Together, they had experienced far more than she and Elian had ever been through because they had never directly worked together. Her husband had been stationed at the military front while she had worked as a psychologist between Jerusalem and Tel Aviv. Now she spent intense periods with Jake on missions.

There was a spark between them and they both knew it. But the danger they both put themselves in meant the likelihood of loss if they took things any further. Morgan worried so much about her twin sister Faye and her niece Gemma, whom she had endangered at Pentecost. After Elian's death and her father's murder, Morgan didn't think she could handle such a personal loss again.

Of course, she could always give up being an ARKANE agent and return to the University of Oxford as an academic. Life would be simpler and safer, but it would also be black and white. With Jake and ARKANE, she lived in technicolor.

Jake leaned over and showed her some pictures of the Taj on his phone. "It's amazing," he said. "I've always wanted to visit. Do you think one of the pieces could be there?"

"It's possible," Morgan said. "But the Taj attracts millions of visitors every year, and from what I remember, it's not full of obvious places to hide a piece of a statue."

"We'll work it out when we get there," Jake said. "Remember Santiago de Compostela in Spain? We didn't have a clue where the stone was hidden, and yet, we still found it, despite it being hidden for so long."

"You had way too much fun that day," Morgan said with a laugh, as she remembered Jake swinging on the chasuble rope, high up in the nave.

He took her hand in his and squeezed, his dark eyes suddenly serious. "We're a good team, Morgan. I'm glad we're doing this together."

CHAPTER 10

Asha walked into the penthouse office without knocking and breezed past the secretary with a cool glance that stopped the woman in her tracks. Mahesh had begun to use the main office before their father had died but now he had truly made it his own. He looked up as she came in and Asha noticed the dark shadows under his eyes.

"What is it?" he said, his voice tired.

"I hear you're heading to Chittagong," Asha replied.

Mahesh stood and ran his hands through his thick black hair. "Yes, I need to build better relationships with the heads of each industry sector." He looked at his watch. "I'm heading to the airport in an hour."

"I want to come," Asha said. "I've never seen the ship-breaking yards before."

Mahesh looked surprised. "I thought you'd focus on the lab and tech side of things now. I can handle manufacturing and mining. Let's face it, the ship-breaking yard is no place for a woman."

Asha bristled at his words, a retort on the tip of her tongue. But she held it in. She walked to the desk. Mahesh was using their father's fountain pen, a Visconti inlaid with walnut wood. She leaned forward and picked it up, taking the cap off to admire the silver nib.

"He used this for all his legal documents," she said. "His private journals too."

"It's too big for your hand," Mahesh replied, plucking it from her fingers.

She let him take it, forcing herself to relax. She needed to keep him onside for just a little longer.

"We can't split everything between us," Asha said in a softer tone, her voice placating. "Father would have wanted us both to understand all aspects of the business. If you let me come to Chittagong, I'll escort you round the labs when we get back. I have some projects that will fascinate you." She paused for effect and then dropped her head, letting a glimmer of a tear glisten at the corner of her eye. "I miss him."

Mahesh rounded the desk and pulled her close, stroking her long hair. "I miss him too, Ash." He kissed the top of her head. "Let's not fight. I need your support as we go through this transitional period." Asha leaned against her brother and wrapped her arms around him in return. For a moment, she felt her father's warmth in his embrace. Then Mahesh stepped back. "Actually, I could use your help. The Board want me to look into a number of discrepancies. Father's illness put them off but now they want answers."

A chill ran through Asha at his words. The labs, the clinic, the Aghori, the hunt for the pieces of the statue, the Kali temple. All were secret, but there would be a money trail.

"What kind of things are they looking into?" she asked, her eyes wide with innocence.

"The details are all in that report." Mahesh pointed at a thick folder on the desk. "I'm going to skim it on the plane."

Asha's eyes darted to the report. She had to know what was in it. She still needed more time to get the rest of the statue and she could not be found out now.

Mahesh looked at his watch. "If you're coming, I'll meet you on the helipad in ten minutes and we'll head to the airport."

An hour later, they boarded the Kapoor private jet and were soon flying northeast towards Chittagong in Bangladesh, on the Bay of Bengal. It was a six-hour flight across the widest part of India, but at least they traveled in comfort. The stewardess brought refreshments over as Mahesh opened his briefcase and pulled out the Board report.

"How about I skim it and give you the highlights?" Asha said.

Mahesh smiled. "I'm glad to have you here, sis." He handed her the Board report. "Just make sure I can answer all their difficult questions."

They both settled into their respective work as the plane flew east. The hum of the engines soothed Asha as she concentrated on the dense text. Much of it was focused on the main business sectors but as she skimmed through, she found questions raised about funds diverted to her own projects.

Asha visualized the Board, those self-righteous, pompous men who gorged themselves on the profits of others, who had grown fat from the industry of the Kapoors and who now questioned how the company was run. But they had forgotten what lay beneath it all. They had forgotten the man who had scraped and worked his fingers to bloody stumps for his first few dollars. Vishal hadn't been afraid to get his hands dirty in order to build a future for his family, and Asha had every intention of making sure the company continued in that vein.

She worked through the report and by the time the plane descended, she had distilled it into a few pages of summary for Mahesh to read as well as recommended actions for the more innocuous projects. That should keep their attention elsewhere for a little while, Asha thought as she packed up the files and buckled up.

They soon landed in Chittagong, a natural harbor and major coastal seaport city that had seen the Portuguese trade here in the seventeenth century, later the Mughal Empire and then the British East India Company. It had become part of East Pakistan in 1947 after Partition of India, and the city had been the site of Bangladesh's Declaration of Independence in 1971.

Asha knew that her father had an emotional attachment to the ship-breaking yards here. He had been a fixer for various archaeological digs and that had led to him solving problems in many different industries, making relationships across huge cultural and logistical divides. He had become involved in the shipping industry and soon saw an opening for the thorny problem of disposal. Most commercial ships had a lifespan of twenty-five to thirty years, and then became uneconomical due to wear and tear.

Vishal always reused everything, finding ways to recycle even the smallest leftovers. She remembered how he had tinkered with their bikes in the early days of the business, soldering on extra parts he'd sourced from local scrapyards. She could only imagine her father's excitement when faced with a huge ship to break down.

Asha had only seen pictures of the huge rusting hulks in the shallow waters of the coast before. This was the first time she would see them with her own eyes. Could there be another piece of the statue here?

"I know Father would want us to keep the yards running," Mahesh said, as they both stared out the window of the car that drove them north out of the city to the coast. He reached for Asha's hand. "But there have to be changes now he's gone. You understand that, don't you?"

Asha heard the implication in his voice.

"Of course," she said. "Did you have anything specific in mind?"

"Your ... guru." Mahesh spat the word. "If you want to be more involved in the running of the company, you have to get rid of him. We can't be associated with such extremism."

Asha pulled her hand from Mahesh's grasp. Her brother couldn't understand what the Aghori meant to her. She could still feel the touch of his bloody fingers on her skin. She could still hear his sacred words. Mahesh didn't know what they planned, so she just had to play for more time.

"As you wish." Mahesh looked over at her demure words and frowned a little. She looked back with wide eyes. "It's all about what's most important for the company now, I understand that."

Mahesh nodded and was silent for a moment.

"Nalika is pregnant," he said finally. "I meant to tell you, but it's not even three months yet, so we're keeping it quiet."

A dark stone settled in Asha's stomach. A baby would be seen as a success for Mahesh. He would be a responsible family man, a worthy successor to her father. The Board would sideline her. She couldn't let that happen.

She leaned in to give him a hug. "Congratulations," she said, beaming. "I'm so pleased. Did Father know?"

Mahesh shook his head. "I whispered it to him at the end but he didn't respond."

"He would have been pleased," Asha said. "Delighted."

She stared out the window again, focusing on the gulf to the west as they sped north on N1. Another child to add to a nation of over a billion people. What impact could that have on a global scale? None whatsoever. She would prove who was the more powerful sibling.

But time was ticking away.

They finally reached the ship-breaking yards, passed the armed guards and stepped out of the car into the heat of the late afternoon. The tang of burned metal and rust hung in the salty air with a greasy edge of oil that seemed to coat the back of Asha's throat. The dirty beach stretched into the distance with the hulks of old ships in the shallow waters, looming above the sand. Some were fully intact, ready to be picked over, others were just shells, stripped of every useful part. The names of the ships faded in the sun, the paint peeling away as they were returned to the elements.

Thousands of men worked here. They crawled through the beached container ships and oil tankers every day, breaking down everything to its component parts, ants under the gigantic propellers and barnacle-encrusted hulls. It was like the Towers of Silence in a way, Asha thought. That which has been created must be destroyed. Everything was reused here, in the same way that bodies were devoured by the raptor birds in the Parsi towers. She could see why her father had loved it here. It appealed on a visceral scale, an impressive testament to man's power over machine.

The foreman approached, taking his hard hat off as he greeted them. He shook Mahesh's hand and gave Asha a respectful nod.

"I'm so sorry about your father," he said. "He came for an inspection only last year."

"We're here to make sure that everything continues smoothly," Mahesh said.

Asha put her hand on the foreman's arm.

"I want to see what my father did when he was here." Her lips trembled slightly. "I want to trace his footsteps through the yard."

A look of surprise crossed Mahesh's face at her emotional words but he remained silent.

"I'm sorry madam, but that's impossible," the foreman said, trepidation on his face. "Everything changes here by the day, as you can see. The ships come in periodically and every day those that are here disappear little by little. You cannot see what your father saw because it's all gone."

Asha looked out over the vista of metallic grey and noted the pools of rust and oil that slicked about the hulls of the ships. Where could her father have hidden the sculpture piece in these ever-shifting sands?

She nodded. "Of course, I understand, but please show me what you can. I want to see through his eyes."

"This way," the foreman said. "We can stay on the boardwalk and keep you out of the mud."

They followed him to the shoreline and onto the rough planks laid down at the edge of the sand.

Men traipsed back and forth through the black mud in bare feet or simple flip-flops. A group of them walked past with a heavy cable over their shoulders as they dragged it towards a newly arrived ship.

"They'll use that to winch pieces of the ship ashore," the foreman said. "We reuse a lot of the materials and chemicals and we find other special items, too. Your father liked to see those. He had his own special place to do it. Come, I'll show you."

A shrill cry suddenly rang out from one of the ships, taken up by the workers around it. The men shouted as they ran from the shoreline, arms waving in warning. A wrenching squeal of metal tore the air. One side of a nearby ship broke apart and a giant hunk of metal crashed to the sand. The noise was like a muffled explosion and the shock rippled under their feet.

The foreman grabbed Asha's arm, steadying her as the moment passed and the men began to walk back towards the ship again, ready to break the piece down and winch it away. Their nonchalance implied such near-death was a regular event.

They walked on further to a hut on stilts, raised above the mud so it had a view out to the ships unmarred by the proximity of the workers.

"Your father trusted me to choose the most interesting things and leave them in here," the foreman said. "Should I continue this in future?"

"Yes," Mahesh said quickly. "Nothing should change for now."

Asha mounted the steps and pushed open the door.

The room was divided into two, separated by a thick curtain. There was a long table under the window and a simple chair behind it, a red metal toolbox on one side, neatly closed. Asha put out one hand and touched it lightly.

"Remember this?" She turned to Mahesh and he smiled back.

"Of course, he used to get it out even if it was just to change a lightbulb. He was always a fixer. But what was he doing in here?"

Asha flicked open the toolbox, checking in case the statue piece was inside. It was a long shot, but there had to be a reason this place had been so special to Vishal.

Mahesh walked to the back of the room and pulled open the curtain to reveal a rack of shelves, each one jam-packed with items, a cabinet of curiosities from the ships. The shelving included a bunkbed, made up with simple cotton sheets and a wool blanket.

"He must have come here to escape sometimes," Mahesh said. "Perhaps it reminded him of what life was like at the beginning."

Asha smiled. "I can imagine him tinkering away at the table, looking out at the ships." She sat down on the bunk. "Sleeping here." She swung her legs up and curled on top of the blanket.

There was a picture pinned to the bottom of the shelf below. Her father would have looked at it every time he lay here.

The Taj Mahal. The iconic symbol of India.

"Look at this," Asha said, scooting over so her brother could lie down next to her. It felt like they were children again, huddling in a den and hiding from the world. She could feel the warmth of him and for a moment, she wanted to lay her head on his shoulder and forget all the plans she had in place.

"That's where he proposed to Mama." His voice was soft and Asha heard the hint of the little boy who had lost his mother so young. "She was performing there, dancing in a crowd scene for a Bollywood movie. He was still building the business back then so he wasn't rich, but she still said yes."

"He never told me about that," Asha whispered.

"He wanted you to be strong and forge your own path. He didn't want you starry-eyed at the thought of love." Mahesh turned his head to look at the picture again. "He loved the Taj. In fact, he was there when it was designated a UNESCO World Heritage Site in 1983. He advised as to how they could ensure it would stand up to the huge numbers of people who would visit."

Asha looked up at the Taj, resplendent in white marble against the blue skies of Uttar Pradesh. If it had meant so much to her father, perhaps he had hidden another piece of the sculpture there. She would go to Agra next.

CHAPTER 11

MARIETTI LAY ON THE hospital bed, his body prone and unmoving. But there was a flickering under his eyelids, lucid dreaming of a past that now came to haunt him again.

Maharashtra, India. April 19, 1982. 2.43pm

The sun beat down as they trekked along the path towards the caves of Ellora. Sweat dripped down Marietti's back, soaking the shirt he wore under his pack. He pulled the brim of his hat down further to shield his eyes and turned to see how the others were doing.

Joseph Manfredi, his assistant from the Vatican Archives, trudged along several meters behind. His face was beetroot red and he still wore the permanent frown he had adopted since they had landed in Mumbai the day prior. Behind him walked Vishal Kapoor, a trusted local fixer and specialist on Indian archaeology, who had worked on a number of digs for the Vatican.

All three men trailed behind Nataline Reed, a young woman of mixed Indian and British heritage whose brisk walk set the pace. Her specialism was rock-cut architecture and Hindu myth, although she was a devout Catholic from the southern state of Goa. She had long dark hair that curled around soft features and her eyebrows arched in a way that reminded Marietti of the Titian Venus of Urbino. Of course, that painting was of a nude and Marietti kept trying to banish the image from his mind whenever he looked at her. For the first time in his life, he regretted his love of art and how he could bring to mind any painting he had studied over the years. He tried to keep his eyes from Nataline's shapely behind as she strode up the hill, wishing he had time to stop and have a cigarette, or some coffee.

"How much further?" Joseph shouted, unable to keep the tone of annoyance from his voice as he brushed yet another fly from his face. The man was clearly at home in the cool, dry stillness of the Vatican Archives, but out here in the heat and abundance, noise and smells, he was lost. Still, Marietti couldn't do this alone. He needed help and until they found something of significance, this motley crew was all he had.

"Not long, Mr Manfredi, sir," Vishal said with a smile, giving that distinctive Indian head-wobble as he spoke. He was a jolly fellow and Marietti instinctively liked the man, with his willingness to help and the knowledge he so clearly had about Indian archaeology.

They walked around a final corner and Marietti's eyes widened at the huge temple complex. The word 'cave' could not possibly describe the rock-cut edifice in front of him. It reminded him of the glories of the rose-red city of Petra in Jordan or the stone churches of Lalibela in Ethiopia. Nataline stood close by, sipping from her water bottle.

"The Hindu caves here were constructed between the sixth and eighth centuries," she said. "The complex design rivals the great cathedrals of Europe that took generations to build. The architects had such vision." She shook her head in wonder and then pointed up at the stone elephant in front of them. "This is part of the Kailasa temple, designed to resemble Mount Kailash, the dwelling place of Lord Shiva in the Himalaya. It's carved out of a single rock, not constructed from blocks as you would think, and covers an area double the size of the Parthenon in Athens."

"How are we going to find anything here?" Joseph wheezed as he sat heavily on a rock to catch his breath.

"We'll split up," Marietti said. "You and Vishal take the east side."

Joseph looked grateful and headed off into the shade of the temple.

Marietti pulled the page from Himmler's diary out of his backpack. He needed to figure out how the directions of the old map related to the physical layout of the temple. He turned it around and compared it to what lay before him. It just didn't fit. So what was he missing? He tried re-reading the German, a frown deepening between his thick eyebrows.

"I still don't know what you're specifically looking for."

Nataline stood before him. The sun was behind her and he could see the curves of her body silhouetted underneath her loose shirt. He took a deep breath, unable to take his eyes off her as she walked closer, breaking the moment.

"I'm …" Marietti struggled to recall what he'd been thinking only moments ago. "We're looking for something specific, the Brahmastra. Do you know of it?"

Nataline nodded. "Of course, it's a mythical weapon. Incredibly powerful. Why do you think this place relates to it?"

He opened the diary and explained the background of Himmler's fascination with India and the Nazis' search for the ultimate weapon.

"Do you know of anywhere in the complex that might fit?" he asked.

Nataline gazed out at the setting sun as she thought. After a moment, she spoke.

"There is something. This way."

She led the way through rock corridors to Cave 19 and stopped in front of a carved panel showing a dancing god. The bottom half was plain rock, but higher up where it was harder to reach there were still intricate paintings in yellow, green and white.

"Shiva Nataraja," Nataline said. "The destroyer and creator of the universe. If anything would fascinate the Nazis, it would be this."

Marietti looked more closely at the carved figure as his undulating arms ushered in a new creation. Then he noticed something. The demon of ignorance under Shiva's feet looked out of place, and the stone had weathered in a different way.

"Look at this," he said. Nataline bent close and he could smell a hint of citrus on her skin, a fresh scent that cut through the dense air. Her eyes narrowed.

She bent to her pack and pulled out a makeup kit in a floral bag, the type associated with more high-maintenance women. Marietti smiled as she opened it to reveal a field archaeologist's kit with files, a mini trowel and brushes of various kinds. He was impressed. Even if she had been searched, it's unlikely these would have been discovered.

Nataline brushed gently at the demon.

"There, look. You can see a seam. This was added later. It's not part of the original carving."

"Can you lever it out?"

Nataline raised a perfectly shaped eyebrow. "And damage a world-famous archaeological site?"

"We can put it back after," Marietti said with a grin. "Besides, I know you're itching to find out what's behind it."

Nataline smiled. "Well, if we have the blessing of the Vatican …" She chose a file from her kit and began to pick at the little carving.

"It's protruding quite far out." She gave it a push and it

shifted. Her eyes flashed to Marietti's, a look of excitement darting between them. She pushed it again, straining a little. "You do it." She moved sideways to allow him more space.

Marietti used both his hands and pressed the demon forward into the rock. There was an audible thunk and a crunch, the shifting of stone on sand, the rubbing of rocks against each other, and then the whole panel shifted back to reveal an entrance. It was no more than half a meter wide, but enough that they could shuffle through. Inside, all was darkness.

"What is happening, sir?" Vishal appeared from behind a corner of the temple. His eyes widened as he saw the entrance.

"We may have found what we were looking for," Marietti said. "But we need light and tools from the packs we left at the entrance."

"I'll go," Vishal said. "And I'll get Mr Joseph, too. He's resting right now." Vishal's smile said it all, and Marietti knew who he'd rather have next to him in the cave. He nodded.

Vishal dashed off, his feet slip-sliding over the rocks in his haste. Nataline looked at Marietti.

"Do you seriously think that the Brahmastra could be in there?" Her beautiful features twisted in concern.

"It's only a myth," Marietti said. "But there's clearly something worth hiding in this sacred complex. Something the Nazis knew about but were never able to get to."

Vishal soon returned with headlamps and Joseph scrambled behind him.

"What's this I hear about a secret entrance?" he said, enthusiasm returning to his voice at the possibility of finding something. He stopped abruptly as he saw the split rock and the darkness inside. His face fell as Nataline and Marietti donned headlamps. "Oh. We're going in, then?"

"You're welcome to wait out here," Marietti said.

"Can I come, sir?" Vishal said, his eyes bright with excitement.

"Of course." Marietti nodded. "You're the expert, after all."

"I'm coming," Joseph snapped, and they all geared up.

After adjusting their headlamps, Marietti stepped inside the dark passageway first. This was what drove him, the anticipation of what they might find. He knew there were ancient artifacts of power hidden across the world and his mission for the Vatican had always been to find them and bring them back before others could use them for dark deeds. But in recent months, he had wondered what happened to the things he brought back and whether, in fact, they were being used in precisely the way he feared. There were dark times coming and he had heard of a group who stood apart from the church, ARKANE, who collected objects of power and kept them from all religious groups, understanding that they each had their own agenda. When he got back to Rome, he intended to inquire further. It was time for a change.

He felt a crunch under his feet and a crack echoed in the narrow tunnel. Marietti looked down to see the path ahead littered with bones. A thick layer of them stretched into the tunnel, a mixture of small animal and human remains. They disintegrated to dust under his boots.

"Watch your feet," he said as he walked on.

The path wound down through the rock.

"This was clearly part of the original complex," Nataline said as they stepped carefully through the residue of death. She shone her headlamp up the walls. "The paintings are more protected here, and I would guess they date back to the eighth century."

Marietti looked up to see a huge painting of Shiva destroying the world. His long hair whirled out and the stars rained down from heaven in fire that consumed the earth.

"Happy times," he said. What the hell was down here?

They rounded a corner and the tunnel opened up into a huge chamber, so wide that the beam of their lights couldn't reach the other side.

"Hello!" Joseph shouted, his voice echoing round the chamber. Marietti spun and grabbed his arm.

"Hush," he whispered through gritted teeth. "This is a holy place."

"It's not our faith," Joseph snapped, pulling his arm away. "It's all just myth and superstition." He strode into the center of the chamber and spun around. His headlamp darted over rock walls, skipping over paintings of Hindu demons, of the goddess Kali devouring her victims as she clutched their decapitated heads in her many hands. Vishal gasped at the scenes as the light flickered over them.

Then a glint flashed and Joseph stopped, turning back to what they had only glimpsed before.

A statue of Shiva Nataraja in burnished bronze stood upon a stone altar, the intricate figure dancing the world to destruction. There were Sanskrit words inscribed on the base. Joseph strode towards it.

"No." Vishal's voice was thin and reedy in the semi-darkness. "Don't touch it, sir."

Joseph lifted his chin and Marietti saw defiance in his gaze. He had no respect for this land, he only wanted to possess it. Joseph reached out and grabbed the statue, picking it up and holding it above his head.

"What? It's nothing. Just a bronze idol, like the Lord God struck down in Egypt."

Then his face froze in a look of horror. "What was that?" He spun round.

Marietti and the others spun too, but there was nothing there.

"Get away from me!" Joseph's voice was stricken as he stared at the pictures on the walls. He backed away as if the stalking gods came for him. He tried to shake the statue from his hand, but he couldn't prise it away. So he used it as a weapon, whirling around, brandishing it like a club as he beat at the air.

"Get back, you demons of Hell!" he shouted.

Marietti moved towards him.

"The guardians of Shiva are here," Vishal whispered. "He has angered them. Don't touch him."

Joseph began to foam at the mouth, his face growing red in the light. He moaned.

Then he began to scream.

The sound made Marietti's skin crawl and he felt Nataline take his arm.

"We have to help him," she whispered.

Marietti took another step forward, but Vishal held him back.

"The statue is cursed," he said.

Joseph dropped to his knees, wrapping himself around the statue, curving his body over and around it as he whimpered in agony. His headlamp went dark as it hit the ground, but they could see the statue glowing, an unnatural light streaming from it. At last, Joseph's cries died and his body went limp.

Then the light from the statue went out.

Vishal released Marietti's arm. "Go to him now, but don't touch the statue. There are stories of this weapon and harnessing its curse, but it must be treated carefully."

Marietti went to Joseph and together with Nataline they pulled his body from the statue, careful not to touch it.

Joseph's face was frozen in a rictus of horror, his eyes wide and bloodshot as if he had looked into the gaping maw of Hell.

"What did he see?" Nataline murmured as Marietti closed the man's eyes.

"I'd say the demons painted on these walls might have something to do with it." Marietti shuddered. "I wouldn't want to meet any of this lot in the flesh."

"A hallucination perhaps?" she said. "Brought on by touching the statue."

"The ancient civilizations were pretty good with curses and booby traps," Marietti said.

Joseph's skin turned grey as they watched, and then his flesh began to shrivel, wrinkling in on itself. They stepped quickly away as his body crumbled into dust.

"What the–?"

Marietti shook his head. Whatever the statue was, they couldn't leave it here. But could he trust the Vatican with it?

"Mr Marietti, sir. Look at this." Vishal's voice wavered and Marietti turned to see him crouching down by the altar, his head-torch illuminating a mural. It showed a Hindu holy man, standing in Vrksasana, the yogic tree pose, his left leg bent at the knee, his arms above his head. He held the statue of Shiva Nataraja in his hands, his mouth open as he spoke a mantra. Around him, a crowd of thousands drew near. Rays of light streamed from the statue and all it touched shriveled before it, their bodies turning to dust.

Nataline walked closer and bent to read the script around the edge.

"It speaks of the Brahmastra," she said, reaching out with one slim hand to indicate the words. "The statue of Shiva concentrates some kind of power … conjured by speaking a specific holy mantra. Then it feeds off the energy of the dead, amplifying it further. If used incorrectly, it burns those who dare to touch it."

She looked over at the pile of dust on the ground.

"There's more writing here," Vishal said.

Nataline turned to look, her fingers brushing over the ancient words. "The weapon is a messenger of death and can harness the power of a thousand suns for those who know how to use it." Her voice shook. "And it speaks of Harappa."

"An ancient civilization in the Indus Valley," Vishal explained. "They found skeletons scattered along the streets there as if some instantaneous death knocked them down where they stood. The skeletons were still radioactive after thousands of years."

"This weapon is what the Nazis sought," Marietti whispered. "Thank God they never found it."

Nataline looked up, her face pale in the flickering light. "But there are others who will seek it. We can't leave the statue here now, not this time. If you found out about it, others will too. And look at the Indian government with their nuclear weapons and the ongoing saber rattling with Pakistan. This is too powerful to leave behind."

Vishal gave his customary head wobble. "I agree, sir. This is very bad for my people."

Marietti spun around and paced away from them into the darkness, not wanting them to see his indecision. He looked back at what was left of Joseph's body, the outline of a human corpse barely discernible against the grey rock. He couldn't be sure that the statue would be safe in the Vatican, even in the Secret Archives. There were too many people with contacts in the shadows, those who would barter such an object for temporal power, or use it to spread chaos.

But they couldn't leave it here. Nataline was right, there would be those who would follow in their footsteps.

He turned to look at his two companions, such different people moving in separate worlds, and an idea began to form.

"We could break it apart," he said. "Each take a section and hide it without telling the others where. I'll explain Joseph's ... accident to the Vatican and you two can return to your own lives."

Nataline stood, her hands out as if to push him away. She shook her head vehemently. "No, not me. I won't touch that thing." She crossed herself. "I promise to be silent but don't involve me, Elias." She looked up at him and he could see that her eyes were wet with tears.

He walked over and pulled her to him, rubbing her back with his hands. "It's OK," he whispered. "You don't have to do anything you don't want to." He could feel her body under her clothes and he felt a stirring within, a desire to protect and shelter her. She was so fragile. How could he even ask such a thing of her?

"I'll do it," Vishal said. "We can take half each and hide the pieces far away."

Marietti released Nataline and nodded.

Vishal crouched down next to the statue. It lay on its side where it had dropped from Joseph's hands.

"It's stopped glowing. Look, it seems to be only metal again." He used a pocketknife to prod it gingerly.

Nothing happened.

"Let's try with gloves," Marietti said. Vishal looked up with doubt in his eyes. Marietti shrugged. "I'll do it."

He pulled on a pair of thick gloves from his pack and knelt down by the statue. He met Vishal's dark eyes. The other man nodded. Marietti put his gloved hands on the statue.

Nothing happened.

Their collective sigh of relief echoed through the cave.

Marietti picked it up. "It looks like it's made up of several pieces anyway," he said. "Perhaps it was hidden separately way back when it was created."

He pulled out the flames from behind the dancing

Shiva and then unscrewed the god from its pedestal and finally split the base in two.

Vishal pulled some rags from his bag, wrapped up one half of the base along with the flames and handed them to Marietti.

"I will take good care of the other pieces," he said.

Marietti nodded. He trusted the Indian, but he also knew that hard times could change anyone's mind. He needed to ensure that Vishal was never tempted to sell the statue. Himmler's diary had other maps in it, and there were treasures hidden in this land that could be useful now.

He put his hand out and shook Vishal's, meeting the man's eyes. "I know you will," he said. "But there's something else I'd like to talk to you about."

A medical alarm down the hallway interrupted Marietti's dream and he was suddenly back in the present, trapped in the hospital bed years later.

Vishal had taken some of the treasure they found later and used it to start a business empire. His natural ability to charm and his entrepreneurial spirit had taken him into the realm of billionaire. Marietti had returned to the Vatican, handed in his notice and joined ARKANE. He wanted to hunt for artifacts but he didn't want to do it under the auspices of the Vatican anymore.

Nataline had returned to Goa and, God help him, he had gone to her more than once. He missed the cool touch of her hands on his fevered skin now. He missed … Marietti sighed. He had given her up for his work, like so much else in his life and as regret circled him, he slipped back into unconsciousness.

CHAPTER 12

Agra, India

MORGAN AND JAKE EMERGED from the taxi in front of the public gates of the Taj Mahal complex. They had flown into New Delhi and been driven the 110 kilometers through the night, both grabbing as much sleep as possible on the way. Morgan felt rumpled from the long flight, her limbs cramped, but she also had a sense of excitement about seeing the mausoleum again.

It was still dark, a few hours before dawn, but already the courtyard thronged with vendors. Some laid out postcards and t-shirts alongside snow globes and brass replicas of the famous dome. Others cooked street food, the sizzling of onions and turmeric filling the air with a heady tang.

"Here, madam," an enthusiastic young man shouted, as he noticed the foreigners arrive. He ran over with his arms full of cheap souvenirs which he brandished in front of them. Morgan was swiftly reminded that the sense of personal space in India differed from the West. He soon gave up at their indifference.

But there was something here that Morgan definitely wanted. She took some small rupee notes and bought cups of chai from one of the sellers, handing one to Jake. The tea was rich with buffalo milk, sweet with sugar, and spicy with cardamom and cinnamon.

"That *is* good," Jake said, and went back for a second helping. He returned with two more cups and some paratha bread and they stood in the semi-darkness, listening to the bustle around them.

"I could drink this all the time," Morgan said as the hot drink revived her. "Chai is one of my favorite things about India."

"I got these too," Jake said. He pulled out a little tub filled with syrupy dough balls. "Gulab jamun. Like sticky toffee sweeties."

Morgan dipped her fingers in and pulled one of the balls out, lifting it to her mouth quickly as the syrup dripped to the ground. It was an explosion of sweetness, almost too much, and she swallowed it down in a moment of extreme pleasure.

"These are Ganesha's favorites," she said and reached for another one. "The elephant-headed god always has one hand full of them."

As they munched happily in a moment of simple pleasure, Jake checked his watch. "Martin said that we should be meeting a professor near the main gate soon," he said. "Apparently, he works here occasionally and has out-of-hours access. Let's head over there."

They walked to the public gate and stood waiting in the semi-darkness. It was impossible to see the famous view of the dome from their position, as the visitor had to walk through a courtyard before reaching the iconic mausoleum. But the area in front of the gate was abuzz with activity and they had plenty of life to watch as they waited.

It would only get busier as the day wore on. Agra was notorious for overcrowding and, at peak times, the crush of tourists in the heat of the sun was unbearable. The smell of sweaty bodies and the shout of tour guides made peaceful contemplation of its beauty impossible. India was often best before the crowds and Morgan was glad that Martin had sorted out a way in before the place officially opened. She looked at her watch.

If the professor turned up, of course.

It was best to breathe and adjust to Indian time. Things would happen when they happened. She sipped the last of her chai as a tinge of pink appeared above the horizon and the black sky turned to shades of indigo.

A few minutes later, a soft voice came from behind the gate.

"Mr Timber?"

Jake and Morgan turned to see a thin, older Indian man beckoning to them from inside. He smoked a hand-rolled *bidi* cigarette, sucking on it as he waved. He wore a faded green jacket with a Nehru collar over dark jeans. Both were ill-fitting and made him look like he'd lost a lot of weight recently.

"This way, please." They followed him to a smaller side gate and went inside. He walked away quickly, gesturing for them to follow. "Hurry. We must get away from the view of the gate."

The man only stopped when they were out of sight of those on the other side. He stubbed the end of the *bidi* out and placed the butt in a nearby bin. He adjusted his jacket and held out his hand in a proper manner.

"I'm sorry to be so hasty, but there are watchers at the gate." They shook hands as he continued. "Some report to people who would not approve of your visit. I'm Professor Chetan Palekar from Delhi University, employed briefly by your good company to show you inside the Taj. I'm an expert in Mughal architecture." He pointed to the next archway. "This way please and you may see the beginnings of the sunrise before the tourist horde."

They walked through the arch and suddenly, there it was.

The mausoleum of Shah Jahan's beloved wife with the iconic dome and four tall minarets, reflected in a long pool of water and flanked by manicured gardens. Morgan gazed up at it, silhouetted against the last stars of night. The early morning mist shrouded the edifice, but every second the sun rose higher and revealed more of its grandeur.

Morgan had stood right here with Elian many years ago but strangely, she didn't feel his loss so heavily now, just a sense of how different she was. She had been someone else back then, caught up in ideology, ignorant of so much that ARKANE had revealed of the world beneath the headlines.

"A teardrop on the cheek of eternity," she whispered.

Chetan nodded. "Yes, indeed. As described by Rabindranath Tagore, one of India's greatest poets. The Taj is a World Heritage Site and one of the jewels in India's architectural crown."

They stood in silence for a moment, then a clang came from behind them as if someone else had come through the gate.

Chetan looked back in alarm, but there was no one there.

"Come," he said, a worried furrow in his brow. "We must get inside before they open the gates. We can't be found here."

He pointed at a footpath off to the side, shielded by a row of cyprus trees so as to avoid the walk down the main boulevard in view of anyone else arriving. Chetan scurried ahead, his long legs striding away and Jake and Morgan walked quickly after him.

"Do you think we should be expecting company?" Morgan whispered. After the unexpected attack in Geneva, Martin had arranged for weapons to be issued on the military flight over, but they had hoped to be in and out of the Taj before anyone knew they were even there. They did not want to be caught with guns at one of India's most important monuments.

"I hope not." Jake nodded towards Chetan. "Because he's not going to be much use in any kind of fight."

As they drew closer to the mausoleum, the complexity of the building became evident. The ivory-colored marble was inlaid with ornate designs of flowers and Arabic calligraphy, the green, red and black highlighted with semi-precious stones. Although the building was heavy marble and anchored to the earth, it seemed light and airy, with decoration lifting the architecture into the realm of art.

Chetan led them under the vaulted archway into the main chamber. Morgan and Jake pulled torches from their packs and shone them around, illuminating the twin sarcophagi before them, surrounded by an intricately designed metal barrier.

"This is the tomb of Mumtaz Mahal," Chetan said. "She was the beloved wife of the Mughal Emperor Shah Jahan and she died during the birth of their fourteenth child. It was built in the mid-seventeenth century and it is said that over 20,000 artisans worked on it."

Morgan looked up into the vaulted dome overhead and then played the torch around the corners of the chamber. It was smaller than she remembered and there were no obvious places to hide a piece of a sculpture, especially that of a Hindu god. This was a Muslim tomb, after all.

Jake was clearly thinking the same thing as he peered through the grating at the sarcophagi of Shah Jahan and his beloved wife. They were beautifully decorated with flowers but otherwise they were quite plain, with none of the embellishments of Catholic monarchs in Europe.

"I don't think we're going to find anything here," he said, disappointment in his voice.

"Oh, but these are not the real tombs," Chetan said.

"So where are the real ones?" Morgan asked. "That's what we need to see."

"Oh no, no." Chetan shook his head. "That's impossible. I can't take you down there."

Suddenly, they heard shouting from outside.

Raised voices spoke quickly in Hindi and the flash of torchlight from outside pierced the interior of the mausoleum.

CHAPTER 13

Morgan pulled out her gun and moved to the side of the main door. Jake slipped silently to the other side. Chetan huddled behind the tomb and crouched near the floor, closing his eyes as if that would make everything go away.

The three of them stood still and silent for a moment as they listened. It was soon clear that the noise was only the jovial banter of security guards doing their rounds before opening up to the public for the day.

As the sound faded away, Jake walked around the tomb and pulled Chetan to his feet.

"We need to see the real tomb."

Chetan nodded, his forehead beaded with sweat at the near-discovery. "This way." He walked quickly over to a side panel behind the tombs. He slid his hand along the marble design, touching the intricate carvings gently as he searched for the entrance. "It's been a long time since I was last here."

There was an audible click and a metal handle popped out from the marble. Chetan tugged it to reveal a door and stone steps spiraling down into darkness.

Morgan shone her torch ahead and walked down into the lower level of the tomb as the men followed behind. The room was simple and stark, with two marble sarcophagi, the Emperor's bigger and grander than his beloved wife's.

The walls were a fine patchwork of marble blocks in hues of pink and grey, the fine grain polished to perfection. It was cool and the air smelled of a light incense. Not a bad place to spend eternity.

She spun around and shone her torch at the walls, but there looked to be nowhere obvious to hide a piece of the sculpture. She shook her head.

"Another dead end." Her voice echoed in the chamber. "There's clearly nothing here."

"What exactly are you looking for?" Chetan asked. "Your employer said only to show you around."

Jake pulled out his smart phone to reveal a picture of the Shiva Nataraja sculpture. "A piece of a sculpture like this," he said.

Chetan paled and his hand flew to his throat in alarm.

"You come here looking for Shiva." He shook his head in despair, his eyes bulging in fear. "I might as well tell you this, but there are those who would deny it and consider it slander. The Taj Mahal is dear to the nation, a flashpoint for emotion." He took a deep breath and continued as he paced up and down in the small tomb. "Some say that this land was not empty when the Taj was created and there are aspects of the building that are several hundred years older. There are rumors that an ancient Hindu temple lies beneath, dedicated to Shiva."

"It's not unusual for kings and conquerors to build over existing holy places," Jake said. "Most of Europe's great churches are built on originally pagan sites. So why is it such a big deal if it happened here?"

Morgan leaned against the cool stone of Mumtaz's tomb.

"The history of Muslims and Hindus in India is complicated and at times, very bloody," she whispered. "So I understand, Chetan. In Israel, there are those who still dispute the ownership of a particular piece of land thousands of years ago, as if that should affect who owns it today. These ancient grudges last a long time."

"But essentially there could be a temple to Shiva underneath," Jake said. "Which means the sculpture piece could still be here. So how do we get to it?"

* * *

Asha Kapoor leaned against the window of the helicopter as they dropped down into Agra, soaring over the city towards the Taj Mahal. She dialed a number on her phone.

"We'll be landing in the Taj Gardens," she said with a tone of authority. "Make sure the public aren't let in until I leave."

Her contact in the tourism department would be well paid for the service, and they would have the time they needed to locate the sculpture piece. Money was useful at times like these, but ultimately it was ephemeral. She was set on a greater goal, a legacy that would last longer than the business her father had created. Asha's heart beat faster at the possibility that she might soon hold the third piece in her hands. The Aghori would be pleased with her and they would be one step closer to the sacrifice.

The helicopter hovered over the manicured lawn of the Taj Mahal garden, its rotors beating the air as it descended. Branches of surrounding trees were whipped into a frenzy at the sudden chop of wind, but as the helicopter engine shut down, calm was restored to the garden again.

Asha climbed out of the helicopter, bending low as she walked quickly towards the mausoleum. Two of her bodyguards followed along, their weapons tucked away as they dragged another man between them.

Gopan had written a book on the existence of a Hindu temple under the Taj Mahal. He had gone into hiding when the book had brought him death threats, but Asha's hackers had found him in little time and they had picked him up on the way from Bangladesh. If her father had left a piece of the Shiva statue at the Muslim Taj Mahal, surely it would make sense that it be located where this fabled Shiva temple was.

Now Gopan would have the chance to prove his conspiracy theory for real. If he was wrong ... well, there was a faster way out of the helicopter to the ground below.

They reached the steps of the mausoleum and Asha turned.

"So, how do we get into this ancient temple?" she said.

She stepped closer to Gopan. He was young, maybe twenty-five, with a poor excuse for a mustache and a straggly beard. Dried blood crusted around his nose and his right eyebrow where a well-placed blow had persuaded him to join the search.

"I ... it ..." Sweat beaded on his upper lip and his breath came fast as he struggled for words.

"There's no need to be scared," Asha said softly. She pulled a handkerchief out, dabbed at his bloody face and then motioned for the bodyguards to let the man go. They dropped their hands and stepped back, silent in obedience. "Your book was so brilliant and I need your help to find this ancient temple. Will you help me?"

Gopan took a deep breath. "It is only a theory," he said. "We might not find anything."

Asha gave a light smile. "I think you'd better try finding something. After all, I've come a long way for this."

Gopan pointed up towards the main entrance. "Then we must go into the main mausoleum and down to the place where the real tombs are. My sources say that the entrance is down in the crypt."

Asha began to walk up the steps.

* * *

Below in the tomb, Chetan vehemently shook his head. "This ancient Shiva temple is only rumored to exist," he said. "And I don't know how we could find it anyway."

"There must be something here." Jake began to search the small tomb again, playing his torch over the walls as he searched for hidden seams that might hide another entrance.

Morgan stood for a moment and watched him search. Something was bothering her. Something about the history of the Taj.

She pulled up the notes from Martin on her smart phone and skimmed the information about the CERN statue and the Taj Mahal. A moment later, she found what she was looking for.

"Look at this," she said. "The same man, Vishal Kapoor, was involved in both the UNESCO World Heritage Site transformation project of the Taj Mahal and the CERN statue. In his early career, he worked on archaeological digs including some for the Vatican. He had to have hidden the piece." She turned to Chetan. "So what was changed here when the Taj became a UNESCO site? Did they make any structural changes?"

"Maybe so." Chetan waggled his head in that Indian way of saying maybe yes or maybe no. "I think they shored up the side closest to the Yamuna River in case of flooding for safety reasons. There was some other minor work, but that would be the most significant. They had many experts here then. Perhaps this man was able to access the old shrine – if it existed at all."

Jake turned and walked to the northern wall of the tomb. "The river is on this side."

Morgan joined him and together they examined the wall more closely. They both ran their hands over the intricate inlaid marble design in the same way Chetan had done upstairs.

The seconds ticked by.

"There's nothing here," Morgan said with disappointment. "Perhaps the sculpture piece was hidden in some other part of the complex. There's more to the Taj Mahal than just the tomb."

"Give me one more minute," Jake said. He bent to the floor and began to examine the flagstones.

* * *

Asha walked into the mausoleum. The dawn penetrated inside now and she could see the cool gleam of the marble tombs in the half-light. She leaned close to the metal grating and gazed in at the two lovers, lying side by side. She had read of Mumtaz Mahal and how she was both wife and mother, but also a trusted companion of the Emperor. She was the equal of Shah Jahan and their marriage had been testament to how much a true partnership could achieve. Asha had once wished for someone to share her life, but the men her father had suggested were weak, with none of the ambition that burned inside of her. She would never be buried in a tomb like this, she would never be loved as Mumtaz had been, but she intended to be remembered for far longer.

She turned to Gopan.

"Where now?"

He walked over to a side panel and ran his hands along the wall. "The way down to the lower tomb is here." His face paled and he pulled his hands away in shock.

"What is it?" Asha asked.

"The door is open," Gopan said. "Someone else is here."

CHAPTER 14

Down in the crypt, Morgan and Jake froze at the sounds coming from above.

"There's no other way out," Chetan whispered, his voice wavering. "And I left the door open. They'll know we're here."

Morgan pulled her gun out and pointed it towards the steps leading down from above.

"Help Jake look," she said softly. "If there is a shrine, now's the time to find it. We can't have a shootout in the Taj Mahal."

Chetan fell to his knees and crawled along the marble slabs, sweeping his fingers across the stones as Jake worked his way from the opposite end.

"Here," Jake said suddenly. "There's a handle. We can pull this slab out. Help me, Chetan."

Together the men lifted one of the smaller marble blocks from the floor, revealing a dark hole below. Jake shone his torch in. It was about six feet deep and there was water and rubble in the bottom where a partially collapsed tunnel doglegged away from the access point.

"It doesn't look too good," Jake whispered. Morgan turned to look briefly, tearing her eyes from the staircase.

"We have to try," she said. "There's no cover in here. We're screwed if it comes to a firefight." In the moment of quiet, they heard the door creak open upstairs. "I'm going."

She clambered down into the hole and Chetan half fell

down after her. Jake came last and pulled the slab over again. Just as he slotted it into place, he saw torchlight flicker on the spiral stairs. It wouldn't take those following long to find the entrance, and there was no way of blocking it from below.

They had to hurry.

* * *

Asha and Gopan followed the two bodyguards down the stairs into the tomb. The men reached the bottom and swung their torches around, tracking the beam with their guns.

"It's clear," one of them said. "There's no one here."

Asha walked into the middle of the room. The atmosphere felt unsettled somehow. The cool air had been disturbed. But there looked to be no exit ... or was there?

She turned to Gopan.

"How do we get to this ancient Shiva shrine?"

"I ... I don't know, madam. Truly, I don't." He grabbed hold of the nearest sarcophagus and leaned against it as he shook with fear. "My sources say it is under here but there's no telling how to get to it."

Asha walked closer to the man. She gestured to one of the bodyguards and he handed her a kukri – a Tibetan machete – from his belt. Gopan's eyes bulged at the sight of the weapon, its blade glinting in the torchlight.

Asha swung it around in two hands, adept in her weapon skills.

"I follow Kali, in her Destroyer aspect," she said. "You know the goddess?"

Gopan nodded.

"Tell me what you know." Asha took a step towards him. The blade flashed before her, torchlight flickering over the silver edge.

"She is garlanded with the skulls of the dead and holds a severed head in one hand." Gopan's voice shook with terror.

"She holds a knife, too," Asha said softly. "The weapon with which she dispatches her sacrifice."

Gopan backed away, his hands out in supplication.

"No, please."

He found himself up against the wall of the tomb, hemmed in by marble.

"If you don't know where the shrine is, then you only have one purpose remaining." Asha nodded at her bodyguards.

They grabbed Gopan and lifted him onto the sarcophagus of Shah Jahan. He struggled and screamed but they held him down as Asha stalked towards her prey. Her pulse pounded and she could feel the incarnation of the goddess rise inside her, hungering to feed.

The shrine would be found, but only through offering a sacrifice. The Aghori often found answers in blood. Perhaps she would be able to read it, too.

She stood at the side of the sarcophagus and lifted the kukri above her head. One of the bodyguards tugged Gopan's head back, revealing his bare throat.

Asha said a prayer to the goddess and asked for her guidance.

She brought the weapon down.

A dull thunk resounded in the marble tomb and Gopan's head was severed from his torso. The bodyguard stepped back from the corpse and the head rolled off onto the floor, its eyes wide and mouth open, frozen in a final scream.

Blood pulsed from the dead man's flesh and ran across the floor. Asha watched the blood trail as it trickled down into the seams of the marble slabs. Then she noticed it pooling around one in particular and she smiled. The goddess had shown the way.

"There," she said to the bodyguards. "Pull that up."

* * *

Morgan ran down the tunnel as Chetan and Jake followed close behind. She had to duck her head so it didn't touch the low ceiling which meant the men behind would be bent over even further. She could hear the professor panting as he struggled to keep up but they couldn't stop. Whoever was behind them wouldn't be delayed for long.

She shone her torch ahead to illuminate the simple structure that held the earth up above their heads. Wooden pillars shored up the sides of the tunnel. It smelled of mold and some of the wood was rotten and splintered from the river water that had seeped in over time. Morgan splashed through muddy puddles as she ran, and with every step she hoped that the tunnel would end up somewhere useful.

A minute later her torch flickered across an entranceway and she emerged into a chamber. The tunnel from the Taj Mahal had clearly been added more recently, but this place looked to be much older than the mausoleum above. Stone slabs had been used to create a circular space, the low ceiling held up by a large pillar. The atmosphere was damp and warm, a primal place where life could grow, and yet the stones were stark and deep grey, like the skies before monsoon rain. On one side of the chamber there was a lingam – a short pillar of stone representing the god Shiva in the phallic principle, the creative energy of God. On the far side, there was another tunnel leading away towards the river.

Chetan and Jake emerged from the tunnel behind her.

"Oh my goodness," Chetan sighed. "It really does exist."

"This place looks pretty old," Jake said as he walked around the main pillar, his eyes flicking over the empty space. "But we really need to find that sculpture piece. It must have been put here much later if indeed it was placed here by Vishal Kapoor during the UNESCO renovations."

Morgan bent down to the lingam and placed both hands upon it. The stone was cool but not as cold as she had expected, as if a latent warmth flowed through it from the earth. It was smooth and she felt an urge to rest her cheek against it, to stop for a moment in this calm place and just breathe.

She smiled at the thought, as she realized why this more austere representation of the deity made her feel more at home. The synagogues she had been brought up with in Israel had no graven images and this place reminded her of that simplicity of faith. She felt more at home here than in Catholic churches with their tortured saints, or in the more elaborate Hindu shrines with their colorful incarnations of the various gods. In contrast, this stone was elemental.

She ran her hands down the sides of the lingam to the base and then looked behind it. There was an oilskin package tucked flush against the wall.

"There's something here." She leaned in and pulled it out. The package was waxy and crinkled, but there was something hard inside.

She squatted on the floor and Jake aimed his torch at the package as Morgan gingerly pulled the edges apart.

"Careful," he said. "We know there's something strange about these pieces, so don't touch it."

Morgan used the side of her own torch to push the edges of the package fully open. She caught a glimpse of bronze in the torchlight before the sculpture piece was fully revealed.

It was the god himself, frozen in his cosmic dance. The detail was exquisite, each finger perfectly formed, each snake undulating around him, a calm smile on his face, even as he looked into the end of the world.

"This is what you came for?" Chetan asked. "I see it is Lord Shiva, but what–"

His words were cut off as a thump echoed down the tunnel.

Whoever was following them had found the entrance.

Morgan quickly wrapped the sculpture piece again and put it inside her pack.

"We'll have to take a chance that the tunnel will get us out of here." Jake pointed his torch into the blackness ahead.

Morgan again took the lead and ran into the tunnel. It angled upwards and as they drew closer to the river, the puddles turned into a more constant water flow and soon the water lapped around her ankles.

Suddenly she could see light ahead and she waded towards it, dragging her feet out of the mud, squelching with every step.

"Come on," she called back to Chetan and Jake behind her. "We're almost there."

They scrambled from the tunnel and emerged onto the bank of the Yamuna River at the northeast corner of the Taj Mahal compound. Dawn had broken and the early sun sparkled on the river. On the opposite bank, women were already out washing and people performed *puja* and yoga stretches on the riverbank, the daily rituals of the morning.

"We can go east from here into the wetlands national park," Jake said, as he pointed towards the edge of a green oasis. "It's a protected bird sanctuary and wild enough that there will be ample cover. It will be hard to follow us and we can hide in there while we arrange transport out of here."

Chetan bent over and wheezed, his breath ragged as he tried to recover.

"I cannot … go any further … I'll make my own way from here."

Morgan grabbed his arm. "No, you have to come with us. You could be in danger."

The professor shook her off and stood tall.

"I have friends here in the complex. I'll head back up to the main mausoleum and into the administration area to clean up. I'll be fine. You go ahead. Quickly now."

Jake looked back down the tunnel. "We don't have time to argue," he said. "We have to go."

"Please, Chetan," Morgan tried one last time. "We can protect you."

The professor spun on his heel and pulled a *bidi* cigarette from his pocket with a shaking hand as he stalked away. Morgan stared after him for a moment. Short of dragging him off, they couldn't stop him. But they couldn't stay any longer either.

Morgan and Jake ran together along the muddy bank and ducked into the wetlands foliage as soon as they could.

As they entered the green perimeter, Morgan turned and looked back. She could just make out Chetan's slight figure climbing the riverbank back up towards the mausoleum. She didn't want to leave him behind, but they had to get the sculpture piece away from here.

She turned and jogged after Jake until they lost sight of the river, cloaked by the thick protection of the national park.

* * *

Asha hurried through the tunnel flanked by her bodyguards, one ahead shining his torch to light the way and the other behind. She would have to call her contact in the Taj administration to clear up the mess in the tomb once they were back up top. She chuckled a little to think of the surprise they would have. But whatever she found down here, if indeed there was an earlier Hindu shrine, it would all be covered up and declared a conspiracy theory anyway. She wasn't worried about any bad press. But she was worried about who had found this place first. There were footprints in the mud and the air was disturbed. Had they found what she herself sought?

"Here, madam," the bodyguard in front said as they emerged into a round chamber buttressed by stone walls. A Shiva lingam was the only feature in the ancient space and Asha knew that the Aghori would appreciate its austerity.

She noticed a patch on the floor where the earth had been recently disturbed. Something had been found here, but somehow she knew it was gone with those who had been here just moments before.

"You." She pointed at one of the bodyguards. "Run up that tunnel as fast as you can. Detain anyone you find and I will follow."

The bodyguard ran ahead, disappearing into the dark. Asha followed behind, relishing the exercise. It was good to be hunting, and she was so close to finding another piece.

She could feel it.

Minutes later, Asha emerged onto the riverbank, her feet muddy and her jeans wet with river water. The bodyguard was out of sight, but she could hear his voice threatening someone nearby and the answering cries of his victim.

"Please, don't hurt me. I don't know anything. I was just out walking before my shift."

Asha clambered up the riverbank back onto the grounds of the Taj Mahal complex. Her bodyguard held a tall thin man by the scruff of his shirt, fist pulled back as he threatened a blow.

"If you were just walking the grounds, why are your trousers wet with river water?" Asha said as she walked closer. Her eyes scanned over the man. "And why do you have earth on your shirt?"

The man's eyes widened in fear. He had been in the tunnel. She knew it.

"I … I was just–"

Asha nodded at the bodyguard. His fist pounded the side of the man's face and knocked him to the ground, then he kicked the man hard in the stomach with heavy boots.

The man moaned and curled on the ground. Asha walked towards him and pulled the kukri from her belt. Its blade was still stained with the blood of sacrifice.

"Look at me," she whispered. The man looked up to see the bloody blade. "You *will* tell me what you're doing here." Her voice was soft.

He bent his head and his shoulders slumped.

"I will tell you everything, madam."

CHAPTER 15

Morgan and Jake tramped through the wetlands and into the forest, sticking close to the cover of the tamarind and cypress trees. Birds trilled at their approach and the air was cool out of the sun. As they walked, Jake held up his phone to try and get a signal, but the reception was patchy.

"If we can get a pickup," he said, "we'll get the sculpture piece to the ARKANE headquarters in Delhi. I know someone there who will help us on the quiet."

"Maybe we can find out who has been following us," Morgan said, her mind still on Chetan.

"Here we go." Jake stopped and dialed, providing details of where they were. The call finished and he turned to Morgan. "They're sending a local driver to take us back to Delhi. We just need to get to the main road further east."

They walked in companionable silence through the lush green national park, one of the few places in Agra protected from the development that had turned the rest of the city into an urban sprawl. The sculpture piece weighed heavy in Morgan's pack. Now they had one of the pieces, there was no way the whole thing could be put together again. But she wondered at Marietti's involvement and why he had protected its secret for so long. What was it capable of?

They soon reached the road to find an air-conditioned taxi waiting for them. They climbed in and the driver handed them bottles of water, frowning only slightly at their disheveled appearance.

"Welcome," he said with a smile. "It will only be a few hours to Delhi on the express highway. Please relax and enjoy your trip."

It was nearing lunchtime as they hit the outskirts of Delhi and the traffic was pretty much as expected for the gigantic Indian city. The sound of horns and Bollywood music permeated the cab even through the windows. The highway soon narrowed into smaller roads as they wound their way towards the central area.

"I am to drop you at the Jantar Mantar," the driver said. "Is this correct?"

Morgan looked at Jake, a question in her eyes. She had never been here before and she was still relatively new as an ARKANE agent, whereas Jake had been on global missions for years. He hadn't spoken of any past experiences in India, but then, they still knew so little about each other.

"Yes," he said. "By the main entrance will be fine."

They emerged into the heat of the midday sun in front of the Jantar Mantar, a huge complex of architectural astronomy instruments completed in 1724 by one of the Maharajas. The usual rush of merchants and beggars crowded about them as Morgan and Jake walked towards the entrance.

A man in a white lungi sat cross-legged on the ground playing a wooden pipe. A woven basket lay in front of him and a small cobra peeked its head out, undulating to the music.

"A real snake charmer," Morgan said as they passed. "I thought perhaps they were an urban myth."

"No fangs," Jake smiled. "All the tourists love a good snake charming. Come on, the ARKANE entrance is inside, away from the hordes."

They walked past the giant instruments, the terracotta shapes incongruous against the backdrop of towering office blocks that had sprung up in the wake of India's phenomenal economic growth.

"We're only a short distance from Connaught Place," Jake said. "The former location of the headquarters of the British Raj. The ARKANE office here was established at the same time as the British Empire. After Independence, ARKANE went underground but even as some of the biggest companies in India developed buildings here, we still retained a foothold. This country has more than enough mystery to keep the local agents busy."

He led Morgan to the very end of the complex, where a shabby breeze-block building sat, ignored by those who only had eyes for the ancient monument. It looked like a disused electrical plant or an abandoned guards' room.

Jake pushed open the door to reveal a storeroom with discarded garden equipment and piles of old boxes. Morgan stepped inside and as she closed the door behind her, the room shifted and changed. Lasers flashed from the walls and scanned their bodies. After a moment there was an audible clunking noise.

"This way." Jake opened a cupboard to reveal a lift inside.

They descended quickly and Morgan felt her ears pop. As in Oxford and London, the ARKANE offices were deep below the earth. It occurred to her that she could really do with some sunlight after way too long underground today.

She pushed that thought aside and focused instead on Trafalgar Square and how that had been breached. Were they putting this place in danger by bringing the sculpture piece inside?

At the bottom, they emerged into a plain room. A door opened in front of them and a stunning woman stepped out. Her long dark hair cascaded to a slim waist, and her tailored burgundy trouser suit did nothing to hide her curvaceous figure. Perfect eyebrows arched over dark intelligent eyes that fixed on Jake.

"It's been a long time," she said, walking over. Jake embraced her and the woman's hand lingered on the nape of his neck. The familiar touch made Morgan suspect that there was something more than professional between them.

The woman stepped back. "I'm glad you're here at last, even under these difficult circumstances." She turned to Morgan and held out a slim hand, her manicured nails dark with indigo polish. "I'm Shilpa Aggarwal, Director of ARKANE here in India."

"Dr Morgan Sierra." Morgan shook Shilpa's hand and met the woman's cool gaze, suddenly aware of the muddy clothing they wore and the smell of the river wafting off them. "I'm Jake's partner."

Shilpa turned back to Jake. "There are rumors that you're working on something unsanctioned. People higher up are asking questions."

"We need your help," he said. "And we have to keep it quiet."

Shilpa nodded slowly. "What can I do?"

Morgan pulled the wrapped package from her bag.

"It's another piece of the Shiva Nataraja sculpture," Jake said. "We presume it's part of the same statue as the piece taken in the Trafalgar Square bombing, but we need it verified. We won't be here long. We don't want a repeat of London, but we could use your help with where the next piece might be." He pointed down at his disheveled clothing. "Plus we could use a shower and some new clothes."

"Of course." Shilpa's eyes flickered over Jake's body and Morgan pushed down a flush of jealousy. What Jake did in the shower was no concern of hers, as long as he hurried up so they could get on with the mission.

Shilpa led them through to the ARKANE labs, the

setup similar to London with self-contained rooms where ancient artifacts were investigated as to their occult properties. Morgan wished they had more time here. There were mysteries in this country she would love to research further.

But there was never enough time.

They walked through into a changing area.

"I'll leave you to freshen up," Shilpa said. "And I'll get someone in the lab to look at the sculpture piece immediately and verify its provenance." She held up a hand. "Don't worry. We'll keep it quiet and won't log anything official."

Morgan handed over the oilskin package and Shilpa walked from the room.

Jake began to strip off his clothes, a cheeky smile playing around his lips. Morgan turned away, not trusting herself to stay so close to him, and headed into the female showers.

She sighed with pleasure as the hot water poured down upon her. It had already been a very long day and it was only lunchtime. She scrubbed the river mud from her skin and it swirled down the drain in grey trails. Her fingers lingered on the scars at her side and she thought of Jake and the scars on his body sustained at the bone church. Was Shilpa touching those scars even now?

Don't be an idiot. She shook her head. *Enough already.*

She got dressed quickly and walked to the communal area to find that lunch had been laid out for them. A number of small dishes filled with perfectly made vegetarian food were arranged next to a pile of roti bread. Morgan's stomach rumbled and she gratefully tucked into a gobi masala, a tangy cauliflower dish that exploded with flavor in her mouth.

Jake emerged a few minutes later, his hair wet from the shower.

"That looks good," he said, sitting down next to her and

tucking in. He smelled spicy and fresh and she could feel his body heat next to her. Morgan quashed the innuendo that rose to her lips and they both ate with relish.

The door opened and Shilpa came in. This time her beautiful face was marred with a frown, her expression grave.

"We've run the sculpture piece through the lab and the radioactive signature is the same as the piece taken from the London vault. It's also a match to a secret cave discovered at Ellora. We suspect the original sculpture was found there. I've been on the phone to Martin in London and it seems that Marietti was in India in the '80s."

"So that's two pieces we know about," Jake said. "But there are still two more. I'd feel more confident if we had another piece. Do you have any ideas as to where to search next?"

Shilpa shook her head. "We're still looking for any other artifacts or places that resonate with that radioactive signature. But it will take time."

Morgan sat silently for a moment. She hesitated to bring a friend into the mission but they were out of ideas.

"There is someone I can ask," she said. "Someone who knew Marietti long ago."

CHAPTER 16

FATHER BEN COSTANZA WALKED through the narrow gate from St Giles and stepped into the heart of Blackfriars, a Dominican Permanent Private Hall of the University of Oxford. Despite the ever-changing matters of faith and internecine squabbles of the Church, not to mention the malleable face of the university, this small quad was one of the constants in Ben's life. Along with his morning constitutional walk around the University Parks, of course, and a neat espresso from Taylors on the corner of Little Clarendon Street. He hummed a few bars from Mozart's Benedictus, a smile on his face as he recalled the early-blooming flowers in the park. It was a blessing to have another day in this beautiful city.

Ben rather liked Mondays. Sunday was always a workday if work related to the church, and his still did after all these years. On Mondays he only had one tutorial session with a Ph.D. student studying the history of the Dominican Order in Britain. Ben was a tutor for the Angelicum, the Baccalaureate in Sacred Theology granted by the Pontifical University of St Thomas in Rome. The session wasn't too taxing and he could soon return to his own private study.

But despite the spring in his step, he was feeling the years more heavily these days, made worse by a spiritual weight caused by the rise in religious fundamentalism both in the East and West. He had seen such things before, of course, and time is ever cyclical. People forget the mistakes of the past so soon, but this time he didn't know if he would live to see the end of the cycle.

As a former archaeologist, he mourned the destruction of the ancient city of Palmyra, recently blown up by Islamic State. But then, the religious had always destroyed what they called paganism. The Christian edict to destroy the great library of Alexandria back in 391 AD was one order he particularly regretted. The classical knowledge destroyed there and later repressed in Europe by vehement Christians could perhaps have prevented the Dark Ages. Even now, humanity continued to repeat those mistakes. Of course, he had the Bodleian, one of the greatest libraries in the world, here at Oxford University but Ben found himself coveting what had lain within those hallowed walls millennia ago.

He walked across the quad and climbed the stairs towards his office, feeling the arthritis in his knees as he made his way up but refusing to let the pain show on his face. He was determined to keep this room where he could see the rooftops of Oxford. He didn't want one of those dark ground-floor offices but he knew some of the younger lot kept their eye on him, like vultures ready to pounce on the dead. But as long as he continued to be useful, he would find a place here.

His phone buzzed and he pulled it out of his pocket. Ben smiled as he accepted the call from Morgan.

"I heard about the bombing in London," he said. "Anything to do with ARKANE?"

"You know I can't comment on that." He could hear the smile in her voice. "But I do have a case to work on and I'm hoping you might be able to help. You'll need to ransack your memory though, and it's about someone you have issues with."

"Marietti."

Ben's shoulders slumped as he felt the veil of time swirl about him. Marietti was a similar age and their history went back years, back to the Vatican, back even to the archaeological digs at Ephesus years before. Ben had told Morgan about the dig where he had met her parents and about his own forbidden love for her mother, who had died from breast cancer years ago now.

But Morgan didn't know everything.

Marietti was bound up in Ben's own emotional history with the Church and at this time in his life, he didn't really want to dig it all up again. But he had promised Morgan's mother, Marianne, that he would always help her daughters, and he saw Marianne's face whenever he looked at her twin girls. As a priest, he would never have his own children, so Morgan and her twin sister, Faye, were the closest he would ever get.

"Of course," he said. "What do you need?"

Ben heard rustling as Morgan shuffled papers.

"We think Marietti found something in India back in the 1980s, a Hindu statue of Shiva Nataraja. It has some kind of relationship to nuclear energy, but we're unsure of the details. The statue was broken into pieces and each hidden. Now someone is trying to put them back together, so we have to find them first. I wondered if you knew or could find out anything about Marietti's Indian trip."

"You can't ask him yourself?" Ben said.

"He was injured in the blast and we don't know when he'll be well enough to speak."

"I'm sorry to hear that. Despite our differences, I still wish him well. But it's strange that the Vatican was even involved in a Hindu dig," Ben said. "I do know why Shiva Nataraja would be associated with nuclear power, though. There's a fable of a weapon, the Brahmastra, mentioned in the Mahabharata, the Sanskrit epic of ancient India. The text influenced Oppenheimer, the American theoretical physicist who helped build the atom bomb. He learned Sanskrit and cited his visit to India as the most influential occasion in his life. The scriptures speak of an ancient battle where this weapon decimated entire armies, destroying crowds of warriors along with war elephants, melting their weapons. Hold on a second, I have the text here somewhere."

Ben placed the phone on the table, switched it to speakerphone, and turned to his extensive shelf of books. The spines were well worn but despite the volume of titles, it was organized chaos of a kind. As an expert in interfaith matters, Ben had copies of many ancient texts sacred to different religions. He quickly located a translation of the Mahabharata, pulled it down and flicked through the pages.

"Here we are. It talks of a weapon charged with all the power of the universe. A perpendicular explosion with billowing clouds rising in expanding circles. An incandescent column of smoke and flame as bright as a thousand suns, and the weapon as a messenger of death which reduced all to ashes. As a result of the explosion, people's hair and nails fell out and birds turned white in the air. Food was infected and soldiers had to immerse themselves in water to wash themselves clean of infection."

"It certainly sounds like an atomic bomb and the resulting radioactive poisoning," Morgan said. "We need to find the pieces and stop the weapon being activated. Can you help?"

In Ben's mind, he saw a mushroom cloud above the spires of Oxford that billowed out over the city destroying all in its path. There were secrets he had buried long ago, but now it seemed time to unearth them again. In his long years, many of those who knew of the past had died, and each time, Ben wondered if he would be the last one standing. With Marietti in critical condition, there were few remaining. Perhaps it was time to unearth this mystery.

"Have you ever been to Goa?" he asked.

CHAPTER 17

THE PLANE BANKED AND the wing tipped and for a brief moment, Morgan stared down into the deep blue of the Arabian Sea. Goa was a coastal state, its long beaches famous for white sand, relaxation and escape from the city grind. Despite India's frenetic growth and economic boom, Goa still managed to hold on to a slower pace of life.

Father Ben shifted in his sleep and Morgan pulled the blanket up around him. They had met him in Delhi and flown on to Goa together. He had slept most of the way and Morgan had been loath to disturb him, despite her curiosity about what he knew. Jake was reading, catching up on the history of western India, but they were still unsure as to exactly why they were heading for Goa.

Martin Klein had sorted the flights quickly and discreetly, keen for them to pursue any new leads while he investigated who inside ARKANE was plotting against Marietti. The repair of HQ continued apace and Morgan imagined the vault and its precious contents disappearing under London again. Of course, the conspiracy message boards were going nuts about what was really under Trafalgar Square based on pictures taken just after the blast, and denials by MI6 and other British government agencies only intensified the speculation. Some of the more sensitive projects had been moved to the labs under the Natural History Museum in Oxford, but no doubt it wouldn't be long until the news cycle shifted attention again.

Father Ben stretched and yawned.

"We're almost there," Morgan said softly.

"What time is it?" He pushed his sleeve back to reveal the vintage Rolex he had worn in all the years she had known him.

"It's 2.15pm local time," Morgan said.

Ben shook his head as he wound the hands forward. "I don't think I'll ever get used to jet lag. I'm sure part of my soul is still back in Oxford and it will take a day or so to get here."

He smiled and Morgan noticed the lines on his face had deepened since she had seen him last. Was she responsible for the added stress in his life? She had certainly brought danger for him in the time she had worked with ARKANE, and she had dragged him into some crazy adventures. He had been almost blown up at Blackfriars, burned to death in the Freemasons Grand Lodge of England and now … well, she didn't even know where this would lead. But since the opening salvo of this mysterious group was to blow up Trafalgar Square, she didn't think it would be a quiet stroll through the backwaters of India.

But Ben knew something about Marietti's early life, and they needed his help.

"It's been many years since I visited Goa," Ben said, as the plane landed and taxied along the runway. His eyes were bright with excitement. "But it has haunted my dreams and I've wanted to return many times."

His words trailed off and Morgan was suddenly glad they could have this time together. Whatever happened, it was worth it for this moment of renewed vigor.

"I guess we're not heading for any of these beaches?" Jake brandished the airline magazine at them. It showed palm trees waving over white sand on the edge of a turquoise ocean.

"This place is more than beaches," Ben said. "It's a

UNESCO World Heritage Site for the Portuguese Catholic monuments. Goa was the capital of the Portuguese Indies from 1565 to 1760, and its convents and churches are protected."

"But what has it got to do with Marietti?" Morgan asked, finally unable to restrain her curiosity any longer.

"You know that he was here on an archaeological dig back in the '80s," Ben said. "But afterwards, he was based here for longer than was strictly necessary. It's unclear what his small team found on the dig – perhaps your mysterious sculpture – but this place was certainly special to him and I've heard that he returned secretly a number of times." Ben smiled, his blue eyes twinkling with mischief. "Elias Marietti is just a man, like any other. Of course, he has been faithful to the Church for many years, but a long time ago, there was someone special in his life. I believe she is still here."

Jake's eyes darkened at this revelation and Morgan wondered what he was thinking. Marietti was like a father to him, but there were clearly so many secrets between them.

After navigating customs, they were soon in a taxi speeding away from the airport towards Velha Goa, the old city. Ben gazed out of the window as they drove through the busy streets, his excitement infectious at the sights.

A group of women walked by in brilliantly-colored saris, saffron and purple, bright pink and yellow, some stitched with gold edging. One woman wore the elaborate clothes of Rajasthan, her skirt embroidered with mirrors. The sunlight flashed in their reflection, each tiny piece of glass catching a different part of street life, as each Hindu incarnation echoed a different part of God.

Harsh exhaust fumes choked the air but underneath, the smell of incense lingered, a sense of ancient faith underlying modern technology. There was a different approach to time in India. Belief in the cycles of creation, destruction and reincarnation meant that waiting a little longer to get anywhere wasn't that important.

Finally, they pulled up in front of the Basilica of Bom Jesus.

Morgan stepped out of the car, grateful to stretch her legs after the long journey. The sun was high, the air tropical, and she could feel a trickle of sweat beading on the small of her back.

She looked up at the facade of the Basilica, the extravagant baroque style incongruous in the heat and verdant green of southern India. It had four towering levels with aspects of red brick and white marble giving the church a distinctly European feel. The first level had a huge door flanked by two smaller entrances, and above that two levels of rectangular and round windows were topped with a heavy sloping roof. A lawn of perfectly clipped green grass surrounded the church and two gardeners watered it while stepping softly in bare feet, heads bent to their work.

"This is where the mortal remains of St Francis Xavier are kept," Ben said. "To some, he is the patron saint of Goa, a man of faith worthy of veneration. To others, his body is a reminder of the dark past of the Portuguese in this area. He requested the Inquisition be brought to India in 1545, and although the records are lost, it's clear that thousands died here, burned alive at auto-da-fé. They forbade the practice of Hinduism and persecuted Sephardic Jews who lived here too." Ben shook his head. "I'm not proud of what the Church did back then, and I'm not surprised that few wish to honor that past. But there are many of faith who love this country and some who try and correct the sins of the past. Nataline is one of them." He pointed to the entrance. "Let's go and find her."

Jake led the way while Morgan helped Ben across the lawn at a slower pace. She could feel how thin he was beneath his cotton shirt and she squeezed his arm gently.

"I'm glad you're here," she said. "We need you. Marietti was so secretive about his past."

"For good reason," Ben said as they entered the Basilica.

The interior was spacious with high ceilings, the wide windows and cream walls lending the light a buttery tone. The main altar was a wall of gold with paintings of angels singing Gloria to God.

Tourists crowded around one of the side altars, a gigantic Florentine mausoleum with ornate carvings of cherubs and stars. The body of St Francis, believed to be incorrupt and still fresh after nearly 500 years, lay inside a casket within the mausoleum.

But they hadn't come all this way to see the dead.

A security guard stood at the side of the shrine. Ben shuffled over and Morgan smiled to see him emphasize the stoop of age. He put out a frail hand to touch the man's sleeve, as if he needed support. The guard looked down with concern.

"Perhaps you could help me, my son," he said. "I'm looking for Sister Nataline. Is she here today?"

The young man nodded.

"She works in the soup kitchen," he said, in heavily accented English. "You'll probably find her out back."

Ben led Morgan and Jake out of the church and onto the lawn again.

"I'm not surprised she's still here," he said. "It's beautiful, a good place to spend one's later years. I can feel my arthritis improving already."

Jake grinned. "So Sister Nataline is a nun?"

Ben nodded. "But back then, when Marietti was first here, she was an assistant on the archaeological dig. She became a nun later, after he left India. Let's walk around to the kitchen."

They found the soup kitchen area easily, marked by the long line of hungry people outside. More emerged from the tiny doorway with bowls of dahl and rice and sat to eat it on the grass.

They waited until the crowd thinned and then entered the kitchen. It bustled with energy and several nuns stood behind the counters washing dishes and serving food to latecomers. One of the women caught Morgan's eye. She wore a light blue habit, her hair covered with a wimple. Her bearing was almost regal, her back straight and she was clearly of mixed race origin by her light caramel skin. Age only seemed to intensify her delicate features and she was still beautiful. She turned as they entered. Her dark eyes narrowed as she looked more closely at Ben.

She put down her dishcloth and walked to greet them.

"You're welcome here," she said with a humble smile, "but you can find places to eat in the tourist area down the road. This is our charitable kitchen for the poor."

"Are you Sister Nataline?" Ben asked. The nun nodded.

Jake pulled out his smart phone, tapped it and then turned it to show her. Her eyes widened and her hand flew to cover her mouth.

"We'd like to talk to you about this man," Jake said. "Do you recognize him?"

Nataline reached out with one hand and took the phone, zooming in with her fingertips to examine the face more carefully. Her eyes darkened as she smiled and Morgan read a secret history there.

"Of course." Nataline's voice was musical, lighter now. "It's been a long time and we're both old now, but I could never forget Elias."

"Is there somewhere we can talk in private?" Morgan asked.

Nataline led them away from the kitchen to a manicured herb garden, sheltered from the sun by a sailcloth tethered by strong rope, a simple yet effective shade.

It smelled of rosemary and thyme, and the soft buzz of insects filled the air.

"We grow these herbs for the kitchen," she said, as they sat down around a small garden table. "I come to think sometimes and it seems appropriate to talk here of the past. How is Elias?"

"I'm so sorry, but there was an explosion and he was badly hurt," Morgan explained. "The attackers took something, a statue of Shiva Nataraja." Jake pulled up the image of the complete sculpture on his phone and showed her.

Nataline paled.

"I didn't ever expect to hear of that again," she whispered. "I thought I would take its secret to my grave. Elias promised that I could walk away, that I would not have to bear the burden, and yet, here you are." She shook her head. "Perhaps we cannot escape the deeds of our past."

"What can you tell us about the statue?" Jake asked.

"Elias found a Nazi map that pointed to a certain cave system where a weapon might be found. I had my doubts." She smiled. "I was young and cynical back then. But in the cave I saw–"

Before she could continue, a scream rang out across the garden.

A volley of shots cracked through the air from beyond the Basilica.

Jake jumped up and both he and Morgan drew their weapons. They spun around, scanning for danger.

"We have to go," Morgan said. "This can't be a coincidence."

The screaming intensified, the sound of a panicked crowd running from gunfire. Morgan knew that they would be outnumbered if they stayed to fight.

They had to run.

"This way," Nataline said, leading the way out of the garden. "We can get round the back of the church and into the streets beyond. We'll lose them there."

They ducked down into an alleyway, Morgan and Jake at the rear to cover their escape.

A bullet pinged near their heads and a rattle of gunfire peppered their location.

"Keep going," Morgan shouted to Nataline and Ben. "We'll be right behind you."

The two hurried on as Morgan and Jake returned fire until the gunman receded.

Morgan spun around to find Nataline and Ben out of sight, the dogleg streets hiding their location. She and Jake ran onwards and rounded a corner into a suddenly quiet alleyway. People had melted into doorways, standing silently. Even the dogs had stopped barking.

"Something's wrong." Morgan's heart pounded. "Where are they?"

She sprinted to the end of the alley to see Nataline and Father Ben being bundled into a sedan car. Men with automatic weapons stood by the vehicle, muzzles pointed at Morgan and Jake.

"Morgan!" Ben's voice was weak, and she started towards him.

Jake pulled her away as the men by the car opened fire, driving them back into the alley.

As they drove off, Morgan pushed Jake away and fell to her knees, her eyes filling with tears as she realized how much she had failed Ben. They had to get after the men.

Jake's phone rang and he answered it quickly.

"We have a situation, Martin."

He fell silent and his face paled as he turned to Morgan.

"They have Marietti too."

CHAPTER 18

THE STREETS BEGAN TO fill again, busy with people continuing with their own daily drama, the little scene quickly forgotten. Morgan and Jake ducked into a side street, away from prying eyes. The heat was now oppressive, the sounds about them threatening. The knife-edge of India had shifted in just a few minutes.

Jake put Martin on speakerphone.

"Marietti was abducted from the hospital twenty minutes ago," he said, his voice crackling a little over the line. Morgan could hear his concern and she felt an echo of it inside herself. "He was unconscious when they took him, but he has a tracker implant. He insisted on having one inserted a few months back. I wondered why at the time, but clearly he's been worried about something like this." A pause, and then Martin's usual no-nonsense voice came back on. "Oh, don't worry, you two don't have one."

"I'm actually thinking it might be a good idea," Jake said, shaking his head. "So are you tracking him right now?"

"Yes, and they're clearly heading towards Heathrow Airport. Of course, I could notify the police before he's taken out of the country–"

"But to find Ben and Nataline, we need to leave him in play," Morgan interrupted. "We have to assume that they'll be held in the same place by the same people who took the sculpture piece."

Jake kneaded his temples with his fists, his muscles

tense with anxiety. "But Marietti is unconscious. The travel might just make his injuries worse. We have to get him back to hospital."

Morgan put her hand on Jake's arm. "You know Marietti. He clearly expected something like this and he kept it quiet, presumably because he didn't want to jeopardize anyone else's safety. From what Ben said about his past with Sister Nataline, he would want us to go after her … and I'm going after Ben, whatever it takes. This is the best lead we have. Please, Jake."

Morgan watched conflict flicker over his features, concern for the man he respected above all others jostling with the desire to follow the mission to the end.

Finally, he nodded. "So be it. Martin, let them leave but keep tabs on that plane and as soon as it's clear where they're heading, get us on a flight. We'll head back to the airport and await your call."

Back at Goa Airport, they found a corner to wait. Morgan curled up on a hard plastic chair and pulled her headscarf around her eyes to block out the light. She could sleep anywhere and while they could do nothing but worry, it seemed better to rest and be ready for the next step. The last thing she saw before she pulled the scarf down was Jake, his jawline taut with tension, his fists clenched on the chair arms, his body braced for action. He had come back from New York a physically stronger man, but he still had his demons. She slipped into sleep.

"Morgan, wake up."

She pulled the scarf from around her eyes, blinking at the harsh light of the airport.

"The plane has landed in Kolkata." Jake held his phone out and she could just make out the sound of tapping.

"There's a plane in the next thirty minutes," Martin's

tinny voice said. "The flight will take just a couple of hours. You'll be there by nightfall. By then, I should know exactly where they've taken Marietti."

And Ben, Morgan thought, conjuring his familiar face. As Jake loved Marietti in his way, so she realized that she loved Ben. After her father had died, murdered in Israel as one of the Remnant, Ben had played the part of mentor and guide.

She had to find him.

"We're on our way," said Jake.

* * *

Each minute seemed like an hour as they traveled east towards Kolkata, formerly known as Calcutta. Jake gazed out the window, lost in thought. He suddenly realized that his fists were tightly clenched and he deliberately relaxed them, exhaling as he tried to release the tension in his body.

He was angry with Marietti for working alone and not telling anyone about his concerns for the sculpture piece. The man was not an island anymore, not when there were ARKANE agents in the field who depended upon him. And yet, Jake knew that his anger was more personal. His own father had been massacred along with the rest of his family in South Africa, and in the last twenty years the greatest impact on his life had been first the military and then ARKANE ... and Marietti.

Jake thought back to that night in South Sudan when they had stood on the veranda of one of the local houses listening to the sounds of the African night. The croak of cicadas, the patter of gentle rain and the smell of frangipani trees were suddenly broken by shouts of surprise and then screams of pain as the militia took more lives in an endless civil war. That night he and Marietti had witnessed harsh brutality and yet they were not allowed to intervene. Nowadays, Jake hated politics and it was a relief to work with ARKANE, spanning the borders of country and religion.

Marietti had spoken that night of a greater evil that lurked on the edge of civilization, how they could not hope to defeat man's everyday violence, but that Jake could choose to join the greater fight. This supernatural battle wasn't about one army or one country, it was about light versus darkness.

That night, the bush around them had reeked of blood and death, the stink of hatred and violence. They couldn't stop that evil but since then, Jake had worked with ARKANE to prevent nights like it. Sometimes they failed, but each win was another chink of light. After some missions, he dared hope that someday ARKANE would triumph and banish that which crept in the shadows for the last time. But now this blow at the heart of the organization. Why hadn't Marietti shared his concerns?

"You OK?" Morgan said. She put her hand on his and squeezed gently.

Jake turned to look into her blue eyes, the violet slash in her right eye brighter as the light from the window rested on her face. In that moment, he wanted to take her in his arms and lose himself in her embrace. What was the point of all this striving if in the end, the darkness triumphed?

Perhaps together they could forget the fight and move on.

No, Jake thought. Morgan was just as addicted to this life as he was and they fought for something greater than themselves.

But as he looked at her, a dark sliver of doubt crept into his heart. He wanted to tell her to leave, to forget ARKANE, because one day he might be just as worried about her as he was about Marietti.

There were few people he really loved left in the world. He couldn't lose her too.

"I could really use a beer," he said and reached up to press the call button. The hostess brought them two cold Kingfishers and Jake took a long swig, banishing his dark thoughts.

"I know you're worried about Ben," he said after a moment. "But they're really after Marietti and what he knows of the sculpture piece."

Morgan sighed. "That's what worries me. Ben doesn't know enough, so why would they even keep him alive? I shouldn't have involved him in this, but he was so eager to help."

"He loves you," Jake said softly. "He'd help you with anything, you know that."

"True, but I think he's forgotten how old he really is." Morgan smiled. "He likes to pretend he's an agent like us."

Jake laughed. "I hope I'm as sprightly as he is when I'm his age." He pulled out his phone and tapped it to bring up the information that Martin had sent. "We might as well check out Kolkata before we land."

He scrolled through the images, a juxtaposition of the extravagant Victoria Memorial, a hangover from the British Raj, and the slums of grey, high-density dwellings where millions eked out a living within the pulse of the city.

Morgan leaned over to see the images more clearly. "I think people in the West associate Calcutta with Mother Teresa, but it seems quite a different place these days as a hub of technology and culture."

Jake pulled up pictures of India's oldest port, situated on the banks of the Hooghly River.

"The capital of West Bengal, the third biggest city in India behind Mumbai and Delhi. How the hell are we going to find Marietti here?"

As the announcement came over the tannoy that the

plane was descending, Jake's phone vibrated and he pulled it out to find a text from Martin. "The tracker has stopped moving."

He clicked the link and a map opened up, zooming in to the detail of the city.

"That's Kalighat." he said. "A temple to the goddess Kali."

"She's an aspect of the goddess Durga," Morgan whispered. "A black goddess, representing the forces of time and destruction. She's usually portrayed with a garland of human heads and she holds a freshly decapitated one. Her hands are bloody from sacrifice and her tongue is red with the blood of the demon Raktabija whose blood she spilled and drank."

"Oh, great," Jake said, and took a final swig of his beer. "This should be fun."

They landed as night fell and jumped in a taxi from the airport. Marietti's tracker had gone dark soon after it had stopped moving, so they could only hope he was still being held at the Kali temple.

"I'm sure he's been taken underground or something. There's nothing to worry about." Morgan's voice was confident, but Jake could hear her concern. He reached for her hand and she let it rest in his.

"Definitely," he replied. "That's the only explanation."

They drove through the city and arrived at the Kalighat temple on the bank of the Tolly canal, which ran down from the Hooghly River further north.

"Some say that the name Calcutta stems from the word Kalighat," Morgan said, as they looked up at the imposing structure. "The river once ran past here but over time it moved north."

The temple was attractive from the outside, with cream domes and archways highlighted in terracotta paint. It was busy with pilgrims come to pay respect to the goddess. Many Indians treated the goddess Kali as a mother figure, bringing her the problems of domestic life and asking for prosperity. A woman bustled past, a wreath of marigolds in her hand, and Morgan and Jake followed her inside the temple through a dark corridor towards an open courtyard.

The sound of bleating made them stop and turn. A goat stood tethered in front of a sacrificial altar, rust red with faded bloodstains. A priest lifted his scimitar and with one quick stroke, he sliced the head from the goat. Fresh blood spurted out onto the altar as the lifeless corpse slumped to the ground, still twitching. Jake understood that animal sacrifice was still common across the world, and if he was honest, this manner of death was more humane than many Western abattoirs. But it still made him shiver a little as worshippers dipped cloth into the blood as a blessing.

They walked on towards the idol, a portrayal of the goddess at the heart of the temple. They moved with the crowd of pilgrims, the smell of bodies and incense and smoke creating a heady atmosphere, until they finally emerged in front of Kali herself. The sound of whispered prayers filled the chamber as pilgrims paraded past the statue of the goddess. It was unusual, with three eyes on black skin and a golden protruding tongue. In two hands she held a golden severed head and a sword while the other two hands were curled into the *mudra* prayer position.

"There's no way Marietti is here," Jake whispered. "Look at this crowd. It's just another temple full of the faithful."

"But the tracker went dead here," Morgan said as they exited the chamber. "So where else could they have gone?"

CHAPTER 19

Marietti heard chanting as he regained consciousness, a repetition of a mantra that vibrated through him. The smell of incense lay heavy in the air and underneath it, the metallic tang of blood. He was bound upright against a pillar of some kind, ropes holding him tight.

He opened his eyes.

He was in an ancient temple with a low ceiling and walls painted with aspects of the divine. Before him, next to a bloodstained altar, was a huge statue of Kali, the black goddess of time and change, creation and destruction. At the feet of the goddess, a dreadlocked sadhu sat cross-legged, his body covered in ash, his dark eyes dilated as he sipped from a human skull. His eyes were fixed at some point beyond the physical realm. Rows of devotees knelt facing their goddess and their bodies swayed as they chanted a hymn of death and blood.

A man was bound to the pillar on his right. His old face was turned away, but Marietti recognized Father Ben Costanza. What was he doing there?

"Elias." A soft voice spoke to his left. A voice he hadn't heard for many years.

Marietti turned his head.

Nataline was bound to the pillar next to him, her face still beautiful, her eyes bright even though they looked hollow in the flickering candlelight.

A sudden realization stabbed through him. The sculpture. The bomb. It was all his fault.

"I'm so sorry," he whispered, his voice cracking with emotion. "I didn't mean–"

"Young love, it's so sweet." A woman stepped out of the shadows behind them. She untied Nataline, releasing the nun from the bonds. "There, go to him."

Nataline rushed to Marietti, her soft lips on his after so long. He closed his eyes and the years fell away. They were back on the beach in Goa, laughing together in the blue waters of the Arabian Sea – before he had chosen another path. Nataline's fingers found his and she began to work on the knots that held him.

The woman pulled her away. "That's enough."

Two bodyguards stepped forward from the shadows and forced Nataline to her knees in front of the altar, their heavy hands on her shoulders. Marietti wanted to shout for them to stop, to take him instead, but he held his tongue. He needed more time to figure out what was going on.

The woman came to stand close to Marietti and looked up into his dark eyes.

"You think you're untouchable, but I was the one who took the sculpture piece from your vault."

"Just one piece," Marietti whispered, a smile playing about his lips. "There is no worth in that and you know it. You don't have all the pieces or I wouldn't be here."

The woman smiled, but he saw the flash of anger in her eyes.

"Do you know of Kali Yuga?" she asked.

Marietti frowned. "The age of vice, or the age of the demon Kali. Supposedly the last of four stages the world goes through as part of the cycle of time."

"When the people are far from the gods and human civilization degenerates," the woman continued. "Then the end will come and Lord Shiva will judge us and the end of time will be upon us."

Marietti raised an eyebrow. "That is not my faith."

"You Christians have a similar apocalyptic vision in the tribulation, a time of great trouble before the end times. So we are not so different. But I believe we can hold this time back by offering a great sacrifice that will make the gods see we are still faithful." She spun around, indicating the devotees chanting behind her. "We are the faithful." She turned back to Marietti. "But I need that sculpture intact. I need the Brahmastra. Tell me where the other pieces are or …"

She nodded towards Nataline, her eyes narrowing.

Marietti stared back at her, his face implacable. But inside, he was screaming. Not Nataline, please God. It was only one life against the possibility of mass slaughter, but it was her life and he had sworn to keep her from trouble. He wanted Nataline to die an old woman in the golden light of Goa after a life of service that made her happy. The thought of her there had kept him at peace for many years, and now she was threatened because of him.

The woman spun to the altar and picked up a kukri, the sharp blade reflecting the light of the candles lit around the temple. A low hiss came from the devotees and their chanting doubled in intensity, their eyes fixed on the blade. Marietti could sense their excitement and bile rose in his throat at what she threatened.

The bodyguards pushed Nataline forward onto the altar, pulling her long hair away from her neck to expose the paler skin there. Skin he had kissed long ago.

"The goddess demands her sacrifice," the woman said. "Now, where are they?"

Marietti hung his head, eyes closed as he prayed for a way out of this, for some sign of what he should do.

"Elias." He looked up into Nataline's eyes as she lay on the altar. He saw love and forgiveness in the depths, and an unshakeable faith that made his own a poor reflection. "Don't let her win."

At her words, the woman turned.

"Hold out her hand."

The bodyguards stretched out Nataline's arm as she struggled against them. The woman raised the kukri and with one swift stroke, she severed Nataline's hand.

It fell to the floor, a pale offering in a growing pool of blood.

One of the devotees cried out as if in ecstasy. Nataline paled, her eyes fixed on the severed limb as her lips moved in prayer. Marietti knew the shock would prevent pain for only a second and she would lose a lot of blood quickly. Desperation rose within him.

The woman went to the sadhu and picked up his skull bowl. She held it to the end of the spurting wrist until it filled with blood. She handed it back to her guru and he drank deep, crimson staining his lips.

Marietti retched, coughing as tears ran down his cheeks.

"The next blow will be her head." The woman's voice was a sick caress, an offering from the dark and Marietti felt like he was on the edge of the abyss. The devil's choice to save a woman he loved and let the rest of the world be damned.

"Even though I walk through the valley of the shadow of death, I fear no evil, for You are with me." Nataline's voice was strong in the temple, loud enough to echo around the walls above the heads of the chanting devotees. Marietti let the words of Psalm 23 wash over him and he was shamed by Nataline's faith.

The woman's face filled with anger and her fingers tightened on the handle of the kukri.

"I will dwell in the house of the Lord forever."

Marietti spoke the final words along with Nataline, their voices joined in prayer.

"So be it," the woman said, and raised the blade above her head, adjusting her position for the final blow.

The bodyguards held Nataline down and one pulled her hair tight so her neck was at the right angle. Marietti wanted to turn away but he had to witness it. He had to see the death he had caused.

The blade flashed down and in one clean stroke, Nataline's head was severed from her body. Blood ran down the altar as a collective gasp rose from the devotees.

Marietti slumped in his bonds, all strength leaving his body as he wept for Nataline, the love he had lost once again, this time forever. Her blood was on his soul, another stain to add to his many sins.

The woman bent to the corpse and dipped her fingers in the pool of blood.

She reached up and forced her bloody fingers into Marietti's mouth. The salt tang made him retch once more.

"Taste it," the woman said. "You could have saved her."

"She gave her life to stop you finding that final piece," Marietti spat. "Nataline believed in God and she is with Him now."

"Then we may as well send another to your God, and my goddess can drink her fill today."

The bodyguards untied Father Ben from the pillar and thrust him forward onto his knees at the altar. He stared down at Nataline's body as her blood soaked into his clothes. He clutched a hand over his mouth and his eyes filled with tears.

"One more chance," the woman said, her eyes fixed on Marietti.

CHAPTER 20

Morgan and Jake moved away from the inner sanctum and stood watching the faithful as they crowded in to see the goddess. What were they missing?

"At some rural places in India, it's reported that human sacrifice is still carried out to honor the goddess Kali," Morgan said. "The severed hands and heads are left in exchange for her blessing. Maybe there are some here who still believe in such extremes?"

"Worth a try," Jake said. "Maybe if Martin can get information on unusual deaths in the city, especially those with missing hands or decapitations, we might be able to narrow down the area to search."

He started to text on his phone, and Morgan continued to scan the crowd. Then a man walked past, looking around furtively. He was thin and he limped, his clothes were ragged and threadbare, and one of his hands was missing.

"Look, Jake. Perhaps he knows something."

Jake nodded and silently they slipped into the crowd after him.

The man stopped at the altar to dip his handkerchief in the blood that still dripped from the goat's body, then he walked to the corner of the compound. He suddenly looked around, away from the crowd, and Jake and Morgan could no longer remain unseen. Jake quickly walked up to the man, his tall physique overshadowing the smaller figure.

"Where are you going?" Jake demanded. "Is there another part of the temple?"

"Please, sir, I don't know of what you speak." The man's English was stumbling but his eyes betrayed a greater knowledge.

Morgan pulled out a wad of rupees, enough to keep the man's family for several months. She hoped it was enough.

"We just want to pay our respects to the goddess," she said. "Will you take us?" The man reached out a shaking hand for the money but Morgan held it back. She handed him a few notes as a promise. "The rest when we're inside."

The man nodded. "Then you must approach with care or the goddess will be displeased. Come, you must prepare."

He dabbed his still-bloody handkerchief on his own forehead and then indicated that they should lean towards him. He pressed the blood against their heads in turn, leaving a scarlet mark.

Morgan could smell the metallic tang of the goat's blood and it sickened her in a way. But another part of her, the ancient side that descended from Jews who worshipped in the temple at Jerusalem, understood the need to sacrifice to a deity.

For what offering was more potent than blood?

The man led them away from the crowded temple and through a labyrinth of corridors, each one angling off the next in a dizzying array of twists and turns. Morgan soon lost her bearings. The walls shifted from the cream and terracotta of the main temple to plain stone as the corridors narrowed and at some point they crossed from the nineteenth-century temple to somewhere far older.

Suddenly they heard voices ahead. The man's steps slowed.

"It is usually quiet here," he said with a frown.

Hope rose inside Morgan at his words.

Jake indicated that the man should go ahead and they walked a few paces behind him, hiding in the shadows of the corridor as he approached a huge ceremonial door. It was decorated with severed heads, each with a different expression of anguish, but all dripped with blood.

The man approached the two guards on the door and they had a brief conversation. Then the man turned away and walked back down the corridor.

"We cannot enter the inner temple today," he said. "There is a special sacrifice for the goddess. I will come back tomorrow."

Morgan handed over the rest of the rupees and the man walked away down the corridor.

As his footsteps faded, she felt the familiar rise of adrenalin in anticipation of a fight. These people had taken Marietti, Ben and Sister Nataline. She and Jake were going through that door. The question was whether these men would stop them.

They both pulled their weapons.

There was no need for words between them and Morgan appreciated that. She trusted Jake, and she could see the excitement in his eyes.

He indicated that he would go left and she could take the one on the right.

They walked out of the tunnel with confident steps.

The guards on the door turned and reached for their weapons.

Morgan and Jake aimed and fired in unison, body shots to bring the men down. The guards fell back against the wall, clutching at their chests. Jake stepped closer and finished them both off.

The goddess had her sacrifice for today.

Together they pushed open the huge double doors. Inside was an empty anteroom, but they could hear chanting through a great arch ahead. The low sound vibrated through Morgan's chest, the repetition of sacred sound a mantra to the goddess.

They continued on, weapons outstretched before them, and walked into the inner sanctum.

A crowd of devotees swayed in prayer, some with hands raised as they chanted. A magnificent statue of Kali towered above them in her Destroyer aspect, her body made of polished black basalt. In her outstretched hands she held a bloody sword and a newly severed head, still dripping crimson drops onto the altar below.

Morgan gasped.

The head was Sister Nataline's.

"No," she whispered and desperation filled her, all caution forgotten in her concern for Ben. She pushed through the crowd. Jake followed close behind until he grabbed her, right on the edge of the altar area, holding her back as they witnessed the tableau before them.

Marietti stood bound to a pillar, his face ragged with sorrow.

The decapitated body of Sister Nataline lay at his feet, one hand cut off as well as her head. A woman stood with a kukri in her hands and behind her sat a dreadlocked sadhu painted with ash.

A bodyguard shoved another bound figure forward.

Father Ben fell to his knees before the altar. He moaned as he saw Sister Nataline and his dusty habit darkened as it soaked in her blood.

"One more chance," the woman said, her eyes fixed on Marietti.

"I'm sorry, Ben," Marietti whispered. "You know I can't. There are too many lives at stake."

The woman raised the kukri above her head.

"No!" Morgan shouted.

She tore out of Jake's grasp and scrambled onto the altar stage. Jake leapt up behind her, gun out. Bodyguards surrounded them, weapons pointed at the intruders.

The woman stopped, her blade hovering above Ben's neck.

"I have the piece you want," Morgan said. She pulled the wrapped sculpture piece from her bag. "Let them go."

"I'd do as she says." Jake stood behind Morgan, his gun pointing straight at the woman's head.

The woman lowered her blade and a slow smile spread across her lips.

"You two beat me to the Taj Mahal. I heard about you from your guide. Of course, he's with the goddess now." She stepped forward. "Do you seriously think that if you shoot me you'll get out of here with your friends alive?"

Jake shrugged. "I'm thinking that you want out of here as well, so I'll take my chances." He kept his gun trained on her as the woman stepped forward to examine what Morgan held.

"Is that the piece from the crypt?"

Morgan nodded. "Yes, and you can have it in exchange for these two men."

"Two men for the final *two* pieces." She raised the kukri over Ben's neck again. "Or the goddess gets her sacrifice."

Father Ben looked up at Morgan, his eyes pleading with her. She saw that he would go to his God in order to save her, but she wasn't ready to give up yet.

"You'll have your two pieces."

Marietti raised his head at her confident tone. His bloody lips were cracked and broken but he managed to speak, his voice hoarse.

"She doesn't know where the final piece is. Only I do."

Morgan's heart thumped as she stood there. Why would Marietti try to stop her? Why did he court death this way? Was the sculpture truly so powerful that he would die before he allowed the piece to be found?

Well, she would not allow it. She would take Ben home and Marietti too.

"I can find it," she said.

The woman narrowed her eyes. "How are you so sure?"

Morgan took a deep breath. She wasn't sure, but something solidified in her mind even as she faced their enemy. The kaleidoscope of what they knew of Marietti's life, the pictures in his photo album and what Jake had said about the destruction in Africa all coalesced into one idea. Marietti had witnessed mass murder before, and if he believed the piece of the sculpture could create such death, then perhaps he would hide it in the place he still had nightmares about.

"He will never tell you where it is," Morgan said. "You can kill us all and he will never tell and you won't complete the sculpture. But he can't hide the footprints of the past. Give me forty-eight hours and I will find the final piece."

The woman lowered the kukri and turned to the seated sadhu. His ash-rimmed eyes looked at Morgan as she stood unflinching before him. She felt him rake her soul and something inside her curled away at his intrusion.

Finally, the sadhu nodded.

"So be it," the woman said. She walked towards Morgan and Jake, her hips swinging in a sinuous manner. She was beautiful, sensual, even covered in blood. "I'll take this as part payment." She reached for the package and Morgan relinquished it into her grasp. "If you can indeed find the last piece within forty-eight hours, then these two will be released. If not …"

She turned and nodded to her bodyguards. They dragged Ben and Marietti away as the men sagged, defeated, in their bonds. Morgan could only hope that they would be able to hang on for just a little longer.

"I want them unharmed," she said.

"Of course." The woman gave a little bow. She turned and spoke to another of the bodyguards. She took his phone, tapped into it for a second and then handed it to

Morgan. "Take this. I'll text the location for you to bring the piece … and I'll send a photo of their heads if you're not on time."

She turned and swept out of the temple.

The sadhu rose to his feet, his eyes empty, like a shadow who lived in the world but was not of it. His footsteps were silent as he walked behind her.

The crowd of devotees melted back into the corridors beyond and within minutes, the temple was empty. The only evidence left was the head of Sister Nataline hanging on the outstretched hand of the goddess Kali, still dripping blood onto the altar.

Morgan fell to her knees, exhaustion suddenly overwhelming her. She felt dizzy and weak. Sister Nataline's head seemed to stare right at her, an accusation of her failure. If only they had arrived earlier. If only …

Jake knelt next to her and pulled her against him. She could hear his heart beating and she rested her head against his chest.

"What were you thinking?" he whispered. "We could have tried to take them."

"You saw how many there were." She looked up at him. "We wouldn't have stood a chance. At least this way we're still alive to fight another day."

"But how will we find the final piece?" Jake's corkscrew scar crinkled at the question, his brown eyes quizzical. "Marietti has never told anyone where it is and it seems that he would die to protect it."

"And let others die for him, Jake. What if it had been you here instead of Sister Nataline?"

He shook his head. "I'm not sure. I thought I knew him …"

"Well, I'm not willing to stand by and let someone I love die." Tears welled and ran down her cheeks. "Marietti may be able to give up, but I won't. Ben didn't ask to be part of this and once again I've dragged him into a mission and put him in danger." She stood and wrapped her arms around herself as the cold night seeped in through the temple walls. "I'm livid with Marietti. How dare he?"

Jake looked up at the severed head of Sister Nataline. "I don't think he knows how to love anymore." He shook his head. "Perhaps he never did. He only sees the bigger picture, the potential for mass slaughter if the sculpture is used as some kind of weapon."

"You and I have faced the darkness before," Morgan said, "and I come from a different faith anyway. The Talmud says that 'whoever saves a life, it is as if he saved an entire world.'" She pointed up at the severed head. "We failed Sister Nataline, but I will not fail Ben."

Jake nodded. "I'm with you. I still want to get Marietti back, even if you're only gonna kill him yourself." He smiled softly. "Right, we have forty-eight hours. Where are we going?"

CHAPTER 21

Kigali, Rwanda, Africa. 11.48am

"It's been a long time since I was here," Jake said, as they emerged from the airport in Kigali. It was just as hot and dusty and busy as Kolkata had been, with taxi drivers shouting for custom and people embracing in tears. He hailed one of the local cabs and they got in. "I had only just started in the military in 1994 and the killing here had already escalated before the world really took notice. We came as peacekeepers to help with the aftermath. I still have nightmares about that time."

"But Marietti was here during the worst of it, wasn't he?" Morgan said, as they drove along the highway out of the airport and headed north. "There was a picture in his photo album in front of a mass grave. He wanted to remember how much it affected him and I think it's why he can't see one death as important anymore. He'll do anything to prevent murder on such a scale again."

"That's why you think he buried the piece here?" Jake said. "But how can you be so sure?"

"I'm not, but I'm staking Ben's life on it. And Marietti's, of course, although I doubt he'll appreciate the effort." Morgan grimaced, imagining the Director's wrath even if they did get him out of the clutches of Kali.

"He's a tough old man," Jake said. "I don't think you or I know how much he has done under the auspices of

ARKANE, or of the horrors he has faced to keep people safe. I know you're angry with him, Morgan, but we'll get through this somehow." He looked out the window. "At least I hope we will."

Morgan pulled out a map marked with five black crosses.

"These are the closest memorials to the city," she said as she showed Jake the proposed route between them. "Marietti was never here very long when he came back to visit, so I'm assuming that the picture we saw is from one of these rather than the others around the country."

They drove through the dirt of the city out to a rural area where rows of green palm trees divided small plots of land. A group of smiling children ran down the road after the car, their white teeth flashing in the sun.

It was a fertile place, rejuvenated in the last ten years as Rwanda invested in crop intensification. Farmers here now made enough to export as well as feed their families. Deep green tea plantations dotted the hills and there were gorillas in the high forests near the border with Congo and Uganda. It was a beautiful country and Morgan wished they could be here under other circumstances. After all, Jake was African and he knew this continent. The knife-edge of glorious life and beauty and intense experience, and the shadows too. India had the same sense of being closer to real life, not separated from it by years of uptight repression as she sometimes felt in England.

They soon pulled up at the first memorial but without even getting out the car, Morgan knew it wasn't the right one. The topography was all wrong. She sighed.

Jake looked at his watch. "We still have time. Let's go on to the next one."

They were hot and tired when they finally arrived at the Murambi Genocide Memorial, a school that had been the site of a massacre during the conflict, and the fourth on

Morgan's list. It was on a hill overlooking fields of green and hills beyond. Chickens scratched in the ground nearby, but the peace and normality hid a troubled past.

"This is it," Morgan said as they got out the car. "It has to be."

A local guide came to greet them, her gentle smile welcoming even as her eyes held great sorrow. She led Morgan and Jake into the compound.

"Tutsis sheltered here to try and escape the violence, but in fact they were herded into such places to make it easier to kill them in larger groups. It's estimated that 45,000 people were murdered here in just a few days. Their bodies were buried in pits and a volleyball court built over the mass grave to hide the evidence."

Her stark words did nothing to hide the horror of what had happened here. The blood of innocents soaked into the earth beneath their feet and Morgan understood, for Israel was the same. Years of conflict, so much blood spilled, and still, no resolution.

The guide led them towards a series of brick huts, her steps heavy. She pushed open the first door.

"Please," she said, nodding inside.

Morgan walked in first and it took a moment for her eyes to adjust to the darkness.

Then she saw them.

Mummified bodies lay on wooden racks, white from the lime they had been exhumed from, the bodies squashed almost flat from the way they had been stacked in death. Some wore ragged clothes, one had a rosary around its neck. One figure had tufts of hair and another lay with its mouth open, frozen in a final scream. Many had limbs missing and cracked skulls, killed with machetes and farm implements. On another rack, skulls piled high, some cracked and broken.

"Most of the dead from the massacre here were given a

dignified burial," the guide said quietly. "But these corpses are displayed openly to stop denial of the genocide."

Morgan nodded, thinking of those who denied the millions of Jewish dead in the Second World War.

"I understand that," she whispered. "The dead are past suffering, but unless we are confronted with the results of such action, how are people to learn from what happened here."

The guide walked to the door.

"Come to the next room. It has the younger children aged three to six years old."

Jake had been quiet but now he visibly paled. Morgan remembered how he had reacted in the crypt of Palermo at the sight of the mummified children. She wanted to reach for his hand to let him know she understood, but he crossed his arms, tucking his hands underneath his armpits, as if he were chilled to the bone.

"I'm going to wait outside," he said, his voice cracking a little. "Call if you need me."

He walked outside and Morgan let him go.

But she needed to see, and bear witness to the atrocity.

In the children's room there were many more bodies, tiny figures curled in death. A wreath of fresh flowers had been left amongst them, the heavy scent of lilies hanging in the air. Morgan wanted to cry, but these were not her people to mourn. A human life was just the flash of a firefly in the night and she could only try to help keep the light alive.

"Why did it happen?" she asked, wanting the woman to tell her story.

The guide took a deep breath. "On April 6, 1994, a suspicious plane crash killed the president, a Hutu, the majority tribe of Rwanda. The Hutus turned on the Tutsi minority in retribution and it's thought that up to a million people were killed in the months following. Neighbors turned against each other and there was widespread rape and maiming as well as murder. Families were torn apart if there had been intermarriage. It was indeed a dark time and it has taken us many years to recover. Of course, we will not forget." She looked down at the bodies. "Some of my own family were taken." Then she looked up, her eyes blazing. "They called us cockroaches. They saw us as less than human, although days before, we were neighbors."

Her words shocked Morgan because it was the same word that Hitler had used for Jews, the same word used even now against migrants and refugees, the same word used to dehumanize the Other.

"I'm so sorry," she said, putting her hand out to the woman and touching her sleeve. She wondered how the guide could stand seeing this every day, but then if everyone moved on, there would be no one left to remember.

Morgan looked around at the bodies, the number who lay dead here. If the statue was put together again, could the Brahmastra weapon really do as much damage as humans had here? Or was Marietti just haunted by a past he couldn't change? Was it all just an exaggerated myth?

Morgan didn't know, but she was certain that she would not let Ben be one of the dead.

"Are there any foreign tributes here?" she asked the guide, turning away from the skeletal remains. "Anything from overseas aid organizations?"

"There is a memorial area," the guide said. "Come. It's through here."

They walked along the corridor into a simple room. The walls were painted a stark white and a row of benches faced a memorial sculpture. It portrayed a family huddled together in polished black stone, their faces upturned to heaven. Two bunches of colorful flowers rested against the plaque on the wall next to it, and a low table in the corner held an open Visitors Book.

"People of all faiths come here to pray," the guide said. "Many of the murdered were Christian, some were Muslim, some of the tribal faith, so this room is where all can come to remember. It was paid for by an anonymous donor."

Morgan looked around the room. There was nowhere immediately obvious where Marietti might have hidden a piece of the sculpture, but the guide's mention of an anonymous donor gave her hope.

"Do you mind if I sit here for a moment?" she asked.

The guide nodded. "Of course, I'll leave you and wait with your friend outside."

She left the room and Morgan sat down for a moment as she absorbed the feeling of the place.

It was desolate, the walls saturated with the collected grief of half a nation. She had felt this before in the chambers at Auschwitz and in the killing fields of Cambodia, and she understood Marietti's reasons for caring so much.

Martin Klein had sent as much as he could find on Marietti's many trips to Africa over the years. The Director had visited Kigali on the anniversary of the massacre most years, but of course, there were many memorials, many other places where he could have left the sculpture piece.

If it was even in Rwanda at all.

It has to be. Because if it isn't …

She stood, walked over to the table and flipped through the Visitors Book. It was sparse and the entries grew further apart as the years went on. Many of the comments were from foreigners, dark tourists drawn to places like this. Proximity to death made the sweetness and brevity of life more prominent, and perhaps that was why she and Jake would struggle to ever leave ARKANE.

The Visitors Book was no use so she walked over to the

plaque next to the memorial. It was a carved piece of stone etched with the dates of the massacre and the number of lives lost in this area.

But then she noticed something.

The stone seemed to float away from the wall. Morgan pressed her cheek against the plaster to try and see behind it.

Her heart beat faster. She didn't want to do anything to desecrate this memorial place, but she had to know if there was something here.

She ran her fingers around the edge and then pulled the plaque towards her slightly to test its movement. It was more slender than she had expected and she was able to lift it up easily. It came away in her hands and she placed it carefully on the floor.

Behind it was a safe with a combination lock.

Morgan's heart fell. They didn't have much time.

She called Martin and he answered on the first ring.

"Morgan, what's going on? Have you found something?"

She switched on the video function on her phone and aimed it at the safe.

"We're at one of the genocide memorial sites and I found this safe but it's a combination lock. I don't even know if Marietti left it here but I need to get inside."

"Zoom the camera closer," Martin said.

Morgan walked forward until the lock filled the entire screen.

"That model is commonly used in Italy and I know Marietti has a version for his personal office safe. There is a chance that he left it here. Let's have a look at possible number combinations." The sound of tapping came from the phone as Martin probed the ARKANE database. "I can look at Marietti's passwords to see if any of those might give us a clue."

Morgan waited in the silence of the room.

"OK," Martin said, a moment later. "Here's something. Try 160867. That's the date Marietti joined the Vatican."

Morgan typed the numbers in.

There was a second of silence then a loud beep.

"That's no good," she said. "And we have to hurry."

Suddenly footsteps echoed down the hallway and the door creaked as it opened.

CHAPTER 22

"Try 521221," Jake said as he walked into the room. His face was calm again, his darkness lifted and Morgan sighed with relief to see him and not the guide or another Rwandan official.

She typed the code into the keypad.

A moment later, the lock clicked and the door popped ajar.

"What does that stand for?" she asked.

"Marietti's favorite Bible quote. Romans, the fifty-second book of the Catholic Bible, chapter 12 verse 21."

Morgan tilted her head to one side as she recalled the words.

"Do not be overcome by evil, but overcome evil with good."

Jake grinned. "Show-off. Bet you didn't know that he has it tattooed on him as well."

Morgan raised an eyebrow. "Seriously?"

Jake nodded. "But if I told you where, I'd have to kill you." He reached for the door of the safe. "Now, let's see what's inside."

He pulled the door fully open to reveal a pile of paper that reached almost to the top. Morgan pulled off the first sheet.

"It's a list of names." She scanned the page. "The names of the dead. It makes sense to have them here behind the Memorial."

She thought of the Holocaust memorials around the world. In the ghetto of Prague, the names of the dead were written on the walls and a voice read them out all hours of the day. In Jerusalem at Yad Vashem, the names were read by candlelight. Here they were kept hidden, but it didn't make them any less real.

Jake leaned forward and lifted the pile of paper out. "There's something behind."

Morgan reached in and pulled out a package wrapped in layers of plastic. It was rectangular, the right size for the missing part of the sculpture base. She tugged open the edge of the plastic to reveal the dull bronze sheen of the final piece.

A huge weight lifted as she realized that Ben would be OK, even though she could see by Jake's face that he considered it a mixed blessing.

"We've got it, Martin," she said.

"Thank goodness," Martin replied over the phone line. "Now you can get Marietti and Father Ben back. Speak soon."

The phone line went dead.

"But what will happen when the statue is put together again?" Jake whispered.

They put the papers back into the safe and closed the door, then rehung the plaque in its original position. It was as if they hadn't even been there, but Morgan knew that she would never forget this place. Her anger at Marietti had dissipated in the face of the past atrocity and if he was worried about this scale of possible death in India, then they still had a fight ahead of them.

Morgan stopped to say goodbye to the guide on the way out and then they walked back to the taxi together, the piece of the sculpture safe in Morgan's backpack.

As they sped back to Kigali, she texted the woman from the Kali temple with a photo of the sculpture piece.

A few minutes later, she received a text in return.

Bring it to Mumbai for the exchange. 12 o'clock tomorrow at the Gateway of India.

Then Morgan texted Martin with an idea. There was a way that they could keep the piece out of Asha's hands and still get Marietti and Ben back. She only hoped it would work.

Mumbai, India. 11.52am

Morgan and Jake stood under the great arch of the Gateway of India, built in the British era to commemorate the visit of King George V and Queen Mary when they visited in 1911. Jake paced up and down, looking at his watch every few seconds but Morgan stood still and leaned against the stone, concentrating on breathing and waiting.

The Gateway perched on the edge of the harbor looking out towards the Arabian Sea. Some would have torn down any symbol of the British Raj but the triumphal arch had symbolic resonance. The final British troops had left through it after India gained independence in 1948 and it was now a symbol of the death of an Empire.

The water was choppy as the wind whipped the waves into peaks. High above, the clouds darkened, heavy with a hint of rain. Tourists thronged the wide courtyard, snapping photos while street vendors hustled with cheap souvenirs. The smell of frying *vada-pav* filled the air and Morgan found her stomach rumbling at the thought of the spicy potato patties served with green chutney. The cry of gulls pierced the air as they wheeled above the harbor diving for scraps, and then a horn blared a deep sonorous note as a ferry docked from the island of Elephanta.

This busy junction had been chosen for its visibility and

it gave Morgan hope that she would see Ben and Marietti again soon. Her backpack was heavy on her shoulders, doubly so because it now contained two bronze sculpture pieces. She had sent Martin the dimensions and photos of the final piece and he had contacted a sculptor in Mumbai who had produced the copy as they had flown back. It really was possible to get anything in India.

The sculptor had delivered it to them this morning, the only difference being that the inscription was not complete. And of course, the radioactive signature would be different. But Morgan carried it next to the original piece with the hope that the fake would pass an initial test, and she was counting on a quick exchange.

She looked at her watch, anxious as the minutes ticked by. They should be here soon.

At exactly twelve o'clock, a limousine pulled up alongside the central archway and two huge bodyguards got out the car. One of the tinted windows wound down with a whirr.

The woman from the temple sat inside, perfectly made up and dressed in an expensive silk sari, her dark hair lacquered. She was the very model of a Mumbai socialite but Morgan knew the reality behind that charming smile.

She beckoned from the window. Morgan walked forward and pulled the fake package, wrapped in brown paper, from her pack.

"Give it to me," the woman said, her bright eyes fixed on the wrapped piece.

"Where are Ben and Marietti?" Morgan demanded.

"Show me the sculpture piece and I'll show you your friends."

Morgan peeled open the edge of the package, enough to reveal half of the bronze base. Her heart beat faster as the woman's eyes narrowed a little.

"It truly is the final piece," the woman whispered. "Oh, you have excelled yourself."

She nodded to the bodyguards and one of them went to the back of the car and opened the trunk. He hauled Ben and Marietti out and they crumpled to the ground, blinking in the daylight. The bodyguard stood over the two men, his hand on his belt to indicate a hidden weapon. Tourists around them ignored the exchange. Just another human drama in a city of millions.

The woman held out her hand. "I keep my word. Give me the package, take your friends and leave India."

Morgan's eyes darted to Ben as he kneeled on the dusty ground. His eyes were pale and unfocused and his hands shook a little. Marietti's broad shoulders slumped and his face was still crusted with blood. They only needed a few minutes to get away.

She handed over the fake package.

The woman barked an order. The bodyguard walked away from the two men, got back in the vehicle and they began to pull out into the traffic.

Morgan and Jake rushed to Ben and Marietti. Morgan threw her arms around Ben and kissed his cheek.

"It's alright, Morgan," he whispered. "I'm OK."

Jake helped Marietti to his feet and the Director stood on shaky legs. But he straightened his back and towered above them, casting a shadow in the midday sun.

He looked down at Morgan, his dark eyes piercing like an Old Testament prophet. He shook his head. "You don't know what you've done."

"Wait," Jake said. "We need to get away from here and then I'll explain–"

His words were cut off by a squeal of brakes.

Doors slamming.

The sound of boots on tarmac.

Morgan spun around to see the bodyguards running from the halted limousine, faces like thunder, hands on their weapons.

There was no time.

She sprinted into the crowd, away from her friends, the backpack with the final piece heavy on her shoulders. If she could just lose them in the busy downtown Mumbai streets …

Angry shouts came from behind her, but no gunshots. They couldn't risk it in such a heavily populated area.

She darted down an alleyway, winding in between shops and insistent vendors, throngs of tourists and colorful merchandise that flashed past as she ran.

Suddenly she was hit from behind, a massive weight bearing her to the ground. The wind was knocked out of her and she gasped for breath.

A fist drove into her side and she retched with pain.

"Stay down," a rough voice whispered. "You're lucky that's not a bullet."

The man pulled the backpack from her and strode off.

People around bent to help Morgan up, chattering in Hindi and pointing after her assailant. But it was too late. She had lost the final piece.

Morgan hung her head as desolation spread through her. Somehow she had believed that they could keep the pieces apart, but now the statue could be put back together. Could it really be used as a weapon?

She limped back to the Gateway.

Jake ran to meet her. "I'm sorry," he said. "I lost you in the crowd. But we'll get it back, I promise."

Together they walked to Ben and Marietti, who sat on a bench near the Gateway as tourists milled around them.

Marietti looked up on their approach. His eyes narrowed as he noticed the backpack was missing. "So they really have it now?"

Morgan nodded.

"Jake, get me away from here." Marietti's voice was cold and Morgan stung with the force of his rejection.

"Wait," Ben said. He reached out and put his hand on Marietti's shirtsleeve, still stained with the blood of Sister Nataline. "There is something that might help. While we were held in the temple, I remembered an ancient story. The Nine Unknown Men swore to protect the most dangerous knowledge of ancient India. It is said that one of their books has the power to stop the greatest weapon, even the Brahmastra."

Hope welled inside Morgan at Ben's words but Marietti laughed, a bark of ridicule. "The books of the Nine Unknown have been hidden for centuries. There's no way we could find even one of them, let alone the right one, in time."

"But it's worth a try," Jake said. "We have nothing left to lose at this point. And…" He held up his phone. "I took a picture of the car. We can trace the number plate and find out who this woman is. Perhaps we can stop her in the old-fashioned way." He looked at Marietti.

The Director's face softened and then he put his hand up to his head as he swayed on his feet. Jake grabbed him around the waist. "But first, we need to get you inside."

The four of them staggered over the road to the Taj Mahal Palace Hotel, opposite the Gateway of India. It was one of the most luxurious hotels in Mumbai, a fitting place to recuperate. They were greeted by attentive staff and shown to their respective suites.

Inside his room, Morgan helped Ben into one of the easy chairs by a wide window that looked out into the harbor. She rang room service and ordered chai.

"I'm not staying here," Ben said. "I want to help you."

"You've already done enough," Morgan said. She knelt by the chair and pulled him into a hug, feeling the frailty of his bones under her fingers. "I can't risk your safety again. Look at what happened to Sister Nataline."

Ben pulled away from her embrace and Morgan could

see the glint of tears in his eyes. "She was calm in the moments before it happened," he said. "Her faith was so strong, not that God would somehow stop the blade from coming down, but that she would see Him soon after. She wasn't scared of death." He paused and stared out the window at the sea beyond. "I only hope that I can meet my end with such peace."

"And I hope that will be a long time," Morgan said. "Which is why I don't want you to stay. So please, go home to Oxford. Jake and I need to finish this ourselves."

Ben looked at her and Morgan felt his eyes search her own. "I'm afraid for you," he said softly. "And not just for you, but for India. These people mean to discharge the Brahmastra and they don't care about individual human lives. They think on a cosmic scale about a sacrifice so big that the gods cannot ignore them." He reached out and stroked her cheek. "I promised your mother that I would look after you and Faye and little Gemma. I fear that leaving you here will break that promise."

"Something changed for me in Rwanda," Morgan said as she stood up. "I understood why Marietti is how he is. He has seen into the heart of mass murder and he can't bear for it to happen again. If I leave with you, the chance of a disaster happening seems much greater. This may be my last ARKANE mission, because I'm not sure that the Director will ever forgive me, but I must stay."

Ben nodded. "Then I'll go home and pray for you, but you had better come back to me, Morgan."

* * *

In the next room, Jake helped Marietti to the bed. The Director sat on the edge of the soft sheet, wincing as he folded his body down. The shadows under his eyes had deepened and his hair had more white in it than Jake had noticed before. Had he aged that much in just a few days?

"I'll ring for the doctor," Jake said. "You should be back in hospital."

Marietti shook his head. "I'm not going back there until this is over." He looked at Jake with sorrow in his eyes. "You should have stopped Morgan from retrieving that last piece. You know what we're up against. There are those, even within ARKANE, who move against me now and try to hasten disaster. This sculpture summons the end ever closer."

"You and I are shadowed men because of what we've seen, but Morgan still has hope." Jake sat down next to Marietti on the bed. "She sees a different world. The years of ARKANE have ground hope from us. We need her, we need a new perspective … We can't beat the darkness in the old ways anymore."

Marietti sighed. "Perhaps you're right. But it's getting worse, Jake. The nights I worked in the lab before the attack, I mapped a global shift in supernatural events. Signs and portents foretold for generations across many cultures are coming together, colliding and building. I fear the end of days, the great battle, may be soon upon us. We have kept so much from being revealed, but soon we will not be able to stop it spilling over."

"But we're not there yet," Jake said.

His phone buzzed with an incoming text.

"It's from Martin. He's traced the limousine." Jake stood up. "You need to rest, but I'm going with Morgan. We'll stay in touch."

CHAPTER 23

Jake rapped on the door of Ben's room and Morgan opened it, her face expectant. Jake smiled. He had missed her even in the few minutes they were apart.

"Martin traced the limousine to a company based here," he said. "Kapoor Industries."

Morgan frowned. "That's the company of Vishal Kapoor, the man who discovered the statue with Marietti in the first place."

"Yes, and there's a daughter. Asha." Jake held out his phone so Morgan could see a picture of her face.

"It's her alright," Morgan said. "Let's go."

They headed out of the hotel and hailed an Ambassador cab. The driver darted through the downtown Mumbai traffic, Bollywood music blaring, and pulled up outside Kapoor Towers soon after.

"Martin called ahead and got us an interview with the brother," Jake said, as they walked towards the glass revolving doors into the skyscraper. "Apparently he's running the place now."

They walked into the lobby and up to reception, where a smartly dressed young woman showed them to a private lift. It zoomed them upwards and at the top they were shown into a penthouse office. Wide glass walls looked out over the dense city in one direction and out to the sea in the other.

"Magnificent, isn't it?" Mahesh Kapoor stood to greet them, walking out from behind a wide mahogany desk. "It reminds me of how insignificant we really are."

He was tall, with the looks of a Bollywood movie star and Morgan noticed how his tailored suit emphasized his muscular stature. There was a photo of his father, Vishal, on the wall, and on the desk, a framed image of a lovely young woman, presumably his wife. There was no evidence of Asha anywhere and Morgan wondered about the relationship between the siblings.

"I hear you have some information about my sister?" Mahesh said, indicating that they should sit in the leather chairs opposite his desk.

"Many years ago," Jake explained, "your father was part of an archaeological dig. They found an ancient statue of Shiva Nataraja inscribed with a sacred mantra that can invoke the Brahmastra."

Mahesh frowned. "That's a mythological weapon, only an allegory."

"No," Morgan said. "We have evidence that it has the potential to inflict mass casualties. The statue was broken apart and your father hid two pieces. The other two were hidden by Elias Marietti, his partner on the dig. Your sister has been seeking the statue and now has all four pieces. We believe she intends to invoke the weapon, but we don't know where or when."

Mahesh paced the room, his forehead creased. His frown deepened.

"Asha has been behaving strangely of late and I dismissed it as grief at our father's death." He turned to them, his arms folded, concern on his face. "But it's more than that. It's the influence of the Aghori, an extremist she follows as a guru. He has no respect for human life, believing all is illusion. He must be the one behind this."

"Either way, we need to find them. Is Asha still here?" Jake asked.

Mahesh shook his head.

"They've gone to the Kumbh Mela at Allahabad," he said.

Jake looked blank at his words.

"The Kumbh Mela is a Hindu mass pilgrimage," Morgan explained. "The largest peaceful gathering of people in one place in the world. Millions bathe at the confluence of the holy rivers Ganga, Yamuna and Sarasvati to wash away their sin. It's said that Lord Vishnu spilled drops of Amrita, the elixir of immortality, at four places while transporting it in a pot, known as a *kumbh*."

"It moves locations between those four sites and last time 120 million people visited the Kumbh," Mahesh continued, his voice soft as he realized the potential horror ahead. "Thirty million of them bathe on the most auspicious day."

The numbers were staggering. Morgan couldn't even imagine that many people in one place. But if Asha wanted a dramatic sacrifice, the Kumbh Mela would be the perfect place for it.

Mahesh bent to his computer and tapped at the keys.

"The best time to bathe is calculated by astrological positions," he said. "It will be the day after tomorrow at dawn. The sadhus, the holy men, will go first and then the mass bathing will begin. It would be carnage if a weapon were set off then. A stampede in a crowd of millions would be just as dangerous as some kind of explosion."

He paused, his frown deepening. Then, he turned the screen so Morgan and Jake could see the *Times of India* article he had found.

"They're reporting a record year at the Kumbh because of a number of miracles in rural areas," he read. "Children with the multiple arms of the goddess Kali and snakes found at sacrificial sites, with the seven heads of the *naga*. Some are claiming these are hoaxes but others are saying that it is a year of blessing and are calling for all Hindus to attend pilgrimage." He shook his head slowly. "I have my suspicions that Asha may be involved in this too. We have to find her in time. I'll put my best security men on it."

"We appreciate your help in finding her," Morgan said. "But we have also heard that there may be a way to counteract the power of the weapon. It's rumored that one of the books of the Nine Unknown may contain a counter-mantra. Do you know of this?"

Mahesh laughed, a hollow sound. "The Nine Unknown Men are equivalent to your Western Illuminati, a secret society founded by the great Emperor Ashoka in 273 BC. He had just won a battle, but the death toll was so great that he found the victory hollow and decided there had to be more to life than conquest. He searched for truths that would stand the test of time, then chose nine men and tasked each with protecting a sacred book, containing knowledge that could change mankind. Some say the books contain the elixir of immortality, the alchemists' recipe for gold, how to travel through time and even tactics of persuasion that could lead a ruler to victory."

"So what became of these books?" Jake asked.

"They are the stuff of legend," Mahesh said. "It's not even certain that they exist, and yet I know my father sought them, as have many before him and many will to come."

"Who were the Nine?" Morgan asked.

"No one knows." Mahesh walked to a bookshelf in the corner of the room and pulled out a journal. He flicked through the pages until he found the one he was looking for. "This was my father's work on the subject. Asha has been reading many of the journals he left in his room, but he gave this one to me a few years back and told me to keep it secret. He said at the time that he could no longer follow the path but that perhaps I might one day."

His fingers ran over the words. "He postulates here

that not all of the Unknown Men were Indian and that influential members of society across the known world were chosen too. The tenth-century Pope Sylvester II was considered one because of his incredible knowledge of mathematics, astronomy and ancient science, way ahead of his time."

Morgan looked at Jake. "The Vatican connection explains how Ben knew about it, but how does that help us now?"

"Can we have your permission to go through that journal?" Jake asked. "We're part of an organization that researches religious and supernatural artifacts. We have a powerful database, so we could cross-reference your father's journal with some of our own information. We may be able to find hints of where the books might be."

"Of course," Mahesh said, "anything you need. While you start on that, I'll get my security staff tracking Asha."

He showed Morgan and Jake to a conference room just down the corridor from his office.

"Please, use this as your own. My resources are yours. I'll send someone to help you tap into our networks and together we'll stop my sister. My father worked his whole life to build this company, and I will not have her drag it down and use what he built for a deadly purpose."

His eyes blazed with anger as he walked out.

Minutes later, a technician came and helped them set up laptops and network access. Jake called Martin on the video phone. The ARKANE librarian sat in his office, coils of cable and old books visible in the background. They could hear the sounds of building work behind him and Martin's blond hair stood up in spikes that were far worse than usual, evidence of his stress.

"I wish you were both back here," he said. "But at least you now have Marietti and Father Ben."

Morgan knew that Martin had a soft spot for Ben after the old monk had helped him when a mission involving the Freemasons had gone horribly wrong. Martin would always be her friend, even if Marietti decided she could no longer work for ARKANE. She hoped that wasn't true, because the thought of going back to academia, to the confines of the university, filled her with dread. Her only hope was that they could stop the weapon in time.

"We need to build a custom algorithm," she said, refocusing on the work. She waved the journal at the screen. "We'll scan these pages so you have them as soon as possible to start cross-referencing. These Nine Unknown Men had sacred books with secret knowledge that could benefit mankind. Some of it was released slowly when needed, but still ahead of its time, so we should find evidence of that somehow."

Martin tapped away on his keyboard. "The ARKANE databases hook into the Vatican Secret Archives and many other sources that we probably shouldn't know about. They'll be something here."

"Tap into the Indian secret archives too," Jake said. "There's no way people haven't looked for these books already."

Martin frowned. "Actually, there's something already coming up. You're going to want to look at this."

CHAPTER 24

MARTIN SHARED HIS SCREEN with them and it filled with the image of a swastika.

"The Nazis searched for these nine books," he said. "There's a rumor that they actually found the book of psychological warfare, and that Hitler's incredible power of persuasion came from its pages."

"Any mention of weapons?" Jake asked. "Psychological warfare is one thing, but we're talking about something more immediately deadly."

"Operation Paperclip," Morgan said suddenly, her face lighting up as she recalled the details. "Of course. It was a program that took the scientists and engineers of the Third Reich and recruited them into the US and the UK in the aftermath of World War II. They officially excluded active members of the Nazi party but we know that much of the research from experiments done under the regime were used by the West. They didn't want to waste such knowledge, even though it came at the cost of so many lives."

"And the Brahmastra is fabled to have the power of a nuclear weapon," Jake said. "So, could one of the books be responsible for the development of a nuclear bomb?"

Martin tapped away again. "Oppenheimer himself researched the Nazis and talked of the Brahmastra so there was definitely a connection, but I think we need to go back even further. Some sources say that King Solomon was one of the Nine and the book of Ecclesiastes was his response to this global search for knowledge and meaning. That would make the myth a lot older than the Indian version."

"Israel is also one of the few countries with a nuclear weapon," Jake said and turned to Morgan with a cheeky grin. "Allegedly."

"Look at this," Martin interrupted. "There is an ancient group of Jews in India." He pulled up an image of a tiny synagogue with blue floor tiles beneath the golden ark of the Torah. "The Cochin Jews are said to have arrived in India with King Solomon's merchants and settled in Kerala as traders. They're also called the Malabar Jews, one of the oldest Jewish groups in India. Their local dialect still has elements of Hebrew and is known as Judeo-Malayalam."

Morgan looked at the clock on the wall.

The minutes ticked on, but they could do nothing until they had a better fix on where Asha was. If there was a chance they could find the book in time, they had to take it.

"We should go down there," she said. "It's only a couple of hours' flight to Cochin."

Jake looked doubtful, but Morgan's face lit with renewed hope.

"Remember how we met the priest on the roof of the Holy Sepulchre back in the search for the Pentecost stones? It was only by meeting him in person that he trusted us enough to tell us of the stone they had protected for generations. Perhaps if we go down to Cochin we'll find someone who can help us locate the book?"

"I can work on the database algorithm while you're doing that," Martin said.

Jake nodded. "It's worth a try."

They called the assistant that Mahesh had assigned to them and the man noted down what they needed.

"We'll have the private jet take you to Kerala within

thirty minutes," he said, and turned away to make the arrangements.

They were soon on a plane heading south, the plush cabin well stocked with local and international delicacies. Morgan browsed the material that Martin had emailed over.

"The Cochin Jews share DNA with populations of some of the most ancient Jews in Ethiopia. There are also the Paradesi Jews, also called White Jews, who settled in Cochin later in the sixteenth century following the persecution in Spain and Portugal. A diaspora indeed." She shook her head. "I don't know why anyone thinks that national borders even matter anymore. We're all just hybrids from generations before."

They landed at Cochin Airport and headed for Fort Kochi, situated on the tip of a spit of land that bordered a narrow channel into the port. The taxi drove around the shoreline past the triangular nets that lined the water's edge, weighted with stones so the fishermen could cantilever them up, filled with pomfret and mackerel. The air smelled of frying fish and masala spices from street vendors who cooked the local catch for passing visitors.

A horn blared and the deep noise vibrated in Morgan's chest as a local ferry docked nearby. The taxi paused as a crowd of people emerged from the ferry and blocked the road. It was warm and humid and sweat pooled at the base of her spine, but she relished the warmth and tropical atmosphere of the place.

They drove on round the peninsula to the old quarter of Fort Kochi, known as Jew Town. It was just a few streets filled with tourist shops and the Paradesi synagogue stood at the end of one road. The street vendors called out from the low doors, offering *mezuzahs*, Hebrew calligraphy and lace, as well as Indian textiles. They were good-natured and relaxed about their pitches, a very different vibe to the intensity of Agra and Mumbai.

If only they had time to stay and look around, Morgan thought as they left their bags in a secure area, a common precaution against anti-Semitic attacks on synagogues all over the world. Jake took one of the paper *kippah*, the circular head covering for men, and placed it on as a sign of respect. They both took off their shoes and walked barefoot, the result of local Hindu influence.

"Two tickets, please," Morgan asked the woman on the door, and she felt the ticket seller's eyes scan over her. They must see a lot of tourists here every day, but Morgan knew she looked Sephardic with her dark hair, even more so as the Indian sun had brought out her skin tone.

They walked through a tiny courtyard into the synagogue itself. The floor was an unusual design of blue hand-painted porcelain tiles from China, the unique patterns drawing the eye towards the Torah ark at the front. There were a couple of information stands but mostly it was plain and simple, as the synagogues Morgan was used to back in Israel. It did feel more like a museum than a place of worship though.

An oriental rug hung on one wall and Jake walked closer to have a look.

"This is a gift from Haile Selassie, the last Ethiopian emperor," he said. "There's definitely a link with the ancient Jews here."

At the back of the room a few pamphlets about the Jews of India sat on top of a heavily protected box. Morgan picked up a leaflet as the last tourists left the room. A few moments later, the ticket seller walked in. She wore jeans and a t-shirt with a mandala on it, her long dark hair held back by a leather strip. She looked like any other young Indian woman in the area.

"That box is said to contain tenth-century copper plates," she said. "They validate the rights given to the earliest Cochin Jews and are inscribed by the ruler in Tamil."

She shrugged. "I've never seen them though. Where are you from?"

"We've come from England," Morgan replied, "but I was brought up in Israel."

"Oh, it must be so different there." The young woman sighed, her eyes bright with interest. "Our community is tiny and the Cochin Jews have no Rabbis so our community is led by elders." She pointed across the room. "There's separate seating for men and women as you can see, but it seems crazy, because I'm the last female Paradesi Jew of childbearing age. There are only six Jews left living in Fort Kochi."

Jake turned at her words and Morgan understood his interest. If there were so few Jewish people left here, it was far more likely that they would discover something useful. And she could see that the woman was lonely, a prisoner of an ancient faith where intermarriage was frowned upon and yet, she had no viable choice of partner in this tiny area. There might just be a way to encourage her to open up.

"What do you think will happen to the Jewish community here in the next generation?" Morgan asked.

The woman smiled but her eyes were sad. "The graveyard is just down the road, a historical site that will be preserved for tourists. I fear that is our future. Soon we will struggle to form a minyan."

Morgan turned to Jake to explain. "A minyan is the number of Jewish adults required to perform religious obligations, usually counted as men over the age of thirteen."

She turned back to the ticket seller. "Then the knowledge of this ancient group will be lost?"

"Indeed." The woman nodded. "A fate that many ancient groups have suffered. But you're from the vibrant homeland, so as ever, the Jews are not finished and never will be. There are other Jewish communities in India too, so we're not the last footprint of the faith in this country."

"And perhaps next year in Jerusalem?" Morgan said. "I believe you'll find a welcome there if you decide to go to Israel."

"Thank you," the woman said. "It's good to meet someone with hope. I'm Rachel, by the way."

She turned to go, but Morgan reached out a hand and touched her arm lightly.

"We're looking for something related to the ancient aspects of this area. A book, rumored to have come from King Solomon himself."

Rachel paled and her jaw tightened. "I'm sorry, but I must go."

CHAPTER 25

"Please wait," Morgan said, rushing after her. "You said yourself that this generation might be the last. What's the harm in sharing now?"

Rachel turned back to them, her eyes darting warily towards the entrance.

"My father left a box," she whispered. "When he died without a son, without any male heirs, he told me to bury it and never to look inside." She looked down and blushed a little. "But I did look and I didn't bury it. There are fragile pages inside from old books."

"Can we see it?" Morgan asked, her heart beating faster with anticipation. "It's hard to explain why, but we think perhaps this book could save many lives and stop a powerful weapon from killing innocents."

Rachel smiled and shook her head.

"These stories of weapons and war, of love and death. This is India. This is what we do." She shrugged. "My own myths are woven with strands of Hinduism and Judaism. Perhaps it's time the box was shared again. I'll take my break and show you. I just live nearby."

They followed Rachel out into the street. The shop owners didn't bother them this time, merely watching as they walked past with one of their own. Rachel turned down a side alley where a few narrow buildings crammed against each other. An old woman burned rubbish at the end, a common sight where rubbish collection was rare.

She poked the embers with a stick and smoke billowed out, the sweet smell of rotten vegetables filling the air.

"Please, come inside." Rachel pushed the door open. "My great aunt will be out at work, so it's just us."

Morgan and Jake walked into a room barely high enough for Jake to stand upright. He seemed to fill the space and backed into a corner while Rachel bustled around them.

She pulled a slim mattress away from the corner of the room to reveal a storage cupboard below. Jake helped her to pull the doors up and she brought out a rectangular wooden box carved with the Star of David and Hebrew script.

"This is what I was told to bury." Rachel handed it to them. "It may contain what you seek. It may not."

Morgan carried it to a low table. She and Jake sat on the floor cross-legged and opened the lid.

A smell of mildew and sawdust rose from the box. There were a stack of loose pages inside, but even without seeing them all, Morgan could see that there was no way this was part of the ancient book they sought. Some of the pages might have been a few hundred years old but it could not be one of the books of the Nine Unknown Men.

She met Jake's eyes across the table and saw her own disappointment reflected there.

Rachel came to stand near them. She folded her arms as her eyes welled with tears.

"My father protected this for his whole life," she whispered. "I don't know what to do with it all now."

Out of respect, Morgan continued to leaf carefully through the pages. There were some texts in Hebrew and others in the local Malayalam language.

"Wait," Jake said. He put his hand out to stop her. "Go back. What's that?"

It was a plain page torn out of a notebook with jagged

and faded edges and a drawing in the middle. A man stood with his arms outstretched as smoke billowed from his fingertips. Beyond him was a field of corpses with roughly sketched limbs sticking up from the ground, and people fell where smoke touched them.

"That sure looks like a weapon," Jake said. "And there's something on the back."

Morgan turned the page over to find several lines of Sanskrit. Copying manuscripts had always been a way to pass down knowledge. Perhaps this was such a copy and there was no telling how old the original might have been.

"Do you mind if we take this?" she asked.

Rachel nodded. "Of course, I think my father would have been glad of your interest."

Jake's phone buzzed. He pulled it out.

"It's Mahesh. There have been sightings of Asha and the Aghori at the Kumbh Mela camp. The private jet will take us straight to Allahabad and we'll meet him there."

They stood to go. Rachel shook their hands, holding Morgan's a little longer.

"Thank you," she said. "Sometimes I forget that there's a bigger world out there, but you've given me hope."

Morgan leaned in and hugged the young woman. "Shalom berakhah ve-tovah," she whispered, a blessing of peace and good things to come.

They drove back to the airport and headed north again.

Allahabad. 7.23pm

Mahesh stood waiting next to a four-wheel drive at the airport with several more vehicles parked behind, surrounded by burly men in black sunglasses.

"Our own entourage," Jake said under his breath as they

walked down the tarmac from the plane. "Not something we usually get on ARKANE missions."

"Let's just hope Asha won't see us all coming," Morgan replied, smiling at Mahesh as he approached.

He shook their hands, his face haggard with worry.

"Did you find anything in Kochi?" he asked.

"Not what we had hoped for, but it might be important." Morgan pulled out the drawing. Mahesh took it and his eyes narrowed with interest. "There's an inscription on the back."

Mahesh turned it over and his lips moved silently as he formed the words.

"You read Sanskrit?" Morgan asked.

"It's been a long time, but yes, a little, even though I don't understand the meaning in this case. The image is disturbing, though. May I keep hold of it?"

"Of course."

"How can a simple mantra be so powerful?" Jake asked, as they got into the lead vehicle.

"The Vedas teach that sound can embody power," Mahesh replied. "Mantras may have no specific meaning, but the sound itself is the reason for speaking them. Take Om, for example. It is the beginning and the end, engraved over entrances to temples and used in private prayer. The sound resonates through the chest and by repeating it you can reach a higher consciousness."

The road became densely crowded as they neared the camp, a mega city created on the banks of the Ganges, a temporary home for pilgrims who stayed only a few days as well as those who camped for the duration of the Kumbh Mela.

Eventually, the crowds became so dense that they halted the car, parking the large vehicles to the side of a couple of smaller, more rugged Jeeps.

"It gets even crazier the further we go in," Mahesh said.

"So we'll leave the bigger cars here on the perimeter with a few guards."

They got into the smaller cars and drove on again. As the crowd thickened, Mahesh ordered one of his men to walk in front with a bullhorn, clearing people out of the way but their driving speed was soon at a crawl again.

It was busy and noisy and smelled of sweating bodies and the smoke of cooking fires. The air seemed to vibrate with the excitement of the mass congregation but Morgan also felt a calm amongst the people, both a respect for life and a distance from it. The collective energy was focused only on God, on community and respect for the holy men who gathered here.

A woman in an orange sari stopped in the middle of the road before them and clutched a cell phone to her ear. She bellowed into it above the noise of the crowd, clearly trying to get directions to her part of the camp. A little boy hid in the folds of her skirt. Morgan smiled at him and he covered his face at the stranger's interest.

"The infrastructure is very well run these days," Mahesh said. "They've used urban planning principles to design camp areas, toilets, drinking water and even extra cell phone towers for coverage." He gestured at the woman on her phone. "If people can find each other easily, there is less need for help from the volunteers or police."

"Police?" Jake looked around. "We haven't seen any so far."

"Oh, they're here," Mahesh said. "But even thousands must be thinly spread in a camp this size. I've sent word to their captain and he's keeping an eye out for Asha. All the different groups of sadhus camp in separate areas so they'll check out that angle. Each group has a *mahant*, a leader, and the police will check with them first."

They passed a group of women who stood together, their hands cupped in prayer. Behind them, others jumped to the beat of a Bollywood song. "There are even female sadhus these days," Mahesh said. "Quite a few are famous now, and they have their own camps too."

"We met Asha's guru briefly," Morgan said, remembering the ash-covered man in the Kali temple.

Mahesh's face darkened and he frowned. "He's an Aghori." He spat the words. "They're ascetics dedicated to Shiva but many Hindus consider them unorthodox. They live in charnel grounds and smear ash from the dead on their skin. They drink from skulls and they use blood in their worship."

"Why would Asha choose such a path?" Morgan asked. "Surely she had everything as the only daughter of Vishal Kapoor. Why choose to follow a man like that?"

Mahesh shook his head. "I think your own scriptures explain this." His voice grew wistful. "The book of Ecclesiastes is an exploration by a young man who has everything but still finds that life is meaningless. He tries all kinds of pleasures, denying himself nothing but ultimately discovers that everything was just chasing after the wind."

"The Buddha too was a prince who gave up everything for a simpler life," Morgan said. "He renounced his riches to witness human suffering and try to transcend it."

Mahesh nodded. "Indeed, and I too have found emptiness at the heart of the rich life of Mumbai's elite. But my father taught me how to help others through our business and use wealth for good. I fear Asha has lost herself to this Aghori because she feels everything but his pure way is pointless." He looked out over the camp, the burning fires below bringing the delicious smells of spice with them. "I have failed my sister but I can still help her – if we can find her in time."

He leaned over suddenly and pressed down the horn in frustration. The blast of noise didn't even impact the crowd in front of them. Mahesh swore in Hindi, thumping his fist down onto the steering wheel.

"I'd like to walk anyway," Morgan said. "I need to stretch my legs after all that flying and it might be quicker that way."

Mahesh nodded and looked at his watch.

"I have calls to make so you should walk ahead. I have a tent booked in the front ranks nearer the water, in the section where there have been sightings of Asha and her guru. It's under the flag of a ship, the Kapoor crest. Just walk straight down the main causeway and you'll find it. If you hit the water, you've gone too far. Just call if you have any problems."

They got out the car and then Morgan leaned back in. "We'll find her in time." She met Mahesh's eyes. "We have to."

CHAPTER 26

Morgan walked with Jake along a causeway that crossed the wide river and joined the stream of pilgrims heading into the main camp area. She looked out over the shallow waters near the edge of the holy Ganges. The river was dotted with people bathing, the brown bodies and dark hair of men as they dipped under, while women in multi-colored saris managed to bathe while still preserving their modesty.

Children splashed each other and screamed with excitement. Naked sadhus painted with ash wallowed in the shallows, tinging the water white. An array of humanity all seeking to wash away sin and be closer to God, and some perhaps, just enjoying the refreshment.

Morgan watched as a man held his hands up in prayer, his eyes fixed on heaven, before he ducked under the water. As he came back up, water streaming off his face, he beamed with a look of pure rapture. She wondered whether he had traveled far and how long he had waited for that moment. It reminded her of baptism, emerging from the water to a new life. She had watched a group of Christians perform the ritual in the River Jordan once, following in the footsteps of Jesus. Water was sacred to all life so perhaps it was no surprise that it was so precious here as well.

"I'm kind of jealous," Jake said as they walked on. "I'd like to believe that washing myself in a holy river would remove all my sin." He sighed. "But the stain is too deep now."

"Then there's a Hindu story you might appreciate," Morgan said. "In the Bhagavad Gita, the great warrior Arjuna finds himself questioning what he's doing in the midst of a battle. He wants to stop and give it up because he can't see a point to the violence. Lord Krishna is with him and tells Arjuna to fight, because it is his duty and his role in life."

Morgan stopped and put her hand on Jake's arm. The sounds of the Mela fell away and in the midst of millions, they were alone. "I know some of what you've done while working for ARKANE," she whispered. "I've killed too, you know that. But we do it to protect the greater good, and if you didn't question what you did sometimes, you'd be a monster."

Jake looked down at her, his dark eyes intense, and for a moment she thought he would bend and kiss her.

And she wanted him to.

A horn blared and they both jumped. Jake pulled Morgan's arm and steered her out of the way as a Jeep piled high with pilgrims rattled past.

"We should head for Mahesh's tent before it gets dark," he said, his voice husky.

Morgan let the moment pass.

They walked down one of the avenues of the vast tent city as dusk fell, just another couple in a sea of people. The tents ranged from elaborate marquees around communal squares to the basic tarpaulin shelters of the poor. Huge banners with the faces of the gods looked down upon them, including Shiva with his trident and cobra, his hand outstretched in blessing. Flags fluttered on high rods above them, marking out the various territories within the camp and used to navigate on the paper maps clutched by new pilgrims.

The stink of cow dung used as fuel for the cook-fires hung in the air along with the smell of human bodies clustered together. There was some kind of irony that they all came to bathe, Morgan thought. Her own cotton shirt clung to her back, sweat dripping down, but she was glad of the full sleeves, long trousers and headscarf she wore. Even with her dark hair, she still stood out amongst the Indian women, although with Jake by her side, no one would bother her.

As they reached the area closest to the river, the campsites shifted from families to sadhus, mainly men, all in different groups. Morgan continued to scan the area as they walked in the hope of catching a glimpse of Asha or her Aghori, but every time she thought she saw one of them, it proved to be a mirage.

A sadhu sat outside one tent, cross-legged in the lotus position, his entire naked body and long bushy beard covered in grey ash. His dreadlocks were tied into a topknot with a marigold wreath wrapped around them and more marigolds draped around his neck and wrapped around his limbs. When so many were naked, the physical body lost its meaning and he sat so still that Morgan wondered if he was asleep.

As they passed, he opened his eyes, dark pools against the ash on his skin. She put her hands together in the prayer position and bent towards him.

"Namaste."

The sadhu nodded back. She found these men alien after coming from Judaism where physical modesty was valued and the holy men spent hours at their books.

Another tent a little further down was alive with discussion, groups of sadhus gesticulating as they conversed of sacred things. The tent was smoky from their *chillum* pipes, the sweet scent of marijuana hanging in the air. Morgan smiled. Perhaps they weren't so different to the

Rabbis who spent years arguing over the finer points of the Torah.

The sky darkened as night fell, but it only became brighter as they reached the camp area closer to the river. Shrines were lit up with lanterns and vehicles passed by, alive with festive electric lights and stereos blaring sacred chants. The yellow glow of the streetlamps all served to create an eerie form of night.

"There." Jake pointed up ahead to where a flag flapped in the breeze. "The Kapoor ship."

They walked to it and pushed open the flap of an ivory-colored marquee, an oasis of calm and cool after the mayhem outside.

Mahesh had commandeered a large tent with separate areas for sleeping and a lounge area for visitors. The festival was a chance to eat together and meet family and friends, as well as worship. A time to celebrate what made life truly worth living, away from the grind of working a city office job or tilling the fields in rural India.

Of course, some could do it in style, Morgan thought, and this tent was a world away from the simple tarpaulin shelters they had seen in the areas further out. Mahesh's assistant brought them cold drinks from the fridge. Sometimes a sweet, fizzy soda was the best thing on earth. Morgan drank deeply.

Mahesh unrolled an aerial map of the camp on the table and pinned the corners down. Morgan and Jake gathered around.

"I got this from one of the news helicopters earlier."

Even at a tiny scale, the camp was huge, stretching for miles in both directions along the banks of the river. It was incredible to imagine the number of individual pilgrims massed in each quadrant, many having come from all over India and from abroad, linked by their desire to commune with God and receive forgiveness for their sin.

Morgan's own belief was complicated. Raised as a Jew by her father in Israel but not Jewish because her mother was Christian, she had always sat on the edge of faith and her work as a psychologist only served to make her question further. But she had seen the supernatural made real in her work with ARKANE, and that kept her seeking. Part of her wanted to believe that the Brahmastra weapon was only a myth, but she had gazed into the Gates of Hell not so long ago and she knew that the darkness was never far away.

"The Aghori sect roam alone through India but there are reports they are congregating around here." Mahesh pointed at one area of the map. "I have men there giving alms to the sadhus and watching for female pilgrims but I believe we should go and search for ourselves." He frowned and rubbed at his forehead in anguish. "If I can only get to my sister …"

Morgan put her hand on his arm. "We still have time."

As they readied themselves to go out into the camp again, the flap of the tent opened and a young boy poked his head in.

"Mr Kapoor," he said. "Delivery, sir." He walked further in with a large cardboard box, sent by courier from Delhi.

Mahesh took it and gave the boy some rupees. He looked at the label and then handed it to Jake.

"It's for you."

Jake grinned as he put the box on the table. "Excellent. This will help a lot." He tore open the package to reveal a quadcopter drone with a camera that could be attached on the mount underneath. The four rotors meant it was easily maneuverable and could be flown by an app on Jake's smart phone. "I got Martin to sort one out via the Delhi office." He focused on fiddling with the controls. "It'll help us search the crowd more easily."

"Even at night?" Morgan asked.

"Oh, don't worry about that," Mahesh said. "This place

is alive by night with fires and torches. If anything, it's busier when it's not so hot, and anything is worth a try at this point."

Jake fitted the battery pack and camera.

"All fully charged and ready to go. You don't even have to actively fly these ones. It can follow the signal from my phone and fly above us as we walk." He grinned, looking every inch the schoolboy with a new toy.

Morgan itched to try it herself, but she knew she wouldn't get a chance while Jake held the controls. It was good to see him smile though, even as the hours counted down to the dawn.

They walked out of the tent into the sprawl of the camp. There were fires every few meters, casting a golden glow over the faces of the pilgrims. Women squatted cooking dinner for their families as the smell of cardamom and curry leaves filled the air. Children ran around, squealing in excitement as they met new friends. It was a social scene, eating and drinking together that was common the world over, in every culture. But as they walked towards the fires of the sadhus, the camp became more alien again.

A group of naked *naga* sadhus sat around a fire, one of them fanning smoke over the rest as they sat in meditation, suffering the heat and fumes in order to transcend physical sensation.

Mahesh led Morgan and Jake onwards towards the Aghori camp, which was nearer the water. Despite the crush of humanity in the area, there were no tents anywhere near their fires. The sect lived as outcasts as they traveled, sleeping in charnel grounds and embracing taboo. Even here they were pushed to the edge of the civilized world. It was eerily quiet and the hum of the camp seemed to fade behind them.

There were no overhead lights and as they walked closer, Morgan realized that most of the Aghori sat around several larger fires, eyes fixed on the flames. They were skeletal thin, sustained by discarded rubbish, eating rotten human flesh and drinking the blood of animal sacrifice from their *kapala* skull bowls.

Mahesh weaved his way around the campfires, gazing at the figures around each of them in turn. Morgan followed him, a few paces behind, as Jake stood back a few meters, checking the drone settings.

A moan rose up from one of the men, turning to a wail as he began to shake and convulse. Mahesh kept walking, scanning for Asha's guru, but Morgan couldn't help but stay and watch for a moment. The other sadhus ignored the man now writhing on the ground as he kicked his heels into the fire. Surely he would burn.

"Lord Shiva comes." The harsh whisper was close. "Kali Ma comes."

Morgan turned quickly to find one of the Aghori right behind her. His breath stank of rotten flesh and his teeth were stained from the *chillum* pipe and the blood of sacrifice. He had bones woven through his long dreadlocks and his body was dusted with ash.

His eyes were glazed, like he was in some kind of trance state or just intoxicated by the alcohol that was part of the Aghori ritual. He held a live chicken in one hand and it squawked as it flapped in his fist. He stepped towards Morgan, backing her towards the fire.

"If we do not offer everything to Kali Ma," he hissed, "we cannot receive her blessing. Only by sacrifice can the world be saved."

Morgan couldn't see Jake or Mahesh anymore. The fires around her filled her vision with flame and she could see it reflected in the Aghori's eyes. The river had faded to black and the sky above lit with blood. Smoke swirled about her, acrid with some kind of herb. She felt dizzy and looked around, suddenly disorientated.

A low chanting began and she saw the other men were now staring at her, some rising to their feet to come closer. Morgan held herself steady even as her heart pounded with fear. There were so many of them.

"Is there a woman here?" she stammered, her voice hoarse from the smoke. "Asha Kapoor. She follows one of your own."

The sadhu leaned towards her and the stink of shit and rotten flesh rose from his skin.

"Only you and the goddess are here tonight," he whispered and bared his teeth. "And she demands sacrifice."

He gripped her arm, his fingers strong and wiry.

Morgan tried to pull away but suddenly, there were naked sadhus all around, pressing their stinking bodies against her as they called to the gods.

There were too many of them and she spun around, pushing them, trying to get away. She was dizzy from the smoke, nausea rising as she tried to scream.

One of the sadhus pushed her and she fell forward onto her knees. The Aghori raised the squawking chicken above her head and held it by the neck.

Then he bent and bit into it, his teeth ripping the flesh away as its blood spurted out.

CHAPTER 27

Morgan felt warmth spatter her face. The copper stink of fresh blood and the sweet intensity of the smoke and the rising chant of the Aghori filled her mind.

In the shadows beyond, she thought she saw a woman with skin the color of a thundercloud and eyes of flame. In her outstretched hand was the bloody head of Sister Nataline, and around her body was a girdle of skulls.

"Kali," Morgan whispered, as the goddess stalked towards her, raising her kukri high above her head.

Then Morgan felt hands on her body and at the edge of unconsciousness, she heard a scream, her own voice in the darkness.

"No!"

Suddenly the Aghori scattered as a huge man loomed from the darkness, fists flying as he shoved the skinny sadhus away. Moments later, Morgan was in Jake's arms and he was half-carrying, half-dragging her away from the campfires.

Back in the light and bustle of the main camp, he lay her on the ground. They were soon surrounded by people clamoring for a look but Morgan didn't care. She focused on Jake's face and tried to banish the horror of what she had seen.

"I'm so sorry." He dabbed at her skin, wiping the chicken's blood off as he held her close with the other arm. "I lost you in the smoke, just for a minute. Then I heard you scream." Jake looked at her, his features creased with concern. "What did you see?"

"I … I thought I saw–"

"What happened?" Mahesh burst through the crowd, then turned and shouted in Hindi for the onlookers to move away. "Oh goodness, Morgan, are you hurt?"

Morgan shook her head. "No, just a little lightheaded. That's some powerful smoke they have there. It's not my blood. The Aghori sadhus had some kind of ritual sacrifice and I stumbled into it."

A look of disgust crossed Mahesh's face. "As Kali drank the blood of the demon Raktabija, so they drink the blood of sacrifice."

"We need to get you back to the tent," Jake said, his arms still wrapped around Morgan, shielding her from the crowd around. She wanted to close her eyes and rest in his warmth, let herself be protected. The attack had been shocking, but had she really seen the dark goddess in the smoke?

Mahesh looked at his watch. "We're almost out of time. They'll start organizing the march down to the river soon. The *naga* sadhus will go first at dawn and then everyone else will mass behind."

Morgan pushed Jake away, stood, and brushed the dirt from her clothes to hide the shaking in her hands. The stink of blood brought bile to her throat. "I'm fine, really. I just need to go and change quickly. I'll meet you back here."

"I'll come with you," Jake said.

"There's no time. I'll be quick."

Mahesh turned and indicated the causeway that crossed part of the river where the main bathing would happen.

"We'll be up there. It's the best vantage point."

Fingers of pink and orange crept into the sky above the camp as Morgan picked her way back through the crowd to Mahesh and Jake after changing. The brief time alone had given her breathing space and she pushed the experience to the back of her mind. Dwelling on it only reinforced the memory, but she still found herself clenching her fists as the dark images resurfaced. She hurried up to the causeway where they had a view over the massed millions, a crush of people stretching way back from the shore.

Dawn was only minutes away now.

And still, they had nothing.

Jake flew the drone above the heads of the crowds, while Mahesh and Morgan scanned the faces on screen for a glimpse of Asha or her Aghori.

"There!" Mahesh said.

Jake circled the drone back for another pass, focusing on the woman he had seen.

"No, damn it, that's not her." Mahesh's voice was desperate now.

A roar came up from the crowd as they parted for the first group of *naga* sadhus, naked but for their ashes and garlands of marigolds. Many carried the trident of Shiva as they marched down to the waters, shouting to the gods as they arrived to bathe at the most auspicious time.

The waters looked dark and forbidding and Morgan found her gaze drawn out to those pilgrims who avoided the crush to bathe from boats in the current. Then she caught a glimpse of white ash against the fading night.

"Out there," she said, pointing at a boat that stood out from the rest of the tourist vessels. It had a metal hull with an outboard engine, and it was elaborately decorated with flowers and paintings of Shiva in his resplendent dance of time. The Aghori stood tall at the prow, his dark skin now white with ash. He held his *kapala* human skull to the sky and his lips moved in a mantra. Next to him sat a woman, her head covered in a saffron-colored scarf.

Jake zoomed the drone towards them, focusing in on the woman's face as she turned to look at what buzzed above.

"Asha," Mahesh whispered, and in his bereft tone, Morgan knew he faced the reality of what his sister had become.

In the frame of the drone's camera, Asha's eyes widened.

"She knows we're here," Mahesh said. "It's only minutes before the alignment. We must get to them." He signaled at his bodyguards and ran towards them. "Get me a boat now!"

"See if you can use the drone to slow them down," Morgan said and then ran after Mahesh, down towards the shore.

* * *

Jake focused on the screen as he tried to shut out the noise of the mass of pilgrims around him. He zoomed the drone down over the Aghori's head, buzzing past Asha and the sadhu. But the holy man ignored the noise, standing unmoved as the seconds ticked past.

At the moment of confluence, when the most auspicious time arrived, the tone of the crowd changed to one of reverence. Some shouted with excitement, others cried out to the gods and still more fell to their knees in silence, crawling towards the water to wash away their sins.

In the tiny camera screen, Jake watched as Asha reached for the Shiva Nataraja sculpture, now fully complete.

They were out of time.

He panned the camera out. Mahesh and Morgan were in a powerboat now, fighting their way through the mass of craft on the water, but they were too far away to do anything.

Asha handed the sculpture to the Aghori and he began to read the ancient mantra on its side, calling the power of the gods down and channeling it through him.

Jake watched his lips move and for a moment, it seemed as if they had worried for nothing.

But then the air crackled and shifted.

A sudden hot wind surged, whipping the river into waves. The clouds above whirled into a vortex in hues of ash and pitch and a veil of gloom obscured the pink of dawn as it began to rain, great thick drops that pelted the crowd.

Pilgrims raised their hands to heaven, calling out their prayers as they turned their faces to the sky in expectation.

Then the screaming started.

CHAPTER 28

The river boiled, its temperature spiking as the Aghori spoke the ancient words. Steam rose as cold rain hit the waves and mist made it harder to see in the semi-darkness. Screams of agony rang through the air and those in deeper waters scrambled for the shore, pushing others under in their haste to get out. But there were so many people crushed into every inch of water that they were trapped as the panic widened.

The faithful crumpled into the waves as their flesh boiled, the animal cries of the dying echoing above the pilgrim throng. In the confusion, those on the shore were pushed towards the boiling waters by those behind. The Aghori held the sculpture to his chest and his chant intensified. Then he cupped his hands as if to push the energy from him and shouted his mantra to the sky as he flung his hands towards the shore.

The air boomed as a wave of boiling water rushed away from him, steam rising into the air in billowing clouds and expanding circles. The wave crashed down onto the pilgrims on the shore, crushing them and roasting them as they died. He chanted on and Asha stood by his side, her face ecstatic at the sacrifice.

A miasma rose up, a fog of rolling death that crept over the waves towards the shore. As it touched the crowd massed by the edge of the water, they began to scream as they tore at their clothes. Their flesh melted at its touch and their bodies burned down to bone before they crumpled on the ground.

Morgan looked around in horror at the carnage on the shore, the bodies that bobbed in the boiling water, but this could only be the beginning.

There were millions more in the camp and the burning mist was heading for them all.

The Aghori took a breath as he prepared for another round and he raised the sculpture again.

"Ram them!" Morgan shouted. "We have to stop him chanting."

Mahesh looked back towards the shore to see the rolling mist intensify, its power growing with every repetition of the mantra.

"It's too late," he whispered, his voice desolate.

"It's never too late," Morgan said. She nudged him aside and took the wheel, angling the boat across the river as she accelerated.

Then she remembered the sketch from Fort Kochi.

"Try the Sanskrit on the back of the drawing," she shouted above the wind.

Mahesh moved to the port side of the boat, fighting to keep his balance as he pulled the slip of paper from his pocket, holding it with both hands as he began to read.

"*Dalla hava mahey mum, yastra hala duvestra hum.*"

His voice was hesitant at first but Morgan felt a shiver at his words. The hairs on the back of her neck stood up and even though she couldn't understand the phrase, she felt the air shift.

Mahesh recited the mantra again, this time with more confidence as the words rolled from his tongue in powerful syllables.

The Aghori faltered and his arms dropped as the counter-mantra touched him. The boiling mist before him softened and sank towards the water.

Asha turned and saw the approaching boat, her brother standing on the prow.

"No!" she screamed.

Morgan rammed into them.

The impact of metal against metal sounded like a gong above the noise of the screaming crowd. Morgan slammed into the deck and slid towards the stern as the boat crumpled at a steep angle but Mahesh scrambled up and over the bow with a roar, leaping onto the other boat as he shouted the Sanskrit phrase in triumph.

The Aghori cowered, covering his ears as Mahesh leapt upon him. They tussled, rolling together, both screaming their ancient words.

Mahesh lunged and they both fell together over the side. The two men sank down into the dark depths of the river, wrestling together even as they writhed in agony in the boiling water, their skin loosening from their flesh as they drowned.

The sound of wailing came from the shore as those still alive mourned their desperate loss. The river swirled with dead corpses and amongst them, Mahesh Kapoor and the Aghori, their bodies twisted together in death.

Asha rushed to the side, reaching down towards the men, her face stricken with loss. For the Aghori. For her brother. For the end of her dreams of sacrifice.

But the men were gone.

Asha turned back to the other boat, her eyes fixed on Morgan. "What have you done?" she screamed. Morgan saw the rage of the goddess in her eyes and realized that Asha still had the sculpture of Shiva Nataraja.

This wasn't over yet.

Morgan reached up, straining to pull herself towards the other boat. But Asha spun and started the engine, revving away so her boat pulled into the current. Her own craft was ruined and Morgan could only watch Asha speed away as the waters calmed. She would soon be out of sight and they would lose her.

Then the drone buzzed overhead.

Hope rose within her, providing renewed energy to continue the chase. Jake could track Asha from above. They could still get the sculpture back.

"Please help me!" Morgan called to the nearest boat. They pulled alongside and helped her in, making sure she didn't touch the steaming water, discolored with human flesh and blood.

The haunted faces of the men in the boat betrayed their shock at what had happened. They spoke to her in their language, and although she couldn't understand the words, she knew what they were saying. The words of grief were universal. She could only nod as they took her back to shore.

As soon as the boat touched bottom, Morgan jumped out and the men headed back out again to help others, or at least bring in more bodies. She ran back along the shore towards the causeway. Jake still stood there, concentrating on the screen, and she could see his hands moving as he directed the drone in pursuit.

She hurried to him, wanting to fall into his arms, needing his support after the horror of the waters below.

"Are you alright?" he said, his voice curt as he concentrated. As ever, there was too much to say and no time to say it.

Morgan looked over his shoulder at the tiny screen on his phone. The drone's camera was still focused on Asha's boat as she headed east.

"Mahesh is gone," she whispered.

"I saw," Jake said. "But he saved millions here today." He zoomed in on Asha's figure. She held the wheel of the powerboat but she slumped against it, her body drooping. "And she is almost finished. Look how broken she is."

"I don't know," Morgan said. "I saw her rage when the Aghori and Mahesh went over the side. She was not just a follower, she's strong. Legend says that the Brahmastra can only be used one time before it needs to recharge, but if we can't catch her, she may try again another time. But at least we're tracking her."

Jake shook his head. "We have a little problem there." He nodded at the screen and Morgan saw the battery indicator was at one bar. "We probably have about twenty minutes left and then the drone will be out of power. I'll stay on her as long as possible but once the drone drops out of the sky, we'll be blind."

Morgan pulled out her own smart phone, navigating to the maps and tracing the river's path.

"The Ganges weaves east to Varanasi," she said. "The holiest city for Hindus. There are cremation ghats, steps on the edge of the river, where they burn bodies day and night. Asha would find other Aghori there and also temples to Shiva and Kali."

"It's our best bet," Jake said. "And we have to try something. I'll stay on her with the drone while you go get a vehicle and we'll head there by road."

Morgan jogged back to the Kapoor tent. Mahesh's assistant stood at the open door, gazing out into the chaos of the crowd as he wrung his hands together in anxiety. The sound of wailing and chanting rose like a prayer to heaven and mist swirled above the heads of the pilgrims, dank with the stench of burned bodies.

"This is terrible, Miss Morgan," he said, shaking his head. "Have you seen Mr Kapoor?"

Morgan took a deep breath and put her hand on his arm.

"I'm so sorry. Mahesh is out there, amongst the people he served – you'll need to retrieve his body. He gave his life to save others."

The man fell to his knees, his face stricken, his hands clasped together and eyes to heaven. He began to pray, his lips moving in ritual prayers for the dead.

Morgan ducked inside the tent. There was no time to mourn while Asha still held the sculpture, and after seeing what the Aghori were capable of, the thought of the weapon falling into their hands was terrifying.

She grabbed the keys to one of the four-wheel-drive vehicles they had left further out on the perimeter. It would be quicker to get out there on foot rather than try to drive out, especially as the camp was in convulsions.

The shouts of police could be heard above the sounds of mourning as they tried to gain control. But the camp was a collective body, mortally wounded, and its suffering seemed to flow across the millions gathered as word spread of death in the holy waters.

Morgan left the tent again, stopping next to Mahesh's assistant.

"I'm sorry but I have to go. Please radio the men at the vehicles further out that I'm coming to take one. We're tracking Asha Kapoor east. She's responsible for this terrible crime."

The man nodded. "Of course, and I know that Mr Kapoor would have wanted me to help you." Tears welled in his eyes. "I must speak to his widow."

Morgan jogged back to Jake. He stood in the same place, but now he gazed down at the bodies lying on the shore below. He clutched the railing, his knuckles white with tension.

He turned as she approached, his dark eyes full of sorrow. Morgan walked into his arms and they embraced. She felt the warmth of his body, heard the beating of his heart.

"I don't know how many more times I can see this," he whispered, his lips against her hair. "Every time I think we're close to some kind of victory, we leave so many dead behind."

"It could have been many more," Morgan said. She tightened her arms around him, pulling him closer. "And we have a chance to finish this now."

Jake stepped back and ran his hands through his hair as he pulled himself together. "OK, let's do this. The drone ran out of power and dropped into the river but she's definitely still on the boat, heading east. In the meantime, Martin's going to see if he can get a satellite lock on her position."

Morgan held out the keys. "We need to get back to the vehicles on the perimeter and then we can head after her. Even though we're behind, the road will be faster. We could still make it to Varanasi before Asha and intercept her on the ghats by the river."

CHAPTER 29

As the river wound away from Allahabad, the sounds of mourning faded and eventually, Asha could only hear the slap of water on the hull. She looked out towards the villages on the banks of the Ganges. A woman squatted on a rock doing her washing. A herd of water buffalo munched in the shallows. Men worked in the fields, their laughter and good-natured chatter rippling out towards her. The sounds of rural India, a background to life that she had never known growing up in the craziness of Mumbai and the privilege of wealth.

Maybe if she had grown up out here, she would have found love and had a family, a simpler life that may have satisfied her. But she would never know those pleasures now.

Asha sighed and brushed away the tears from her cheeks. She had lost her brother to the boiling waters along with her guru. The other dead pilgrims meant nothing to her, but those two men had been precious and their loss cut to her heart.

The goddess had asked for a sacrifice, but perhaps her demand had never been for pilgrims. Perhaps she had only ever wanted Asha's dearest, or perhaps the timing had just not been right.

She looked down at the sculpture of Shiva Nataraja, the bronze glinting as the sun rose higher in the sky. If the carving truly was the Brahmastra mantra, she could use it again.

And it wouldn't have to be in India.

She could take it to London or New York, anywhere the casualties might be even higher than the Kumbh Mela.

A piercing cry rang out over the river. She looked up to see a peacock on the edge of the bank, its feathers spread in a perfect semi-circle of brilliant blues and purple.

It stared right at her, its piercing eyes glinting as it screeched again.

"Mayura," Asha whispered, the Sanskrit word for peacock. The bird was sacred to Hindu mythology, depicted as killing a snake, the symbol of the cycle of time. Was it meant to be a warning?

Confusion swept over her. What did the goddess want?

She had to get to the Aghori in Varanasi. She would join their rite and in the blood and the fire, she would see the goddess again and learn her true wishes.

* * *

Morgan and Jake drove into the outskirts of Varanasi. The highway had been swift but as they wove through the streets into the central city, it became useless to drive any further.

Skinny cows with jutting ribs wandered the streets chewing on whatever they could find, as birds of prey wheeled overhead. A woman squatted next to the road with a tray of pomegranates, one split open to show the red flesh inside. A flower seller with marigolds spattered by the rain hawked his wares next to jasmine flowers and huge gourd-like cucumbers, dried coconut and piles of colorful dye for offerings. The sound of horns and radios playing Bollywood tunes filled the air, blaring horns and bells and the crush of pilgrims overwhelming anyone who stood still. A scooter zoomed past driven by a man with his wife and three children plus a chicken piled around him.

"Something like that would be much faster," Jake said as they sat in a traffic jam.

"Let's do it," Morgan said.

They left their vehicle at the side of the road and hailed a bicycle rickshaw.

"Where to, ma'am?" the young driver asked, his bare feet ready on the pedals.

"Is there a temple to the goddess Kali on the ghats?" Morgan asked.

"There is a shrine near Dashashwamedh Ghat. I will take you there?"

Morgan nodded. "Yes, please."

He darted down a side street and into the warren of the ancient city, ringing his bell as he clattered along. Morgan held onto the side of the cart, leaning into Jake to try and avoid getting slammed into the walls as the young man rounded corners at speed.

They shot through an intersection, weaving in between sacred cows and buses filled with people. The traffic was like a shoal of fish, moving together, inches apart and yet somehow not colliding, as if a sixth sense sparked between them. Decorated trucks with multi-colored paintings and tinsel bore down on their tiny vehicle but at the last minute the driver swerved, grinning back at them in triumph.

"Look at the damn road," Jake shouted. He turned to Morgan. "Maybe you have to see life as cyclical here, so you can stop worrying about dying every five minutes."

The city was dirty and dusty and the buildings drooped into one another as if they might tumble like dominos any minute. But despite the dense humanity packed in like sardines, there was a pervading sense of calm. This place was truly sacred and to die here meant an escape from the circle of reincarnation. For if the ashes of the dead floated in the Ganges at Varanasi, the soul would ascend to heaven with no need to come back to the agony of life. Some days,

Morgan could see why such a belief would be so precious.

After a short journey, they paid the driver and walked down onto the ghat. Sadhus sat in lotus position on the bank, their backs straight and bodies still as they stared at the horizon. Beggars held tins out as Morgan and Jake passed. They asked for a few rupees for firewood for their own pyres, because it took a great deal to burn a human corpse to dust. Even death was hard here.

Near the steps of the ghat, a man drove his buffalo herd into the water and began to wash them, while just downstream, a dhobi-wallah washed a pile of clothes, slapping the bright material on the steps. A woman stood in the shallows, weeping as she released a wreath of flowers onto the holy waters.

Morgan and Jake found the Kali shrine in a parade of other gods, her black face and red tongue as well as the severed heads marking her out. Pilgrims prayed next to it, leaving flowers and other offerings. The sound of prayer cymbals and the smell of incense emanated from the shrine.

But they couldn't spot Asha in the crowd of pilgrims.

Jake's phone buzzed.

"Martin says that the satellite shows she definitely alighted from the boat here at Varanasi, but further downstream at the burning ghats."

"That's the cremation grounds where the Aghori would congregate too," Morgan said. "Let's head in that direction."

Shadows lengthened as they walked along the edge of the river, and when they eventually reached one of the main cremation ghats, it was getting dark. The pyres burned here twenty-four hours a day, seven days a week, to process the huge numbers of dead, and as they walked through, Morgan glimpsed the different stages of cremation.

A group of men carried a body down to a pyre that was

stacked high, ready for burning. The corpse was wrapped in orange silk and garlanded with flowers. The men lifted it high and placed it onto the wood and a young man leaned forward to light the kindling, his face contorted with grief. Later, he would have to crack the skull of the dead to release its spirit, but for now, he bore witness to the end of another life.

Flames hissed and popped and the sound of sonorous bells rang through the air. The heat was intense and as they wove through the fires, Morgan was reminded of the story of the furnace of Nebuchadnezzar, when three young Jews walked in the flames unhurt because of their faith in God. This was a primal place and staring into the flames here meant watching a human body return to bone and ashes.

"There," Jake whispered suddenly.

Towards the end of the ghat, in the shadows beyond the main pyres, a group of Aghori sat in front of a huge fire. They sat so close that it seemed impossible that their skin didn't burn. Their *kapala* skulls sat before them, bone glinting in the flickering light and the ash on their naked bodies marked them out in the darkness.

Between the men, Jake and Morgan saw the smaller figure of a woman.

They approached slowly, weaving between the fires until they reached the perimeter of the Aghori circle. One of the sadhus looked up at them with dark eyes.

Morgan was wary after her experience at Allahabad and she could smell the sweet smoke that had blinded her back then. The *kapala* skulls were filled with blood and ritual alcohol and the men would be intoxicated as they sought the way to the goddess.

Asha sat within the circle, surrounded by Aghori sadhus. The sculpture of Shiva Nataraja sat between her crossed legs and she stared into the fire. Her eyes were glazed and she seemed to be in a trance. The blood of animal sacrifice marked her face, daubed in thick clots and scattered with ash.

A bell rang out, its dull note sounding three times.

The Aghori began to chant.

Asha's face changed and tears welled, dripping down her face as she wept in anguish, leaving trails through the blood and ash.

She swayed in place as the Aghori's chant grew louder, and changed to a repetitive mantra of harsh words, guttural and raw. One of them offered his *kapala* skull to her and she drank deep, her head tipped back as she finished the bowl of bloody alcohol.

The Aghori rose and Asha stood with them, her eyes fixed on the flames. She held the statue of Shiva tight against her chest.

Suddenly Morgan saw her intention.

"No," she whispered and stepped forward, her hands outstretched.

But the Aghori closed ranks, protecting the circle as Asha walked into the ring of fire and sank down into the circle of wood. She made no sound at first, her eyes glazed over as the chanting rang through the air.

Then the flames pierced her consciousness. She threw her head back and screamed.

Morgan tried to fight her way into the circle.

"Let me help her," she begged, but the Aghori blocked her path, their wiry muscles strong and unmoving.

"It's no use," Jake said, his hand gentle on her arm. "She made her choice."

They watched as Asha's skin blackened and she crumpled to a heap, mercifully out of sight. The corpse crackled as the Aghori fed the flames.

Through a crack in the piled timber, Morgan caught a glimpse of the bronze statue as the metal flames surrounding Shiva danced in the heat of true fire. The etchings of the mantra carved into the statue rippled in the heat and the words dissolved into one another.

"Look," Morgan whispered, pointing it out to Jake. "The weapon can't be invoked again. At least not that way."

He nodded and took her hand. "Now Asha is dead and gone, I don't want to see what the Aghori do with her body."

Morgan shuddered at the thought of their cannibal rituals. "You're right. It's time to go home. There's just one more thing I want to do."

CHAPTER 30

Morgan and Jake stood on the edge of the Ganges looking east as the sun rose over the horizon and cast a fiery trail across the water.

"How quickly things change," Morgan said. "Yesterday we stood waiting for the dawn with Mahesh and now he's gone. Asha's dead, and so many more are with their gods."

"And we're still standing," Jake said. "Be thankful for that, because one day, you or I will stand alone." He took her hand and kissed it, his dark eyes intense as he looked at her. "I hope that won't be for a long time."

Together, they crouched next to the water and lit tea lights inside little cardboard boats, used to carry prayers onto the sacred waters. They sprinkled marigolds around the flames and pushed them gently into the current.

Morgan put her hands together in the prayer position over her heart.

"Namaste," she whispered, her thoughts with Mahesh. They watched until the little lights were lost in the encroaching dawn.

"Let's go home," Jake said.

Hours later, as the plane took off, Morgan looked down at the city of Varanasi as it grew smaller beneath them. She pressed her nose to the window so she could drink in that last look and then it was gone, lost below the clouds.

Jake was already on the edge of sleep, his eyes closed, a

shutter against the world. But Morgan felt a strange sense of loss as they headed west. People had traveled to India for generations seeking meaning and enlightenment. There was even a myth that Jesus had not died on the cross, but ended up here instead. Those who stayed in the country could spend a lifetime looking for meaning, and some lucky few found what they sought. But those who left could not forget, and India lingered, like the scent of a lover.

Morgan suddenly felt the truth of that and longed to stay, to immerse herself in the rich culture, the colors and extremity of experience that made her feel so alive. India was like Israel in that way, a place on the edge of life and death where an unexpected turn in the road could take you into the heart of an ancient ruin or the hands of a mob. The very unpredictability of it was part of the thrill.

India was full of life and laughter and people here lived in the moment, because who knew what tomorrow would bring.

She would come back here. She was sure of it.

Morgan closed her eyes and let sleep come.

London, England.

Morgan and Jake slipped into the city before dawn and arrived in Trafalgar Square by taxi from Heathrow Airport.

"Terrible thing that bombing," the cabbie said, shaking his head as he took their fare. "But look at how quickly it's all been rebuilt. The terrorists can't crush Londoners."

The square was quiet as they walked beneath the facade of the National Gallery. The reconstruction was well underway, with the square rebuilt and the fountains almost finished. Nelson's Column stood proud again and although the lions closest to the blast area were still missing, they would be rebuilt soon enough. No one would ever notice the difference and within months, the city would forget, its attention distracted by the latest headlines.

They entered ARKANE through the basement of St Martin-in-the-Fields church, going through multiple levels of security including new biometric scanning.

Morgan held her breath as she faced the machines, still wary of Marietti's anger at her actions. But it beeped green and they walked together down through the lab area towards Martin's office.

"Morgan, Jake. Wait." The voice boomed through the corridor and they turned to see Director Marietti at the entrance to one of the labs. He held a cane and rested against the door frame, his body still weak from his injuries. But his eyes were steel hard. He would not back down in the face of danger, whether inside ARKANE or out in the world.

Jake went to him and embraced his mentor, then stepped back, aware that he had overstepped the mark. But Marietti smiled.

"It's good to see you back safely." He looked at Morgan. "Both of you."

His eyes met hers. It was as close to an apology as she was likely to get. And that was OK.

"I know you've just returned but there's something we need to work on together." He beckoned them into the lab, where Martin Klein stood next to an artifact on a bench. "Something that threatens us all."

AUTHOR'S NOTE

I love India and I've wanted to set a story there for a long time. Of course, it's impossible to do justice to such an incredible culture in one action adventure story, but I hope that you enjoyed the attempt. I always enjoy hearing from readers who have looked into the research behind the book, so here are some of the aspects that went into it.

The initial idea came from a statue of Shiva Nataraja that I saw in the Museum of Delhi back in 2006 when I visited the Taj Mahal and Varanasi, which also features in *Stone of Fire*, ARKANE book 1. Then I read about the huge statue at CERN, Himmler's fascination with Hinduism, and the phrase spoken by Oppenheimer, and the conspiracy was born.

You can find the pictures behind the book here on Pinterest: www.pinterest.com/jfpenn/destroyer-of-worlds

India

I tried to make the Indian locations as close to reality as possible, although I haven't visited all the sites in person. I did visit the synagogue in Fort Kochi on a cycle trip through South-West India and many of the other places have a flavor from my own travels, supplemented by other research from books and documentaries. Here are some of them:

The Story of India by Michael Wood. Book and documentary series.

Sacred India documentary.

Ganges documentary.

West Meets East. Kumbh Mela documentary with Dominic West

In the Land of Shiva. Book by James O'Hara

The real tomb of Shah Jahan and his wife Mumtaz are beneath the main room of the Taj Mahal, and there are conspiracy theories of a Shiva temple below. The Aghori truly are a pretty scary sect, and the worship of Kali does range from mainstream temples to reported child sacrifice in rural areas, although of course, I have used extreme examples for an exciting novel!

Rwanda

In earlier books, I hinted at Marietti and Jake's experience in Africa and as I thought about the idea for *Destroyer of Worlds*, it seemed to me that Marietti would have wanted to stop the same thing happening again. I was nineteen in 1994 when the genocide happened and I remember seeing pictures of the mass graves. Researching the atrocity was difficult, but part of the reason that I write is to challenge my own thinking. If you want to read more, I recommend *We Wish to Inform You That Tomorrow We Will be Killed With Our Families: Stories from Rwanda* by Philip Gourevitch.

END OF DAYS

AN ARKANE THRILLER

J.F. PENN

For Jonathan.

Thank you for being by my side in Israel.

"Then I saw an angel coming down from heaven, holding in his hand the key to the bottomless pit and a great chain. And he seized the dragon, that ancient serpent, who is the devil and Satan, and bound him for a thousand years, and threw him into the pit, and shut it and sealed it over him … until the thousand years were ended."

Revelation 20:1-6

"The female of Samael is called Serpent, Woman of Harlotry, End of All Flesh, End of Days."

The demon Lilith, as described by Rashi, a medieval commentator on the Talmud and the Hebrew Scriptures

PROLOGUE

Two weeks ago. Ruins of Babylon, Iraq.

IT WAS DARK WHEN Massoud went back to the tomb. The moon was high and silver light glinted on the sands of Babylon, like the edge of a knife before it lodged in the heart of its prey. The sound of the camp filtered across the dunes, the crackling of fire and the voices of men trying to forget what they had seen in the light of day. Their tales of bravado steeled them to face another dawn.

But Massoud could not forget.

He clutched his tool bag tighter and scrambled across the ruins towards the edge of the excavations. Before the war, Saddam Hussein had been rebuilding the ancient city and much had been renewed. The tyrant had remounted the Lion of Babylon, a black rock sculpture over 2600 years old, and carved his own name into bricks alongside that of the ancient king, Nebuchadnezzar. For the glory of Iraq, he had said.

But now Saddam was dead and gone. Iraq was broken by war and crushed under the feet of fundamentalists, fighting for the scraps of what remained. This ancient city had been pounded by mortar and bulldozed by western soldiers, grinding what was left of proud Babylon into the dust of the desert. Massoud shook his head. It was all madness, but for now at least, there was good money to be made digging for archaeologists who wanted to make their names in the desert once more.

And there was a way to make more than just the daily cash in hand.

It was dangerous but it was worth the risk. There were those who would pay handsomely for a piece of ancient Babylon if it could be smuggled out, and he had glimpsed something earlier today at the very edge of his patch. If he could just get it out then his family would not go hungry this winter and his daughter would have her medicine.

A sound came from up ahead. A scuff of boots on stone and the hacking cough of a night watchman.

Massoud froze and ducked down behind a rock. If he was found here at this time of night, he could be beaten … or worse. His heart pounded and his tongue stuck to the roof of his dry mouth.

But then the clouds shifted over the moon and darkness hid him as the guard passed only meters away. Massoud scurried to the tomb, clambering over the remains of the military base. He reached the very edge of the dig where they excavated part of the city that had not been explored before, revealing treasures unseen for millennia, a glimpse of its great past. Babylon had once been the largest city in the world, a hub of commerce and art and the pinnacle of civilization. Massoud smiled and shook his head. How the mighty had fallen indeed. A lesson that the Americans would learn some day, as the British and every other empire learned before them. Man was not built to last and days of glory passed quickly in the blink of history. All that mattered were the people you loved in this lifetime, and that was why he was here now.

He made it to the tomb and crouched at the edge of the pit that led to the entrance. His fingers dug into the red dirt and he hesitated as he felt a shadow at his back. He turned his head quickly.

There was no one there.

He shivered, then took a deep breath, steeling himself before clambering down into the pit. He pushed aside the wooden barrier and crawled within. He couldn't risk the torch yet, not this close to the entrance so he scrabbled in the dark, feeling his way.

Massoud breathed in the air of the tomb. He had dug at many ruins in the deserts of Iraq and he knew the smell of a ruined city. This one was not like the others. Where before he had smelled only the dust of the long dead, here he could smell the earth, freshly turned, as if something was alive down here.

As if the city could spring awake again.

He crawled into the darkness and felt the shadow of a presence, slipping along behind him in the dirt. A whisper in the dark.

The crackle of dry skin rasping across sand.

Sweat broke out on his brow but he kept going. He couldn't turn his head in the narrow tunnel and he knew he would see nothing anyway. Perhaps it was a djinn of the desert, a demon of this cursed city. But there were so many demons in Iraq now and Massoud was more afraid of the human kind than the ethereal. The extremists had taken his cousin away one night and his body had never been found. They had beaten his old father in the market when all he had done was play music at his stall. Yes, the demons in human form that stalked the country now were surely worse than anything under the sands. Massoud crawled on.

At last he made it to the dogleg in the tunnel, out of direct sight of the entrance. He turned on his head-torch. The dull yellow light drove away the shadows and finally he crawled into the tomb itself. Lamplight flickered across rough-hewn walls, revealing a mosaic in bright colors, undimmed by buried years. It was both magnificent and terrible, the image searing itself on his memory. A massive serpent undulated across a map of the known world, its mouth gaping to swallow a bound woman. Its hooked fangs pierced the body of a screaming sacrifice while its huge coils wrapped around countless other dead. Massoud couldn't read the cuneiform text below the serpent, but he had been in enough tombs to know that it was a warning.

When the archaeologists had opened the tomb a few days ago, they had found myriad skeletons of long-dead snakes amongst human bones, evidence of sacrifice to this demon serpent. Massoud shivered to think of being left down here in the dark with hissing death. A primeval terror, especially for a desert people.

Suddenly, he heard a slither in the dark. Something moved at the edge of the torchlight, just outside the warm glow.

Massoud jerked his head around.

Were there still snakes down here?

Stop being a fool, he chastised himself. *The faster this is done, the faster you can get out of here and turn this old stone into a fortune.*

He turned back to the wall. A black stone slab lay at the corner of the mosaic, carved with the giant serpent on a smaller scale against an inlaid pattern of stars. Cuneiform text wound around it, disappearing into the rock beyond. He couldn't excise the whole slab, but it was still a priceless piece of art that was also small enough for him to smuggle out.

He pulled his mason's hammer and chisel from his tool belt and bent to place the blade carefully behind the stone slab. The metallic tapping obscured the rustle of snake skin from behind him in the shadows. The sound echoed down into the depths of the earth, calling to the darkness to rise again.

CHAPTER 1

Appalachian Mountains, Kentucky, USA.

Lilith stepped over the threshold into the tiny church. The white walls were duller than she remembered, marred by time and stained by the breath of believers, reeking of tobacco and the residue of communion wine. It had been years since she had visited, but the smell of the place instantly took her back to her childhood. Back then, the Appalachian Pentecostal church had been her home, her escape, the only place where she felt part of something bigger in a miserable life of poverty.

She had come a long way since then.

Lilith wore a shapeless dress of muted color, the traditional style for women in these parts, having left her smart tailored clothes behind in the city. Her face was bare of makeup and her titian curls hung loose about her shoulders. Her work colleagues at Viperex Pharmaceuticals wouldn't even recognize her.

But she needed this. She had been away too long. There was something only this place could give her and today, she was coming home.

Orphaned as a toddler, Lilith had passed from foster family to foster family around the poor neighborhoods on the border of Kentucky and Virginia. She had a propensity for silence and shied away when people tried to hug her.

These things kept her apart and made even the most loving mothers think she was touched in some way. Then one day, here in this church, she had discovered that which brought her alive. She had never been drawn to people, but here she had found her true passion.

In the last month, the serpents had called her back, haunting her sleep. She woke most nights with her hands in the air, reaching for the weight of them, wanting to dance. Perhaps today …

"Hello dear." Lilith jumped as a woman touched her arm. "Are you visiting with us today?"

Lilith turned and looked down at her. There was something familiar in the hunched frame, the faint smell of lavender and the woman's pattern of missing teeth.

"Are you sister Beatrice?" Lilith narrowed her eyes a little, trying to remember.

"Why, yes, child. I am. How would you know?" The woman looked more closely at her. Then a smile lit up her face, making her blue eyes crinkle and the gaps in her teeth protrude even more. "You're Lily. Well my goodness, it's been many years since we've seen you here, sweetie. Since that day …" Her words trailed off as her eyes dimmed at the memory. Then she patted Lilith on the arm. "Well now, you're welcome back. I'm sure Pastor John will be pleased to see you."

The woman bustled away as the small community filled the church and the sound of greetings filled the air. Lilith stood at the back in a white wooden pew, eyes down and demure. She clutched a hymn sheet in shaking hands, anticipating the service to come. She didn't want to draw attention to herself – not yet, anyway.

The plinky-plonk of piano keys filled the room and the congregation stood to sing a rousing folk song with clapping and shouts of praise interspersing the notes. Some shook tambourines, the rattle of tin beating time. The energy in the room stepped up a notch and Lilith felt the rise of a smile on her lips, buoyed by the faithful who came here to escape their miserable lives every Sunday.

"I'm going to tell you children, do you know what Jesus Christ said?" Pastor John began in his singsong voice, the final words rising to a high note. He stepped forward, his hands raised towards heaven.

And at his feet, a locked box.

Lilith couldn't stop looking at it. She knew what was in there even though she couldn't hear the rattle from this far away. Her eyes stayed fixed on it as Pastor John continued, his tone rising and falling as his flock thrust their hands high.

"And the gospel of Saint Mark says that these signs shall follow them that believe. IN MY NAME they will cast out devils, and speak with new tongues. IN MY NAME they shall take up serpents and if they drink any deadly thing, it shall not hurt them. IN MY NAME, they shall lay hands on the sick and they shall recover."

"Hallelujah!"

"Praise Jesus!"

A man a few meters in front of Lilith began to shake in place, his whole body wracked with convulsions. Those around him calmly laid hands upon him and prayed. Another woman fell to her knees in the aisle, crying and speaking in tongues.

Lilith watched, waiting for the atmosphere to rise even further, for the spirit-fueled hysteria to grow. Back in her university days, when she had trained as a scientist, she had researched mass hysteria and tried to explain away what happened in this little corner of the world. Some would say these people were caught up in the Spirit, others would think they were crazy. Lilith was still unsure what she believed, but her own truth lay inside that locked box.

As the piano thumped into another tune, Pastor John bent and opened the lid.

"When God anoints you, when the Spirit prompts you, you can take up serpents IN HIS NAME!"

Lilith's heart raced as she caught a glimpse of the snakes within. Three timber rattlesnakes, deep brown chevron markings on their muscled bodies. She ached to touch them, to feel their cool skin against hers. She licked her lips, hardly able to stay in place.

Pastor John lifted out one of the snakes and held it high. It wrapped itself around his wrist, tongue flickering as it tasted the air. He bounced to the music, shuffling around and singing loud as it wound around his hands.

The man who had been convulsing just a few minutes ago stepped into the aisle. His forehead gleamed with sweat and patches of it formed under his armpits, staining his shirt. He fixed his eyes on the snake as songs of praise swelled and filled the little church.

Those who spoke in tongues shouted their guttural praise to the Lord as the man walked to the front of the church.

Pastor John nodded at him and held out the rattlesnake. From behind, Lilith could see cords of muscle on his back standing out through his sweat-drenched shirt. His fear was palpable and she knew the snakes would sense it.

He reached out for the rattlesnake.

Lilith clutched the edge of the pew, her heart hammering at what could happen if the rattler struck him. But the snake seemed merely bemused by its handling, curious to taste the skin of the man. Its flickering tongue tasted his salt, head wavering over his arm.

She relaxed a little at the snake's behavior, confident that it wouldn't bite him for now. Lilith was a herpetologist by day, working with snakes in a lab where they were specimens to be tested, farmed and milked to make antivenom. She understood snakes' body language but in the lab, she was a scientist, clinically detached.

Whereas here the serpents were primal beings, and she craved their touch.

More in the congregation were shaking and crying now, the frenzy growing. The pianist just kept playing as people stamped and prayed, some falling down.

"Getting high on Jesus is better than cocaine," a man next to Lilith said with a toothy grin, as he joined the growing number of dancers in the aisle.

A woman brought her baby up to Pastor John. With one hand he cradled the child and with the other, he picked up another rattlesnake from the box.

"IN MY NAME they shall take up serpents and if they drink any deadly thing, it shall not hurt them. And we claim this now for your child, Lord."

Lilith felt an echo of her once-strong faith. She had been the youngest child in the congregation to handle snakes at aged seven, considered a blessing on the church, a miracle of sorts. Until that day …

It was time to face them again.

She stepped into the aisle, her green eyes fixed on Pastor John, who held the baby in the crook of one arm, the snake in his other hand.

He looked up and saw her approach. His eyes narrowed and then recognition sparked.

"Praise Jesus," he called aloud. "A daughter returned."

But Lilith could see hesitation in his eyes. He remembered. She had taken up serpents nearly every week until her fifteenth year, when she had been struck.

Pastor John had handed her the snake that day.

She remembered the initial sting, the shock of the hit, and then burning physical pain as the venom had raced through her blood. Her arm had begun to swell immediately and the world had swayed and then collapsed into colors and sounds.

Lilith remembered a curious jealousy in the eyes of

those who had watched her fall to the ground. She had been given a chance to test her faith. Would the Lord take her? Was it her time? Or would she demonstrate faith by not succumbing to the poison?

They had laid her in the Pastor's office on a blanket and prayed for her and over her and with her. Whispered words of faith in the hallucinations of the night, but nothing for the pain.

No hospital treatment. No anti-venom.

Just the rustle of snake skin in the dark.

Then she had recovered just as the Lord had promised. A sign to the faithful. But fear had crept in and she had never handled in church again. She had stolen money and run to the city. Over time, she had been drawn back to snakes, training as a herpetologist and working for one of the foremost producers of anti-venom.

Now years later, she was back here again.

Lilith held out her hands, her eyes fixed on Pastor John.

"I take up serpents because the Bible says I will not be harmed," she said calmly, loud enough for him to hear over the music. "It is the confirmed word of God."

She knew he couldn't deny her the chance. He nodded and handed her the rattler.

Lilith took hold of it. The heaviness of its body, the smooth scales, so cool to her touch. She raised it to her face, let its tongue flicker over her features, let it taste her. It felt like coming home and she wanted more.

She bent and picked the final snake from the box, letting it wrap around her other arm. Then she reached out to the sweating man and lightly took the rattler from his shaking hands. The relief in his eyes was palpable and he fell to his knees in prayer.

Now Lilith had three rattlesnakes winding around her, two in one hand and one in the other. She raised her arms high, standing still and silent while the congregation whirled and stamped around her. Tambourines rattled. The faithful cried out to their God. She closed her eyes and felt the power of the serpent running through her, like a current into the ground beneath. Its ancient power rising and channeling through her blood.

Then she felt it. A whisper like that in her dreams.

The heartbeat of the Serpent of Serpents.

He was coming.

CHAPTER 2

London, England.

"MORGAN, JAKE. WAIT." THE deep voice boomed through the corridor of the ARKANE headquarters, deep under Trafalgar Square in central London.

Dr Morgan Sierra turned to see Director Marietti at the entrance to one of the labs. He held a cane and rested against the door frame. His body was still weak from the injuries he had sustained in India during the hunt for the Brahmastra weapon, but his eyes were steel hard. Morgan knew that he would not back down in the face of danger, whether inside ARKANE or out in the world. She was part of that fight now and even though they had just returned from a mission, she was ready for whatever came next.

Jake went to Marietti and embraced his mentor, then stepped back, aware that he might have overstepped the mark. But Marietti smiled.

"It's good to see you back safely." He looked at Morgan. "Both of you."

Marietti's eyes met hers. They had almost come to blows over her actions in India, when she had made a decision against his orders, but it seemed that was now forgotten. His words were as close to an apology as she was likely to get.

And that was OK.

"I know you've just returned," Marietti continued, "but there's something we need to work on urgently. Something that may threaten us all."

He beckoned them into the lab. Morgan followed Jake into the room, one of the sterile environments used for examining ancient artifacts, down in the hidden chambers that few knew about. The public-facing side of the Arcane Religious Knowledge And Numinous Experience Institute consisted of funding academic discourse on religious topics, but ARKANE was actually a secret agency investigating supernatural mysteries around the world. There were secrets down in the vault below that Morgan had almost died to protect and many more left to uncover.

Like the artifact Marietti pointed at now.

Spotlights illuminated a black marble tablet mounted on its side. Even with the bright lights in the room, the temperature felt cooler around the slab, as if the stone sucked in the light and warmth around it.

Morgan shivered a little as she bent to look at the tablet more closely. It was roughly cut around the edges, as if excavated in a hurry and one end was missing. A huge serpent curled across the face of a map of the known earth as it was millennia ago. Its jaws gaped wide and its fangs dripped poison as it pierced the body of a sacrifice heaped upon a pile of corpses. People cowered around it, some rapt in worship, others with faces contorted by terror. The precise chisel marks of cuneiform text ran around the tableau.

"The cuneiform words tell of an ancient evil."

A man stepped from the shadows in the corner of the room. He wore a black amaranth-piped cassock with pellegrina, a purple fascia and a gold pectoral cross. A scarlet skullcap topped his white close-cropped hair. His eyebrows were bushy above piercing blue eyes and he moved with the silent, lithe grace of an athlete.

"This is Cardinal Eric Krotalia," Marietti said. "He's an expert on eschatology, the End Times. I've been consulting with him about the tablet. He's one of our ARKANE advocates in Rome."

"Good to meet you, sir." Jake held out his hand and Krotalia shook it firmly.

Morgan thought Marietti's tone was just a little reserved, but if he trusted the Cardinal then she should respect his opinion. She nodded a greeting but kept her distance at the other end of the table. The man was just a little too good looking for a Cardinal, more like Sean Connery playing the aged hero than a crusty Vatican scholar.

Cardinal Krotalia walked up to the table and pointed at the carving.

"According to legend, the serpent will appear at the End of Days to devour the earth. The language is close to some of the biblical prophecies, although of course this tablet is much older than extant texts."

Marietti's dark eyes were haunted at he gazed at the marble. "It was smuggled out of Iraq as part of a network of archaeologists trying to save what's left of ancient civilizations. After the destruction of Palmyra, there are many who worry what else may be lost in the darkness of religious extremism."

Morgan reached out a finger to touch the edge of the slab. It was exciting to be this close to a piece of that iconic civilization and one of the reasons she loved working for ARKANE. "The mythology of the snake is in every culture," she said. "Why is this tablet so important?"

"Because of the timing." Marietti pointed to one part of the marble slab. "This references a particular pattern of rarely seen star constellations. We've cross-referenced with data from multiple sources and this particular stellar alignment only occurs once every four thousand years. This one coincides with a series of blood moon eclipses that intersect with Serpens, part of the constellation Ophiuchus, believed to represent Laocoon –"

"– who was killed by sea serpents," Morgan finished for him.

"Let me guess," Jake said, raising an eyebrow. "It's happening soon."

As he spoke, Martin Klein entered the lab. ARKANE's brilliant archivist bobbed up and down on the balls of his feet and brushed his ragged blonde hair back from his face. He pushed his wire-rimmed spectacles further up the ridge of his nose as he spoke with excitement, his words tumbling over one another.

"You're right, Jake! The alignment will happen in only ten days and we will be here to witness it." Martin grinned and clapped his hands a little, bouncing in place like a child delighted with a new toy. "What was prophesied so many thousand years ago will now come to pass."

Marietti held his hand up and Martin stopped bouncing, his smile fading at the Director's grim face. "While this *is* academically exciting on the one hand, it's also worrying. The text tells of a serpent who will destroy the earth, a warning of apocalypse at a time when too many already seek oblivion for humankind."

The Cardinal raised his hands as he intoned the words from the book of Revelation. "He seized the dragon, that ancient serpent, who is the devil and Satan, and bound him for a thousand years, and threw him into the pit, and shut it and sealed it over him … until the thousand years were ended."

"But the serpent is a representation of many things," Morgan said, resisting the pronunciation of doom. "Renewal in the shedding of skin, rebirth and eternity in the ouroboros, the snake eating its own tail. Why are you so worried about this in particular?"

Marietti sat down heavily on a chair by the marble

tablet. The penumbra of the spotlight caught the side of his craggy face, deepening the shadows under his eyes. His skin was sallow, his shoulders drooped. Morgan saw a broken man on the edge of what he could handle. Marietti sighed and shook his head.

"I haven't told you what's been going on at ARKANE these last few months. The hierarchy and politics are generally kept hidden from field agents, so you can concentrate on your jobs. But you know ARKANE has teams all over the world, across many faiths and cultural divides. Up until recently, we all agreed that the supernatural world we face should be kept away from the public."

He shook his head and the Cardinal continued for him.

"Now it seems there are some who want to hasten the End Times, those who believe the Great Battle should come soon, and who believe that in trying to keep the supernatural away from the world, ARKANE somehow blocks the cosmic plan. We are concerned that this serpent will be used somehow to hasten the End of Days. When Director Marietti told me of the tablet, I knew we had to act."

"Sounds just as crazy as what we usually face out there," Jake said. "So what can we do?"

"The cuneiform script tells of a great pit where the serpent lies bound," Marietti said. "An echo of the Revelation verse, so I give it some credence. I want you both to find the pit, because others search for it too."

Martin picked up his tablet computer, fingers flashing across the screen. "The group we suspect to be involved wears this symbol." He turned it round to show Morgan and Jake a tattoo of a coiled snake poised to strike, inked in emerald green. "They call themselves Roshites."

"From the Hebrew word *rosh*, meaning poison or venom," Morgan said, recalling the Hebrew. Although she hadn't lived in Israel for a number of years now, she had been brought up there by her father, murdered as one of the Remnant, and Hebrew was her second, fluent language. She felt a fleeting need to speak it again as the word formed on her lips. She thought differently when she spoke the ancient language, even dreamed different dreams.

"Indeed," Martin continued. "The Roshites are devotees of the Great Serpent, an ancient sect that can be tracked through history. The snake goddess sculptures at Knossos depict women holding writhing serpents aloft. Then there's the prophetess Pythia of the Delphic oracle in ancient Greece. Wadjet, the snake goddess of the uraeus crown in Egypt. And then of course, the biblical history –"

"The brazen serpent on Moses' staff," Morgan interrupted. "So that when anyone was bitten by a snake, they could look at the bronze idol and be healed. From the book of Numbers, chapter twenty-one."

Jake had been quiet but now he spoke. "And let's not forget this ancient serpent of Revelation, bound and cast into a pit, until the thousand years are ended. That seems to be the most important aspect right now."

Marietti put his hand on Jake's shoulder. "That's what I fear. It seems that the serpent was buried to keep it from the world, so at least our ancestors were able to vanquish it once before. But this prophecy suggests it is coming again."

"Perhaps it's just allegory," Morgan said. "The sin of the world, the knowledge of good and evil, that's what is destroying the earth. The Anthropocene era, as they call it now, demonstrates how man has brought this destruction upon himself."

Marietti looked at her, his eyes full of sorrow. "I wish it were so, Morgan. But you've seen the other side of allegory as an ARKANE agent. You know what we have to keep from those outside." He gestured down towards the vault beneath them. "You know the secrets we keep. You saw the demon in the bone church, the creatures from the Gates of Hell, the power of the Brahmastra. How can you now doubt that this could also be real?"

Morgan smiled. "You can't take the scientist out of the girl. But I take your point." She ran a finger over the curls of the snake, following its path across the slab. "This isn't uniform," she said. "Perhaps it's some kind of map?"

"My thoughts exactly." Martin tapped on the tablet again and spun it around. "This is a map of ancient Iraq and I've indicated the possible route of the snake based on the undulations on the slab. It heads directly east through Asia and out into the Western Pacific. Beyond the boundaries of what they would have known as the earth at the time, right out into the ocean."

"Whatever it was, it looks like they went to a lot of effort to get rid of it." Jake pinched the screen and zoomed in on the map. "That's near the Mariana Trench, the deepest place on earth."

"Not somewhere we can just rock up and search then," Morgan noted.

"There is something else." Marietti took the tablet from Martin and pulled up an image of the Ishtar Gate, a massive arch with bright blue bricks decorated with images of dragons and aurochs bulls. "The tablet was found at the back of where the Ishtar Gate was originally excavated. But there's information missing so perhaps there is a more detailed clue at the gate."

"Guess we're heading to Iraq then." Jake smiled. "It's been a while."

Actually, it's closer than that," Marietti said. "The Ishtar Gate is in Berlin at the Pergamon Museum."

"I'll make the arrangements." Martin tapped on his device. "By the time you've swapped your gear over from the India trip, you'll be good to go back out."

Morgan and Jake walked out into the corridor, heading

for the weapons room. It was a short turnaround but they could kit up and be on their way again later tonight. Morgan loved the adrenalin of the mission and was keen to get going.

But there was one thing she had to know before they left. One thing that could put them both in grave danger.

CHAPTER 3

Appalachian Mountains, Kentucky, USA. 10:12pm.

LILITH'S EYES FLICKED OPEN, suddenly wide with the knowledge of what was coming. As she gasped with the rush, she saw a man at the back of the church. His dark eyes were fixed on her. His close-cropped hair receded over a broad forehead, green eyes so like her own staring back at her. He wore a black shirt open two buttons and she could see a tattoo winding up his neck. The coils of a serpent in green and yellow.

He beckoned to her, then turned and walked out of the church.

Lilith felt the serpents shift in her hands. She had lost control and they would soon grow restless. As the faithful continued to sing, she bent and placed the three snakes back into their box at the feet of Pastor John.

Then she ran from the church out into the night.

The man leaned against the bonnet of a weathered SUV, his features shrouded in darkness. He was tall and powerfully muscled, with the scuffed boots and latent power of a ranger in the mountains.

"I know you felt it," the man said, his voice sensual, languid. "Do you want to know more?"

Lilith took a step towards him.

"Know more about what?" Her voice sounded fragile

out here in the night, drowned out by the singing still audible in the church behind her.

The man went to the door of the car and opened it. The light from inside lit his face from beneath, his eyes dark hollows. He pulled his shirt away from his neck to reveal more of the snake tattoo. Lilith found herself walking towards him until she could see the detail of each scale. She stood so close she could feel the heat from his body and smell the musk from his skin. She wanted to lick his flesh with an outstretched tongue like the rattlers would.

"The time of the Great Serpent is close," he whispered. "Those of us who practice mithridatism know it."

Lilith inhaled sharply and stepped back. How did he know of her secret addiction? The practice involved injecting small amounts of venom regularly, in order to build up immunity to the poison.

That's how it started anyway.

Deep down, Lilith knew she chased the high she felt in the depths of poisoning, the hallucinations that took her out of her body into another realm. The small amounts she self-administered took the edge off the craving, but she always wanted more. The toxins were building up in her blood – they could kill her at any time.

But she couldn't stop.

"There's a venom you haven't tried," the man whispered. "One that will take you into the realms of what I know you crave." He bent close to her ear. His breath made her shiver. "Because I crave it too."

Lilith's heart hammered in her chest. He was hypnotic, dominant. She wanted what he offered, in so many ways.

"Who are you?"

"My chosen name is Samael." He smiled, and Lilith heard a dark humor under his intensity. "Call me Sam. And you, Lilith …" He stepped closer to her, cupping her chin and lifting her face. "You were born to be part of this."

His lips brushed hers with the gentlest of touches and something in her blood called to him. But the coils of the Great Serpent lay heavy in her mind.

"Part of what?" she said, putting her hand on his chest and pushing him back.

Sam stepped away and reached into the car. He pulled out a tablet computer and swiped the screen a few times. He brought up a picture of the night sky and zoomed into a star system.

"This is Serpens, part of the constellation of Ophiuchus. The picture was taken two nights ago." He was all business now, speaking with authority as he swiped the screen again to display an image of a black marble tablet inlaid with the coils of a great snake. "This is a tablet from ancient Babylon, a prophecy that tells of the rising of the Great Serpent at the End Times." His eyes flashed with sudden anger. "That piece is lost to me now, but we have detailed photos. The pattern of the stars on the tablet match the constellation for the first time in four thousand years. My men are heading to Berlin to get the final piece of the puzzle, so we will soon know where the Great Serpent lies."

It sounded crazy and one part of Lilith, the scientist, wanted to mock his words. She would expect talk of the End Times and the Great Serpent from the fanatics inside the church. And yet, his words captivated her. Venom ran through her veins and his words made her blood sing.

"And then what?" she asked.

"Then we bring him back," Sam said, his eyes flashing with fire. "You felt the power of those tiny snakes here, so imagine how powerful the Serpent of Serpents will be. We will serve him and reign in a new world order. But I need your help."

The thought of this powerful man needing her brought a smile to Lilith's lips.

"Why? What can I do that you can't?"

Sam sighed and shook his head. Lilith sensed a form of jealousy running beneath. "There is no other who can handle the venom levels you have already survived. Believe me, we've tried a number of subjects and there's no time to waste anymore." Lilith fleetingly wondered who those subjects had been, and whether they had died in the spasms of venom poisoning.

"I've even tried myself, but you … you're the only one who can reach him." Sam's voice was flattering, even respectful as he continued. "I know you must have heard him in your dreams and in your venom trance. Only you can find him now. Come with me, please. Help me bring him back."

Sam reached into the car and pulled out a vacuum flask. He unscrewed the lid and a plume of dry ice wafted into the air with a puff of exhalation. He pulled out a tiny vial.

"If you come with me, this is yours."

Lilith reached out a hand for it, but Sam held it out of her reach.

"What is it?"

"Inland taipan."

Lilith gasped and the hairs on the back of her neck prickled, her skin rising in goosebumps. The inland taipan had the most toxic venom of any land snake in the world, ten times as venomous as the Mojave rattlesnake. The venom was also a legendary hallucinogen, incredibly dangerous but also rumored to give the user an experience out of time.

"You'll see the other side, Lilith. You'll experience pleasure unlike any you have before. Just come with me tonight and learn more. If you choose to leave later, then of course you can go back to your old life."

Sam put the vial back into the vacuum flask and sealed

the top again. He walked around to the passenger side of the car and opened the door for her.

Lilith saw a new future in his eyes. One she wanted to be a part of. She had spent too long in the labs, clinically milking the snakes, reducing them to chemistry. She was easily replaceable by any other lab technician. But Samael offered a chance to be part of something greater. She had glimpsed the Great Serpent, and now she would tear down the veil to reach him.

And she wanted that venom.

Lilith got into the car.

They headed south until they reached a private airfield. A helicopter sat waiting, the pilot ready for takeoff.

"I'll bring you back if you change your mind," Sam said.

She walked towards the chopper. "I'm ready."

* * *

Grand Canyon Snake Valley Retreat, USA

Two hours later, they landed at a private helipad and Sam helped Lilith from the helicopter onto a path that led towards a lodge. The wind blew her hair about her face as they walked up the path. Artful spotlights in cactus beds lit the lodge in a subtle manner, giving the wood and stone a mottled effect that made it almost blend into the rocky ground.

"The Colorado river winds like a snake through the very earth of the United States," Sam said, as he led her into the lodge. It was stark inside, the walls decorated with a few chosen pieces. An Aboriginal dot painting of the Creation Snake. An enlarged photo of the head of a green mamba, the brilliant color bright against the white wall.

"Come outside." Sam beckoned and Lilith followed

him out to a wide wooden deck that stretched out over the edge of the Grand Canyon.

The breeze wafted the night air over them, bringing the scent of sagebrush and ocotillo, the heady aromas of the mesa. Lilith stepped closer to the edge and looked down into the darkness below. The black deepened as the valley fell away before her and Lilith held the edge of the railing to steady herself as her vision adjusted. It was a long way down.

Sam came and stood behind her, his breath tickling her neck. Lilith wanted him to touch her, craved his lips on hers, but there was a question in her mind.

"How did you find me?" she asked softly.

"Viperex is my company," Sam said. "I heard the call of the Great Serpent when I was deep undercover in Africa years ago. I was drugged and scared, tied up in a cell, under threat of execution by terrorists. But the King of Snakes calmed me and when I made it out of there, I returned to the US and started Viperex."

He put his arms around her and she could feel his arousal against her back.

"The company attracts those who feel drawn to the serpent, and I let vials of venom be released for the mithridatists. I wanted to find those who could take it. Those who could take all of it."

He brushed her hair away from her neck and kissed her softly.

Then he bit down and she shivered at the sensation of his sharp teeth on her bare skin. He lifted his head and turned her to face him, his eyes dark with longing.

"I've been watching you for so long, Lilith. When the Babylon tablet was uncovered, I knew it was time."

Her name was soothing on his lips and as he bent to her, she closed her eyes, giving herself to the serpent within.

CHAPTER 4

London, England.

ONCE THEY WERE OUT of range of the lab, Morgan put a hand out and stopped Jake in the corridor. "Are you sure you're OK with this mission?" she asked, acutely aware that not so long ago, Jake had been bitten by a nest of vipers in the hunt for the Gates of Hell. The poison had left him on the edge of death and she knew it had broken something in his mind too, a phobia of snakes re-awakened from his childhood in South Africa.

Jake looked down at her, the corkscrew scar above his left eye crinkling a little as he smiled. His brown eyes were warm and inviting, like the first chestnuts of autumn. Morgan trusted him implicitly, but she couldn't let his phobia jeopardize the mission or their lives.

"Something happened when I was in New York," he said quietly. "I haven't told you, or anyone, the details." He shook his head in disbelief. "To be honest, I'm not sure how much of it was real. But you know I came back changed, you saw evidence of that in India. My body has healed and my mind too. I can't explain it, but –"

Morgan put a finger up to his lips, stopping his words. "If you're sure you can handle the whole snake thing, then I'm happy." She moved her hand to his chest, acutely aware of how close he was. She could feel the beat of his heart, slow and steady, and smell his pine forest aftershave. "Most of what I've seen with ARKANE has been inexplicable anyway," she continued. "If we ever have time to stop and think too much about it all, we'll both go nuts."

Jake smiled and put his hand over hers. "Maybe we can go nuts together."

A noise came behind them in the corridor. They broke apart quickly and walked away to get their gear for the mission.

* * *

Berlin, Germany.

Morgan shivered as they walked the back streets of Berlin towards the Pergamon Museum. The night air was cool and a light rain fell. She pulled her leather jacket closer about her as the sound of laughter drifted out of an all-night bar as they walked by.

"Fancy a drink?" Jake said, his voice low.

"Absolutely." Morgan smiled, wishing that they could just forget everything for a night. Jake raised an eyebrow and she gave a rueful smile. The apocalypse waited for no one. "But I guess we'll have to leave it for another time."

The city was young, a party town full of start-ups and trendy bars, but affordable enough that the tech and art scenes still thrived. Like London and Paris, Berlin never slept. But at this time of night, it was at least quieter, and they remained in the shadows as they headed towards Museum Island on the River Spree.

Morgan and Jake were no strangers to breaking and entering, but Martin had assured them that one of the local ARKANE agents would meet them at the museum and take them to the Ishtar Gate. They crossed a pedestrian bridge, turning away from the grand main entrance to walk down the side to a goods delivery door. A figure stood in the dark, the glow of a cigarette by his side. He raised a hand in greeting as they approached.

"I'm Christoph," he said, shaking their hands. "Berlin office."

He was young, Morgan noticed with a rueful smile, even though his hipster beard made him look older. His eyes weren't yet lined by the years and there was no evidence of pain in his body as he moved to open the door for them. She felt the scar from the demon's claw throb at her side and, for a moment, the exhaustion of India threatened to overcome her. The darkness made her want to sink down and sleep in a corner of this quiet place.

They walked into the museum along a service corridor, their footsteps echoing in the dim hallway.

"So, you're here to see the Ishtar Gate?" Christoph asked.

"We don't know what we're looking for exactly," Jake said. "But we have a stone tablet from Babylon that dates to the same period so we're looking for cuneiform inscriptions that might match."

Christoph stopped at a doorway. "This way." He grinned and Morgan couldn't help but smile at his infectious enthusiasm. "Brace yourself."

He pushed open the door and they stepped into a gigantic open space with high ceilings. In front of them stood a massive three-sided edifice, a reconstruction of the ancient Greek Pergamon Altar from the second century BC. Spotlights from below touched the faces of Olympian gods battling giants on a sculpture frieze. It was a piece of classical history brought to a modern world, a juxtaposition of the past in a city that surfed the web into the future.

"Pretty cool place to work, huh." Christoph led them to the right of the altar into another chamber dominated by a two-story marble structure. It loomed over them in the semi-darkness and Morgan was just able to make out ornate friezes covered in bulls and flowers.

"This is the Market Gate of Miletus," Christoph said. "We go through it to the Ishtar Gate. Come." He beckoned them to follow him through the middle arch.

As they stepped through, Morgan thought she heard something clang further out in the museum. It was faint and neither Christoph nor Jake seemed to hear it. But she still checked her gun in its shoulder holster. After some difficult moments in India, she wasn't going on a mission without a weapon for a while.

She stopped and listened for a moment but all was quiet again.

Christoph turned on more lighting in the room ahead.

"Wow!" Jake was clearly impressed and Morgan hurried to catch them. She emerged into another room, through the middle of the Ishtar Gate. After the dark night and the cool white marble of the ancient Greek monuments, the stunning colors of the edifice filled her vision.

The glazed bricks were cobalt blue, the color seemingly unfaded by time. It was decorated with bas-relief dragons and aurochs bulls in gold, symbolizing the gods Marduk and Adad. A flower frieze ran around the base, each petal perfectly rendered.

"It was constructed around 575 BC by King Nebuchadnezzar, the eighth gate to the inner city of Babylon," Christoph explained. "These are mostly the original bricks."

Morgan stepped closer to it, running her fingers lightly over one of the dragons. To think that Nebuchadnezzar himself had seen these bricks. She shook her head. It was truly amazing.

"You wanted cuneiform. Well, there is something strange on the side. An inscription that has puzzled Near Eastern scholars." Christoph led them around the side of the gate and pointed at a cuneiform inscription above a pattern of dots.

"The dots could be constellations?" Jake bent closer.

"Yes, they thought of that," Christoph said, "but there were no star patterns like this in ancient times."

"But did they check for when the stars might be in this alignment?" Morgan asked.

Christoph frowned. "I'm not sure, I'll have to find out. But there's something else. Down here."

As he bent to the lower bricks, a sound of movement came from the room beyond. Then a short exclamation of pain as someone tripped, wrong-footed in the dark.

Morgan and Jake pulled their weapons out.

Christoph froze. "I don't know who else could be here," he whispered. "But I'm sure it's fine, just one of the curators."

Morgan glanced quickly around. They were tucked into a corner out of the main line of sight, but if anyone walked through the gate, they would be seen. Perhaps it was just a night watchman, but something made her uneasy.

"I'll deal with it," Christoph said. Before they could stop him, he walked back out into the main hall. He pulled a notebook from his jacket and began to write something, looking up as if in surprise at the noise from beyond the gate.

"Hello," he said. "I'm just catching up on some research before the tourist horde arrives later. I wasn't expecting anyone else to be here."

He walked out of sight between the main pillars.

Round the corner, Jake nudged Morgan. "We've got to get out of here," he whispered, gesturing towards the darkness of the halls beyond, where they could just make out looming statues of Assyrian gods. "That way."

Morgan pulled out her smart phone and took a few silent pictures of the top inscription and the bricks that

Christoph was about to explain. There was no time to figure out what they might mean and no way of getting the bricks out of the gate.

Then she peered round the corner.

Christoph backed into the main hall, his hands held up as if in surrender. He spoke in rapid German. Morgan knew enough to understand he was offering to help with anything they needed.

A man came into view, black hair pulled back into a ponytail and one side of his face drooping and disfigured as if he'd had a stroke. A tattoo of a serpent wound up and around his neck. He held a Glock in front of him, the gun pointing at Christoph's face. Two more men walked out behind him, one of them holding a large bag.

Morgan ducked back out of sight, gesturing for Jake to get down low. They could take the three men out between the two of them, but a firefight in central Berlin and bodies piled up in this eminent museum wasn't quite what she'd planned for tonight.

Plus it would hold them up, and she really needed that drink.

The voices faded a little and Morgan guessed that Christoph was leading the men round to the other side of the gate to look at an alternative inscription. She stuck her head out slowly. Sure enough, they were out of sight.

She indicated to Jake to stay low. They ran quickly and silently around the back edge of the hall, ducking down behind a table with a replica of the ancient city of Babylon as the men emerged behind them.

"Wo ist es?" The gunman's voice was harsh and threatening now.

"Diesen Weg, bitte." Christoph's tone was placating, and Morgan guessed he would have to take the men around to where they had been standing only seconds before.

The group walked in front of the table.

Jake tensed behind her, readying himself if they needed to fight.

Morgan held her breath as they passed and she heard the brush of one man's shoes on the stone by her head.

So close.

"Hier. Schau." The relief in Christoph's voice was palpable as he must have realized they'd moved. But they would be seen easily if the men turned around.

Morgan looked up. The dark corridor was only meters away.

They would have to sprint for it, and she only hoped the men were more concerned with the bricks than with following them. She reached back and squeezed Jake's hand, letting him know to be ready.

She peeked under the table. The men gathered around the inscription and the man with the bag unzipped it, revealing power tools inside.

Morgan ducked low and ran into the darkness, Jake right behind her.

"Scheisse!" A voice rang out in the hall behind them and then the pinging of bullets on stone echoed through the corridor. Morgan raced away down the south wing, along the edge of the Processional Way, past stelae and cuneiform tablets, winged statues with curled beards looking down as they passed.

"Sie waren nur Studenten," Christoph pleaded, his voice fainter now. *They're only students.*

Morgan could only hope the men believed him.

"This way," Jake whispered and they ducked down a side corridor towards a fire exit. They charged through the door and out into the dawn.

As they ran through the streets away from the museum, Morgan wondered what was so important about the inscription. Why were the men so desperate to take it?

CHAPTER 5

Grand Canyon Snake Valley Retreat, USA

SAM'S PHONE BUZZED IN the balmy night. He unwound himself from Lilith's sleeping form and padded out to the deck to take the call.

"I've sent pictures." Krait, his second-in-command, was gruff as ever. "That should be all you need. If you want the actual bricks, we're gonna have to tear them out the wall. I've got myself a hostage in case we need more time so I can do it, but we'll have to hurry."

"Give me a minute to check the resolution." Sam could barely contain his excitement. Finally, they were so close.

He ended the call and went to his wall screen, logged onto his secure email and opened the images that Krait had sent. The brilliant blue of the Ishtar Gate bricks filled the screen, a series of strange dots superimposed over them. Then the other brick was revealed. A cuneiform inscription he had never seen before.

He called Krait back. "It's enough. Get out of there and wait for me to call with where to head next."

Sam padded back into the bedroom and gently shook Lilith's shoulder. She opened her eyes and smiled up at him, a languid look of satisfaction on her face from their earlier time together. He bent to kiss her and her tongue flickered over his lips. Part of him wanted to take her again. But there was something far more important for them to do now.

"It's time," he whispered.

She gasped, her eyes widening in anticipation of the venom he had withheld.

"I have a room prepared." Sam handed Lilith a robe to tie about her naked body. "Come."

The sanctuary sat at the very corner of the lodge, with a wall of glass that gave a 180-degree view over the Canyon and a ceiling that opened to the stars above. The lights were dim and as they walked in, Lilith sensed something else there.

She smiled as she heard the soft rattle.

All around them in the walls were snakes in individual habitats. A desert striped whipsnake, a common king and a beautiful wandering garter snake. She would enjoy handling these another time, but right now she craved the venom trance.

Lilith sat on a pile of cushions facing the open glass wall, looking out towards the Canyon. She settled herself, taking long, deep breaths to prepare.

"The shamans call it spirit walking," she said. "Others call it astral projection."

Sam nodded as he prepared the dose, drawing the inland taipan venom up into the syringe. Lilith watched the level fill, higher than she had ever taken before. It would be intoxicating.

Or it would kill her.

She bit her lip in anticipation, speaking softly to calm herself.

"Each time I've seen things I couldn't know of, visited places I've never traveled to. Each time I hear the voice of the Great Serpent more clearly."

Sam turned to her. "I believe you," he whispered. "Hear him now. Find him so we can bring him back to his rightful place."

He walked towards her with the syringe.

"I prefer to administer it myself," Lilith said softly. He nodded and laid it down gently next to her on a tray. He placed the images from the museum by her side and she fixed those images into her mind. Sam moved back into the shadows, out of her line of sight.

Lilith waited, breathing in the night air, letting her mind reach out into the world of reptilian awareness.

In the moments before she injected, she always questioned her motives. There was a great tradition of mithridatism and her purest reason was surely pragmatic. As a scientist, she worked with snakes and inoculating herself against a possible bite was practical. She had survived once, but that didn't guarantee she would make it through next time. The little death of each tiny shot was protecting her future.

But she knew it was more than that now.

She no longer denied her addiction, but how else was she to rip through the veil to the other side of perception? How else could she tear the world from her eyes and see clearly? This physical realm was just one part of the whole and the venom pierced it.

In the beginning, the serpent tempted Eve with fruit from the Tree of the Knowledge of Good and Evil. This was her temptation even now, for when she took the venom, she saw beyond reality.

She put on the tourniquet, tightened it and quickly injected herself, dropping the needle. It clanged in the tray. Sam let out a sharp intake of breath behind her and moved forward to help. Lilith put out a hand to motion him away.

She shut her eyes, wanting to feel every second of the rush.

The burn was hot, stinging, right on the fulcrum of pleasure and pain. The venom shot through her, spreading like fire through her veins. Everywhere it touched became as molten gold. Her blood sang. She was on fire as the heat curled through her belly, down to her sex.

Lilith began to undulate on the cushions, her hips writhing as she felt the serpent rise within her, taking control of her body. She lay back on the cushions and looked up at the stars, her mind expanding into the night sky above.

Then she felt His touch upon her.

The Serpent of Serpents called her name with a deep longing. She tilted her head to hear Him better as He told her of what she must do. His sibilant hiss vibrated inside her skull as she flew out of her body into the stars. Her breath was forced from her chest as the air rushed past.

Then she was diving back down towards an ocean, drawn forwards by a mysterious force.

She plunged down into the waves, cold seeping into her skin as she felt herself inhabit the body of a sea snake. She was drawn down into the violence of the deep, passing creatures that preyed on the unsuspecting. As the water darkened, she saw bioluminescence, winking lights of anglerfish and dragonfish predators.

A five-foot-long frilled shark buzzed past, baring its rows of razor-sharp, three-pronged teeth. A living fossil, the eel-like shark was rarely seen. Lilith shivered as it passed and she continued down into the abyssal zone.

Deeper still, a dumbo octopus swam past, its ear-like fins swiveling towards her. Part of Lilith's conscious mind logged how deep she was. This creature was considered an extremophile, one of those that lived at extreme depths of over 10,000 feet below the sea.

A plume of what looked like smoke caught her eye as it erupted only meters away. A black smoker, a hydrothermal vent spewing out superheated water.

Near it, she saw something rectangular. It looked manmade in this alien environment and she felt a jolt of recognition.

Then something flashed from the dark.

Lilith saw a long snout like a rhino's horn and rows of nail-like teeth. A goblin shark. The creature rushed towards her, teeth bared, and she pulled out of the trance, panting and sweating.

She was suddenly back in her body, back in the lodge, back in the air above the canyon. She shivered uncontrollably as she gulped air into her lungs. Lilith hugged her arms around herself, trying to warm her skin after the experience of submersion.

Sam knelt next to her and pulled her close. "It's OK. You're back now." He rocked her back and forth and rubbed her arms until her shivering subsided. He helped her to drink a little water as she recovered.

"How long was I out?" she whispered.

Sam glanced at his watch. "Nearly two hours. I was worried."

Lilith turned to him, saw the concern in his eyes. "You needn't have been. I heard His voice. He led me to the depths. He's ready to emerge."

"Where?"

"Deep in the ocean. I recognized some of the species, so we should be able to triangulate the position using the museum images as a starting point. I need to check."

Sam handed her his tablet computer. Lilith searched Google for the marine creatures she had seen.

"Definitely the Pacific." She paused, then tapped away on the screen again. She felt certainty settle within her and then smiled. She opened the Maps application, turning it so Sam could see.

"There. The Mariana Trench, the deepest part of the ocean."

Sam nodded, and she saw no doubt in his eyes.

"Ready yourself," he said, pulling out his phone. "We'll leave as soon as we can."

* * *

Berlin, Germany.

As first light dawned, Morgan and Jake found a park and hunkered down behind a closed coffee shop. Jake video-called Marietti while Morgan sent the picture of the bricks to the Director and Martin.

"We were interrupted," Jake said when they connected. "Another group arrived, men with guns. We couldn't stop them, but we got a picture of an unusual inscription. Morgan's sending it over now."

"I'll get Martin working on it." Marietti frowned. "Did you see this other group?"

"One of the men looked like he'd had a stroke," Morgan said. "He also had a snake tattoo winding around his neck with green and red scales."

"We'll search the criminal databases for him." Then Marietti frowned, recalling a memory. "I knew of a man with a similar tattoo once, but the scales were green and yellow." The Director shook his head with regret. "He was one of us once, but terrorists took him in Africa while on a mission, tortured him under the influence of hallucinogenic drugs. After he stumbled out of the desert and made it back, he was a broken man and resigned from ARKANE. He calls himself Samael, although back when we worked together, he had another name."

"Samael means Venom or Poison of God," Morgan said. "An archangel from Talmudic scripture, a seducer and a destroyer, considered both good and evil." She paused. "Also known as the Angel of Death."

"Indeed," Marietti said. "In the Kabbalah, Samael was said to be the serpent who tempted Eve, who seduced her and fathered Cain. He then became the consort of Lilith,

Adam's first wife, and had demon children with her."

"Happy families indeed," Jake said.

"Wait a minute," Marietti said. "I'm going to get Martin in on the call."

Martin came on the line, his shock of blonde hair standing up in clumps. He had a tendency to pull it as he thought. And he did a lot of thinking.

"I've checked this second inscription from the gate against the database. I'm still checking the locational data, but it's brought back something else I can't understand."

Morgan heard confusion in his voice, which was strange because Martin had designed the ARKANE database, hacking into the world's most secret archives to cross-reference across cultures, religions, languages, and even time. There was little he couldn't find out.

"There's only one other example of this image I can find. An unusual destination indeed."

CHAPTER 6

Western Pacific Ocean, above the Mariana Trench.

A BANK OF CLOUD FORMED a dark curtain on the horizon, turning the ocean to ink.

"We have to turn back," the captain said. He gestured at the weather report. It showed a gigantic storm approaching from the northeast. "It's too dangerous. We can't deploy the ROV in this. We're heading back."

Sam turned and nodded to one of his bodyguards. The man pulled a cell phone from his pocket, thumbed a few buttons and then turned the screen. The captain paled at the sight.

"No," he whispered.

"Your wife and son will be fine as long as you help us find what we're looking for," Sam said. "They haven't been hurt … so far. If you help us, you'll be able to retire on the cash bonus. But turn back now, and my men will gut your family like the fish you ate last night."

The captain nodded slowly. "Then we have to hurry. I need the coordinates."

"Start preparing for a dive," Sam said. "I'll get what you need."

* * *

Lilith sat at the very top of the boat, above the captain's deck. There was a private viewing area up here with reinforced glass that gave a 360-degree view of the ocean. As the research vessel rolled with the gigantic waves, the room dipped towards the water, swaying back and forth. She had sat here for the whole trip so far, hearing the hiss of the Great Serpent in the sound of the waves. They were getting closer, she could feel it.

She remained in a state of trance, a light edge of intoxication but Sam carefully monitored her dose. If she could just get hold of the vial …

As a scientist, Lilith understood that venom blocked the acetylcholine receptors in the brain to produce an altered state of consciousness. But the mechanism for how it worked no longer concerned her. It was a drug, pure and simple, and she craved the insight it brought her. Each time the venom entered her bloodstream, she was catapulted into another realm, her senses heightened to exquisite perception.

She heard Sam's footsteps on the stair and her heart beat faster in anticipation. She wanted his touch on her skin, but she craved the venom high even more.

"It's time." He entered the cabin, bracing himself with the handrails against the roll of the boat.

"I'm ready," she said.

He prepared the dose, triple what she had taken before. Lilith knew it was a risk, but she snatched it from him, injecting herself and then lying back with a sigh as her mind took flight.

* * *

Lilith's eyelids flickered and it seemed to Sam that the woman behind the green eyes disappeared. She swayed, her head tipping back as the venom took hold. She shuddered, first gently, then with violent convulsions that turned into writhing.

Had he given her too much this time?

Sam put more cushions around her to contain her movements. Moments later, she began to calm.

Then her mouth opened and she hissed, a low sound that vibrated through Sam's chest.

"Ssssouthwest," she whispered. "See the signs."

Sam wanted more, something that might help further. But Lilith's body sagged and she collapsed unconscious. That was all he was going to get from her right now. But it was enough to get them started.

Sam brushed Lilith's hair back from her face. Her skin was smoother somehow, with the pearlescent look … of scales, perhaps. He pushed away his guilt at what Lilith was becoming and left her prone on the cushions. He would come back up later to see if she was alright. He only hoped she would survive the dose. After all, he would need her again soon. He would not risk his own life, even to channel the Great Serpent.

Back down in the captain's cabin, the rain hammered on the windows, a staccato beat above the throb of the engine. Sam watched as the crew launched the small Remote Operated Vehicle with a splash into the whitecapped waves.

"The little one's fastest," the captain said coldly. "If we find anything, we'll send down the Big Boy to bring it up. Ted here'll be your guide to the deep." He turned his back on Sam, pointedly ignoring him.

Ted, the ROV pilot, sat close to the screen. He used a joystick and manual controls to drive the ROV through the water as it submerged.

"The water is almost as cold as ice further down," he said, "but then there are hydrothermal vents that shoot out superheated water close to 700 degrees Fahrenheit. The black smokers belch minerals from the core of the earth, but the water can't boil because of the water pressure down there, over 155 times that of the surface. There are creatures living in that hell, thriving on the extremities of what we thought possible."

"Like what?" Sam asked, as he scanned the screen for anything that could be considered a sign. What the hell did Lilith's words even mean?

"Like these awesome giant amoebas, xenophyophores, the size of a man's fist. There's millions of them, like the zombie horde." Ted's enthusiasm bubbled over. "There's an underwater volcano too, with a full-on lake of molten sulfur. It's such a cool place."

"There may be even more than you know about down here," Sam said quietly.

Minutes passed into hours and Ted fell silent as the ROV camera saw nothing in the water column except the occasional deep-water prawn and jellyfish.

The darkness of the storm encroached and the captain finally snapped. "We have to get back. How long do you want to watch the emptiness go by?"

Sam whipped around, a snarl on his face. "As long as it takes, old man. Think of your precious family and wait, or I will take their eyes for your impudence."

"Oh, my. Look at this." Ted's voice was tinged with awe. "I've never seen anything like it."

Sam turned back to see the screen filled with writhing sea snakes of all colors, dancing in the water, undulating together. Their heads all faced towards the deep.

"This is more than weird," Ted said. "They shouldn't even be around here. They're solitary creatures but this is like a swarm. Oh man, this is so cool."

"Follow them down," Sam said.

Ted pushed the joystick forward and the ROV dived

amongst the writhing snakes, moving faster into the deep. There were thousands of them, tiny ones that darted in front of the camera and huge, thick, long ones that slowly headed deeper.

"Holy crap," Ted said as he watched the fathometer reading. "I've never taken her down this far."

"Keep going."

Minutes later, they reached a seamount covered in writhing serpents, the dying snakes convulsing on top of the already dead, a sacrifice to the deep.

"What are they doing? What's attracted them here?" Ted wondered aloud.

"Take the ROV closer," Sam said. "There's something on top."

As they drew closer, the outline of a large rectangular shape could be seen. It was still covered by piles of snakes, but through the gaps between their bodies, Sam could see what looked like stone.

"Bring it up." The voice from the door was cold and clear.

Sam turned to see Lilith standing there, her green eyes fixed on the screen, her titian hair loose about her face. The silk dress she wore was moulded to her body and as she walked towards them, it was as if she undulated like the sea serpents in the depths. She exuded sex appeal and Sam felt a tightening in his groin. He wanted her, and he could tell by the way Ted shifted uncomfortably on his seat that he felt the attraction too.

But there was also something terrifying about her eyes. They were cold as emeralds, the pupils narrowed to almost vertical slits.

Snake eyes.

"Do what she says," Sam snapped at the captain.

The crew hurried to launch the bigger ROV with grabber arms that would attach balloons that could lift even the heaviest of deep-sea discoveries.

Ted attached the mini ROV to the rectangular object and then piloted the larger vessel down to meet it. He attached balloons to the corners, then manipulated the controls. The balloons began to inflate.

Slowly, the object lifted from the seamount.

The dead snakes fell away, revealing the shape of a sarcophagus, a massive stone box covered in encrusting life and the sludge of the deep. As it rose, slime dripped off it to pool in the waters below.

The captain came to stand close to the screen. "Are you sure we should bring that up here?" he whispered.

"Yesss, it's time." Lilith fixed her green eyes on the man.

He gulped and backed away. "I'll ready the deck for cargo."

The sarcophagus ascended slowly from the deep ocean but, finally, broke the surface by the side of the boat, held up and buffered by the balloons. The waves were high now, the storm almost upon them. The crew battled the driving rain and rolling movement to attach a winch and drag it onto the deck.

The ancient stone was covered in pelagic sediment, a mustard-yellow viscous ooze composed of shells, animal skeletons and decaying organisms that had sunk down to the bottom of the ocean. It smelled of sulfur and rotten fish and the stink of dead snake carcasses. Sam covered his face, trying not to gag as he bent to it. He could just make out carvings under the sediment, twisting in the undulating curves of a serpent. He had waited so long for this, but now he was apprehensive. The next steps were unknown.

Lilith stood grasping the boat's rail in just her thin dress, oblivious to the cold, her eyes fixed on the casket. As powerful waves crashed onto the deck, she walked forward and gently placed her hands on it.

She bent and laid her head upon it, eyes closed, her left

ear pressed to the ancient stone, as she listened for something within. Sam marveled to watch her so transformed, so self-assured in the face of the chaos around them.

After a minute, she stood upright again, her dress soaked through, revealing her slender frame. The wind whipped her hair about her face, her green eyes a reflection of the dark ocean around them. She was beyond a woman now, Sam realized.

She was a goddess.

For a moment, he doubted his purpose. He had thought he could use her to find the power he sought, but now he wondered who was really in control.

Suddenly she stumbled, her legs wobbly on the rolling deck. He went to her and grasped her arm. Her skin was freezing, goose-bumped from the chill water.

"It's quiet inside," she whispered in her own voice, her eyes suddenly normal again. "I can't hear him."

"We need to get the casket back to shore," Sam said. "You can take the venom again then." He led her away from the sarcophagus as the men on deck moved to strap it down for the trip home. "Come, rest now. Sleep, and soon we'll be home."

Lilith leaned against him and he half-carried her into their cabin, helping her out of her wet clothes and into bed. Her naked body glistened as she turned away to sleep. Behind her neck, just below her hairline, he saw scales. He brushed her hair over them and stroked her forehead.

"Sleep now," he whispered. She gave a half smile as her breathing shifted into unconsciousness.

* * *

As the captain steered towards home, finally heading out of the storm, Sam went back out on deck. He walked to the sarcophagus and put his ear to the stone. He could hear nothing but the whoosh of the ocean beneath the boat, the slap of the rain on the deck and the engine motor. But there had to be something inside. The prophecy foretold it.

He had to be sure.

He brushed away the remaining dead snakes that hung on the edge of the sarcophagus, and then scraped the stone free of algae along the top half. There were indentations along the edge, carvings reminiscent of cuneiform and underneath, what looked like Greek.

He scraped the pelagic sediment from the front of the sarcophagus, needing to be sure. The Roshite scriptures told of a seal that would unlock the burial chamber. He pulled a small ebony box from his pocket, carved with the whorls of a coiled snake. It had been passed down for generations, believed to be the seal. He opened it and lifted the amulet out, checking the carvings on it with those on the sarcophagus.

His heart beat faster and a smile spread across his lips as he found, with relief, that they were the same. This was indeed the resting place of the Serpent of Serpents.

But as he brushed away the remnants of the deep, Sam found that there were seven indentations in the stone, each with a separate carving.

He had only one seal. So where were the others?

He headed inside to call Krait. It was time for the next phase.

BBC NEWS REPORT

The spate of extreme weather conditions across the globe continues this morning. The most powerful hurricane to hit Florida in living memory made landfall last night, leaving hundreds of thousands with no power and several hundred people dead.

In Taiwan, a super-typhoon lashed the coast, destroying property and causing chaos at airports.

In New Zealand, aftershocks continue to pummel the North Island after an earthquake measuring 7.1 on the Richter scale occurred deep off the northeast coast.

In Ecuador, a double earthquake has left thousands dead and many thousands more homeless as aid workers scramble to reach those affected. And in Great Britain, more than one hundred flood warnings have been issued as torrential rain and flooding pummel the country.

Some are taking the strange weather as a sign of the times, pointing to the imminent End of Days. Pastor Louis Masterson of Tallahassee stood on the steps of his church in ankle-deep water, palm trees whipping about his head, as he spoke to reporters. "As Luke's gospel, chapter twenty-one says, there will be strange signs in the sun, moon and stars. And here on earth, the nations will be in turmoil perplexed by roaring seas and strange tides."

As politicians call for calm, scientists explain the confluence of freak weather events as being due to a series of super moons combined with an incredibly rare lunar cycle.

CHAPTER 7

Ouidah, Benin.

MORGAN SHIELDED HER EYES against the bright sun as the *zemidjan* motorbike-taxi sped through the outer limits of the city. Tamarind and jasmine trees lined the streets. People walked along the dusty roadside, deftly avoiding the motorbikes and stray dogs as they headed for the central market. Only a few days ago, she and Jake had been back in Africa, further east in Rwanda, and now they were both in this sliver of a country in French West Africa.

Here in Ouidah, the landscape was marked by a dark past. The oldest area of the city was filled with the elegantly crumbling architecture of empire, the relics of wealth built on the backs of slaves. They passed an eighteenth-century Portuguese fort built to administer the slave trade, and several grand Afro-Brazilian houses built by emancipated slaves. Those lucky few who made it back from the Americas.

"This was once the Route des Esclaves, the Slave Route," the taxi driver explained, clearly used to ferrying tourists around. "You can still trace the final walk made by thousands of slaves to the coast of the Atlantic Ocean. There was once a Tree of Forgetfulness here. The slaves would walk around it nine times in order to forget their old life and family, so they could be happy in their new life across the ocean."

They drove on to a desolate beach fringed by palm trees on the edge of the Gulf of Guinea, where a gigantic arch stood in shades of ochre, black and white.

"The Door of No Return," the driver said. "The last stage of the journey to slavery."

Morgan felt an urge to look at the monument more closely. "Can we stop a minute?" she asked.

"Of course, it is a sacred place."

The driver pulled over and waited as they got out. Jake wandered away, silent with his own thoughts. Morgan took off her shoes to feel the sand under her feet as those chained would have done before boarding the ships. So many died on the way over, the rest dying across the ocean, far from those they loved. She looked up. On the top of the arch, chained slaves marched towards stylized ships with heads bowed. On each side of the memorial, voodoo gods stood to welcome the souls of dead slaves back to their homeland.

Morgan looked out at the ocean, the waves turquoise in the shallows and darkening towards the horizon. The air smelled of salt and fish caught and processed further down the coast. Tears pricked at her eyes as she considered the many thousands taken from here to bleed and die on foreign soil.

Of course, it was unthinkable to unravel how history might have panned out if the evil of the slave trade had not happened at all. Like much of man's inhumanity to man, once events had been set in motion, the resulting effects echoed through history. The Shoah – the Holocaust – had the same resonance for Jews. Without Hitler's abomination, would there be a modern state of Israel? Without the slave trade, would there have been a black President of the USA?

Morgan felt an echo of her own history here, a people uprooted from their homes and treated like animals across the seas. But when she returned to Israel, she felt it was her home. She wondered how the diaspora Beninese felt when they came back generations after slavers took their ancestors to the Americas. There had also been native people here who were complicit in the slave trade, tribes raiding other tribes for slaves to trade with the westerners. Like the *capos*, Jews who helped guard the death camps. Just as in the rest of life, there was good and bad on both sides. No race came out with completely clean hands.

One of the resulting effects of the slave trade had been the transplant of voodoo beliefs to Haiti and Brazil, and Morgan felt the throb of those vibrant cultures here. Voodoo was the state religion in Benin, followed by sixty percent of Beninese. In Haitian voodoo, Damballa, the creator loa, was represented by a serpent and there were water loa in serpentine form. Morgan wondered what they would find in the city of Ouidah.

They got back in the taxi and drove into the town. They passed Zomachi, the Remembrance monument, built in 1998, part of a ceremony to ask forgiveness from God for the sins of the ancestors who aided in slavery.

Eventually, they stopped on the edge of the market. Morgan leaned out as they passed a voodoo stall to look at a pile of ritual objects. The air reeked of decomposition and a musty dryness. She tried to work out what she was looking at.

Suddenly, Jake screwed up his nose. "Oh, no. That's a hippo foot. Gross."

Once she realized they were animal parts, Morgan could make out a dog's head, what looked like a pickled chameleon, and a crocodile snout, all used in voodoo ceremonies.

"But no snakes," Morgan noted. "We have to go further."

They finally arrived outside the entrance of the Python temple. Morgan had been expecting something grand and ornate, like the Indian Hindu temples, but the bricks were plain, a muted pink with white panels. *Temple des pythons* was painted in blue and red over the metal doorway, and she could see simple huts with straw roofs inside the compound.

The driver pointed behind the temple to trees beyond.

"Hundreds of years ago, King Kpassè of Ouidah was defeated in a war and he fled to the forest to escape those who came to capture him. The Royal Pythons saved him and in their honor, he built the temple here and another beyond in the forest. The python represents the voodoo god Dan, and people here will not kill a python for fear of bad luck striking them." He smiled and waved them towards the gate. "I will leave you here. May the blessings of the Great Serpent be upon you."

Morgan and Jake paid the driver and walked into the compound. Three huts with painted doors flanked a central open area, each door propped open to provide a glimpse of the snake pits within. In the center was a sacred Iroko tree, under which a couple of pythons curled, languid in the heat of the day. A man sat in the shade of one of the huts, relaxing under a straw awning that kept the strong sun off his head.

And off the python curled around his shoulders.

He looked up at them with curiosity in his eyes as they entered, but he didn't move. He just nodded and Morgan returned his greeting with a smile. The man fingered a set of *Fa* beads, threads of eight wooden disks, just as a Catholic would count his rosary. But Morgan knew that the *Fa* beads could be cast and the positions read to interpret the will of the gods. Mediums channeled spirits here in Benin, and possession was almost normal during worship. The supernatural was part of everyday life.

They walked into one of the round huts. It was dark and smelled musty. The sound of slithering over straw came from the pit in the center. As Morgan's eyes adjusted to the dark, she could see the pythons that lay on the steps around them, a few on the top levels and more in the pit below.

Jake stayed near the door.

"They look pretty chilled," he said. "So what exactly are we looking for?"

"Something that looks similar to the image from the Ishtar Gate." Morgan walked around the outside of the pit, her hands running over the smooth walls. Jake walked in the opposite direction, both of them checking for any hidden niches. But the walls were plain and smooth. There wasn't even an altar. Perhaps they offered food directly to the snakes, Morgan thought, glancing into the pit.

She wasn't scared of snakes particularly, but she had no desire to get any closer if they didn't have to. They walked back round to the doorway.

"Perhaps we should –"

Morgan's words were interrupted by voices shouting from outside.

A gunshot. A sharp howl of grief.

They ducked down and Morgan looked around the edge of the door. In the courtyard, four men stood with guns trained on the old man who sat in the shade. One of the pythons lay unmoving before him, blood seeping from its body.

The leader of the group was the man with the snake tattoo she had seen in Berlin.

And there was no way out of this room.

"Where are they?" the tattooed man said, his voice brusque as he addressed the old Beninese in English, then in French. "Qui est là? Où se cachent-ils?"

"He's asking where we're hiding," Morgan breathed in Jake's ear, and she saw his own concern matched hers.

They only had seconds before they were discovered.

A snake caught Morgan's eye as it moved within the

deep pit, writhing over the others. There were holes in the sides of the pit, cool alcoves for the serpents to hide in when the sun became too high.

"Are you really sure that you're over your snake phobia?" Morgan whispered.

Jake followed her gaze to the pit of snakes. "I guess we're going to find out."

They heard the old man talking as they clambered down into the pit. "Je pourrais savoir. Je pourrais pas savoir." *I might know. I might not know.*

Then the sound of the *Fa* beads cast upon the earth. Morgan realized that he was asking the spirits for direction.

In her concentration on the sounds, she narrowly missed putting her hand on a python's head. It hissed, flickering its tongue at her, tasting her passing.

Jake placed his feet gingerly between the coils, heading for one of the alcoves out of direct sight of the door. He seemed to be doing OK so far, but then he wasn't lying in a confined space with the snakes yet. Morgan was acutely aware that he had almost died the last time she'd gotten him involved with snakes. She hoped he was right about being healed in New York.

A moment later, the old man's voice came again.

"Il n'y a personne pour vous ici."

There's no one here for you. He wasn't giving away their position, but it was a small compound and the men could still find them soon enough.

Moving slowly so as not to disturb the snakes too much, Morgan knelt down and then lowered herself to lie flat, curling around the serpents that were already down there. Jake was in the alcove next to her, his face white, sweat pooling on his brow. His eyes were wide. All the hallmarks of fear.

"They're pythons," she whispered. "They shouldn't bite you."

"Just squeeze me to death." He mouthed the words and Morgan smiled. He was clearly managing.

They both lay flat, easing into the alcove as the sound of men searching came from above. Morgan heard footsteps. Then the sound of breathing from the lip of the pit.

CHAPTER 8

Morgan imagined the man looking down into the pit. If he caught a glimpse of them, they'd be easy targets.

And if Jake freaked out, they'd be caught for sure.

"A lot of damn snakes, but there's no one in here," the man called from above, his voice getting softer as he walked away towards the door. Then the scuff of boots as another man joined him.

"Samael will be properly mad if we don't find the second seal. It must be here somewhere."

Morgan frowned. The second seal? That implied they had one already and there were more to be found.

"Il y a un autre temple." The voice of the old Beninese filtered down from the courtyard. "Dans la foret. Là bas."

He must be pointing them to another temple in the forest behind. She and Jake would have time to escape if the men went looking.

Moments later, the footsteps receded. The men were gone.

Morgan and Jake slid from their respective alcoves. Jake wasn't sweating any longer, and he even stroked one of the pythons with a bemused smile as they clambered out. Morgan wondered anew what had happened in New York, but it seemed that whatever it was, it had worked. And for that, she was grateful.

They tiptoed to the edge of the hut and peered around. The courtyard was empty except for the old man sitting in the shade, looking down at the *Fa* beads in the dirt in front of him.

He turned his head and beckoned to them, the other hand still stroking the python that curled around his shoulders.

"Les esprits me disent de vous montrer quelque chose. Viens."

"He says that the spirits have told him to show us something," Morgan said, as they walked back across the courtyard.

The old man pulled himself upright and lifted the serpent from his shoulders, laying it gently on the ground in the shade. He shuffled ahead of them to a scruffy prefab building, what looked like a maintenance shed in the corner of the compound.

He pushed open the door and beckoned them again.

They followed him in and he pointed to the corner of the dirt-floored hut.

"Creuser," he said, motioning a digging action.

Jake raised an eyebrow at Morgan and picked up a spade that stood propped against the wall. After digging down a few inches, he struck metal. He looked up for permission. The old man nodded.

Jake dug his fingers into the soft dirt and pulled out a metal box. Something rattled inside.

He opened it to reveal a round stone carved with intertwined snakes.

"The seal?" Morgan lifted it out, judging its weight. It matched the markings from the Ishtar Gate. It was just three inches in diameter, the perfect size for sealing important documents … or a sarcophagus.

"Les esprits disent que vous devez prendre cela et aller."

The old man glanced behind him at the forest. "Maintenant, et rapidement."

The spirits say to take this and go. Morgan turned to him, the seal in her hand.

"Are you sure? This must be precious to your people."

The man must have understood her expression, if not her words. He put one hand on her head as if to bless her, and with the other, he curled her hand around the seal.

"We should get going," Jake said. "The others will be out of that forest soon if they can't find anything."

"Thank you," Morgan said as they passed the old man at the doorway.

He nodded. As they walked away, Morgan heard him whisper, "Ne me remerciez pas, ma fille. Le sceau est une malédiction et non une bénédiction."

As they left the compound, Jake turned to Morgan.

"What did he say as we left?"

She clutched the seal more tightly as they hailed a taxi. "He said not to thank him. The seal is a curse, not a blessing." She looked up at Jake. "I think this is only the beginning."

* * *

As soon as they reached the airport, Morgan and Jake found a quiet corner and called ARKANE HQ.

As they recounted what had happened at the temple and the man's words, Marietti paled, the color draining from his cheeks. "The Seven Seals. It must be."

"What do you mean?" Jake asked.

"The book of Revelation talks of Seven Seals at the End Times," Morgan said. "As each one is broken, they release terrible things upon the earth, including the Four Horseman of the Apocalypse. Most would say they are allegory, but perhaps they are actually real."

"The seals open the sarcophagus," Marietti said, his voice faint. "The rumored resting place of the Great Serpent, bound for a thousand years."

"But all seven are needed to open it, right?" Jake noted. "So let's get the rest and destroy them before this serpent crew have them all."

Marietti nodded, and then shook his head as if to clear it. "You're right. I was forgetting myself. For so long, we have tried to keep these prophecies from coming true. But in the end, we are but pawns in the long game of eternity. Martin, do you have any leads on the other seals?"

Martin tapped away on the screen. "I've got the database running now, looking for images from ancient civilizations that relate to serpent gods. There are so many, so I'll need to narrow them down."

"Start with those that are closer to Babylon physically," Morgan said. "The Australian Aboriginal people have a creation snake but I can't think that a seal would be hidden so far, millennia before the continent was discovered by westerners."

Martin nodded. "I think I have a place for you to start. Your old stomping ground, Morgan. Considered by many to be the beginning of the End of Days."

* * *

Grand Canyon Snake Valley Retreat, USA

A military helicopter lowered the crate into a massive hole dug into the ground outside the lodge. Wooden slats protected the ancient sarcophagus as it creaked with the strain. Wind whipped the loose earth into flurries around it, obscuring what was within.

Sam's men guided it down into the hole and onto a

custom-made trolley. From there, they wheeled it along and down into a specially prepared vault.

Lilith stayed close, her hand resting on its side, her concern like a mother hen for her chicks. She hadn't let it out of her sight on the journey back. She knew something was inside, although that something didn't have a heartbeat and she hadn't heard His voice since the boat.

But then Sam kept the vial of venom close to him and he wouldn't let her have any more until they were sure of the next step. Until he had the other seals.

She glanced over at him as they rolled down the tunnel. He was weak, spineless.

He was not worthy to open the sarcophagus. The serpent had chosen Eve in the Garden of Eden, as He chose Lilith now. The curves of the serpent were her curves. Samael could try to tame the serpent's power, but only she would channel it to glory.

She would have to be careful of Sam, keep him close for now. But in the end, only one of them would stand in front of the Serpent of Serpents.

* * *

Sam noted the change in Lilith's posture as the sarcophagus rolled towards the vault. Her steps became a glide and she hovered close, her hands fluttering near the stone as if protecting something precious. He felt her eyes upon him and the hair on his neck prickled with awareness. Could he still trust her? His hand moved instinctively to the vial within his jacket pocket. As long as he controlled her addiction, he could control her.

His phone buzzed. Krait's name appeared on screen.

Sam turned back down the tunnel to answer the call.

"Someone else was there in Ouidah." Krait's voice was

harsh over the line, his anger barely contained. "The seal was taken from under our noses. We returned from the forest empty-handed, clearly sent on a wild goose chase, to find the guardian of the temple gone. There was a hole dug in one of the huts. Something was taken." He paused. "I'm wondering if the supposed students in Berlin were those seeking what we are looking for, too."

Sam frowned. He hadn't considered that others might be on the trail. He had backing from powerful groups affiliated with the Vatican, extremist Islam and fundamentalist Jews. They all had a vested interest in bringing forward the End of Days, so it wouldn't be any of them. There was another organization, though … He'd been expecting them.

ARKANE.

Memories came flooding back and he walked back out into the dust of the mesa to clear his head.

With his Egyptian-American heritage, Sam had been an agent based out of ARKANE's New York office, sent to work undercover in Egypt. His mission had been to infiltrate a cell, part of an antiquities smuggling ring. Powerful relics were being passed to terrorist cells in the Middle East, traded as occult objects believed to have great power in the battles to come. Hitler's elite troops had sought artifacts that would influence the supernatural realm; now, those who sought to expel the US and Britain from the Middle East were seeking the same. Sam had believed he was doing the right thing … until that fateful day.

Sam sighed and touched the locket around his neck. It was hidden under his clothes, a sign of weakness he didn't let others see. He thought of Leila, her smiling face, her dark eyes filled with love. But she was lost to him now, her body broken and buried by a targeted bomb from his own country.

* * *

They had been out in the desert of Libya, having finally been invited to one of the terrorist camps where the exchange of archaeological objects took place. He had been gathering the final evidence needed to take them down.

A high-pitched whistle, screams and then blackness.

Sam's hands shook as he remembered the terror of waking beneath the crushing sand. His rising panic as he couldn't breathe. Clawing his way up to the surface. Screaming for Leila as burned ash rained down on body parts strewn around him.

He hadn't found her remains, but as one of the few survivors and a stranger, he had been swept up by the surviving militants and taken to a camp deeper in the desert.

The torture was sweet punishment after his loss. He longed for death, begging the men, goading them. They injected him with snake venom and during his hallucinogenic visions, he told them whatever they wanted. He roamed the earth above his body in those times, taken higher by the drugs. It was then that he heard the voice of the Great Serpent for the first time.

His captors didn't believe his story of ARKANE and its quest for supernatural artifacts. They wanted American military spies, hostages they could trade, and in the end, men they could behead on video. Another propaganda win in an unequal war.

When they dressed and hooded him, then dragged him to another room, he had expected it to end with the hack of a jagged blade.

But they sliced away his bonds.

When the hood came off, there was only one other man in a room dimly lit with lamps. A tray of sweet mint tea sat in front of him with two small glasses, typical of Arab hospitality.

"Drink," the man said softly. He sat down across from Sam. "Here, I will show you it is fine." He poured two glasses and sipped out of one. "It's good."

Sam reached out a trembling hand. The first sip was nectar on his parched throat. The man watched him, his dark eyes interested but patient. When the tea was finished, he called for more.

"In the depths of your torture, you called for Leila." The man pulled a phone from his pocket and showed a picture. "Is this her?"

Sam felt tears prick and his voice wavered. "Yes. She died in the drone attack."

"A drone attack by the US government." The man's words were matter of fact. "Your government."

Sam lifted his chin. "I'm half-Egyptian. My father always talked of home, but he was driven out by extremists. So to whom am I meant to be loyal?"

The man chuckled and shook his head. "We live in mixed-up times. Migration and inter-marriage make us all brothers and sisters and yet we still tell stories of murder and injustice by the Other." He leaned forward. "But you are not who we thought you were. The hallucinogens we gave you were based on snake venom. I've used it in smaller quantities myself for the journey trance, but you were able to take much higher doses."

The man reached for his phone again and played a snippet of sound. Sam heard his own voice, or what sounded like his voice, but it hissed and spat.

"It isss time. The Great Serpent awakes. Ssseek his resting place."

"What does it mean?" Sam asked, even as he felt a deep resonance within him, a desire to heed the voice.

The man took a deep breath and grasped Sam's hand. "The thousand years are ended."

* * *

A night bird called and Sam found himself back in the mesa on the edge of the Grand Canyon. The wind rustled through the rocky landscape and the chirp of the cicadas anchored him back to the land. That long night of discovery in the Libyan desert had led to this day. If only his mentor Farid had lived to see it. But the Brotherhood of the Serpent now awaited his word, for if the Great Serpent emerged, the End of Days would be ushered in.

The world would be remade.

ARKANE couldn't stop him now because the seals were in reach. Their organization was weak, pathetic, nothing in the face of the powerful allies he had. There were only a few places where the seals could be. He would send Krait to the next location to intercept them.

CHAPTER 9

Israel.

MORGAN SMILED AS SHE and Jake drove north from Tel Aviv along the coast road. The air smelled of salt from the Mediterranean Sea and the fresh scent of pine trees. The sky was blue above and she relished the sun on her face. After the flight from Benin, it felt good to be in control of how they traveled. She pressed down on the accelerator of the two-seater convertible, reveling in the speed and the wind in her hair. She felt at home in England now, but when she returned to Israel, she knew this place would always be the closest to her heart.

After their parents divorced when she was little, her twin sister Faye had remained in England with their Christian mother, and Morgan had been brought up here in Israel with their Jewish father. The twin sisters were close now and Morgan loved her niece Gemma deeply. But she knew that Faye would never understand the part of her that was Israeli, the part that thrilled to be out in the desert, to be on the knife-edge of conflict and to be part of a history that still played out its daily ritual of blood vengeance. England was undoubtedly safer, but Morgan felt more alive here. Her father was gone now, buried in a graveyard further north in Safed, the Kabbalah heart of Israel, but she still had friends here. She still felt the throb of history in every kilometer they drove.

"Happy to be back?" Jake said from the passenger seat, as he leaned his head back to catch more sun.

"Surprisingly so," Morgan said. "I know it was a little crazy last time we were here." In the hunt for the Key to the Gates of Hell, they had criss-crossed Israel, even diving in the depths of the Dead Sea before Jake had been evacuated from the salt pillars of Sodom in the Negev desert further south. "But hopefully there'll be less shooting this time around."

"So tell me about Megiddo," Jake said. "Why is Martin so sure that there's a seal there?"

"First of all, it's the biblical Armageddon," Morgan replied. "The site of the final battle in the End Times, described in Revelation chapter sixteen. The archaeological dig there has found twenty-six layers of ruins, so it's likely the apocalyptic reputation comes from the number of times it was destroyed and rebuilt due to its strategic location."

They turned off the main highway, heading east towards Nazareth.

"But it's what they've found in the excavations that we're here to see. Serpent cult objects from the Bronze Age, when snakes were used as part of the Canaanite religion."

The sun was low in the sky by the time they drove into the Jezreel Valley and on to the kibbutz at Megiddo, past olive and citrus trees that filled the air with a fresh scent. There was a bigger settlement nearby but they were staying in the more original housing, kept for tourists who wanted a taste of how kibbutznik had lived in the early days of the state of Israel. This particular kibbutz had been founded in 1949 by Holocaust survivors from Hungary and Poland.

A young woman walked out of the guest accommodation as they pulled up. Her long brown legs peeked out of denim shorts and she had a red checked shirt tied around her waist. Her dark hair hung loose around her face, and

Morgan caught a glimpse of her own younger days. She and her husband Elian had spent many happy nights up here in the north, when he was off duty from fighting at the front and she could get away from her job as a military psychologist for the Israeli Defense Force.

Their nights had been filled with feasting and song and laughter and they had thought they would live forever. But Elian had died in a hail of bullets in the Golan Heights, defending the country they both loved. Would he even recognize her now? Morgan wondered. She had changed so much since joining ARKANE, and her beliefs and loyalties had been challenged at every turn. She was a world away from the young woman she had been back then.

But she still loved this land with fierce passion.

She and Jake got out of the car.

"Welcome to our home. I'm Rachel," the young woman said. "I'll be your guide to the Tel."

"Is there time before it gets dark to visit the site?" Morgan asked.

Rachel nodded. "Of course. Your organization called ahead. I've arranged for the snake artifacts to be brought to one of the viewing rooms so we can see them after the dig visit." She smiled. "And of course, you'll want to be back for dinner." The smell of garlic and the sound of sizzling came from the kitchens beyond. "My mother is the chef here. Her Orez Shu'it is to die for."

"White bean stew," Morgan explained to Jake as they grabbed their bags from the car. "You'll love it."

"So let's get over to the dig and then hurry back. My stomach's rumbling already."

They jumped in the back of a battered, dusty truck and Rachel drove them the short distance to the dig.

"The city of Megiddo guarded a narrow pass on the ancient Fertile Crescent," Rachel explained as they parked up by the visitor center. "That's why it was so sought after.

There's been a settlement here since the early Bronze Age, around 3500 BC. We've uncovered part of what's considered the largest structure in the Near East, so this was a powerful city."

The sun was setting as they got out of the car and looked out across the Jezreel Valley, the deep green of the lush National Park alive with birdsong.

"Amazing to think of the battles that have been fought here," Jake said, shaking his head. "We think our current empires are so important, but we all disappear with the march of time."

"Megiddo has stood for 5000 years," Rachel said. "Come, I'll show you the main dig before it gets too dark."

She led them down some steps into the dig itself, where a path wound through levels of the city, with plaques indicating the time period of each.

"The city gates would have been here," Rachel said. "This area is called the Ivory Palace, as a significant cache of ancient ivory objects and jewelry were discovered here. Some of them are in the visitor center."

She walked on until they reached a circular pit with a metal staircase attached to one side.

"This shaft goes down twenty-five meters and then extends seventy meters west to the spring that kept the city alive when it was under siege. It's an incredible feat of ancient engineering and enabled the city to survive much longer than others of the area."

A metallic smell came up on the air from the pit, a tang of water deep below. Morgan peered down into the dark. How many feet had descended these stairs, she wondered. Had her ancestors trodden these very paths?

"It's too dark to go down now," Rachel said. "But would you like to see the serpents?"

"Definitely," Jake said.

They walked back to the visitor center and Rachel took

them into a special, atmosphere-controlled room. She swiped her security pass against the door and they went in. Two long bronze snakes lay in the center of a white table, their surfaces pockmarked with age. Morgan pulled on a pair of white gloves and picked one up. There was nothing on it that matched the seal. The other one was just as plain.

Disappointment welled within her. "Where were the snakes found?"

"In the Bronze Age stratum." Rachel turned to a replica of the excavations, cut through to show the different sections. "Over here. The dig is still ongoing but there are a number of other objects associated with the serpents, currently undergoing testing."

"We're looking for a round stone, carved like a seal. Have you seen anything like that?"

Rachel frowned as she thought. "I'm not sure, to be honest. The dig is jam-packed with objects from all eras. You can't help falling over things, but I can take you into the research area tomorrow when the curator is back on deck. He doesn't like people in there without him." She smiled ruefully. "He's my PhD supervisor, so I have to stay on his good side."

"Of course," Morgan said, with a sideways glance at Jake. "Tomorrow, then."

They drove back to the camp and joined the kibbutznik around the campfire. They shared a meal together and Morgan enjoyed the camaraderie that stemmed from a country surrounded by enemies, people who worked the land together and turned the desert into bountiful produce. The Orez Shu'it was everything Rachel had promised, chased down with a fruity, full-bodied Syrah from the Golan Heights. There were moments when Morgan forgot the mission and just enjoyed being here with Jake and new friends in the country she didn't live in anymore, but still called home.

***

Later, as they headed back to the guest accommodation, Morgan took Jake's arm, walking close to him through the olive grove.

"We can't wait until tomorrow to see if there's a seal in the research area," she whispered. "If it's there, we need to take it and they're hardly going to let us do that during office hours."

Jake nodded. "See you at two a.m., then?" He grinned and the moon caught his corkscrew scar as he turned towards her. "A little night adventure, just the two of us." He pulled Rachel's pass from his back pocket. "This might help."

Morgan smiled. "Good one."

They stopped for a moment and she wanted to lean into him, to feel his hard body against hers. Being back in Israel made her brutally aware of the shortness of life, of how fleeting pleasure could be. And this place, this Armageddon, cast a shadow over her, filling her with a foreboding she couldn't shake.

Morgan pushed the feeling away, and they walked on to the huts.

"See you later," she whispered as they entered the separate rooms.

***

In the darkness of the olive grove beyond the camp, Krait stood over the body of an unconscious Israeli guard. The man was bleeding and hog-tied but he'd live. No point in causing an international incident … just yet.

He waited until the two had entered their accommodation and then checked his camera. With a long lens, Krait had shot photos of the pair laughing with the kibbutzniks around the campfire. He knew they had one seal from Benin and he ached to repay the humiliation of that loss. It wouldn't take long to slice their throats in the dark, or maybe he'd spend more time on the woman.

But he had to wait.

Krait emailed the photos to Samael with a text. *They don't have the seal yet, but it's definitely here. Do you want me to take them tonight?*

He sat down in the darkness, one hand on his knife, itching for blood, and waited for the reply.

CHAPTER 10

Grand Canyon Snake Valley Retreat, USA

SAM LOOKED AT THE photos Krait had emailed, the carefree smiles of the two who held one of the seals he needed. With a word, Krait would finish them tonight and he would hold the seals by tomorrow, one step closer to opening the sarcophagus.

They didn't deserve to touch the sacred objects. They were his by right.

He began to text back, his decision made.

"Ssstop." Lilith's voice was soft but strong. "Let them find the others." Sam turned abruptly to see her standing right behind him. He started at how close she had gotten without him realizing. She had become quieter since they had returned from the deep and Sam felt a rising concern at her growing powers.

But Lilith was not the only presence now.

Her green eyes were empty, the pupils dark and slitted like the snake she had wrapped around her neck, one of the rock pythons from his terrarium. She stroked it with gentle fingertips. Had she gotten to the vial of venom? He needed to be more careful and control her trance states.

"We will take the ssseals when it is time, Samael."

Sam nodded, unsure to whom he spoke. But for now, he could bide his time.

He deleted the text he'd starting writing to Krait.

Lilith stared at him intently, as if she could read his doubts about her.

Sam typed a new message. *Let them find the seal tonight and then follow them.*

Lilith smiled and slipped away, her body undulating back to the stairs of the vault as she headed back down to the sarcophagus. He imagined her lying across it, her flesh against the cool stone. Part of him wanted to go down there and take her against the casket. He would show her what was real life and what was still just dead stone.

But what if she was channeling the Great Serpent even now?

He banished these darker thoughts and turned back to the pictures of the two ARKANE agents. He would let them find the next few seals, but in the meantime, he would find out who they were … and who they loved. He would not leave the next phase to chance.

* * *

Megiddo, Israel.

The moon was in shadow when Jake heard the light tap on his door. He was ready to go in dark clothes, with a small pack containing a head-torch and tools in case they needed them. He opened the door to see Morgan standing outside, her beautiful face alive with excitement, and he smiled at her enthusiasm. For all their missions together, she still made him feel alive.

The last time they had been in Israel together, he had been poisoned by snake bites in the salt caves of Mount Sodom. His phobia was like another life now. The experience underneath New York really had changed something within. Call it a miracle or merely some kind of psychological shift, it didn't really matter, Jake thought. The result was the same. He could be a worthy partner for Morgan again, and for that, he was grateful.

They walked out into the dark together, easy in their silence, and padded out past the kibbutz towards the Tel. They didn't dare drive in case the noise brought the guards, but Morgan was confident they could pass the night security on foot. This was her land and with her training in the Israeli Defense Force, Jake trusted her to get them back into the archaeological dig without a hitch.

It crossed his mind that Morgan didn't really need him; that she could do all this alone.

But then she reached for his hand in the dark, a moment of connection while the night hid their faces. There was something between them that went beyond just ARKANE partners, something they had come close to acknowledging a number of times, but a relationship was impossible with their dangerous lifestyle. Perhaps they really did need each other, though – not just to watch each other's backs, but to keep the other grounded. After all, the things they saw on ARKANE missions would make the sanest person a little crazy. He squeezed Morgan's hand back, hoping that she could feel what he could never say.

They walked together through the olive groves and onto the road. The air smelled of lemon thyme. Clouds covered the moon. Once they reached the perimeter of the kibbutz, they jogged to the Tel site, slowing as they reached the outer gate. The guards weren't in sight, so Jake swiped Rachel's pass and they went inside, heading straight for the research center that they had skipped past earlier.

At the door, Jake tried the pass again. The light flashed green.

Morgan exhaled with relief and they pushed the door open.

Even though the shutters were closed, they put on head-torches with bulbs dimmed, so as not to attract the guards. It was organized chaos inside, a cornucopia to be explored, much like the dig itself. A number of white plastic boxes were piled on top of one another, each with a separate object inside. Rough handmade clay vessels, each a smaller size as they nested inside one another like an ancient Russian doll. Delicate gold earrings next to a seal ring with a fish etched into it. Rows of tiny beads made of gold, silver and carnelian.

"Hmm." Jake bent to one of the boxes. "There are labels on all these, but they're in Hebrew. I have to admit that mine is a little rusty."

"We can't pull all the boxes apart," Morgan said. "It will be obvious that someone has been here." She looked around at the piles. "But I don't see any other way to find the seal unless there's some kind of index."

"Probably computerized. We could get Martin to hack in?"

"No time," Morgan said. "I guess the other option is just to make it really obvious someone was in here. They're going to discover the seal is missing anyway – if we find it – and the longer we're here, the more chance of discovery." She glanced over to Jake. "Let's just not break anything. There's some serious history in here."

They took half the room each and methodically worked through the trays, moving each out the way to see into the trays beneath. Jake noted that Morgan was slower than he was, distracted by the interesting objects she uncovered. When she had first joined ARKANE, she had been an academic and if he was honest, he hadn't considered her an appropriate partner for missions.

But here they were.

He had underestimated her back then. Now he watched her lean closer to one tray, her fingers reaching out as if to touch something. Her blue eyes, the right with a brilliant violet slash, fixed on the object. Then she felt his gaze and turned to him.

"Have you found something?"

"No." Jake shook his head. "I just like watching you."

A smile played around her lips.

"No time for that now," she said softly. "But come look at this. I think this might be it."

Jake walked closer, aware of her slight curves next to him in the semi darkness. Her head-torchlight played over a grey lump of what looked like hardened clay, the color of storm clouds over water.

With gentle hands, Morgan picked up the clay piece and turned it over. There was a round seal set inside the lump. The carvings were faint, but Jake could make out the undulations of a serpent, a different design from the one they'd found in Benin, but similar enough to be related.

"It certainly looks like the other one," Jake said. "It seems strange that the seals are so far apart, though."

"I love how they're part of a diaspora, just like the Jewish people." Morgan smiled. "These ancient objects are passed down through families who move across the face of the earth, taking their most precious possessions with them. It's not so strange. There's been a trade route into Africa for millennia, and there were great kingdoms there long before Europe rose to power. Remember the Pentecost stones, handed down by the Keepers and spread from Iran all the way to America?"

Jake nodded.

"I think the seals will be spread out, too." Morgan ran her fingertip across the clay around the seal. "If you take Revelation as only part allegory, then someone bound the serpent in a pit. Someone sealed it and then presumably made sure the seals were hidden."

"You really think there's some kind of real serpent in a real pit."

Morgan shrugged. "I didn't believe in the literal Gates of Hell until I saw them with my own eyes. Sometimes that night seems like a dream, like it didn't happen, but in my nightmares I still see the dark wraiths."

Jake thought of what he had seen under New York. "I know what you mean," he whispered. "Let's get out of here."

Morgan wrapped the lump of clay containing the seal in a jersey she'd brought with her and put it in her backpack alongside the other one.

Two down, Jake thought. Not a bad start. The question now was where they would look for the next one.

They left the research hut and headed back through the dig, careful to avoid the guards. Once they were out of hearing range, they could talk freely again.

"I think we should just get up and leave early," Morgan said. "If we go tonight, it will raise suspicion."

Jake nodded. "But if we leave before breakfast, we can say goodbye in a civilized manner and be at the airport by the time the research team gets to work and discovers the seal is gone. Good plan."

They headed back to the kibbutz across the fields.

As they crossed the olive grove, Morgan's phone buzzed in her pocket. She pulled it out to see Martin's number on the screen.

"Strange that he'd call this early," she said, answering the video call.

His face was haggard, his features drawn, his eyes wide with concern.

"Morgan, I'm so sorry. Your family has been attacked."

CHAPTER 11

Megiddo, Israel.

MORGAN'S HAND FLEW TO her mouth, tears springing to her eyes.

No, please not Faye. Not Gemma.

After her sister and niece had been abducted during the hunt for the Pentecost stones, she had sworn never to endanger their lives again.

"What happened, Martin?" Jake said, taking control as Morgan sank to the ground in shock.

"It's been quite a night, but don't worry, they're safe now."

"Damn it," Morgan exploded with anger, grabbing the phone back. "You scared me, Martin."

"Sorry. I thought you'd want to know straightaway. We installed a special alarm at the Price's house in Woodstock after the Pentecost stones were retrieved. We have something similar in place for the families of all our agents. It was triggered earlier and countermeasures were successfully deployed."

Morgan looked sideways at Jake when she heard the words, but by his raised eyebrows, he clearly didn't know what Martin meant by countermeasures either.

"Several of the intruders were injured," Martin continued, "but Faye and David, and of course, little Gemma, all escaped unharmed. They're staying in the visitor quarters at ARKANE in Oxford until we can ascertain who attacked."

Morgan remembered her first visit to the labs there, buried deep under the Pitt Rivers section of the Museum of Natural History. It was a fascinating place, and she imagined little Gemma walking wide-eyed through the exhibits at night. But then she thought of her sister Faye, who had survived once before. The sisters didn't speak of any lasting trauma, but it had to be there.

"It looks like we might have disturbed the viper's nest," Jake said. "It has to be Samael and the Brotherhood of the Serpent. They must know of us."

Morgan nodded.

"Are you sure no one can get to my family now, Martin?"

"Of course, we have extra security in place. Don't worry."

She sighed with relief. They were safe for now, but Morgan felt the weight of guilt bear down on her. She considered herself to be independent, beholden to no one except maybe her cat Shmi, back in Oxford, who even preferred the neighbor these days. She and Jake took risks with their own lives for ARKANE, but she had thought her family would be safe. But the night she had seen Faye on top of a pyre, about to be burned as an offering at Pentecost, still haunted her nightmares.

Now her choices had put her family at risk again.

The truth hit Morgan hard. How could she continue at ARKANE when she placed those she loved in danger?

"We've had word from an ARKANE source in the Philippines," Martin continued, breaking into her thoughts. "A deep-sea scientific vessel reported bringing up a large sarcophagus from the depths of the Mariana Trench."

His words cut through Morgan. Could the deepest part of the ocean be the pit described in Revelation? Could the sarcophagus really contain the Great Serpent? The scientist part of her would have laughed at something so crazy not so long ago, but now she wondered.

"If Samael has the sarcophagus," she said, "he will definitely want the seals." She looked out into the darkness. Suddenly her land felt threatening, as looming clouds covered the moon. "We have to get out of here."

"Agreed." Jake stood looking out into the fields around them and Morgan could see that he sensed a heightened danger too. "Where should we go next, Martin?"

"Follow the snake motif through history. You need to head to Greece, to the Pythia."

"The Oracle of Delphi," Morgan whispered. "Of course."

"I'll sort out the flights so you can be on your way as soon as possible." There was a tapping on the line. "I can get you out of Haifa tonight. It's only forty-five minutes' drive."

"Can you get Marietti to give the Tel Megiddo authorities a call?" Jake said. "It might help avoid an incident over taking the seal."

"Sure," Martin said. "Safe travels."

Morgan hung up the phone and sat for a moment, breathing deeply to calm her concerns. Her family was safe inside the ARKANE compound. There was no need to worry about them. She could speak to Faye in the morning, so why did she feel so jumpy?

"Are you OK?" Jake hunkered down next to her, his face a map of concern.

She smiled. "Not really, but we have to get going. I'd like nothing more than to fly back home and cuddle my niece, but we have to finish this. If Samael really has the sarcophagus, we have to hurry."

She stood and they walked back towards the kibbutz together.

"I know you're worried, but aren't you also curious to see what's in that sarcophagus?"

Morgan laughed. As ever, Jake was able to dissipate her fears. "You're right. If it really has been buried for over a thousand years, I want to see inside. It's probably just a pile of dust."

Back at the guest accommodation, they packed their things quickly and left the kibbutz. As time ticked towards dawn, Jake drove them towards Haifa airport in the west while Morgan called Faye on the video phone.

Her sister answered within two rings. Faye's blonde hair was loose about her face and her blue eyes were ringed with dark shadows. The twins had inherited opposite features from their parents, Morgan's dusky features from their Sephardic Jewish father, and Faye's Celtic looks from their Welsh mother. But their eyes were both blue, the unusual slash of violet in Morgan's right eye and in Faye's left the only thing that made them look related.

"Oh, Faye, I'm so sorry. Are you alright? How's Gemma? And David?"

Faye smiled a little. "We're fine. I know you want to be here but none of us are hurt, just a little shaken. David was so paranoid after Pentecost, so Director Marietti at ARKANE helped us install safeguards. I'm sorry we didn't tell you but I didn't want to worry you any more than I know you already do."

"For good reason, clearly." Morgan sighed. "I wish I was there."

"I'll hug Gemma for you. She misses her Auntie M."

"I'll be back soon, I promise. Maybe we can go away for a holiday or something together." Morgan knew she sounded desperate, that she was clinging to an ideal of family life that didn't represent their true relationship. There was so much of the past unsaid and unacknowledged, but Gemma was the real bond between them. A murmur came from beyond the screen and Faye turned her head to mouth something over her shoulder.

"We need to sleep now, Morgan, and we'll be fine here. Gemma loves the ARKANE lab, so it will be like an adventure. Stay safe now."

"OK, sleep tight."

The screen went black and Morgan stared at it for a moment. She was relieved to see her family, but bereft to be so far from them. Not for the first time, she felt a twinge of jealousy at the security of Faye's marriage and the love for her daughter.

Was she fated to run around the world trying to stop bad things happening to people who didn't even notice the darkness around them? Would she spend her life chasing demons, only to die alone in some forgotten corner of an ancient ruin?

Jake put his hand on her arm, glancing over from his focus on the road.

"They're alright?"

Morgan nodded. "Yes, they're fine. Let's finish this so we can go home."

Jake shifted gear and they accelerated into the night towards Haifa airport.

* * *

Grand Canyon Snake Valley Retreat, USA

Lilith loved it down here, curled up on the cool stone of the sarcophagus in the darkness of the sanctuary. Although she had to go upstairs every few hours to bathe in the warmth of the sun and renew her strength, she preferred the chill down here. Layers of deep-sea growth had now dried on the casket, giving it a spongy texture and she lay on top of the softness, still and silent.

Waiting.

Listening.

But as much as she tried, she couldn't hear his voice clearly unless she was in a venom trance. Samael said she must wait and he kept the venom close to him, rationing it, keeping her on edge.

Lilith sighed and dangled one hand over the side of the sarcophagus, touching her fingertips to the indentations. Sam had promised the seals would be delivered in time but she felt an edge of unease, a tension in her spine that could only be released by the opening of the casket.

She longed to see what was inside.

Sam did too, but she sensed his distance now. When she had been just a girl coming out of the church that first night, he had been the one with all the power. He had drawn her, hypnotized her as the serpents within the church had. She had felt languid in his arms.

But now … now he watched her when he thought she wasn't aware. And his gaze was more clinical, as if she were a specimen that he should keep in a case, like his reptiles in the viewing room upstairs.

She heard footsteps on the stair and she froze.

Sam entered the chamber, his gait wary. Lilith slid off the sarcophagus and crouched behind, peering around the end. He narrowed his eyes and squinted in the half-light, unable to see her.

"Lilith?"

She could see him clearly in the dark, but his eyes had not adjusted. For a moment, she saw fear in his expression. Fear of where she might be … Of what she might be.

Lilith smiled, relishing his response. She left him hanging for another few seconds before revealing herself.

"I'm here," she said, straightening.

A look of relief flickered across Sam's face.

"The agents have taken the seal from Megiddo and gone to Delphi in Greece." He frowned. "I know you said to leave them. Was that …" His words trailed off and Lilith knew he didn't want to question the Great Serpent.

"What's wrong?" she asked. "You'll be able to get the seals when they have them all."

"I'm concerned," Sam said. "Krait is excellent and he'll track the agents, but …"

Lilith came closer and pressed her body against Sam's. His heartbeat was fast, a pitter-pat underlined by fear. He didn't belong down here, he was a creature of the mesa and the light.

"But?" she asked.

"I need leverage," Sam said. "The woman's family is now in an ARKANE safe house. Krait's men tried to take them but the attempt failed and now they will be doubly wary." He looked down at Lilith and she sensed that he wanted to be far from her, and far from the sarcophagus. "This is something I need to deal with myself."

"You're going to Europe." Lilith smiled.

"Will you be alright while I'm gone?"

"Will you leave me enough venom?" It was the only thought on her mind.

Sam frowned. "I'll leave enough to keep you going, but we need to save the strongest dose for when we have the seals and can open the casket. Don't take it too far, Lilith." He paused. "I need you."

She could tell it hurt him to admit that. She walked away from him to curl again on top of the sarcophagus. "Don't worry. Just find the seals. He is anxious to emerge and every moment we wait, his anger grows."

* * *

An hour later, Sam boarded the helicopter to take him off the property to Flagstaff airport, then on to Phoenix and London. As they banked over the canyon, he looked down at the lodge as it faded into the mesa, expertly landscaped and camouflaged.

He thought of Lilith down there in the crypt. When he was close to her he was confused, but as the chopper pulled away, he felt like himself again. He shook his head at his previous words.

She was no snake goddess, channeling the Great Serpent.

She was just a junkie he had sought out for her willingness to go into the venom trance, to save his own sanity. But when he found what he sought, when he was finished with her, well, she could have all the venom she wanted.

He texted Krait, determined to regain control. *Get me those seals and finish the agents.*

CHAPTER 12

Delphi, Greece.

THE SUN WAS HIGH as Morgan and Jake reached the town of Delphi and drove up towards the ruins of the ancient sanctuary. After snatching a few hours' sleep on the flight, they had taken turns driving north from Athens and now Morgan turned the car into the carpark. She switched the engine off and got out of the car quickly to stretch.

"Oh, it feels so good to move." She rolled her neck and shoulders, reaching her arms up towards the sun before turning to the view.

Delphi perched on the southwestern slope of Mount Parnassus, surrounded by groves of dusty-green olive trees in a landscape that was similar to the Jezreel Valley they had left just yesterday. It felt timeless, a place of spiritual resonance where seekers journeyed to discover their future.

They headed into the ruins, walking through the ancient classical city along the Sacred Way, the main route through the Sanctuary of Apollo. A group of tourists clustered around the remains of a colonnade, some holding umbrellas to shield them against the Mediterranean sun. Their guide talked into a microphone as he waved his hands with enthusiasm.

"This is the *omphalos*," the guide said. "The very center of the world. It is said that Zeus sent two eagles flying from either ends of the earth and where they crossed, right here, was considered the center."

Jake chuckled a little as they passed by. "Like Rome for Christians," he said under his breath.

"And Jerusalem for Jews." Morgan grinned.

"And Mecca for Muslims. Religion never changes, despite the centuries," Jake said.

"There's a lot of serpent symbolism in various religions too. Ancient Greece had Medusa with her hair of snakes and the Hydra, the nine-headed snake."

Jake put his hands in a prayer position and turned his eyes to heaven. "Please God, don't let us have to battle one of those." He stopped by the ruins of a temple. "But I've got to admit that this place is pretty cool."

The remains of the Temple of Apollo perched on the edge of the hill, with its six Doric columns stretching up into the blue sky. Below them, cypress trees dotted the landscape. Life in the midst of sun-bleached ruins.

"So what happened here, then?" Jake asked.

"There was a shrine, an inner sanctum, where people came to seek the prophecies of the Pythia, the priestess considered the Oracle of Delphi. She sat on a tripod seat over a crack in the earth and the fumes gave her visions of the future. Even kings came to ask the gods for help here."

Morgan understood the desire to ask for guidance from some spiritual force. She felt in need of some herself right now.

In many ways, ARKANE gave her exactly what she needed. A constant stream of fascinating new places, ancient artifacts and puzzles, with an edge of excitement and violence that she now acknowledged as an integral part of herself. She'd tried to shut down that side after leaving the Israeli Defense Force, but it hadn't worked. She'd found academia just too boring to focus on that alone, and her private psychological practice had been repetitive cases with no real challenge.

So why was she now considering leaving ARKANE? And what would she do instead?

"How cool is this, Morgan?"

Jake's voice broke through her thoughts and she turned to see him on a lower level, examining the wall below the temple base.

She smiled at his enthusiasm.

If she stayed at ARKANE, would she and Jake remain just friends, always flirting with the subtle chemistry between them, helping each other stay alive?

If she left, perhaps there would be a chance for them to be together. But then he would always be off doing exciting things, and what would she do? Stay at home and wash dishes?

Like Faye.

Her sister seemed happy being a wife and mother as David performed his duties as the pastor of a church. But as much as Morgan sometimes craved that stable life, she knew she'd probably want to kill something within a week or two.

"Come and see. It's a weird wall," Jake called. Morgan clambered down to see what he was looking at.

The stones that made up the platform were cut into polygonal shapes and carved with ancient inscriptions. One of the stones had the whorl of a snake cut into it, a shape similar to the two other seals she carried in her backpack. But this wasn't a seal. It was just a carving on a stone.

Morgan bent closer. There was something else carved next to it.

"What do you think this is?"

Jake bent to look at it, squinting to try and make sense

of the lines. "Maybe a spring? Something to do with water anyway."

"There is a spring here," Morgan said, "where the priestess would ritually wash before entering the temple." She looked at the plan of the ruins and then pointed up to a rocky gorge east of the precinct. "It must be that way."

They walked past the tourists again as they trooped towards the theatre. The semi-circular construction had an incredible view across the valley and Morgan wished they had more time to explore. Instead, they walked onwards towards the Castalian Spring and down a rocky path. Dappled sunlight filtered through the trees. It was a beautiful day, but Morgan felt a prickling on the back of her neck as they reached the bottom. Someone was watching them.

She turned suddenly but there was no one there.

"What is it?" Jake asked, spinning around to look as well.

Morgan frowned. "Maybe nothing, but let's stay alert."

They finally emerged onto a rocky platform that led to the cliff face where two fountains had been cut into the rock within an alcove. A trickle of water came from one.

Jake raised an eyebrow. "That's underwhelming."

Morgan nodded, scanning the area. "This can't be the real place. There's been an ancient spring here since the sixth century BC so this is probably just for the tourists. We need to get to the source, where the origin of power emanated, the most holy place for the serpent." She pointed at a cleft in the rock just around the corner, surrounded by abundant foliage. "That way."

At the edge of the rocky outcrop, they clambered over a low wall and into the dense bushes and trees that hid the cleft in the rock. Jake pushed straight through but Morgan stopped at the edge, turning again as she felt that prickle on the back of her neck.

But once again, there was nobody there.

She frowned and sighed. She usually trusted her instincts, but she knew she was off kilter after the scare with her family. She turned and pushed her way into the trees, finding Jake next to a rocky outcrop.

"Look at this." He stood aside so she could see into the cleft. "It goes a long way back. You think we'll fit?"

"I will." Morgan smiled. "Not sure about you, though."

Jake fake punched her on the arm, sucked his belly in and turned sideways to ease past the rocks. Water dripped down and ferns brushed against Morgan's skin as they twisted up the cleft, eventually reaching the entrance of a cave.

"What *is* that stink?" Jake wrinkled his nose. "It's disgusting."

Morgan bent down to look inside.

"In ancient times," she said, recalling the myth, "the Python was an earth-dragon who made its home here and who became the oracle for Gaia, Mother Earth. But the god Apollo decided he wanted Delphi as his own oracle and killed it. It's said that the priestess, the Pythia, drew her powers from the rotting corpse of the dead snake." She tilted her head to one side and looked up at Jake. "Of course, it could just be bat shit."

Jake snorted with laughter. "Ladies first." He waved towards the entrance with a bow.

Morgan knelt down and opened her pack. She pulled out a head-torch and put it on before crawling into the low tunnel. The stone was wet and it did indeed stink, but within a meter or so, the tunnel expanded out so she could stand. The tinkling of water came from further on. She looked up and the light from her head-torch caught the whorls and loops of a gigantic snake carved on the ceiling. She turned and called back to Jake.

"Get in here and look at this."

Moments later, he crawled in with his own head-torch on and looked up.

"Oh yeah, that's a snake alright."

"And its head points further in."

Morgan felt a rising excitement, a sense that this place was the true sacred spot on the mountain, not the manmade columns of the temples outside. This place was closer to the Gaia, Mother Earth, and closer to her creatures. Closer to life … and death.

She shone her head-torch in the direction of the snake's head and at the back of the cave, there was another hole. They walked over to it.

"This is quite a bit narrower than the entrance." Jake frowned as he shone his light through. "But it's quite short."

"Do you want to stay here while I go on?"

"No way. Where you go, I go." Jake grinned. "Most of the time anyway."

Morgan pushed the backpack ahead of her through the hole and wiggled in. She stretched her hands out in front and pulled herself along while using her feet to push. She tried not to think about the tons of rock above her.

Once in the next chamber, she helped pull Jake through and he collapsed on the floor.

"A little too tight for my liking," he said, after regaining his breath. "It better not get any narrower." Then he looked up and his torchlight played on the walls. "But maybe we don't have to go any further."

Morgan turned to look.

The entire chamber was decorated with carvings, the rock hewn with images of nature. Deer leapt over fish swimming in streams, while birds flew overhead. A cornucopia of nature's bounty. The colors had faded with time but clearly there had been worshippers here more recently. A wilted bunch of wildflowers sat on the edge of a spring. It was just rough-hewn rock with edges discolored by minerals that flowed from within the mountain. But something about it made Morgan's breath catch in her throat. The sound of tinkling water resounded in the cave, a constant hymn to the Creator.

Behind the glistening water, Morgan caught sight of a circular object.

"There, behind the spring."

Jake diverted the flow with his hands, the fresh water splashing over his shoes while Morgan took a closer look.

"It's the seal," she said. "It's a similar size to the others, but the snake is curled in a slightly different way."

"Can you lever it out?"

Morgan pulled a multi-tool from her pack and began to lever the rock from the spring. How long had it been here? Who had put the seals in places sacred to serpents around the world? Part of her wanted to study the stone carvings, to try and work out what their power was. She was fascinated by how old they could be. But part of her wanted to find a way to crush the stones into powder as fast as possible, ending their mission so she could go back home.

The stone popped free and Jake let the spring run in its natural place again. He cupped some of the water and brought it to his mouth.

"Tastes good," he said. "Despite the smell."

Morgan took a sip. Perhaps the Pythia of ancient Greece had drunk from this spring long ago. She smiled to herself at the romantic thought.

"Let's get out of here," she said, after a moment.

Jake eyed the tunnel and Morgan caught the look on his face.

"I'll go first and help you through again, you big baby."

She pushed the backpack in again and crawled after it. Jake huffed behind her, his breathing shallow as he tried to make his substantial size much smaller. She emerged into the cave tunnel.

"I need a hand," Jake called from back inside, his light flickering around her.

Morgan placed the backpack with the seals on the cave floor, needing both hands to help him through. She squeezed halfway back into the tunnel and reached for him.

"Grab my hands and I'll pull while you twist."

As she tugged, Jake wriggled and by inches, he made his way through the tiny space.

Then a noise came from behind her in the cave.

Morgan couldn't see, couldn't turn around quickly. Her startled eyes met Jake's.

"Go, I can make the last few inches," he said.

Morgan shuffled backwards into the cave and turned her light to the floor.

The backpack was gone.

With all three seals inside.

The sound of running footsteps came from the tunnel that headed towards the entrance. She sprinted towards the noise, her light bobbing through the cave. Behind her, she heard Jake swearing and a thud as he pulled himself out of the tunnel. Then he joined in the chase.

Morgan turned a corner and saw a man silhouetted at the low entrance.

He ducked under.

She heard a click and then a series of popping noises. She knew the sound from her time in the Israeli Defense Force. She threw herself back and down on the floor.

"Down, Jake!" she shouted, as the cave exploded around her.

CHAPTER 13

As the dust from the explosion settled, Krait emerged from the cypress tree he had sheltered behind. He crouched down and checked the backpack for the three seals and smiled as he examined each in turn.

Samael would be pleased.

He glanced back at the now-buried entrance to the cave. There was no way of checking whether the agents inside were still alive but they should at least be trapped and injured, hopefully dead. Whatever state they were in, they were delayed and he had the seals. But the noise of the explosion would bring rescuers soon enough, so he needed to get away from here.

Krait texted Samael. *I have them. Where shall I meet you?*

He walked back down the rocky path towards the carpark where site officials busied themselves for a rescue operation. Tourists bustled around taking pictures of the drama, confusing the scene. Krait walked into a pack of them, a concerned look on his face, well-hidden amongst the many nationalities represented. Using their cover, he made his way back to the car. As he drove out the carpark, joining the throng heading away from the mountain, his phone beeped with an incoming message.

Excellent. Come to London.

* * *

Inside the cave, Morgan stirred. She felt a sense of crushing weight upon her as she woke from the blackness. Her head pounded and she tried to lift her left arm.

There was something on it. She couldn't move.

Pins and needles prickled her flesh. A trapped nerve. Not good.

Her right hand was free, though, and she lifted it to her face, gingerly touching her temple where the pain was greatest. Her fingers met sticky wetness and she probed a dripping wound. She winced as she tested the edges but it felt shallow, nothing serious. Her whole body ached but after years in the military and plenty of injuries with ARKANE, she understood her own pain levels. She would be alright – if they got out of here soon.

But what the hell had happened?

Morgan opened her eyes. It was pitch black. The air smelled of tar under the sickening stench of the rotten python, or whatever the hell that smell was. The bastard who stole the packs must have set off an explosion as he left.

"Jake?" she whispered in the dark. "Are you OK?"

A deep groan came from her left.

Then she felt a hand reach out for her. She gripped it and for a moment, they just lay there in the dark, the physical connection all they needed. Morgan took some deep breaths, letting calm wash over her. They were alive. They were together.

"He took the backpack," she said eventually, as she began to feel a little better.

"Of course he did," Jake growled. "But he could have just stolen it. Why the hell did he have to blow us up?" The sound of rocks shifting echoed in the cave. "At least you didn't make it to the entrance, though. Another twenty meters closer and you'd be buried."

Morgan heard the concern in his voice. She remembered the explosion they'd been in at the Palermo Capuchin crypt and how his injuries that night had filled her with the same worry. At least they weren't surrounded by broken bits of mummified bodies in here.

"I can't move my arm," she said. "Any chance you can help?"

"Just a sec." A tiny light flared and then grew in warmth. Morgan saw Jake's face in the light of the yellow glow-stick. "Good job I still have my pack." Jake grinned and Morgan couldn't help but smile back, despite the pain in her arm and her head. There was something primeval in having light in the darkness. It made everything instantly better.

He clambered over the fallen rocks towards her. "Right, let's get you out of there."

* * *

It was another four hours before they heard the clunk of stones being removed and the shouts of voices beyond the cave-in. Morgan had fallen asleep, cradled in Jake's arms, but woke again as he moved at the sound. The pounding in her head made her nauseous and her arm throbbed. Thoughts of her family rose in her mind. Faye strapped to a pyre. Gemma unconscious in the arms of a madman. She knew they were safe, but she longed to be with them.

"Stay there," Jake said, gently stroking her face as he helped her sit back against the cave wall. He rose and went to the pile of broken stone.

"We're in here!" he called through the cracks.

A triumphant shout came back, the words unintelligible, but soon they saw torchlight as the rocks at the side of the tunnel were pulled away.

Jake joined in, hefting stones until he could touch the hand of one of the rescuers beyond.

"Hang in there," the man said. "Here, I'm passing through provisions." He pushed through a parcel and a flask. "We'll have you out soon. Is anyone injured?"

"My friend's arm was crushed in the fall and she might have concussion from a minor head injury."

The rescuer nodded. "We'll hurry."

Jake took the food and drink over to Morgan, pouring hot coffee from the flask and handing it to her. "Here, drink this." He helped her to sip the bitter black and Morgan felt a wave of relief sweep over her. Coffee always helped.

They devoured the sweet pastries together and the sugar buoyed them both as they waited for the tunnel to be widened further.

The rescuers broke through soon after. A medic tended to Morgan's arm, before they scrambled from the cave out into the late-afternoon sun.

* * *

A little while later, Morgan sat in the back of an ambulance. Her arm was patched up and in a temporary sling. Her head was bandaged, and with a full dose of painkillers, plus sugar and caffeine, she was feeling comparatively better. Jake was on the phone to Marietti.

"Yes, the seals are gone but we're just about OK. I think we can travel." He looked over at Morgan and she smiled back, nodding her head that yes, she was alright. "Where do you want us to go next?" He paused. "Right. Later then."

He hung up and turned to her. "Marietti wants us back in London. There are too many options for where to go next. And he wanted me to tell you that your family are still safe."

Morgan looked out at the setting sun over the valley. It was beautiful, a timeless place where so many had come to seek the will of the gods. The smell of olive trees and warm earth lingered on the air. "Let's not rush back."

CHAPTER 14

ARKANE Headquarters, London.

MARTIN KLEIN WALKED AROUND his desk to the wall of his office and examined the colored markers arrayed in a rainbow from light to dark. This called for crimson and cerulean blue. He picked up the particular pens and began to draw directly on the office walls, allowing the critical part of his mind to relax as he shaded and cross-hatched and spiraled across the white.

Despite his many technological tools, Martin had learned that his mind sometimes just figured things out this way. While some people had ideas in the shower, he found inspiration in drawing. It distracted his analytical mind and enabled him to find the most peculiar connections. Of course, his office had to be repainted every few months, or whenever he had solved whatever problem was most pressing. A small price to pay for clarity.

Most of Martin's time was spent immersed in computer code as part of his role as ARKANE's archivist, although he was basically a hacker on behalf of the agency. He had yet to come up against a system he could not get into. His main concern was the knowledge locked away in physical texts and symbolic objects, that which was *not* digitalized.

And that's what haunted him now. Because something was very wrong indeed.

The hunt for the seals was just one aspect, but there were too many other things happening at the same time. The news reported developments daily, an increase in violence done in the name of religion, a sudden influx of natural disasters and death caused by extreme weather, earthquakes and rising oceans.

And then there was the series of blood moons, which drove the fundamentalists crazy as they claimed that biblical prophecies were coming true.

So it had to be one of two things.

Either it really was the End Times, the final days of Earth as humanity knew it and the imminent beginning of a new order ushered in by celestial trumpets and great destruction by the Almighty …

Or, someone was pulling the strings from behind the scenes, engineering a growing crisis that could spill over into something unstoppable. God helps those who help themselves, after all. World War Three would not be sparked by one event, but tensions were mounting. All it took was one significant flashpoint to trigger the end.

Something itched at the back of Martin's mind, and he had grown to trust that feeling. When he had first joined ARKANE, Jake had fondly nicknamed him Spooky for his uncanny ability to find connections in the mass of data and knowledge. Martin was proud of the title and wanted to remain deserving of it. There were few people he valued in the world, and Jake was one of them. Perhaps he would even count him as a friend, although the rules of such a relationship puzzled Martin a little.

He understood his own condition. He'd spent time researching why his parents had been so disappointed with him despite his incredible academic achievements. A PhD from Cambridge by seventeen years old, and yet they just wanted him to get a girlfriend. Asperger's would have been a handicap in any other era but in this technological age, it was a true gift.

Martin understood the world of numbers and code and logic, but he couldn't understand why people behaved the way they did, and why they didn't say what they really meant. ARKANE had been a haven and Director Marietti had taken him in, allowing him to push the boundaries of his gift, accepting him for who he was with no pressure to conform to any societal norm. But then ARKANE was a haven for all kinds of misfits. It suited those who wanted an extraordinary life, not those whose idea of fun was watching Netflix on a Friday night with a pizza and a bottle of wine.

Jake had been friendly from the start, and Morgan … Martin smiled at the thought of her. Morgan seemed to truly understand him. Perhaps there was a touch of his own dysfunction in her fierce independence.

Marietti, Jake and Morgan were his true family and he sensed they were in danger now. He had to figure out what the hell was going on and for once, his computer couldn't help him. All the hacking in the world couldn't find something that wasn't codified in bits and bytes.

He stopped drawing and ran his fingers through his hair, tugging at the roots. Some of the strands came out in his fingers and he brushed them to the floor. It was a bad habit, but pulling his hair out actually helped him think, and he certainly wasn't bothered by what people thought of his appearance.

So far, the picture on the wall undulated with the coils of a massive serpent. He began to draw the various clues they had found around it, and then expanded it into the signs that had appeared in the world. The freak weather events, high tides and super storms that rocked every continent. The sarcophagus found in the deepest ocean, thought by some to be the resting place of the Great Serpent.

But that wasn't all.

In the last weeks, Director Marietti had been targeted

by those who wished to stop him investigating the Babylonian prophecy of the serpent. Because they knew he would send Morgan and Jake to find out more. They knew he would try to stop whatever had been set in motion. The bomb that had blown open the vault was directed with deadly accuracy and only someone on the inside would know the vault's exact location.

What if the whole India mission had been planned to keep ARKANE occupied while the End Times progressed towards its inevitable conclusion? If Marietti had been killed, ARKANE London would have been crippled. So, who had known about all of this?

Something pricked at the corners of his mind.

Martin went back to his computer and checked the inventory of the vault, recently updated after the damage from the bombing. Amongst the priceless objects and artifacts of supernatural power, there were also records from the earliest days of ARKANE that he had discovered in the aftermath of the explosion. The original annals, the founding documents. Records that were so old they had to be read in a climate-controlled atmosphere.

Records he had yet to digitize.

Martin scurried from his office and headed down to the lower levels in one of the lifts. The whole area had been reinforced with extra security, so he scanned his retina and then typed in a passcode to get the lift moving.

At the basement level, the door opened onto a corridor reinforced overhead. It wouldn't stop a bunker-busting bomb, but it would prevent pretty much anything else getting through.

Martin walked to the thick metal door overlaid with ancient wood. It was inscribed with occult patterns that once upon a time might have made someone think twice about entering. But now the door was criss-crossed with modern steel bars and protected by a high-level electronic security system updated after the last attack and protected with a steel cage. Martin typed in another code and then placed his finger on a pad. It was sensitized to certain individuals within ARKANE; if their heartbeat was too fast and fell outside the normal range, the system went into security lockdown.

Martin calmed his breathing. The door clicked open.

He stepped inside the vault and breathed in the rarefied air as he walked past individual rooms containing treasures that the world thought lost to history. Part of ARKANE's job was to recover powerful artifacts and hide them here, away from the clutches of those who might use them for evil. Morgan and Jake had placed the Pentecost stones here, the Devil's Bible, the staff of Skara Brae and other objects that needed protection.

Or that the world needed protection from.

But there were also records of ARKANE, the annals of its birth and growth, lists of Directors and the agents who had given their lives for the secrets down here and yet could never be acknowledged in public. Martin hoped that the Director would never have to inscribe Jake or Morgan's name in these books.

He walked to the back of the vault to a special area filled with towering shelves loaded with great leather-bound books. He found the right date range and then used the wheeled ladder to climb a meter up. He ran his finger along the cracked spines until he located the book he wanted and then pulled it down. The dates 1880–1900 were etched in gold on the spine.

The escalating news cycle from Israel had been bothering Martin the most, as biblical prophecies stated over and over again that the Jews must be back in their ancient homeland for the End Time events to occur.

It could be argued that the Chosen People had been protected over the many generations they had been persecuted, broken apart and spread across the world in a diaspora that spanned the globe. But despite oppression by Egypt, Assyria, Babylon, Persia, Greece and Rome in ancient times, and from much anti-Semitism, pogroms, death camps and more in modern times, the Jewish people had survived. Perhaps God really did have a hand in their survival, but Martin had his suspicions that there was more to it.

He found the page he wanted, an account from 1897, when ARKANE representatives had been at the first Zionist Congress supporting Theodor Herzl in the goal of reclaiming the land of Israel. He looked at the names, recognizing the title of a Cardinal from the Vatican. Not unusual by itself.

But then Martin found something curious.

Minutes from a meeting between the same Cardinal and the Mufti of Jerusalem, a Muslim. There was nothing concrete, only veiled references to a long-buried cistern and a joint project that would safeguard the future of both religions even as Israel expanded.

Martin narrowed his eyes. There must be more.

He climbed the stairs again and pulled down more books, pushing them to the floor with a series of crashes. He clambered down and sat cross-legged, pulling each one onto his lap as he scanned for more such meetings.

A note from the Imam of Iran thanking the ARKANE Vatican liaison for support. A receipt for services rendered during the Gulf War. A picture of a multi-faith group of men in front of the statue of Laocoon, with the priest and his sons dying in the grip of writhing serpents.

The more he read, the more Martin realized that the Vatican and ARKANE seemed to be part of a bigger plan that also involved fundamentalists on both the Jewish and the Muslim sides.

They were sworn enemies, but they also desired a

new world order, albeit of a different shade. All wanted to hasten the apocalypse. What if the mortal enemies engineered a world-ending battle together?

Could anyone stop that?

Until the thousand years were ended. The words spoken by Cardinal Krotalia echoed around his head. He needed to get this to Marietti.

Suddenly there was a clunk and a click. The lights went out in the vault.

Martin spun around, his hands still on the book. The vault door was closed. A hissing came from nozzles above. He had installed the upgrades to the security himself.

A poisonous gas would flood the vault in the next three minutes.

CHAPTER 15

ARKANE vault, London.

MARTIN SCRAMBLED TO HIS feet and ran towards the door, slipping on the polished floor in his haste.

"Stop. I'm still in here!" he shouted, hoping it was a mistake. Maybe Marietti had come down for something. He reached the massive door and pounded upon it with his fists, but no sound came from outside. Whoever had shut him in was gone.

The hissing sound grew stronger as the gas escaped from the nozzles above.

He coughed and covered his mouth, bending lower to the ground to keep his face away. If he succumbed before he could get out, then the ARKANE vault would be his final resting place. As much as he loved it here, that wasn't how he intended to go.

Jake had told him once of a rumored escape route from the vault, something placed here just in case. Like so much of ARKANE, there was always another way. Nothing was left to chance.

But where was it?

Martin wracked his brain trying to remember the offhand conversation. He hadn't paid much attention at the time, but it was something about a curse of kings channeled through a woman of heaven …

He stumbled to one of the side vaults marked with symbols of ancient Egypt, noticing anew the stylized uraeus cobra on the crown of the pharaohs. The serpent was everywhere and he cursed it now. Dizzy, Martin sank to the floor. He crawled into the vault, willing himself to go on. Jake wouldn't give up, and thoughts of his friend spurred him on.

The space was filled with boxes covered in stamps and labels, each one containing something precious and powerful. But none of those could help him now. Martin's eyes fixed on the standing sarcophagus against the back wall. The anthropoid inner coffin of Seshepenmehyt, carved from sycamore fig and dated to around 600 BC.

He dragged himself to the coffin and looked up. The face of the long-dead noblewoman painted in dark green stared down at him. Under the decorated collar, the goddess Nut spread her wings, goddess of the sky and the heavens.

Doubt flooded Martin's mind but as the opaque gas began to fill the room, he knew it was his only chance. He pulled himself up, desperately feeling for any way to open the sarcophagus. His fingers found a notch in the side and he pressed it. The door swung open.

He gasped in horror.

The mummy stood wrapped in bandages, brown with the patina of age. He imagined scarab beetles crawling through the layers, eating the dead flesh inside.

But then his logical mind kicked in.

There was no way a real Egyptian mummy would be kept in the ARKANE vault, even with its special climate control. It must be a fake.

He grimaced with disgust but steeled himself to reach out and pull the mummy from the case. It crashed down to the floor and he pushed it away with his foot, the spongy corpse making him shiver. The hiss of gas increased its frequency and Martin began to feel faint again. He clambered into the sarcophagus and pulled the door shut with a click, trapping himself in darkness. He could sense the boundaries of the tiny space, the wood only inches from his nose. It smelled of incense and the sweet, cloying scent of death. His breathing grew shallow and he panted and coughed, wheezing with pain.

He had made a terrible mistake.

With a horrible dread, he felt for a catch on the inside of the sarcophagus, his fingers desperately scrabbling for something that would get him out of here again. Was he trapped? Would he die here in the vault?

Martin tried to channel Jake's confidence. What would his friend do? If this was really the emergency way out, it wouldn't be obvious. The mummy was a decoy, of that he was sure, so there must be something else here. He pressed himself back against the rear wall, his fingers sweeping the wood from side to side as he shuffled up and down, desperation rising in his chest.

Suddenly, he felt a groove in the wood.

Martin pressed a finger inside and heard a faint click. Relief flooded through him and he let out the breath he hadn't realized he had been holding. The lower half of the mummy case behind him dropped away, creating enough space for him to back out and crawl into a thin, low tunnel. Emergency lighting in the floor meant that he could see a little way into the darkness. The shadows threw an eerie light before him.

He bent over to walk down the low tunnel, scurrying away from the vault. He didn't know who had locked him in, but he couldn't go back to the ARKANE office now. He needed to get to Jake and Morgan. They would know what to do.

* * *

Delphi, Greece.

Morgan sat on the edge of the pool at the Delphi Palace Hotel. Her legs dangled in cool water as the sound of cicadas filled the balmy air. It smelled of lemon thyme and the coconut of spilled suntan lotion and she smiled, enjoying a moment of normality in the craziness of an ARKANE mission. Right now, there was nothing else to do but wait.

Jake walked out of the hotel room carrying two glasses, ice chinking against the side as he sat down next to her.

"Gin and tonic," he said. "Local gin but hey, it's better than nothing."

Morgan took the drink. "Cheers."

They touched glasses, eyes meeting in the semi-darkness. As ever, there was too much to say but Morgan understood Jake's relief at her recovery. She hadn't enjoyed seeing him in hospital, but thankfully this time, they had both escaped severe injury.

She took a sip, letting the aromatics fill her senses. She sighed. "That is so good."

They sat for a moment in silence, savoring the night air. Jake's leg brushed against hers in the water and Morgan entwined her ankle around his.

He turned to her. "Morgan, I–"

His phone buzzed in his pocket. The moment was broken. Jake pulled it out and answered.

"Martin, what's up?" His face paled and he stood up on the water's edge. "It's OK. Calm down. Here's what you need to do."

Jake paced up and down by the side of the pool as he explained an escape plan from London. When he finally hung up, his face was serious.

"Martin was almost killed in the ARKANE vault. Someone shut him in there."

Morgan frowned. "Someone on the inside."

"Exactly. I've sent him to one of my emergency drops so he'll be able to make it out."

Morgan raised an eyebrow. "Emergency drop?"

Jake hunkered down next to her, his face inches from hers, his eyes amused. "Oh, I expect you have several, Ms Sierra." He smiled, his corkscrew scar twisting with humor. "Perhaps I'll get to see them one day."

Morgan laughed. It was good to be here with Jake, just a pair of secret agents now apparently on the run. "Is Martin coming here?"

Jake walked back towards the hotel room. "Sorry, but we're going to have to break up the party. He saw something in the archives that he thinks might be important, so we're going to meet him in Rome."

* * *

Vatican City, Rome, Italy.

"This is terrible coffee." Jake grimaced as he gulped the black liquid down.

Morgan gestured at the grand entrance to the Vatican Museums in front of them. "But look at the view." She checked her watch. "Martin should be here by now. I hope he's alright."

"I supervised his mandatory field training. He'll be fine." Jake took a bite of his flaky cornetto pastry.

They had driven back to Athens and flown out on the last night flight to Rome. Jake had stayed in touch with Marietti, but neither had mentioned Martin's escape. ARKANE was clearly compromised and the Director would find out something was up soon enough. In the meantime, they would try to get ahead of whoever was trying to sabotage the mission.

Morgan's head had been pounding by the time they landed and found a hotel. Jake had insisted on sleeping on the couch in her room, worried about concussion. She had watched him in the dark, wanting him to hold her but saying nothing. She had slept soon after and woke in the morning light to find him sorting out tickets to the Vatican Museum. They had arranged to meet Martin in the closest cafe to the entrance, hence the bad coffee. Still, any coffee was better than no coffee at this point.

She looked across the road to the entrance, the marble door carved with the words Musei Vaticani. It was flanked either side by a towering wall and tourists snaked in a line away down the hill. Morgan knew from bitter experience that the queue could go on for several kilometers, which is why they had sorted tickets in advance using ARKANE connections.

Just then, Morgan saw a tall man with a shock of messy blonde hair scurrying up the hill towards them.

"Un altro caffè, per favore." She gestured to the waiter and he brought another espresso just as Martin reached their table. There were deep shadows under his eyes, barely concealed by his wire-rim glasses and he rubbed his hands together in an anxious, repetitive movement.

Jake pulled a chair out for him. "Sit down, Spooky. Take a breath. We can't go in yet. They haven't opened the gates."

Martin sat down with a pained expression. Morgan could see he was disturbed by his flight from the ARKANE offices. She didn't know where he called home, but he spent so much time under Trafalgar Square that it was likely he had a bed there. She knew what exile felt like, and she wanted to reach out a hand to comfort him. But Martin wasn't one for physical contact, so she just pushed the espresso over to him. He gave a half smile and a long exhalation, then leaned across the table towards them.

"I'm worried about going in there," he whispered. "I found things in the vault that suggest the Vatican is involved in this End Times conspiracy. Perhaps one of their own shut me in the vault."

Jake snorted with laughter. "Of course they're involved. That's not news. The Church has a vested interest in keeping people believing in the End Times. No doubt the fundamentalists within want to usher in that day of reckoning."

Morgan nodded. "Jake has a point there. The question is whether this is a move towards something more concrete."

Martin pulled out his smart phone. "I think this goes beyond eschatology in the academic sense." He swiped to find a picture and turned it to show them. "This is an inter-faith meeting. This man is Jewish, this one Muslim and these are Cardinals. Look where they're standing."

Morgan took the phone and zoomed in. "That's the statue of Laocoon. That's why we're here." As she spoke, the massive gates opened in front of them and early-bird tourists began to file into the museum complex. "Let's go see what we can find."

"And try to get out again before anyone knows we're here," Martin said.

Together, they walked into the Museum. Morgan wished they had more time because it didn't matter how many times she visited, there was always more to see here. The Vatican Museums were a treasure trove of history, a place to delve into the magnificence of what humans could create in the name of God. The Jewish tradition she came from wasn't big on over-decoration but she appreciated the extravagant beauty of the Vatican, even though the current Pope deplored the wealth of the Church and wished to give it all away to the poor. Perhaps those who opposed his reforms were part of this End Times plan.

They walked on through the corridors, heading for the Museo Pio-Clementino, one of the sculpture museums surrounding the Cortile del Belvedere. They passed the porphyri sarcophagi of Constance and Saint Helen, a gilded bronze of Hercules, the sleeping Ariadne and a grouping of Apollo and the Muses. Morgan was grateful for the acceptance of these pagan images within the hallowed walls of the Vatican. After all, it was these classical statues that inspired Michelangelo to paint the figures on the ceiling of the Sistine Chapel, the glorious male nudes that were the models for Adam and God himself.

They finally reached the courtyard where the Laocoon statue stood in a niche. Morgan walked around it slowly. Despite the number of significant classical figures within the museum, this one stood out in its portrayal of human agony. The marble sculpture immortalized the perfection of the male nude, outlining each straining muscle of the tortured priest. The classical themes of suffering and death pervaded the Vatican, but this statue was pagan, depicting a death that did not end in redemption. Thankfully the Christians of the modern era were not so threatened by these ancient gods that they had destroyed all mention of them.

Morgan bent closer to examine how the fangs of one snake sank into the priest's thigh, just as an official Vatican guide walked up, leading a group of tourists. A few keen photographers crowded near the front and the usual bored teenagers trailed behind their parents, tapping away on their screens. Morgan wondered briefly if Pokémon Go had made it into the Vatican. Perhaps it would rejuvenate the interest of the young if they made it part of the experience.

"Laocoon was a Trojan priest of Poseidon who tried to stop the Trojan horse destroying the city by revealing what was inside." The guide's delivery was clipped, a practiced speech. "But the Gods had their own plans and he was punished for his attempt to disrupt the path of Fate. Poseidon sent sea serpents to devour the priest and his sons for daring to meddle with the divine plan."

She took a breath before continuing. "The style of the sculpture is known as Pergamene baroque from Greece and Asia Minor around two hundred years before Christ. The most famous example is demonstrated on the Pergamon Altar, reconstructed in the museum named after it in Berlin."

Morgan started at the mention of the Pergamon Museum and her eyes darted to Jake's. He looked as surprised as she did by the revelation. Could this be the link they were looking for?

CHAPTER 16

Jerusalem, Israel.

THE ENTRANCE TO THE vault was hidden at the back of a guesthouse run by the silent Sisters of Charity. It was used only by select members of the Vatican, those who were part of the greater plan, whose theology leaned towards the eschatological. Cardinal Eric Krotalia glanced at his watch as he stalked through the house. He was going to be a few minutes late after a hold-up at the airport and then the rigmarole of trying to lose any potential tail in the warren of the Old City.

But the precautions were important at this stage. They were so close now.

He hurried to one of the cupboards and pulled out a suitcase. He couldn't proceed without changing and removing all traces of his true identity. He took out the hooded robe of plain hessian and put it over his casual jeans and t-shirt attire, not what most would expect from a Cardinal in Jerusalem. His running shoes peeked out from below the robe, necessary for the unstable stairs and walk ahead. Despite his sixty-five years, the Cardinal felt fitter than ever.

More than ready for the times to come.

He paused as he reached for the snakeskin belt. He ran a finger along its length, reveling in the texture of raised scales. It was brilliant blue with a red stripe along the length, skin from a California red-sided garter snake, caught within a few miles of his own home in Monterey County. According to the ancient tradition of the Brotherhood, he had caught, skinned and treated it himself. He stroked the snakeskin and smiled with pride as he picked it up and tied it around his waist. It was thinner than the scarlet fascia he wore as part of his official choir dress, and he liked how the two were a line between his alternate worlds. One must walk in the darkness to fully appreciate the light. And to usher in the End Times was a crucial role indeed.

He took off his Cardinal's ecclesiastical ring and laid it by the bedside. As the final step, he picked up the matching snakeskin mask that would obscure the top half of his face, turning his eyes into serpent-like slits so as to protect his identity. He would put that on downstairs, just in case he surprised one of the nuns.

It was time to go.

He walked back downstairs and out towards a plain wooden door in the kitchen. It looked just like a pantry but behind it, stairs had been cut into the rock that wound down and under the city. They led to an ancient cistern, one of thirty mapped by Sir Charles Wilson in 1864, back when the Temple Mount was not such a flashpoint for religious extremism. It was forbidden to go down in the cisterns now.

At least officially.

But the old maps had been useful to locate this particular cistern, and it served the Brotherhood's purpose well. The houses were closely packed here in the Old City and this corner of the Jewish Quarter backed almost directly onto the Temple Mount, one of the holiest Islamic shrines and controlled by Muslim authorities. Armed guards walked the perimeter, automatic weapons at the ready. At the same time, Israeli soldiers patrolled the site of the Western Wall, both sides preventing extremists from either religion from doing anything that might disturb the fragile knife-edge of peace in this city.

But the time was coming when the commonalities of the great religions would matter far more than the differences.

The tunnel had taken many years to form, the rock dissolved by special acids and then chiseled away so as to be almost silently constructed. The price for being discovered would be instantaneous and catastrophic but so far they had avoided detection. The status quo of the Holy Land site remained untouched, put in place by the Ottoman Sultan in 1757 to protect freedom of worship. The Cardinal knew that the Christian emperors and kings would never have allowed such a ruling, but the current Israeli administration enforced respect for the status quo and as such, the Temple Mount was under the protection of the King of Jordan.

But the status quo would not stand for much longer.

The Cardinal opened the door and clicked on the lights inside. Dim bulbs hung on metal brackets illuminating stone steps, a dull yellow light casting a sulfur glow. Water dripped down the walls and he walked slowly down, holding onto the lumps in the stone to prevent himself from slipping in the wet patches.

He wiped a bead of sweat from his brow as he descended. There was so little time left and much more to do. He worried more about discovery after what had happened at ARKANE. After Marietti had somehow gotten hold of that tablet, he had tried to direct their agents away from the truth. But now their archivist had escaped his trap and would be investigating further. He couldn't be seen around there anymore. It was imperative that Samael focused on retrieving the seals.

The air smelled musty, like an animal lair where half-digested carcasses lay in the corners. He had tried to direct fresh air into the cistern below, but it still held the scent of death and decay. Perhaps that was only natural. After all, this particular spot in Jerusalem had been the site of thousands of years of conflict, of blood spilled on all sides. It was only right that it absorb the scent of death. And there was much more blood to come, if their plans proceeded on track.

The Cardinal finally reached the bottom and hurried as much as he could down the tunnel. He didn't like to be late. There was enough jostling for position in the Brotherhood as it was and he didn't like to leave the others alone for too long.

Raised voices echoed in the tunnel and his pulse raced at the thought of the sound filtering up to the Temple Mount above. Sometimes he wondered whether his trust in them was even justified. The other two had their own entrances and he didn't even know where they emerged, so secret were the details of their construction. Each understood the consequences of discovery, but tensions were rising between them.

He put his mask on as he turned the final corner and pulled up the hood of his tunic to cover his head as he entered the main chamber. The cistern had been used in the time of the First Temple, later buried by the double destruction of the city above. It lay directly under the Dome of the Rock and to the east of the Western Wall, a secret compartment only meters from two of the most contested sacred sites in the world.

The Cardinal stood silently for a moment as the other two men turned at his entrance.

"Brothers, be calm," he said quietly. "We're so close now. What could be more important than ushering in the climactic battle between Good and Evil at the apotheosis of history? We must work together in these final days."

The two men fell silent and shuffled to the center of the chamber to meet him.

The Cardinal glanced around. The three of them were the highest ranking of the Roshites, the Brotherhood of the Serpent. Each wore a snake around his waist and covered his face. Although they were meant to be anonymous, the Cardinal knew enough about each man. As they likely knew the truth of his own double life within the Vatican. But together, they had a more important mission.

The End of Days.

"It is true. Our differences are nothing." The man known as Cerastes wore a desert horned viper and spoke with an Iraqi accent. He was bent with age but his grip was still iron hard. He controlled a vast army of devotees under the auspices of what some called freedom fighters, and others called terrorists. Cerastes believed he was living in the era of the return of the Mahdi, a messianic figure prophesied in the *hadith*, a collection of the Prophet's deeds and sayings.

Some days, the Cardinal was jealous of Cerastes. It was easy for him to incite his followers to violence and decisive action, whereas the American congregations he was responsible for were much happier giving money than their lives to the cause.

But that would change soon enough because there would be something to unite against.

"What news, brother?" The third man, Echis, was tall and lithe and moved like a soldier with barely restrained violence. He wore a saw-scaled viper, the dark and lighter brown stripes tied almost double around his waist, evidence of how big the creature had been in life. The Cardinal imagined Echis crushing it with those meaty hands in the desert sand, his dark eyes showing no compassion as he broke its skull. Echis was an extremist Jew and a Zionist, the final side to their triangle.

Between the three of them, they represented the great

monotheistic religions, the faiths that believed in an end time and together they would usher it in.

Each believed the others to be wrong about the details of the coming apocalypse, but they had enough in common to begin the countdown together. God would know his own once the slaughter began.

"There have been a few setbacks." The Cardinal dipped his head in a slight apology.

Cerastes coughed, a wet sound that echoed in the chamber. "Where is the sarcophagus?"

"In a safe place."

"In America, you mean."

The Cardinal nodded. "But it will be transferred in the next few days. The details for shipping are being finalized. It will travel with objects for an exhibition at Hebrew University. Don't worry. It will be here in time for the alignment."

Echis nodded. "I can confirm the transit details and will ensure the sarcophagus is brought here as soon as it arrives."

The Cardinal took a deep breath. "There is a woman who will travel with it. Samael believes she can hear the Great Serpent speak, that she channels His thoughts."

Echis grunted. "You believe this?"

The Cardinal hesitated, thinking of what Samael had told him about Lilith. Then he nodded. "The risks are too great to lose one of us to the other side of the venom trance. She is a conduit until He is risen."

"And when we bring her here?" Cerastes grunted.

The Cardinal nodded. "She will be the first sacrifice to the Great Serpent, as it has been foretold."

"There has always been a woman in the prophecy," Cerastes said. "But what about the seals? The alignment is only days away."

"We have four of them. There are still three more to

find." There was a heavy sense of disappointment in the room and the Cardinal felt it was all directed at him. It was time to change tack.

"What of the preparations for the battle at Dabiq?" the Cardinal asked Cerastes pointedly.

The city in Syria was mentioned in a *hadith* describing events of the *Malahim*, roughly translated as Armageddon. It was meant to be the site of one of the End Times battles between Muslims and modern Crusaders, one of the reasons that extremist groups had captured it and lured western forces into battle there. The Rome of Revelation was represented by the troops of the United Nations and the European Union.

"We're continuing to bait Allied troops," Cerastes said. "We captured some western reporters and we will be–"

"I don't need to know the details." The Cardinal held up his hand. It was much better not to know the atrocities that Cerastes had set in motion, although a few lives mattered little now.

After all, life was not about maximizing human wellbeing. It was about doing God's will and being His instrument to bring about the End Times. The serpent was just one of the important parts, a visible symbol of the end. Once events had gone far enough, the End Times would be declared and the Unbelievers would be punished.

The Cardinal knew that he would be the only one left standing. His faith was unshakeable. The Great Serpent would destroy these others and the world would be cleansed of the Unbelievers in the days after.

When he had first joined the Church, he had believed that the whole world could be saved and that somehow people would turn back to God. But over the years, he had seen enough to know that they just needed to start again. It was time for a purge, a cleanse, another type of Flood.

God's reset point on the earth.

"Ezekiel prophesied that fire and brimstone would rain down on the enemies of God's people," Echis said, interrupting his thoughts. "Have you organized the Allied troops?"

The Cardinal nodded. "If Cerastes amps up the atrocities, I can guarantee that there will be more bombs from the Allied forces. We will spark the tinder box, don't worry. The more violence in the Middle East, the more the fundamentalists claim the End Times. When the Great Serpent emerges, the battle will truly commence."

Echis grinned, his teeth glinting in the semi-darkness. "Then we have much to do, brothers. I'll send word when the sarcophagus is here."

"The thousand years are ended." The men intoned the words together and then went their separate ways into the dark.

CHAPTER 17

Vatican City, Rome, Italy.

THE MENTION OF THE Pergamon Museum made Morgan start. It had only been a few nights since she and Jake had run through it to the Ishtar Gate to find the pictures that led them to the seal. Her anger still simmered at losing it again. With the attacks on her own family and then on Martin, Morgan was determined to beat Samael to the remaining seals.

The tourists crowded even closer as the guide ignored Morgan's small group in the typical Italian way and continued her talk.

"There are copies of the sculpture in many of the great museums of the world, including the Louvre in Paris, the Uffizi in Florence and the Grand Palace of the Knights of St John in Rhodes."

This last comment caught Morgan's attention.

The Knights of St John were also known as the Hospitallers, a medieval Catholic military order with a papal charter to defend the Holy Land. Unlike the Templars, who had been destroyed or at least driven underground by persecution in the fourteenth century, the Hospitallers persisted through history. Like the Church itself, they had survived the rigors of history and still protected secrets held since the Middle Ages.

This original Laocoon statue was such a tourist attraction within the walls of the Vatican that Morgan couldn't imagine how a seal could still be hidden here. But people didn't visit Rhodes for a replica of the Laocoon.

As the guide moved off, Morgan sidled back around the sculpture to Jake and Martin.

"Fancy a dip in the Aegean?"

* * *

Rhodes, Greece.

Morgan waited for Jake and Martin at a cafe on the edge of the harbor near the ruins of Our Lady of the Castle cathedral. The guys were sorting out accommodation and it was good to have a little time out. The pace of the ARKANE missions could be brutal and her bruises still smarted from the bombing at Delphi.

She looked out across the azure sea and sipped a cold Mythos lager, enjoying the refreshing fizz while the alcohol helped her relax. Rhodes was closer to Turkey than the mainland of Greece and the island was a haven for sun seekers, particularly as winter descended on Northern Europe. Morgan was grateful for a sliver of sun on her face. The climate here was similar to Israel and even the air smelled similar, salt fish on the breeze with a hint of citrus and olives. But she had no ties here, no memories and no chance of bumping into people she knew. Here she could pretend to be just a tourist, not a secret agent on the hunt for what might prevent the End of Days. Part of her wanted to melt into the tourist crowd, find a little place overlooking the ocean and just rest.

"Not a bad spot you've got here."

Morgan looked up to see Jake beaming down at her.

He'd changed and now wore a blue striped t-shirt and light chinos. He looked ridiculously good. Morgan smiled back.

"Glad you like it."

"I think more of our missions should involve Mediterranean islands." Jake sat down next to her. "Martin's back at the hotel room. He's calmer now so he's sifting through piles of ancient data on Near Middle Eastern seals. Fascinating stuff." He faked a yawn. "But we're field agents, so we need to be in the field." He gestured to the waiter for a beer. "Important agent things to be doing, after all."

He was quiet for a moment and they both looked out over the water, finishing their beers as they watched people stroll by. A couple stopped on the waterside in front of them, arms woven around each other. Their loving smiles were a glimpse into a relationship that Morgan found herself envying.

Jake cleared his throat. "Time to go?"

Together, they walked up the hill along the Street of the Knights towards the fortress, passing tourist trap shops along the way. The Palace of the Grand Master of the Knights of Rhodes was as imposing as its name, a medieval castle that towered above the town and the harbor, looking out over the ocean. Built in the Gothic Provencal style in the fourteenth century, two massive crenelated towers flanked the entrance. Silhouetted as they were against the blue sky, Morgan could easily imagine archers leaning over to shoot down invaders of old. The past was drenched in blood and the Catholic Church had shed more than its fair share. But then how different were she and Jake to the warrior priests of the Hospitallers?

They entered the gates into the inner courtyard. It was lined with a colonnade that offered shade from the hot sun.

"This is a pretty cool place." Jake's grin was infectious and Morgan couldn't help but smile back.

They walked into the inner fortress and entered the Great Hall. A grand staircase filled one end of the room and at the top, Morgan could see the Laocoon replica. It overlooked the lobby in full view of the tourists below, who clumped together in a few groups around other areas of interest. Security guards were spaced out around the room and despite their Greek nonchalance and air of relaxation, they carried guns on their hips.

As they headed slowly towards the statue, Morgan took Jake's arm.

"Remember what you did at Santiago de Compostela?" she said in a quiet voice.

He nodded.

"I might need some kind of distraction like that again if I find something."

"Gotcha. I'll wait for your signal." Jake headed off in the opposite direction.

Morgan climbed the stairs towards the sculpture and a moment later, she stood in front of it. This Laocoon was clearly inferior to the original. It was a little smaller and although all the essential features were there, it was missing the smooth lines and the overall impact was less emotionally intense. Whereas the sculpture in the Vatican resonated with the death throes of a father trying to save his sons, this one merely seemed like decoration in a castle built for fighters, not art critics.

But there was something about it that puzzled her.

She examined it more closely, trying to remember the Vatican statue … then she saw it. The altar that Laocoon the priest sat on was marked in a different way. There was a carving of a serpent on it, the ouroboros, the snake forming a circle with its tail in its mouth. Morgan couldn't recall seeing that on the Vatican statue. It looked like some kind of button.

She turned around and looked across the hall. Jake was

standing on the other side facing her, right next to a painting of Hospitaller Knights marching towards Jerusalem. He had his head stuck in a guidebook but she could see that he was alert for her signal, watching her out of the corner of his eye. She nodded at him.

His shout rang out across the hall as Jake fell to the floor and began rolling around, faking an epileptic fit by the look of it. The guards turned towards the sound and ran to the balcony. Morgan only had a minute before calm would be restored.

She quickly turned to the statue and ran her fingers over the ouroboros. She pressed it hard and a little drawer sprung out the back with a small round package wrapped in dull ivory cloth inside. She picked it up, slid the drawer closed and put it in her backpack, then walked swiftly towards the exit. Behind her, security dealt with the continuing uproar as curious tourists huddled around the drama.

By the time Jake strolled back to the bar on the waterfront an hour later, Morgan had ordered two more beers and was halfway through hers. She looked up at his approach.

"Took your time." She pushed back a chair for him.

"I had to convince the nice doctors I was OK to leave."

"Nice work back there."

Jake gave a fake bow. "At your service. Now what did you find?"

Morgan pulled open her pack to show him the wrapped package. "It's definitely another seal. It matches the others."

"Do you really think these are the seals of Revelation?" Jake asked.

Morgan stared out at the blue ocean before them. She and Jake rarely talked about what they believed in terms of faith, but both of them had seen enough strange things to believe the seals could be real. "Patmos is only a few islands northwest of here."

Jake raised an eyebrow quizzically.

"That's where John, the author of the book of Revelation, had his visions. Some say he was the apostle John, the one that Jesus loved, and the same author as the gospel of John. But textual analysis says otherwise. He was more likely a Christian exiled to the island during the persecution of Domitian. Father Ben once told me that he was likely in a fasting state when he wrote some of the visions but he certainly used a lot of Jewish prophecy in his work. Verses from the books of Daniel, Ezekiel, Psalms and Isaiah pepper the text."

"And the seals?"

Morgan shrugged. "Seven is a sacred number in various numerological traditions and it's used over 700 times in the Bible. Seven days to create the earth. The Sabbath is on the seventh day. There are seven hills in Jerusalem, and seven trumpets to sound the end."

"Seventh son of a seventh son."

"That's not actually in the Bible."

Jake grinned. "Iron Maiden is just as inspirational."

"What's puzzling me is who hid the seals," Morgan said. "If they are some kind of device that will open a sarcophagus, then why hide them near snake symbols?"

"Perhaps they were hidden by those who worshipped the serpent?" Jake mused. "Think about it. You've lost your sarcophagus. Some ancient do-gooders have buried it far away but you still have the seals. You know you won't live to see it opened but you trust that the Brotherhood of the Serpent, or whatever it's called, will eventually rise again and find the sarcophagus. So you hide the seals where they would know to look, in the very places that are sacred to the snake."

Morgan nodded. "Makes sense, I guess. So where's the next one?"

As she sipped her beer, Martin came scurrying along

the waterfront, a sheaf of papers clutched in his hands. His shock of blonde hair stood up in clumps where he had been pulling it. The frown had deepened across his forehead, making him look much older.

He came to sit at their table and without so much as a hello, he thrust the papers at them, finger stabbing at an image on the top. "This must be it!"

CHAPTER 18

Rhodes, Greece.

MORGAN LOOKED DOWN AT the image Martin pointed at. It was a stone carving of a serpent curled around a circular object, its body wound through an ankh symbol. Next to it, the falcon god Horus wore the crown of Egypt and another cobra sat proudly at its feet. Martin stumbled excitedly over his words.

"The ouroboros you saw on the Laocoon, the snake eating its own tail. It's an ancient Egyptian symbol representing renewal and rebirth in the cycles of life. In the Book of the Dead, it's related to the god Atum who rose from the chaos of primordial waters in the form of a serpent. Later sources use it as a symbol in alchemy, linked to the Philosopher's Stone."

"Egypt?" Jake looked hopeful. "It's been a while since I've visited."

Morgan thought back to when Jake had lain in hospital, injured by the demon in the bone church while she had gone hunting for the Ark of the Covenant. Egypt had been a revelation, but also a place of violence and death, and she had no desire to return anytime soon. But it seemed she would have little choice in the matter.

"So where's this carving?" she asked.

"The goddess Wadjet, portrayed as an Egyptian cobra,

is on the wall of the Temple of Hatshepsut in Luxor," Martin said triumphantly.

"That circular object certainly looks like a seal." Jake peered more closely at the picture.

"It's a sun disk," Morgan said. She tipped her head on one side, trying to recall the symbolism associated with the goddess. "But I seem to remember that the first image of a snake curling up a staff was Wadjet shown as a cobra curling up a papyrus leaf in the pre-Dynastic era around 3100 BC. The symbol was later adopted by many Mediterranean cultures in various forms, such as the biblical graven serpent and the Greek caduceus."

"Exactly," said Martin. "I've run algorithms over the remaining cultures of the world that relate to snakes. But all the rest are much further away: the nagas in India and the Far East, the Rainbow serpent in Australia, and Quetzalcoatl in Central America. All these fall outside the parameters of what are considered likely to relate to the seals. But Egypt …" He shrugged.

Jake raised his glass to the setting sun.

"To Luxor next, then. But for now, I just want to finish this beer."

* * *

Grand Canyon Snake Valley Retreat, USA

Lilith knew she was taking too much of the venom, but increasingly she preferred the altered state of consciousness to her real life.

She spent her time curled up on top of the sarcophagus, crooning to the hidden life she knew pulsed beneath her. In her more lucid moments, she recognized that she was on the edge of what many would call madness. But something greater called to her. He whispered dark truths in the darkness and she listened, storing up the drips of poison in her heart.

Time seemed to both slow and pass like lightning. She barely ate and her ribs showed through the thin skin of her chest.

But she liked that.

She counted her ribs in the mirror every morning and watched the vertebrae of her backbone undulate. Although she had a pathetic thirty-three vertebrae and twenty-four ribs while the serpents had several hundred. Her body was inferior but it could still be useful. He had whispered that to her.

She would be His vessel.

She didn't know how, but she had to make sure she was there when the sarcophagus was opened. So she waited as if in hibernation in the darkness of the crypt. The time would come when she would act.

Lilith wasn't surprised when the door finally cracked open. The voices of men filtered down from outside and the sound of footsteps echoed through the vault. She rolled from the sarcophagus to stand in front of it. Her heart beat fast and she felt a little dizzy as she stood. She needed another shot of venom, but Samael had the vial she really wanted. Perhaps he had returned?

But it was Krait, the boorish security man, who walked down the stairs. He looked at her, his expression momentarily shocked before he hid his response.

In his eyes, Lilith saw a glimpse of what she had become. She must look like a physical wreck, but the man had no idea where her mind had been. He would be far too weak to take the venom trance.

She raised her chin, standing tall, her hand resting on the sarcophagus. But now she noticed the dirt under her nails and how ragged they were.

"What do you want?"

Krait pushed her aside. "Samael's orders," he said gruffly. "We're shipping the casket out of here. You're coming too." He glanced at her disheveled state. "Get changed and pack. We're flying to Israel this afternoon."

"Where's Samael?" Lilith asked, desperate for her next dose of the purest venom.

"Egypt," Krait grunted.

* * *

Luxor, Egypt.

The plane banked over the dark green curve of the Nile, and Morgan looked down on the ancient city of Thebes. It was an open-air museum and a mecca for any wannabe archaeologist. The massive temple complexes of Karnak and Luxor dominated the heart of the city. On the opposite side of the Nile lay the West Bank Necropolis, with the temples and tombs of the Valley of the Kings and the Valley of the Queens. Much had been discovered under the sands of the desert here, but surely much was still buried, hidden well and now forgotten. How little our lives matter in the grand scheme of history, Morgan thought. But that was comforting somehow, for when her body was dust, these magnificent monuments would continue to stand.

Unless of course, it really was the End Times.

She smiled to herself. As in all her ARKANE missions, Morgan battled her own scientific skepticism when it came to matters of faith. Despite what she had seen, she still clung to rational argument. Because if she became a true believer in the nature of evil and a supernatural battle was to come, then she might crumble. After all, what could one woman do against forces of that magnitude?

Jake snorted in his sleep. She looked sideways at him and Martin, both snoozing next to her on the plane. Well, one woman and two sidekicks.

If their foes were human and temporal, then they had a chance. She had to believe that. Those who wanted to use the seals to usher in some kind of apocalypse could still be stopped.

The plane touched down and they emerged into the bright sun of an Egyptian day. The air was like a furnace.

"It's good to be back in Africa." Jake smiled, striding down the stairs and stripping off his jersey to expose his brown arms to the sun.

Martin stood holding the railing, cupping a hand over his eyes to shield them. "It must be over forty degrees Celsius," he said in a weak voice, clearly wilting in the heat. "No one knows I'm here, so maybe I should just wait at the hotel for you to return? I could work on the possible locations for the final seal."

Morgan heard stress and deep fatigue in his voice, the longing for a cool room and some quiet time. They wouldn't be at the temple complex for long so he should be safe enough. She looked over at Jake. He nodded, concern for his friend visible in his eyes.

Morgan opened her pack and handed him the package from Rhodes. "You can keep this one safe for us too."

She was glad that Martin would be safe out of the way. The last time she had been in Egypt in the hunt for the Ark of the Covenant, things had gotten very dangerous indeed. She didn't worry about herself and Jake, but she hated to put Martin in danger. He wasn't cut out for fieldwork but until they knew who had shut him in the vault, he would be best off near them.

But maybe not too near.

They had told Marietti that Martin was here to provide backup in the field. The Director had sounded suspicious but he trusted them enough not to question what was going on. Clearly the threat was within the ARKANE organization itself, so the less he knew, the better.

After getting Martin settled at the Luxor Palace Hotel, Morgan and Jake caught a taxi over to the Mortuary Temple of Hatshepsut. It was a grand funerary complex, cut out of the towering cliffs at Deir el Bahari. As they drove up, a bank of cloud formed above the temple, casting dramatic shadows over the limestone cliffs as the wind whipped the air into an afternoon storm. Fat drops of rain spattered the earth. A roll of thunder rumbled in the distance.

"Storm's almost here," the taxi driver said, as he took their payment. "Better shelter inside."

Morgan and Jake ran the tourist gauntlet of the hawkers and headed up the long path to the temple, half jogging to get out of the rain until they reached the first level of colonnaded walkway. They turned to look back across the valley as rain pounded the dusty earth before them.

A crash of lightning split the sky, forking down onto the rocky plateau.

This place would have looked similar over three thousand years ago when they built it, Morgan thought. It was a spectacle of death in the Egyptian way, made even more resonant by the massacre of sixty-two people, mainly tourists, in 1997 by a fundamentalist group intent on disrupting the Egyptian economy. Layers of history piled up, alongside the bodies of those who died along the way.

As the rain eased, they walked out of the first colonnade and up the massive ramped staircase in the middle of the triple tiers to the second level.

"Hatshepsut ruled around 1500 BC," Morgan said. "The second historically confirmed female pharaoh. Her temple is dedicated to the sun god, Amun."

"It's pretty stark," Jake noted.

"It would have been hung with gardens back then,"

Morgan explained. "Frankincense and myrrh trees as well as many other foreign plants."

"So where's the carving?"

As they reached the top of the ramp, Morgan pointed through the colonnade to the inner temple. "Somewhere in there."

They walked through slowly, checking the walls as they went. Relief sculptures told the story of the divine birth of the female Pharaoh and an expedition to the exotic land of Punt on the Red Sea coast. There were statues of Osiris and columns with the cow-head of the goddess Hathor. But as Jake said, it was pretty stark with little personality.

"Her stepson, Thutmose III, destroyed a lot of the statues after her death," Morgan noted. "But once it would have been magnificent, an oasis in the desert. It's aligned to the winter solstice so the sunlight would pierce the inner temple and strike the statue of Osiris."

They walked around a corner and found an impressive wall of carvings in a sheltered niche. A vulture flew with wings outstretched, each feather detailed in blue and green with accents of crimson. Above it, eight cobras in strike pose inched along a frieze, each with a sun disk in a crown on their heads. It was stunning, but not what they sought.

After weaving around the temple behind a group of tourists, they finally found the carving, the original far more impressive than the picture Martin had showed them. Morgan imagined the chisel of the ancient sculptor, his hammer blows ringing out in the temple complex. The Egyptians were builders, that was for sure, and they were right in ensuring a physical memory. Walking lightly on the earth was all very well, and leaving no trace was an admirable philosophy, but what endured if no one built anything? And what would remain of the increasingly digital world when the silicon chips it ran on returned to dust?

"They don't make 'em like this anymore," Jake said, admiring the wall.

"They're still building the Sagrada Familia in Barcelona," Morgan replied. "You loved it there."

"Shame about the circumstance of our visit though." Jake frowned and Morgan knew he was thinking of the death of Santiago Pereira, the beginning of their hunt for the Key to the Gates of Hell not so long ago. He looked around them at the empty temple.

"I'm not sure where we're meant to hunt for this seal. The temple is almost stripped bare."

Morgan nodded. "I agree. Short of setting up a full archaeological survey, we won't find anything here. But there must be more images like this in some of the other tombs. Let's go and ask one of the guides."

Together they walked back to the tourist group who now milled around taking selfies with the colonnade as a backdrop. The guide stood in a corner, checking her phone. She looked up as Morgan and Jake approached and smiled in welcome.

"Can I help you?"

"We're looking for a portrayal of Wadjet, or some kind of serpent, in a tomb," Morgan asked.

"There are plenty of tombs around here." The guide smiled. "Can you be more specific?"

"Something unusual," Jake said. "Something that you wouldn't expect, rather than the usual cobra images."

The guide smiled up at him and thought for a moment. "Probably the best serpent in the valley is portrayed in Ramses I's tomb. It's in the Valley of the Kings, number KV16."

"Thank you, that's –"

Jake's words were cut off by the rattle of gunfire from the plaza below the temple.

Then the screaming started.

CHAPTER 19

THE GUIDE'S FACE WENT white with fear at the sound.

"Oh no, not again." She started shouting for her group. "This way, please. Follow me."

There were procedures in place since the terrorist attacks in the 1990s, but Morgan thought this was something different. As the tourist group streamed back through the colonnade, she and Jake slipped out to stand behind the pillars, shadowed by the darkness within. They looked down onto the lower level of the temple. A group of armed men cleared the area, herding the tourists away while another man stalked up the ramp towards them.

Morgan could just make out the snake tattoo on his neck.

"Samael?" she whispered.

Jake nodded. "He must have had the same idea as us."

They slipped back into the temple, following the tourist group, hoping there really was another way out. Or pretty soon, Samael would make it up here and find them.

The guide led her group of tourists deeper into the heart of the temple and then veered right down a small tunnel. She pointed in front of her, herding them through.

"Quickly now," she whispered. "Follow the tunnel down. It's carved through the cliff behind us and emerges in the carpark at the Valley of the Kings."

The group ran down into the tunnel and eventually the sound of gunfire faded, replaced by the dripping of water and the rasp of breathing as the tourists hurried away. Morgan and Jake stayed at the back, just in case anyone came after them.

But no one did.

As they walked down the tunnel, Morgan imagined Samael scouring the funerary complex for any trace of the seal. But he would come up short and likely head for the tombs of the other pharaohs next.

They had to stay ahead of him. She redoubled her speed.

Ten minutes later, the group emerged into the carpark, a wide tarmac area that held back the sands of the desert cliffs around them. The rain was heavier now and the guide corralled her tourists together, pointing them in the direction of coaches parked a little further away. Morgan and Jake turned towards the entrance to the Valley of the Kings, an unimposing start to the magnificence hidden inside the cliffs ahead.

Storm clouds whirled overhead and the rain intensified, hammering down. Morgan and Jake ran onwards, passing groups of tourists with colorful umbrellas heading back out again. The Valley of the Kings looked just like a load of caves cut into rock from the outside, but in the 500 years between the sixteenth and eleventh centuries BC, tombs had been dug here for the great pharaohs of the time. They ranged from simple pits to elaborate complexes, one with 120 chambers that would have been packed with precious objects for the afterlife. Each tomb was marked with a number. Sixty-three in all, most pillaged by grave robbers in antiquity, but Morgan was sure there was more to find in the desert out here.

By the time they found KV16, the tomb of Ramses I, Morgan and Jake were both soaked through.

"I love running in the rain." Morgan laughed as they ducked into the low tunnel.

"Definitely exhilarating." Jake grinned as they both dripped rainwater onto the cave floor.

The tomb was lit with dull electric lights. They attempted to preserve the incredible painting on the walls and ceiling, but also enabled the tourist horde to proceed without tripping over the rocky floor. At peak times, these tombs would be crowded with sweaty groups, flashing pictures while ignoring the No Flash signs and elbowing others out the way to get a better shot of the Egyptian funerary art. It was macabre tourism drawn here by the dead who had lain here for thousands of years.

But Morgan doubted that people would be so interested without Howard Carter and the curse of Tutankhamun. The discovery of the nearly intact tomb in 1922 sparked worldwide press reports and a renewed interest in Egyptology. The mysterious deaths of those involved had driven the hysteria even higher. The curse was considered by most to be complete fabrication, but the ancient Egyptians had certainly believed in magic. Supernatural forces still swirled about these places but Morgan didn't sense a threat here now. Even so, as they walked down the tunnel, it was clear that the paintings on the walls were meant to keep evil at bay, helping the dead into a happy afterlife.

After several chambers full of interesting paintings, Jake sighed.

"I'm having my doubts that this trip was worth it." He indicated the wall frieze. "Look at this. More servants with more grain and more animals to feed the Pharaoh in the afterlife, but no serpent."

"Just a little further," Morgan said, refusing to believe this was a wasted trip. Especially if Samael had the same idea.

Then they walked into the next chamber.

The wall painting portrayed a gold and green funerary barge. Slaves in white loincloths manned the oars while the Pharaoh sheltered under a canopy. Lines of hieroglyphics ran from top to bottom and Morgan could make out some symbols like the bird with a human head, known as the *ba*, the soul. Beneath the barge, a large serpent curled in six figure-of-eight loops, an intricate dance of death.

"Now that's what you call a serpent." Jake stepped closer to examine the detail.

"Its shape looks unnatural," Morgan noted. "More like a map. What do you reckon?"

"Could be. You want to go deeper into the tomb?"

Morgan nodded, a sense of excitement growing within her. At this point, they had nothing to lose. She took out her smart phone and took a picture of the curves of the snake.

They walked on through the tomb, quickly arriving at the first turn in the tunnel. There were two options. Morgan looked at the snake image and chose the left, following the undulations of its body.

Soon they reached a safety barrier indicating that the way ahead was closed and dangerous to proceed. A large stone had been rolled in front of the way to stop inquisitive tourists. Jake heaved it aside and they went on.

The lights grew dimmer as they continued following the turns, until only the light from Morgan's phone illuminated the way ahead.

"We must be almost there," she said. "One last turn."

They turned again and Morgan almost fell into blackness as her foot stepped onto air. She put her hand out to brace herself on the wall. Jake caught her round the waist, pulling her to him briefly.

"Careful," he whispered. "I don't want to lose you."

Morgan shone her light forward and down into a pit before them. In the middle was a stone altar with a smaller sarcophagus on top, carved with the undulating shapes of a serpent.

"We have to get down there." Morgan knelt down on the edge. "It's not too far. Can you lower me down?"

Jake held her hands and lowered her as far as he could. She dropped the last meter, landing with bended knees onto soft earth. It smelled damp, as if the rainstorm had found its way through the rock above, down to the chamber beneath. In a strange way, it felt more alive than the dusty tomb that the tourists visited, as if people had worshipped here more recently.

Morgan tried to pull the top from the smaller sarcophagus, but it was too heavy.

"Sorry," she called up to Jake. "You're going to have to come down and help me with this."

"Shine the torch over here."

Morgan turned the light to help him see his way down. He lowered himself as far as he could and then drop-rolled to the ground. Then he came over and heaved the top off.

"Good to know you can't do without me."

Morgan smiled. "Just making you feel useful."

She reached in and pulled out a stone roundel.

"This is it," Morgan whispered. "The sixth seal. It's beautiful."

The intricate carving of the snake wound around the circle, each scale perfectly cut. The others had suffered the ravages of time, but this one had been preserved down here.

With wide eyes, she handed it to Jake and he cupped it in his bigger hand, weighing it slightly.

"It's easier to believe the seals have some kind of intrinsic power when we're down here," he said quietly. "Or at least to think that someone once believed they did."

Suddenly they heard a scuffle in the tunnel above. Torchlight played along the walls, alighting briefly on the faces of the impassive gods.

Someone else was here.

Morgan looked at Jake with alarm. Together, they softly moved directly under the doorway.

"I know you're down there," an American voice called from above. "And I know you have the sixth seal. But I have something you want too."

The sound of someone pushed to the ground. A groan of pain. Then the click of a gun.

"I'm so sorry." Martin Klein's voice filtered down to them in the dark of the crypt. "Please don't –"

A dull thud. A cry of pain, and Martin's words were cut off.

"I have the other seal and your friend. The question is how much do you value him?"

Jake stepped away from the wall with no hesitation. Morgan moved to his side and they both looked up.

"What do you want?" Jake asked.

Samael stood in the doorway at the top of the crypt. Martin knelt before him, face bloody and streaked with tears, one of his eyeglass lenses broken.

"Throw me the seal. You will have your friend back and I won't shoot all three of you. You're fish in a barrel down there, after all." Samael put his hand on his heart in a slightly mocking way. "You have my word."

Jake weighed the stone object in his hand. "This is the sixth seal, so there's still one more to find."

"True. But after I find it, the sarcophagus can be opened. Such a shame you won't be there to see it."

"Alright," Jake said. "On three."

Samael nodded.

"One, two, three."

On three, Jake threw the seal up towards Samael. The man caught it with one hand, but Martin remained kneeling at his feet.

"You gave your word," Jake said.

Samael laughed. "Of course."

He shoved Martin forward so he tumbled into the pit. Jake rushed forward to break his fall and the two of them ended up in a heap on the rocky ground.

"I promised not to shoot you, but you'll find the tomb sealed up for renovations, if you ever make it out of here. Perhaps the archaeologists of the next generation will find your bodies mummified down here." He smiled. "Now I'm going to retrieve the next seal." He started to walk away, then turned back. "You think those you love are safe, Morgan Sierra. I almost wish you could make it out of here to see that they are not."

He smiled and walked off, followed by his men. Their footsteps echoed up the tunnel. Moments later, there was the sound of a muffled explosion.

Samael had sealed the door.

They were trapped inside the tomb.

His last words echoed inside Morgan's mind. How could he be going after her family again? Faye and Gemma were safe inside ARKANE. Then she looked down at Martin, as Jake helped him dust off his clothes. They had gotten to him inside the vault, the heart of ARKANE London headquarters. So, how hard would it be to get to her family in Oxford?

She had to get out of here.

CHAPTER 20

MORGAN RAN TO THE wall below the doorway.

"Help me up!"

Jake leaned over and she put her foot into his hands. He boosted her and she sprang up, clambering back to the ledge above. She turned to call back to them.

"I'll go check the exit. Back in a minute."

Morgan ran down the tunnel the way they had come. Her heart hammered in her chest, not from the exercise but from the fear of what Samael planned for her family. Surely he couldn't get to them?

She made it to the safety barrier but as promised, the tunnel was blocked by a cave-in. They'd used enough explosive to bring it down but not enough to make sufficient noise to bring the guards. It was unlikely that the Egyptian authorities would check this far down into the tomb complex until morning.

"Help!" she shouted, hoping that somehow her cry would make it through the cavern. But the storm still hammered the valley outside, cloaking any sound. The tourists would all have gone back to their luxury hotels for the night, to be entertained with belly dancing and cocktails with pyramid-shaped ice. The guards would be huddled in their buildings, sheltering from the rain. There was no one to hear them. Samael had made sure of that.

Morgan banged her fist against the rock as she frantically considered the other options. They could explore the rest of the tunnels and look for another exit. But they might just end up lost in the caverns dug into the cliffs, their voices joining the whispers of the long dead. This was no time to go wandering away from the light.

She hefted one of the rocks away, her back muscles straining as she moved it just a few inches. Perhaps together they could shift enough to make a passage through.

Morgan jogged back to the pit and looked down at Jake and Martin. Their faces were ghostly in the semi-darkness and it was as if she saw them in the grave.

"The exit's blocked but we might be able to dig ourselves a way out. It's our only chance to get out of here before the morning security rounds."

Jake boosted Martin up and then clambered up after them himself. The three of them jogged back down the tunnel, their footsteps echoing through the chambers until they reached the barrier.

Jake raised an eyebrow. "He did a decent job of that." He turned to Morgan. "But at least you weren't under it this time." He bent his knees and hefted a rock up into his arms. "Guess it's time for a workout."

Morgan followed suit and Martin joined in, each of them working in silence punctuated only with the exhalation of breath.

An hour later, Morgan sank to the floor.

"Time out, guys."

Jake and Martin stopped shifting and sat near her. Jake wiped the sweat from his brow and looked over at the pile of rocks.

"We're making good progress."

Morgan laughed and shook her head. "Nice try, but we've barely touched it."

A knot of worry sat heavy in her stomach as she considered that they might not get out of here until morning when the security rounds began, or even when tourist groups arrived. There was no way they could shift all the rocks from the cave-in themselves.

"It's only six hours' flight from Luxor back to London." Morgan's frown deepened. "Samael could get to Oxford before dawn tomorrow."

"But the ARKANE labs there are pretty much impregnable," Jake said. "And when we fail to report in, Marietti will make sure your family is protected."

"Like he protected Martin in the crypt?" Morgan snapped back.

Martin huddled into the wall at her words, wrapping his arms around himself as if to ward off the truth.

"I'm sorry," she said with a sigh. "I'm just so worried."

Jake stood and walked over to where she sat. He sank down next to her and pulled her into a hug. There were no words that could help at this point, but Morgan was grateful for his support.

As they settled in for the night, she could only send positive thoughts to Faye, David and little Gemma. *Be safe. I'm coming as soon as I can.*

* * *

Oxford, England. The next morning.

Father Ben Costanza walked out of the Radcliffe Camera onto the square. He blinked a little as he emerged and breathed in the scent of the air after rain. The circular interior of the library was a haven in the middle of the busy city, part of the Bodleian Library. It held the theological texts he consulted in preparation for his lectures, although truth be told, he could have found them all online now. But he liked to get out of the hallowed hall of Blackfriars and feel part of the wider university. This was one of his favorite places, especially in the early mornings when no one else was around.

Sleep was a minor part of his life now and most nights he only rested for a few hours. One of the minor benefits of age perhaps, as he had more time to read and think. But this morning, he had woken while it was still dark with a sense of foreboding, a twisting in his gut that something was wrong. It had happened several times since returning from India, with nightmares of the Kali temple and a shadow of violent death that still lay heavy upon him. So he came here and had been deep in study since the early hours, but now he had to get back for a morning tutorial.

Ben loved his life at Oxford. After years of working for the Vatican, he enjoyed the relative freedom he had to pursue his studies as well as teach the next generation everything he knew.

Or at least some of it, he thought.

Much of what he had learned over the years was best left buried.

He gripped the handrail and slowly walked down the stone stairs, one step at a time. A couple of students bustled past him, laughing together as they strode towards their bikes, chained up in the tangle in the rack at the edge of the square.

Ben smiled to see them go, even though they didn't even notice him. The old were invisible, he thought. That had always been the way of things and he was more than ready to give way for the young. They would learn their lessons in time and he wished them many years before they faced the inevitable pain that would come.

Such was the wisdom of the old, Ben thought with a rueful smile, feeling the twinge of arthritis in his knees as he stepped down. The familiar pain heralded the beginning of autumn, when damp pervaded the stone wall of his rooms back at the college and seeped into his bones.

But autumn and winter had their own pleasures and he preferred Oxford in the darker days, dusted with snow, although that was rare these days. Mulled wine and Mass by candlelight, nights telling tales of old … and his books.

Always his books.

Despite the digitalization of the Bodleian Library and the march towards all things online, he still valued the weight of tomes filled with knowledge on his shelves. Amongst them, a rare Wettstein New Testament in Greek, a first edition of *The Pilgrim's Progress*, an illuminated Book of Hours from the Tudor period and an Armenian antiphony, a liturgical book used by the choir. Books he had collected on his travels in the Middle East, illuminated by the hands of monks long dead before him.

The many map books were amongst his most precious things, proof that borders meant nothing in the path of history. Most people assumed that countries were fixed, that nationalities were more than just an idea. But the map books Ben had on his shelves proved how the world had shifted over time, as men who cared more about resources like oil rather than people remade the borders to suit themselves. Maps proved the world was mutable, the edges porous, ever changing.

He thought of Morgan, off on another ARKANE mission. She worked on the edge of supernatural mysteries, as he himself had once done back in his Vatican days. He had thought those days were over, but on the trip to India, he had faced evil incarnate. He remembered the darkness of the Kali temple, the blood of sacrifice pooling before him and the thought that he would certainly be next.

He shivered and pulled his robe closer about him. He

was glad to be back here, far away from the demons of the east. There were more than enough of his own to conquer.

Once on the main path, Ben shuffled along the cobblestones through the archway into the tiny square of the main Bodleian Library before walking out past the Sheldonian Theatre onto Broad Street. Students cycled past on their way to lectures, bells ringing to encourage the tourist photographers out the way. It was too easy to forget the glorious surroundings when hurrying to the next tutorial. The rarefied air of Oxford became just another city when an essay deadline loomed, and Ben supposed the romance of getting into the university soon faded with the reality of the workload.

But he was grateful for every day he was able to walk these ancient streets, for every moment he had left to breathe the air that so many brilliant scholars had before him. Time was ever more fleeting the older he became.

Would he swap his life for that of a newly minted student? Ben chuckled at the thought. No, he couldn't keep up with all the technology anyway and thank the Lord, he had a good life in these twilight years.

He turned at the church of St Mary Magdalen and walked past the Martyrs' Memorial, commemorating Anglican bishops Cranmer, Latimer, and Ridley, who had been burned at the stake in the sixteenth century. An unwashed man crouched on the steps, holding a bottle in a paper bag. The smell of booze emanated from his skin. He looked up as Ben passed, his eyes narrowing a little as if expecting some kind of reprimand.

Ben rummaged in his satchel for some coins and handed them to the man with a smile.

"For your supper."

It was hard being poor in a city like Oxford, where the elite were well catered to but the unfortunate of the city were unwelcome. Especially near the colleges.

Ben crossed the road to head up St Giles as he hummed a few bars of Liszt's *Bénédiction de Dieu*. Outside the Ashmolean Museum, just before he reached the haven of Blackfriars, a white transit van swerved in.

It pulled up right next to him on the pavement. Ben stopped in surprise.

The door opened and a man jumped out, a tattoo of a snake winding up his neck.

Before Ben could even shout, the man shoved him through the side of the van, jumped in after and slid the door shut.

The van pulled out into the main road, heading north.

CHAPTER 21

Oxford, England.

BEN CLUTCHED AT THE sides of the van and pulled himself upright in the moving vehicle as it sped up the main road. The man sat watching him, his dark eyes unfathomable.

"What do you want, my son?" Ben asked.

"Father Ben Costanza." The man's tone was a threat. "Dominican monk based at Blackfriars. Tutor for the Angelicum, but once an archaeologist specializing in the Near East. Friend of the Vatican."

"Yes, all that is true." Ben nodded. "But what do you need from me?"

The man didn't blink. "Mentor to Doctor Morgan Sierra."

Ben froze at Morgan's name. He knew that her sister Faye and her family had gone into hiding with ARKANE in the last twenty-four hours but he didn't know the details why. Was this who she was running from?

The man smiled. "I see your fear, old man, but don't worry. If you help me, you need have no concern about your safety. Morgan Sierra has nothing I need now ... but you do."

Ben sighed and shook his head a little. "I'm old and much of my life has been conducted in the shadows. I've traveled many places and seen many things. You'll have to be more specific."

The man nodded. "Soon."

The van turned sharp left and moments later, it turned down a bumpy road. Ben considered where they might be. Given the short distance, it was likely they were in the more rural area near Wolvercote. It was close to the city but there were still farmhouses that seemed in the middle of nowhere.

There would be no one to hear him shout for help.

His tutorial student would wait ten minutes and then take advantage of his absence to go work on his essay again. No one would miss him until tomorrow's breakfast when the professors, monks and students gathered in the Hall. Even then, sometimes he skipped it when fasting. He was at the mercy of this man for at least twenty-four hours.

But it couldn't be any worse than the Kali temple. An image of Sister Nataline flashed through his mind, how her faith had sustained her even as she faced certain death.

Could he be so brave? Would he have to be?

The van stopped and the man pushed the door back to reveal a small cottage on the edge of a wide-open green field. Port Meadow, the closest Oxford came to wilderness, a large area of common land recorded in the Domesday Book of 1086 ... and a haven of peace and quiet. Nothing like the busy city only a few kilometers away.

The man got out and reached in a hand to help Ben clamber down. Another man emerged from the front of the van and went to open the cottage door.

"We won't be disturbed here." Ben heard the edge of threat in his voice. "Krait," the man called. "Prepare the room."

Ben balked at the words, but there was nowhere to run and they would soon catch him even if he could break away. His old legs were not meant for much more than hobbling these days.

But at least he could go with some dignity.

Ben stood tall, shaking the man's hand from his arm. He walked towards the door, trying to be steady on his feet. He'd seen Morgan fight before and for a moment, he toyed with the idea of channeling her strength. Perhaps he could get away from the man.

He saw a spade by the edge of the garden. It was only a few paces away on the diagonal. The edge was sharp and he could swing it as a weapon.

"Don't even think about it," the man behind him growled. "Go inside."

Ben stepped under the ivy-clad doorway into the cottage. Deep grey flagstones led into a homely kitchen, but the place smelled musty and unused.

The other man, Krait, stood inside. He waved a hand towards the sitting room. Ben turned in and gasped at the sight.

A wooden chair had been placed in the middle of the room and the floor covered with black plastic. Beside the chair was a small table with a series of knives laid out upon it.

He grabbed hold of the door, backing away.

"No, please!"

Krait forced him forward.

* * *

Valley of the Kings, Egypt.

The clunk of metal on stone and the yammering of voices woke Morgan from a restless sleep filled with nightmares. She opened her eyes to see a chink of light appearing at the top of the cave-in.

She rolled to her feet and clambered up, trying to see out of the crack.

"Help! We're trapped in here."

An Egyptian security guard appeared at the hole.

"I'm so sorry, miss. This is terrible. Please move away from the rocks and we'll have you out soon."

Morgan slid back down to the bottom of the pile. Jake rubbed his eyes as he got to his feet. Martin uncurled himself from the floor, stretching his stiff limbs. The sound of the rescuers grew louder as they redoubled their efforts to clear the way.

"Hopefully it won't take them long to get us out of here," Morgan said. She felt a dawning sense that everything could possibly turn out OK. The Egyptian authorities were very concerned that tourists had a good experience here and after gunfire at the Hatshepsut temple yesterday, it was likely that they wanted to prevent any further negative press. They would hurry.

She looked at her watch, calculating the time in England. She imagined Gemma waking up, the little girl reading one of her favorite books in bed with her cuddly toy dog. Faye would be there, arms around her daughter. Morgan smiled at the thought and then her smile faded. If Samael touched them … she couldn't bear to consider it.

She picked up another rock and hefted it away from the pile. Jake and Martin joined in, redoubling their efforts. She had had quite enough of being trapped in caves.

* * *

It was another hour before there was enough space for them to squeeze out the top of the cave-in into the chamber beyond. Morgan slid down the other side into the waiting arms of the Egyptian security team. There were medics on site who insisted on checking them for any injury.

"I'm fine, really. I just need a phone."

As a medic cleaned some of her superficial injuries, Morgan managed to get a mobile from one of the security guards. She called Marietti and the Director answered on the first ring.

"Damn it, Morgan. Where have you been?"

She quickly told him what had happened.

"But we're all fine. It's my sister I'm worried about. Samael threatened those I love."

"Just a minute. Hold the line and I'll check."

Marietti kept the phone line open so she could hear him call the Oxford ARKANE labs. One of the agents answered and Morgan heard the rumble of low voices, but couldn't quite make out the words. Then Marietti came back on the line.

"They're OK. Gemma slept well and she's having breakfast. Faye and David are coping well despite the shock of the attack. They're safe. I've told the agents to activate the shut-down protocol until further notice. No one is getting in there."

Morgan sighed with relief, the weight of concern lifting a little. But how many more times could she put her family in danger? Was her role at ARKANE just too risky for those she loved?

Then a cold fear tightened around her heart.

"Ben," she said. "Is he safe too?"

Marietti was quiet for a moment. "He refused extra security when we returned from India," he said. "But let me see if we can locate him."

Once again, Morgan heard his low voice, but this time there was a darker tone.

"He's not in his office and he didn't show up for breakfast, but the Porter says he often works at the Rad Cam in the early mornings. I'll send someone to find him, Morgan. You just get to the airport and come home."

As he cut the line, Morgan sat unmoving in the tomb

as the medic swabbed her wounds. The smell of antiseptic filled the air, the hubbub of voices around her as security teams tried to get everything under control. But she could only see the wall in front of her, a portrayal of the death of the Pharaoh, his heart weighed against the feather of truth as he left this world for the one beyond.

CHAPTER 22

Oxford, England.

KRAIT PUSHED BEN INTO the chair as the other man entered the room behind them. Together, they bound him, arms pinned by his sides, legs taped to each chair leg, a final piece of tape over his mouth.

Then they left the room.

Ben broke out in a cold sweat as he looked at the table of knives by the chair. His heart beat so fast he thought it might burst from his chest. Lord, give me strength. Martyrs had suffered torture and pain for the sake of Christ. They were in glory now. If he could just calm himself … but his eyes kept lighting on the knives and he could almost feel the sharp edges on his flesh. This body was old and he feared that he would not be strong enough to withstand the pain.

What did the man want?

Ben wracked his brain for something that they could be interested in but the years jumbled together in his mind, the many archaeological digs he'd been on, the artifacts he'd worked with at the Vatican, the people he had wronged along the way. He had sought forgiveness, praying for his own soul and those of others, but all leave a wake in the path through life. Sometimes those ripples have unintended consequences.

The sharp whistle of a boiling kettle pierced the air.

A minute later, the first man entered the room with two steaming cups. He placed one on the table next to Ben, alongside the knives.

"Hot, sweet tea. Helps with stress. Can we talk a little?"

Ben nodded.

The man pulled the tape away and lifted the cup for Ben to sip. Sweetness filled his mouth and the taste calmed him a little. The man wiped a little dribble from his chin, an almost tender gesture.

"Forgive my brutal tactics but I'm going to be honest with you, Ben. We don't have much time. So we need to begin now and I need you to cooperate. I hope I don't have to use these." He nodded to the knives. "Let's begin with introductions. My name is Samael."

His words sent a chill down Ben's spine. The archangel of death, the seducer and destroyer. For a man to take such a name, he had to be committed to the dark.

"I seek the seven seals of Revelation."

Ben paled. It was worse than he had thought.

Samael took up one of the knives, his hand hefting its weight.

"I dislike such crude measures of torture, so I have something that will help you remember. Something that will make your compliance pleasurable." Samael walked out of the room and then returned a minute later with a hypodermic needle. The liquid within was a pale green. "Your kind have always been wannabe martyrs, resisting pain with the power of faith. But with this, you won't be able to control your response. Even your God won't be able to stop you speaking of the past."

Ben squirmed on the chair, pushing himself as far away as he could but he was pinned.

Samael advanced towards him and pulled Ben's collar down. He grabbed Ben's hair and yanked his head sideways. He plunged the needle into the muscles of his neck.

Ben felt the sting and then pressure as the liquid forced into him, burning like fire as it spread.

"This is a hallucinogen distilled from the venom of the coral cobra, one of God's most beautiful snakes, with distinctive red and black bands." His voice was mocking. "There is no cure for the venom but this is just a tiny dose." Samael pulled the needle from Ben's neck. "You might even enjoy the experience, as it dulls the real world around you."

Samael sat back in the chair opposite Ben and sipped his tea as he waited for the poison to take effect. Minutes ticked past and it seemed that the silence expanded to consume the space. All Ben could hear was the dry rustle of snakeskin across the floor behind him.

Or did he imagine that?

Samael's dark eyes raked his soul and Ben felt that the man saw something inside him, the darker part, the aspect of himself he wrestled to deny, that he prayed on his knees to subdue.

But all men had a drop of darkness within them and Ben felt the poison caressing that part of him, a tendril of truth after a lifetime of hiding.

He wanted to confess. He wanted to give up the secret he had held for so long.

"I found a seal." Ben heard himself from a long way off. It didn't even sound like his own voice anymore. "On a dig in Ephesus many years ago." His mind slipped back into the past, back to the days when he was young and he was in love with Marianne, Morgan and Faye's mother. He had watched her that summer and doubted his calling to the Church. But she had loved another.

"Continue." Samael's voice snapped through his memory.

"I was part of a series of digs, investigating what was left of the seven churches named in Revelation. The Vatican believed that much of the book wasn't allegory but real. We found seven lampstands in the ruins. And although there weren't seven seals, I did find one."

"Where is it now?" Samael snapped.

"I didn't give it to the Vatican like I should have." Ben's voice trailed off.

Samael slapped him across the face, the jolt of pain anchoring Ben to the here and now. "I don't have to hurt Morgan and her family, but I will. Answer me."

Ben couldn't remember why he ever thought to hide the seal, but whatever the reason, it was nothing compared to those he loved. He was at the end of his own days, and theirs were just beginning.

"It's in the Ashmolean," he whispered. "Within their extensive catalogue of ancient Near Eastern seals, hidden in plain sight. No one would think it was anything special and when they collected other seals from the period, I donated it."

"Why is it special?"

Samael bent close. Ben could see each scale of his snake tattoo, the pulse in the vein in his neck giving it a semblance of life.

He frowned. It was important not to say the words but he couldn't resist. The venom freed his tongue. Perhaps this was God's will anyway. He was a mere wisp in the wind, blown apart by forces much bigger than himself. He took a deep breath and uttered the words he had never before spoken aloud.

"I fear it is one of the seven seals that will usher in the End Times."

As he said the words, Samael smiled with triumph and began to free him from the chair.

"Krait," he called. "Get the van. We're going back into Oxford."

Ben couldn't move. His head rolled onto his chest as the bonds loosened. His limbs felt disconnected, as if they weren't his own and he was dimly aware that his heart rate was much faster now, his pulse skipping beats. He heard it thudding in his chest like a countdown.

As the two men helped half-drag, half-carry him to the van, Ben realized that hours had passed. The night air smelled of autumn leaves and a hint of wood smoke. With his heightened senses, he could separate the scent of decaying flowers in the mulch of the earth from the tang of his own cold sweat. He could feel the muscles of the men by him and sense his own wasted body. The filters of reality shifted and for a moment, Ben felt as if his own flesh melted into theirs. He was just a tiny part of a whole organism. Wonder flooded his mind.

Krait pulled open the door and they lifted him inside the van, laying him on the floor.

Ben could feel the cool metal against his skin, a welcome balm to his heated flesh. Visions of the martyrs from history came to him and flames danced across his flesh as they drove back into Oxford. But his eyes were fixed in another realm and he smiled at the sheer beauty of it.

In what seemed like moments later, Samael and Krait walked him into the delivery entrance round the back of the Ashmolean.

"Is he alright?" a gruff voice said. One of the security guards, clearly paid off to let them in.

Samael pulled a wad of cash from his pocket, the roll of hundred pound notes silencing the guard. They walked on.

Now that he was inside, Ben felt pulled to the seal, as if it called to him through the museum corridors.

He had been in to visit it over the years. It always pleased him to see it sitting side by side with seals used for official correspondence, the disinterested public not seeing the true meaning of the stone. The gaudy and shiny objects attracted more attention. As it was with so much of life.

"That way," he panted and his words seemed to linger in the air.

Ben led Samael and Krait into the labyrinth of corridors. Like so many great museums, the Ashmolean was an overwhelming cornucopia of ancient delight, a treasure trove of objects, each of which had a story spanning generations. Ben had spent many of his days here over the years, as it was just next door to Blackfriars and he enjoyed the company of strangers without having to talk to them. The sense of history soaked through the walls of the place. The colors around him were brighter now and Ben wished he could stop to look once more at some of his favorite objects.

But there was no time.

He led Samael and Krait to the ancient Near Eastern section and stopped in front of a glass-fronted case.

"It's that one." Ben pointed at a round stone seal with the undulating curves of a serpent clearly visible on its surface. He remembered digging it from the ground of Ephesus that summer, a symbol of an ancient belief that even pre-dated Christianity. Now he could feel the tightening of the serpent's coils.

It was suddenly hard to breathe.

Ben sank to the floor, clutching at his chest through a haze of pain. He watched as Krait pulled a crowbar from his backpack and hammered the metal into the glass.

It cracked. An alarm rang out.

"Hurry!" Samael shouted. Krait smashed the glass again, then levered the end of the crowbar into the hole and pulled the shards away.

Samael took the seal from its case, a triumphant smile on his face. "The seventh seal."

At his triumphant words, Ben felt a jolt of pain flash

through his chest. In the depths of the venom trance, he sensed his end approach.

It was past time.

He summoned Morgan's face to his mind, the daughter he never had, the woman he was so proud of. There was only one thing now that might stop the Great Serpent from consuming the world. He hoped she would find it.

But he could do no more.

A violent spasm wrenched Ben into blackness.

CHAPTER 23

As dawn broke over London, Morgan looked out of the plane window at the sleeping city nestled around the curves of the River Thames below. Millions of people lay down there with no idea of ARKANE and the secrets they kept, no clue about the edge of destruction averted so many times. She had once been one of those unknowing, and now she could never go back to that state.

Even if she left and returned to her university position in Oxford, she would always be aware that Jake and the other ARKANE agents walked the earth, hunting down dark secrets.

She looked over at Jake now, his face relaxed in sleep, the corkscrew scar the only physical evidence of the battles he had faced. Could she really have a normal life on the outside?

As the plane touched down soon after, Morgan turned her phone back on. When they had boarded the plane a few hours ago, Marietti still hadn't located Father Ben and she had spent the flight worrying. She hoped he was lost in some manuscript in one of the lesser-known libraries around the university, head bent over ancient Greek words. He had forgotten the time, that was all. Just an old scholar lost in his manuscripts. But she also felt a rising sense of desperation, and she held back her tears as her phone beeped.

There were several voicemails and a text message.

Morgan's heart beat faster as she opened it.

There's a car waiting for you at Arrivals. You need to get to Oxford.

She took a deep breath, trying to calm herself.

Ben was more than a mentor. He had been her mother's friend a long time ago and when her parents divorced, Ben supported Marianne and helped her care for the twin daughter, Faye, that she left behind when she died of breast cancer. Morgan had met Ben later in life and he had helped her settle in at Oxford, providing guidance to the academic political quagmire.

He had helped her and Jake on so many ARKANE missions, risking his life for her in the flames of the Grand Lodge of the Freemasons and almost dying in India in the hunt for the Shiva Nataraja statue. He was an old man, for sure, but he had an inner strength that made him seem so much younger.

Morgan summoned Ben's face to her mind, his quiet smile, the depth of his faith despite what he had seen in the darker side of religion. It was never God who erred in his mind, only His creation.

Jake stirred and opened his eyes. He frowned as he saw the concern on her face.

"What's wrong?"

"It's something about Ben." Morgan clicked the voicemail button and listened to Marietti's words, color draining from her cheeks as she heard what had happened.

Morgan, I'm so sorry. Father Ben was found at the Ashmolean Museum next to an exhibit of Near Eastern seals. He died of a massive heart attack and his body showed signs of poisoning by snake venom. One of the seals is missing. We're sure that Samael and the Brotherhood of the Serpent were involved.

"No!" Morgan couldn't help her cry of despair. Tears

welled up and ran down her cheeks. Jake pulled her close, rocking her as Marietti's voice continued the message.

His body is at the John Radcliffe hospital morgue. The car waiting at Arrivals will take you straight there. Again, I'm so sorry. Despite our differences, Ben was a good man. Call me when you can.

Morgan wept as Jake held her. He said nothing while she sobbed and for that she was grateful. Sometimes, there were no words.

The worry and pain of the last few days overflowed and Morgan let it all out. Not long ago, she had fought for Ben's life in a bloody temple in India. She had expected many more years together, and now he was gone.

Her tears finally slowed and Morgan felt the stirrings of a white-hot anger. She raised her head and wiped her eyes.

"Samael will pay for Ben's death." Her voice was calm. "I'm going to Oxford to say goodbye and then we'll track the bastard down."

Jake nodded. "Do you want me to come with you?"

"No. I need to do this alone. Can you work with Martin on where Samael might be going next? If he has all seven seals, we need to find where he's planning to use them."

* * *

A few hours later, Morgan arrived at the John Radcliffe Hospital in Oxford and headed for the morgue. Although Ben's body had been identified already, Marietti had arranged for her to visit before it was released to the funeral directors.

The clinical white corridors smelled of antiseptic, an attempt to reverse the stench of sickness and decay of death. The scent took her back to the tomb in the Valley of the Kings. Death comes for all in the end and cannot be held back for long. Ben had been old, and of course, Morgan had expected this day would come at some point. She had hoped he would go to his God in his study surrounded by books, in the comfort of the life he had built for himself. But then few are able to choose the manner of their own deaths.

She entered the morgue and signed in, before being escorted to the viewing area. In a small white room, a body lay on a metal gurney under a white sheet, face covered.

Now she was here, Morgan hesitated.

She had seen death so many times, but this was different. After her own father had been blown up in what had seemed like a suicide bombing in Israel years back, Ben had been like a second father to her. She couldn't bear the thought of seeing his face now, lifeless on a slab.

Morgan steeled herself. She needed to be sure, and she owed Ben these last moments. She walked to the body, and stood by the head. She nodded and the lab tech pulled the sheet down, revealing the face of the corpse.

Ben's face.

Tears sprang to her eyes and ran down her cheeks as Morgan looked down on his dear features one last time. White hair swept back from a strong brow. Lines that had been earned through living and working hard for his God. She didn't know too much about Ben's past but she knew that he had given much for his belief. And he would have done anything for her.

She took one last look, understanding that this physical body wasn't the man she had loved, just his temporary shell. The Ben she knew had gone.

"Thank you."

The lab tech covered him again. Morgan turned and walked out. She would remember Ben as he was in life. At his funeral, the remains of that physical body would be lowered into the ground, but his kindness and faith lived on in her memory. She would honor that.

She would also make sure that the man who sent him to his grave would beat him into the ground. She would find Samael.

First, she needed to check Ben's office. Martin had sent through security footage showing Ben being taken from St Giles and many hours later, being escorted through the halls of the Ashmolean. A seal had been stolen, but Morgan was puzzled as to how Ben knew about it.

She needed to get to his rooms before the college cleared them out.

A short time later, Morgan arrived at Blackfriars, her heart heavy. Tears pricked her eyes as she walked towards the staircase that led to Ben's study rooms. She passed the green quadrangle where students lay on the grass, laughing and joking together. The sound rang hollow for her, even though she knew that Ben kept his window open so he could hear the students. They kept him young, he always said.

"Dr Sierra?"

The voice came from the window of the Porter's Lodge. Morgan turned to see an old man dressed in a three-piece suit poking his head out and waving at her. Fred, the Porter, took his job as the gatekeeper to the college very seriously.

She hadn't signed in. Morgan walked back over.

"Sorry, Fred. I'm just here to visit Father Ben's room one last time. Is that OK?"

"Of course. And you know how sorry we all are to hear of the Father's passing. He was a good man. With the Lord now though. A better place."

Morgan didn't share Fred's faith but she nodded. "I'm going to miss him so much."

Fred reached a hand out and squeezed her shoulder. "He certainly thought a lot of you, Dr Sierra. In fact, he told me to give you something. It was a while back, before he went to India. He must have been worried about traveling at his age, I s'pose." Fred opened a tall filing cabinet and rustled around in the papers. He pulled out a manila envelope and handed it to her. "He said that if anything happened, I was to give you this."

Her name was written on the front in Ben's handwriting.

"Thank you. Do you mind if I read it up in his room?"

Fred waved her away. "Take as long as you like. We're not scheduled to get the room cleaned up until after the funeral at the end of next week."

Morgan walked back across the quad and up the stairs to Ben's room. She pulled a key from her pocket and opened the door. It was dark inside and she went to pull the curtains open. The room smelled of cinnamon and nutmeg, the spices of the chai tea that Ben loved so much. She took a deep breath and closed her eyes, hoping to feel him here somehow.

But Ben was gone.

Morgan opened her eyes and looked around at his study, dominated by shelves piled with books. Ben had never defined himself by physical possessions, but he certainly loved to read. She had sat here so many times asking him convoluted theological questions and he had always pulled down exactly the right tome to find the answer. He had retained his quick mind and inexhaustible memory to the end.

Who would she ask her questions of now?

Martin Klein? Google?

Morgan smiled at the thought. Then she looked down at the letter in her hand. She sank down to the chair and opened the envelope. It contained one sheet of paper covered with Ben's spidery handwriting.

My dearest Morgan,

I write this as I head to Goa to meet you. The Lord only knows what we shall face together this trip. Part of me is excited to join you on a mission! But time passes and I grow weaker and I worry that I won't have time to tell you what I need to. So this letter is just in case and if you're reading it, then I am gone.

Don't be sad that I've passed beyond the veil. I've been so tired these last years so it will be a relief to go, although I will miss seeing your future triumphs. And they will be triumphs, dear Morgan, whatever you choose to do. I will miss seeing little Gemma grow up and I hope you and Faye will find your peace with each other.

Take whatever you want from my study, whatever will help you or leave it all. It matters not.

Except one thing.

There is a box that is for you and you alone. Do not tell ARKANE of it for I know that Marietti would dearly love what is inside. Remember the day we discussed the role of Spirit-inspired prophecy vs. the effect of fasting in the Revelation of St John? You will find the directions in the book we talked of then.

Be safe, Morgan, and know that I have always loved you as the daughter I could never have.

Ben

Morgan let the silent tears come as she re-read his words. At his age, the end could have come at any time, and Ben had been ready to face it. But he should not have died in agony without those he loved around him, and her rage would not abate until she avenged his death.

But first, she had to find this box and her curiosity was piqued as to what could be within. ARKANE had vaulted rooms under Trafalgar Square in London, containing precious objects from all cultures across history. What could Ben have kept that ARKANE could possibly want? She knew that Ben and Marietti had a history together, a distrust from their past at the Vatican and both kept secrets she would never know. She smiled. Trust Ben to leave a mystery, knowing she would be unable to resist the hunt.

She looked up at the wall-sized bookshelf and tried to remember the conversation he referred to. It was a few winters ago, before she had even joined ARKANE. She had a client at her private psychology practice, a survivor of a cult. The girl had believed the End Times prophecy, but much of their cult practice involved extreme periods of fasting. Morgan had gone to Ben to understand his perspective, since fasting was a common spiritual practice in many religions and Ben specialized in multi-faith disciplines.

She stood and scanned over the titles, running her fingertips along the oversize spines.

This one.

She pulled the book from the middle shelf, a treatise on fasting by Rabbi Jonathan Sacks. Not a book that many would expect in the library of a Dominican monk.

There was something in the pages and as she shook the book, a postcard fell to the floor.

Morgan picked it up. There was no writing on it but the distinctive spire of the building on the front caught her eye.

CHAPTER 24

Salisbury, England.

MORGAN AND JAKE WALKED down the path through the expansive green lawn around Salisbury Cathedral. The tallest spire in Britain towered over the town, and Morgan looked up as they approached.

"It was built in the thirteenth century to the glory of God," she said quietly, "but there are a lot of interesting things about this place."

"Stonehenge is only up the road a little way, isn't it?"

The prehistoric standing stones were thirteen kilometers north, constructed over 4000 years ago as a pagan worship site aligned with the sunrise of the summer solstice and the sunset of the winter solstice. Like the Egyptian temples, light would strike a particular stone on a particular day, evidence of the continuation of the gods' pact with mankind.

Morgan realized that Jake was trying to distract her from dwelling on Ben's death. She appreciated his attempt, but truthfully, this place really was fascinating. While Martin worked on trying to locate the sarcophagus, they had some time and Salisbury was only a few hours' drive. Martin had relocated to the vaults below Oxford, and promised to keep an extra eye on Faye and Gemma. While Morgan wanted to go to them, she needed to finish things with Samael first to ensure they would be safe. She would not see her sister's face on a mortuary slab.

"This cathedral, the church of Old Sarum, and Stonehenge are said to be placed on a ley line," she said. "They're considered by some to be ancient trackways of pagan Britain, mystical alignments that have a certain energy."

Jake raised an eyebrow. "Sounds like fun. What are we expecting to find here?"

"Ben's note implied some kind of box, but your guess is as good as mine as to where it might be. Or what's inside."

They continued up the path towards the church. The Great West Front portico featured sculptures of the patriarchs, prophets, apostles and saints, many heavily weathered over time. Morgan recognized Abraham with his knife, Daniel with a lion at his side, and a horned Moses with the tablets of the law. There were even some women, Saint Katherine with the wheel she was martyred on, Saint Barbara with a palm and castle. In the Jewish faith that Morgan was raised within, such images were never used, but she had to admit that these churches were spectacular. A myriad of stories in stone.

Some of the more weathered sculptures had been replaced with newer statues and Morgan was surprised and pleased to see one with clearly African features, evidence that Salisbury Cathedral moved with the times. After all, the church was far more active in sub-Saharan Africa, Latin America and Asia these days than it was in the historic centers of Europe.

She consulted the notes that Martin had provided about the church.

"That's Canon Ezra Baya Lawiri," she said, indicating the sculpture. "A Sudanese teacher who translated the Bible into the local Moru language. He was killed in the Sudanese war in 1991."

"I don't think I've ever seen an African face carved on

an English cathedral," Jake noted, smiling up at the serious figure clutching his Bible. "It's incredible to think that they didn't have the Bible in their language until he translated it so recently."

They walked through the great door into the cathedral, emerging into the colonnade of the cloisters. Arched stone windows looked onto a square lawn beyond with a massive cedar tree dominating the space. With the rain dripping down outside, it was peaceful but there was a chill here too. Morgan imagined the faithful coming here over the last 800 years, walking the cloister quadrangle as they prayed for their health, for enough to live on, for the safety of their families. People weren't so different now, although perhaps more distant from the spiritual energy of a place like this. But the stone had soaked up the faith of years and Morgan could still feel the imprint of the past here.

They walked into the cathedral nave and stood for a moment at the back. It had a Gothic vaulted ceiling, the lines of the arches accentuated by the use of darker grey Purbeck marble against lighter Chilmark stone walls. Light streamed through stained glass windows either side.

A modern font in the shape of a curving Greek cross reflected the high ceilings above. Biblical sayings ran around the edges. *When you pass through the waters, I will be with you.* Isaiah chapter forty-three. So often these Christian churches used words from the Jewish scriptures and the simple use of water made Morgan feel closer to God than the grand architecture around them. Any belief she did have was rooted in the needs of a desert people, and water was always precious.

They walked on past the niches that lined the nave where noblemen had been buried over the years. Morgan glanced into each of the side chapels as they passed. She didn't know what they were looking for, but she trusted

Ben enough to know she would recognize whatever it was when they found it.

They walked down to the far end of the cathedral. A stained glass window in hues of deep blue and shades of red cast a darker light onto a small altar. A candle wrapped in barbed wire stood before it, representing Prisoners of Conscience imprisoned for their faith around the world. It was striking, but not what they were looking for. They continued on in front of the choir stalls, emerging before the altar. It was simple, a juxtaposition to the ornate stone and wood carvings around it.

Then Morgan glanced up.

"Oh!" She couldn't help the exclamation of surprise as she caught sight of the strange window above the altar. She pointed up to a series of glass panels.

Moses stood in the center, a golden serpent wrapped around a pole next to him. At his feet, people lay on the ground writhing in pain while snakes slithered around them. Underneath, they could faintly make out the words, *Even so must the Son of Man be lifted up*, from John's gospel, chapter three.

"That is a strange image to have above a Christian altar," Jake said.

"I know," Morgan replied. "I've never seen the brazen serpent image used in such a prominent place before. The book of Numbers, chapter twenty-one recounts that God told Moses to make a bronze serpent so that any who were bitten could be healed by it. As we saw at Megiddo, the snake was a cultic object in ancient Israel. There was a serpent in the Holy of Holies, known as Nehushtan, before the reforms of Hezekiah, before the First Temple was destroyed. The serpent was also known in other ancient cultures as having healing properties."

"Like the rod of Asclepius in ancient Greece."

"Exactly. But it's strange because graven images were

considered anathema to the Jews. They were punished for the golden calf in the desert, and yet this snake remained a symbol. And now the church uses it as an analogy for Jesus."

Jake frowned. "It's a bit of a stretch to compare Jesus to a serpent, isn't it?"

Morgan nodded. "I've always thought so, although perhaps it relates to healing in some way. A supernatural remedy for snakebite is something truly precious to a desert people."

"So what's the significance? Why would Father Ben send us here?"

Morgan's face crumpled at Jake's words and he reached out a hand to grasp hers.

"I'm sorry," he said softly.

Morgan wiped the tears from her eyes. "I miss him so much already, but I'm determined to find what he left me. Samael is mine when we find him, Jake."

He nodded. "Understood."

Morgan looked up again at the stained glass. "We need to ask who worked on this or whether there are any other artifacts that relate to the serpent here."

They walked back down the nave and into the little shop at the side of the cloisters. Morgan spoke to one of the ladies serving and they were directed back towards the document archives.

An elderly man met them at a rickety desk.

"We're interested in the Moses window," Morgan said. "I think a friend of mine had something to do with it. Father Ben Costanza?"

The man's eyes didn't flicker. Morgan saw no indication that he recognized the name.

"The preservation of the stained glass windows will always be an ongoing project," he said. "That window was threatened because it needed so much work. To be honest,

I think some in the church consider it an inappropriate image to have above the altar." He smiled. "But I quite like it. Ties us to the past and let's say, the exotic beginnings of our faith. Reminds us to remember the Middle East in our prayers."

Morgan wanted to encourage his friendliness but they didn't have much time.

"It was threatened, you say …?"

"Yes, but then there was a large donation, specifically tied to that window."

"Do you have any records of the details, or anything that was left behind along with the donation?"

The old man rubbed his chin. "Hmm, let me see. I'll have to go out back but you've piqued my interest, young lady. Why don't you wait in the Chapter House and I'll come find you when I've had a look."

Morgan didn't see that they had any choice. She nodded.

"Thank you, I really appreciate your help."

She and Jake walked back down the cloisters towards the Chapter House.

"The world turns on the curiosity of one man," Jake whispered. "But I'm glad we don't have to break in here and look for it ourselves."

"That's if he finds anything."

They walked into the octagonal Chapter House, bright with sunlight that poured in through high windows. A decorative medieval frieze circled the interior above the stalls, alive with figures from Genesis and Exodus. Morgan recognized Adam and Eve, Abraham, Noah and even the Tower of Babel. A gigantic display case dominated one side. A group of tourists huddled around it as their guide explained the manuscript within.

"This is one of the four surviving original copies of the Magna Carta, the Great Charter or peace treaty that promised protections against a tyrannical King."

The guide continued to explain the history of the document but Morgan tuned out her words. She looked at her watch. Time ticked on. She imagined the old man rifling through boxes in a long hall of records. Would he even find anything?

The sound of footsteps came from the corridor and then the old man emerged.

"I found this." He held up a small rectangular package wrapped in brown paper, dusty from the storeroom. It had her name written clearly on the front in thick black ink. "Are you Morgan Sierra?"

Morgan pulled out her driver's license. He looked at it, nodded and then handed her the box.

"I'll just go and photocopy this for the records," he said. "Back in a minute."

The tourist group walked out of the Chapter House and they were alone.

"I'm not waiting any longer."

Morgan crouched down on the floor and peeled open the package. Inside was a plain cedar-wood box. There were no carvings as would be expected from a Dominican friar. Morgan smiled. Ben was never one for over-decoration or fussiness.

She opened it.

CHAPTER 25

Inside the box was a note and another package, wrapped tight in oilskin. Morgan opened the note first. Ben's spidery handwriting stood out on the cream paper.

My dearest Morgan,

If you nd this, I'm gone and I'm sorry to leave you with this burden. I found this vial with the seal in Ephesus. The carvings in the tomb where I discovered it referenced a serpent trapped for a thousand years and suggested that this was some kind of antidote or weapon. I don't know which, or what it's for. But I know enough of evil to trust how important this is. Whether the serpent is real or allegorical, this may help in the ght against it.

May God guide you and give you His strength,

Ben

Morgan unwrapped the package.

It contained a vial made of thick glass, tightly sealed with creamy wax. The glass was opaque but the color within was a deep scarlet.

"Blood?" Jake suggested.

"Could be." Morgan held it up to the light. The liquid inside was viscous and stuck to the sides as she swirled it. "I should get this to Martin to test in the labs, right?"

Jake nodded. "That would be the best plan."

"But Ben said specifically to keep it away from ARKANE …"

"And given what happened to Martin," Jake continued, "it might not be safe to take the vial into HQ right now."

Morgan nodded. "So we keep it with us until this is done."

Her phone buzzed with a message from Martin.

The confluence of the stars is imminent and the eclipse will cover Jerusalem tomorrow. We've had reports of a sarcophagus being taken into the Old City of Jerusalem by night. Flights booked out of Heathrow for you both.

Jake checked his phone for the details. "Looks like we need to get going."

Morgan slipped the vial into her backpack. "Let's finish this."

* * *

Jerusalem, Israel.

Deep underneath the citadel, the sound of dripping water echoed through the tunnel. Then came heavy breathing from the men who hauled the massive stone sarcophagus towards the central chamber.

"Careful!" Cardinal Eric Krotalia shouted as it bumped

the walls, leaving a chip off the stone. But he could do nothing to widen the tight tunnel and he waved the men on, standing back as they continued down.

He wiped the sweat from his brow, more from anxiety than physical exertion, since Samael's men were the ones doing all the work. Samael himself was at the head of the group, directing the sacred object towards the chamber. His man Krait heaved at his side, and the woman he had brought, Lilith, slid sinuously ahead of them. She wore a green silk robe, hood covering her face, but he thought he glimpsed scales on her skin and a flash of green eyes in the torchlight.

Truth be told, he was nervous about bringing the sarcophagus down here. Somehow it suddenly made everything real. The ancient Brotherhood of the Serpent had survived as a secret organization for longer than history recorded, perhaps unbroken since the times of ancient Egypt, when Moses raised his brazen serpent in the desert. As much as the Cardinal believed the apocalyptic rhetoric, he had not seriously believed that he would be part of the End of Days.

Until he had seen the markings on the sarcophagus earlier.

Now it was here and doubts crept in. He didn't know what would happen when it was opened. What if he couldn't control the following events? His plans were for an earthly battle, the positioning of pawns on the chessboard of military strategy, enhanced by religious conflict. A changing of the guard in the Middle East, where it was time for Christianity to take a stronger role again, as it had in the Middle Ages. It was likely that Cerastes and Echis thought exactly the same thing: that they would be the ones to triumph once the status quo was gone. But what if none of them were able to contain whatever was in here?

The Cardinal sighed and pressed his hand against the

cold stone of the tunnel wall, letting the physical sensation anchor him to what was real. It was all superstitious nonsense. The Great Serpent was allegory. There would be nothing but dust in the chest.

But he had to make sure.

He had promised to wait until Cerastes and Echis arrived before opening it, but he needed to know what they were dealing with.

They finally rolled the sarcophagus into the cistern and Samael dismissed the men, sending them back up to the Old City with enough money to keep their mouths shut. He indicated Krait should stay.

After the footsteps and coarse laughter faded into silence, only four of them stood in the chamber looking at the sarcophagus.

"Do you have the seals?" the Cardinal asked.

Samael put down his pack and opened it up. He pulled out each stone seal in turn and placed them on the floor in front of him.

"There. Seven in total."

Lilith knelt by the seals, her fingers reaching out to touch them. The Cardinal bent to pull her away.

"Don't touch them! You're not worthy."

As he yanked back her shoulder, she turned her face up. The hood fell away. She hissed at him, sibilance echoing in the chamber.

The Cardinal gasped, his hand flying to his mouth in shock. The woman's face was skeletal thin, her green eyes slitted and glazed, her tongue forked as it flickered towards him.

Samael put his hand on her shoulder. His eyes met the Cardinal's, warning him away.

"It's alright, Lilith. The Cardinal was just trying to honor the Great Serpent. He didn't realize how close you are to Him. How well you have taken to the venom."

"I …"

The Cardinal didn't know what to say, but if this was what the venom could do, then he was glad he hadn't taken it himself. He straightened his robe and took a deep breath. "Well then, perhaps we should take a look inside."

"Yesss. It is time." Lilith's voice made the Cardinal shiver, as if it called to something base inside, the part of him that descended from a common vertebral ancestor.

He glanced over at Krait.

Samael saw his look. "Oh, you can trust Krait, and he deserves to be here."

The Cardinal nodded. Part of him wanted to be one who opened the casket, but he couldn't risk himself. Let Samael take the chance. "Proceed."

Samael picked up the first seal and pressed it to the sarcophagus on top of the indent matching the seal's markings. His fingers shook a little as he slotted it into the ancient stone.

Nothing happened.

"Do the next one!" the Cardinal ordered.

Lilith handed Samael the next seal and once again, he pushed it into the waiting space. Nothing.

Impatient now, he quickly added the next and Lilith joined him, adding the others until all seven were tucked into their spaces on the edge of the sarcophagus.

The Cardinal held his breath, waiting for something … He didn't know what. But all this effort couldn't have been for nothing. His heart sank as he considered possible failure.

Then something inside the stone casket clunked.

A crack appeared along the side.

The sound of thunder rolled through the cistern as if a storm crashed directly overhead. The great pillars cracked and chunks of masonry fell from above. The Cardinal fell to his knees, protecting his head with his arms. Lilith cried out in an exclamation of excitement.

The top of the sarcophagus creaked open. Just a crack, but it was enough.

Samael turned to Krait. "A crowbar, quick."

Krait grabbed one from the corner of the room. Together, they wedged the end into the crack and began to lever the heavy lid up and away from the side, managing to push it up an inch further.

A salty musk of decomposition rose from the opening. Both men recoiled, hands clutched to their faces in disgust. The Cardinal coughed and tried to swallow down the retching that threatened to overwhelm him.

Something had died in there. A long time ago.

But Lilith bent to the crack. She put her face close to it, inhaling the noxious smell as if it were roses, her face contorted in ecstasy. What the hell did she sense that he couldn't?

"Pusssh it further." Her eyes glinted with excitement. "So we can see inside."

Samael wedged the crowbar back into the gap and between them, he and Krait managed to lever the lid even further, sliding it back until it crashed on the floor behind the open casket.

Lilith was the first to look at what lay inside. Her hands flew to her mouth in shock.

"No!" she cried.

The Cardinal stepped forward to stand next to the sarcophagus, Samael and Krait next to him. He looked within.

It was half-filled with grey-green dust, like a powdered form of algae. A deep disappointment filled his body, along with a rising anger.

Samael pushed the end of the crowbar into the dust, raking it around a little just to check if anything was beneath. There was nothing. He turned to Lilith.

"I guess you were wrong."

Her eyes flashed with anger. She wrenched her hand back, putting all her weight into slapping him across the face.

Her serpent ring caught his lip and a drop of blood flew from his mouth to land in the green dust.

"You bitch –" Sam's words stopped abruptly as he saw the blood droplet soaking up the green powder. It changed, hardening and shimmering in the torchlight until it was a perfectly formed bright green polygon.

The Cardinal bent to pick it up and held it to the light.

"Is that what I think it is?" Samael said softly.

The Cardinal nodded. "It's a scale."

Lilith plucked it from his fingers. "We need more blood."

CHAPTER 26

THE CARDINAL BACKED AWAY from the sarcophagus, retreating to the corner of the cistern. Sam met Lilith's gaze, understanding flashing between them.

He spun around with the crowbar, smashing it into Krait's face.

The man flew backwards, stunned at the sudden attack, clutching his broken face as he moaned in pain. Sam whirled the crowbar round again, whacking Krait in the kneecap. The man went down, roaring in pain. Sam raised the weapon to swing the final blow.

Krait surged up from the floor, like an angry bull charging for its life.

He smashed Sam into the side of the sarcophagus. Sam doubled over as the air was driven out of him.

The crowbar fell clattering to the floor. Krait's hands found Sam's neck and squeezed, even as the blood from his injuries dripped down onto the floor.

"You bastard," Krait grunted. "After everything I've done for you and the Brotherhood."

As the edges of his vision began to fade, Sam saw Lilith pick up the crowbar. She swung it at the back of Krait's head.

It connected with a sickening thunk. Krait's hands dropped away and he spun to face the new attacker. It looked like the blow had done nothing but anger him further. Sam fell to his knees, choking on the floor, trying desperately to catch his breath.

Lilith backed away, her hands raised in supplication.

Krait advanced on her. "It's about time you …"

His words trailed off as he faltered. His hands clutched at his head, and then he slumped unconscious to the floor.

Lilith rushed to the fallen man. She grabbed his hands and pulled him back towards the casket.

"Help me! He won't be out for long."

Sam stumbled to his feet and helped lift Krait's body. Together they heaved him over the edge and into the sarcophagus. He thumped down into the grey-green dust, some of it rising to hang in the air around him.

Lilith pulled a knife from her belt. Her green eyes glinted with black slits again, and Sam wondered once more who she had become. She pulled back on Krait's hair with one hand, exposing his throat.

Then she plunged the knife down and tugged it towards her, slitting his jugular vein.

Blood gushed from the wound, pumping out on to the dust. It began to transform into scales that drew themselves together, coalescing into clumps, then tiny worm-like creatures. They wriggled over Krait's body, dissolving his skin and slipping inside, becoming part of him. Eating his body from the inside out. It was mesmerizing to watch.

Suddenly, Krait's eyes flew open in agony.

He tried to sit up, gurgling through the bloody wound at his throat. Sam and Lilith pushed him back, holding him down in the dust as he became a writhing, pulsating mass of bloody flesh.

The Cardinal joined them at the edge of the sarcophagus once it was clear that Krait was really dead. They stood in silence as the body was consumed. By the time it was done, a long chain of scaly lumps lay writhing on the top of the grey-green dust. It wasn't a serpent yet, but Sam could see the beginnings of what it might become. He could feel a twinge of excitement in his belly. This mess of half-formed thing was nothing, but there was still a great deal of grey-green dust remaining.

Lilith still held the bloody knife. She turned towards Sam and the Cardinal. "None of us go in there. Agreed?"

The Cardinal nodded. "Of course. There are plenty more we can find to pay the blood price." He looked down at the writhing mass. "How many do we need?"

A smile played across Lilith's lips and she flickered her forked tongue in the air as if tasting the sacrifice to come. "Ssseven is the sacred number."

Sam had plenty of contacts on the darker side of the city. He looked at his watch. "Give me a couple of hours."

The Cardinal nodded. "Hurry. The confluence of stars and the full moon eclipse coincide at 9:33 p.m., when Jerusalem will be in darkness. My brothers will be here and together, we will greet the Great Serpent."

* * *

Morgan and Jake got out of the taxi at the Damascus Gate. Originally built as a triumphal entrance in Roman times, the existing sixteenth-century gate had been built by the Ottoman Sultan, Suleiman the Magnificent. It was hot and noisy since the ancient place was right next to a busy bus station and highway intersection. Jerusalem had ever been a vibrant city, concerned more with the living than the empires of the dead. Tourist groups headed into the city following guides with colorful umbrellas, while locals expertly dodged those taking photos.

Jake finished paying the taxi driver.

"Martin said that a sarcophagus arrived last night as

part of a shipment for Hebrew University but it never arrived. It was diverted to a residential area in the Jewish Quarter of the Old City."

"We'll head that way then," Morgan said. "Through the Arab souk."

They walked together under the arch. The Old City walls towered above them and Morgan felt a renewed respect for the city she had grown up with. It seemed she only came back here at times of crisis these days. When she did, the longing to stay welled up within her. But there were so many ghosts of her past here, Elian and her father, old friends who had moved on. She had another life now.

The narrow streets of the bazaar bustled with people. Tourist shops catered to all religions here, some stalls selling Jewish *yarmulke* alongside olive wood crucifixes and gilt plates inscribed with Arabic calligraphy. The smell of falafel wafted from one tiny shop, the fried chickpea balls with salad in pita bread a Jerusalem favorite.

Old men sat outside their shops drinking tiny cups of thick black Arab coffee, flavored with cardamom. Women in hijab haggled over the price of vegetables while the sound of the muezzin drowned the noise of the market in the call to prayer. As they walked past the Stations of the Cross, a group of Christian pilgrims chanted as they carried a life-size wooden cross on the route Christ himself had walked.

At the edge of the Jewish Quarter, Morgan stopped at a fruit stall piled high with light green melon and brilliant red pomegranates. Plastic cups filled with chopped pieces of juicy fruit stood at the front of the stall. She paid a few shekels to the vendor and picked two up. For a moment, she and Jake just stood on the edge of the market relishing the diversity of the city, enjoying sweetness after a long journey.

The sun warmed Morgan's face and the sounds of the

souk swirled around them. Morgan tried to embrace the moment. Even without Ben in her life anymore, she had her family. She had Jake. Yet she was walking into danger once again, and her anger had driven her here. It was hubris to think that they could somehow stop the End of Days. This city was threatened daily by destruction, but it had continued to survive for thousands of years. Fruit sellers had sold to weary travelers since the earliest days in this very spot. Romans, Crusaders, Ottomans, Jews. They would continue after she and Jake were long gone.

Morgan took a final bite.

"Right, let's find this sarcophagus."

They ducked through an ornate arch and emerged into a square. Morgan looked towards the golden Dome of the Rock on Temple Mount before them, a sense of foreboding rising within her.

"Parts of the Jewish Quarter are awfully close to the boundary. I wonder …" Her words trailed off as she stared up. "There are rumors of tunnels underneath the Temple Mount. Excavation isn't allowed, of course."

"But what if there was a way to get underneath?" Jake shook his head. "This would be the perfect place to kick off the End of Days."

Morgan pulled out her phone and called Martin.

"Can you scan through the plans for this area of Jerusalem? I want to know who owns the buildings, particularly the ones closer to the edge of the Temple Mount."

"Give me ten minutes."

Morgan turned to Jake. "Let's keep walking. We might find something."

The white stone reflected the heat of the sun, keeping the interiors cooler. There were no gardens in this densely packed neighborhood but flower boxes bloomed in little windows, a glimmer of color against the pale walls. There were *mezuzahs* on the doorposts, little decorative boxes containing parchment inscribed with specific verses from the Torah, the prayer of Shema Yisrael.

Hear, O Israel, the Lord our God, the Lord is one.

Morgan remembered the *mezuzah* by her father's door in Safed, decorated with the sacred blue of Kabbalah. Israel had taken so much from her, but its intensity was the bedrock of her life. Maybe the ghosts were not those of the dead who remained here now, an echo in the olive groves and ancient ruins. Maybe she was the ghost. Flitting around from country to country, living on the edge for the mission and leaving a piece of her soul behind every time.

A buzz on her phone.

"I think I've found it." Martin stumbled over the words. "It has to be him, it has to be that man, that –"

"Slow down, tell me what you've found."

"There's a Vatican retreat house a few streets from where you are now. Three years ago, plans for interior modification were filed with the Jerusalem council. The name on the application was Eric Krotalia."

"The Cardinal?"

"The very same."

"Send through the details and we'll head over there now."

* * *

This time he would make sure everything would be done properly and with ceremony, as befitted the momentous occasion. The Cardinal lit the final candle and looked around in satisfaction. Golden light flickered in the corners of the stone vault, dancing over the open sarcophagus and its writhing inhabitant. He shivered a little, and he knew it wasn't the cold.

Thoughts of the Great Serpent had filled his mind

since he was a boy in the hills of rural Greece. As a young orphan he had been taken in by the local monastery and it was there he had started his rise within the Church. He had been recruited as a young priest into the Brotherhood, drawn to them by the promise of a rapid ascent through the layers of ecclesiastical hierarchy. And now he stood at the crux of history and yet …

He walked to the open sarcophagus and looked down at the pathetic creature within. It was just a big lump of green and grey flesh, writhing with some kind of life force imbued by the death of the first man, Krait. It was base and gross. The Cardinal shook his head and exhaled slowly. Where was the majesty? Where was the terror?

What would Cerastes and Echis think when they arrived? Had they really sent the world into turmoil for this?

He turned away, disgusted at his own lack of faith, but he couldn't look at the thing any longer. He could only hope that Samael brought enough bodies to turn it into something worthy of his allegiance.

The sound of singing came from the corner of the room. Lilith sat on the ground, painting her skin with swirls like the undulations of the serpent. He had forgotten she was even there. She looked up at him, her green eyes flickering.

"You doubt, Cardinal. He knows thisss."

Her smile was predatory and he wondered again at her sanity, but he also felt a white-hot jealousy at her seeming trust in the serpent. He made up his mind. He would take the venom at the time of sacrifice. He would join her in her deep faith as the Great Serpent was resurrected.

There was a scuffle of footsteps in the tunnel. Samael walked in with a group of men, each carrying a body wrapped in a shroud over their shoulders. The men laid their burdens down in front of the sarcophagus and retreated back up the tunnel, hurrying away with the haste of those fleeing certain death.

As Samael began to unwrap the first body, two figures emerged from the shadows across the cistern. Cerastes and Echis.

"Welcome, brothers." The Cardinal's confident smile returned. "You're just in time to witness the resurrection."

CHAPTER 27

THE ECLIPSE WAS ALMOST at its zenith as Morgan and Jake reached the house that Martin had identified. The darkness was nearly complete and the sky was a dull rust.

"The sun will be turned to darkness and the moon to blood before the coming of the great and dreadful day of the Lord." Morgan looked at Jake. "The book of Joel, chapter two."

"Or, it could just be a lunar eclipse," Jake said. "The earth's shadow on the moon's face appears dark until it covers the moon entirely and then it looks red. The earth's atmosphere changes the light spectrum, filtering out the green to violet, leaving only the red behind."

Morgan smiled and punched his arm. "Where's your sense of occasion?"

Suddenly, the door of the house slammed open. A group of men darted out, eyes wide with panic. They ran off down the road as if demons chased them.

"What the –?"

Morgan was already running for the door they had left wide open behind them.

"Come on, we have to find what they were running from."

They ran into the house and found another door open in the kitchen. A stone staircase led downward, lit by weak lights. A metallic smell of blood and the stench of decay emanated from beyond.

"This must lead under the Temple Mount," Morgan whispered.

Jake nodded. "And by that smell, I'd say they've started without us. Let's get going."

Together, they descended the steps, careful to walk as quietly as they could.

Morgan heard chanting as they reached the bottom of the staircase. She peeked around the corner to see a vault hollowed out of an ancient stone cistern. A group of people stood around a stone sarcophagus watching something inside. Four bodies lay on the ground next to them.

Something lifted out from the sarcophagus.

A green curve of a snake's coil, its body as thick as her own waist.

* * *

Lilith watched as Samael lifted the next body and heaved it into the sarcophagus. A young Arab, his muscles honed from manual labor. She nodded her head in approval at his choice. The man's strength was worthy for the offering.

She bent with the knife and sliced his throat. Bright blood gushed out over the coils of the serpent, bathing it in gore. She felt the other men's eyes on her, and understood they feared her in some way. But she no longer cared for their opinion. She only had eyes for the serpent.

It shuddered with a kind of ecstasy as it consumed the sacrifice and began to pulsate as it grew yet again. She reached out with one hand and stroked its skin. The green scales were iridescent and variegated, like the feathers of a tropical bird, like emeralds at the heart of the earth. They were cool and hard, almost metallic to her touch but underneath, she could feel the pulse of its blood.

She could hear His voice more clearly now. The last of the venom was gone, coursing through her veins but Lilith knew she wouldn't need it again. Now she would commune with Him directly. Her entire life had led her to this moment, to this encounter, and she vibrated with the energy of His resurrection. She thought back to the church where she had first held snakes, her misdirected belief that it was God who wanted her to take hold of them. When really, it had been the Serpent of Serpents, calling her to His side.

Now she was here. Now she was ready.

Echis looked at his watch.

"We have to hurry, the eclipse is at its zenith."

The Cardinal glanced at the remaining bodies. "If we each lift one, we can finish this."

He dragged one of the bodies to the other side of the sarcophagus, pulling the man's neck to the edge. Echis took another and Samael helped the old man, Cerastes. They held the final three offerings on the lip of the stone casket.

Lilith cut each neck in turn, each slash making her sigh with pleasure. The blood rained down on the serpent. It writhed in the gore, bathing itself, coating its scales as it absorbed the fluid and flesh. They pushed the bodies in.

The coils started to grow faster.

The sarcophagus creaked and cracked as the serpent's muscular body pushed against the boundaries of the casket. Lilith stepped back as she realized what was about to happen. He could not be contained any longer.

A loud crack resounded in the cistern.

The serpent exploded from the sarcophagus. As the stone fragmented, its coils tumbled from the prison it had been held in for a thousand years.

Lilith felt His exultation at being free. He reared up even as He grew even faster, His massive head turning towards the men below. His eyes were hard emeralds, a shifting intelligence behind an animal physicality.

The Cardinal fell to his knees in front of the serpent, his hands lifted in supplication. "Great Serpent, we serve –"

The snake reared back and struck with lighting speed, its fangs like swords piercing straight through the Cardinal's body. His words broke off, his eyes widening in horror as he died.

Echis darted towards the tunnel but the serpent swung its gigantic tail, knocking the man off his feet and crushing him beneath the writhing coils even as it absorbed the Cardinal's flesh.

Cerastes stood like a statue, his old frame shaking a little. He smiled, almost with resignation, his eyes wide at the glorious, terrible sight.

"The thousand years are ended!" he shouted in triumph. The serpent wrapped its coils around him, crushing the air from his lungs and absorbing the man within its ever-growing form.

Samael darted behind a pillar, crushing himself as far into a corner as he could, making himself small so as not to catch the snake's attention. Lilith could smell his fear even from this distance. These pitiful men. They should have understood that they were only here to be consumed. He needed their blood for His power.

Come to me.

She heard Him speak as He had through the venom, but now He was here. Lilith's heart pounded in her chest as she stepped forward in front of the Great Serpent, offering herself to Him. His giant head swung around, His eyes fixed upon her. She thought she saw recognition there. Her blood was mostly venom now, her body already transforming into a serpent.

This was her fate.

In a flash, the massive serpent whipped its coils around her and crushed her body to Him. Lilith heard her bones snap as she was broken apart, but the pain was part of another life. The venom took her mind above the agony and she relaxed into His embrace, releasing the air from her lungs as He crushed her ever closer.

She felt a burning, melting sensation and her skin began to morph and ripple as she was absorbed. The snake pulsated around her and she became a part of it, fusing with its flesh.

In the last moments, her awareness spread, separating from the pain. She was no longer an empty bag of flesh and bones, no longer a frail woman. She was in the serpent. She was part of Him. She could feel the undulations of His thick musculature, the slip of cool stone underneath. She could sense the vibrations of others nearby.

Above and around, out there in the city, there were so many more.

With every sacrifice, she would grow stronger and bigger, more powerful. The city waited. But first …

The serpent turned back towards the corner where Samael cowered.

* * *

Morgan watched in horror as Lilith was crushed and twisted and then somehow, became a part of the Great Serpent. It grew as her body was absorbed into its skin and suddenly, there seemed an all-too-human glint in its eyes, a female intelligence.

Its giant head whipped around and stared at Samael cowering in the corner. His face contorted in terror as it slithered across the cistern floor.

"I am your servant." His hands pushed at the coils of flesh as they pushed against him. "Lilith. No!"

Morgan watched the snake toy with him a little, its head swaying hypnotically. Then it reared back to strike.

Samael had killed Ben. He had left them to die in Egypt. Morgan felt nothing as the serpent's head darted forward, its gigantic fangs slicing down. Samael's scream echoed in the chamber as he was pierced, crushed and consumed.

But the serpent would not be occupied for long with Samael's meager body. It would soon want more. Its coils were almost at two meters thick now, hugely powerful, growing with every sacrifice it absorbed.

"We need to leave," Jake said, heading up a few stairs. "Get a military strike team down here and blow this freak of nature to bits."

"It's too late." Morgan watched as the snake grew even larger. "It will burst out of the cistern soon. The Temple Mount is above us, the Western Wall is so close. Who knows what power this thing will have once it gets too big and escapes into the city. We have to stop it down here." She stepped out of the tunnel into the cistern.

"No, Morgan." Jake ran back down and grabbed her arm, but she tugged out of his grip.

This was her city.

She could not let this unholy thing destroy the sacred places around them. It would spark a religious war not seen here since the time of the Crusades. Blood would run in the alleyways of Jerusalem again and she would not allow it.

She took another step into the chamber. The Great Serpent swung its head around, blood dripping from its fangs. It fixed its eyes upon her.

CHAPTER 28

THE GREAT SERPENT HISSED and undulated across the stone floor towards Morgan. It grew with every breath, its body expanding with thick muscle and shimmering dark magic. It was magnificent now, with a strange and terrible grace. Its emerald green eyes sparkled in the candlelight and Morgan was hypnotized by the stark beauty of it. Lucifer was said to have been the most beautiful of the angels. Was that dark presence in this creature now? Was anything left of those it had consumed?

Then she remembered the vial that Ben had found with the seal. Perhaps those ancient protectors had known this day would come.

"The vial, Jake. Quickly!"

Morgan feinted in one direction as the snake's giant body slid through the blood left from the sacrifice. Its mouth opened wide, its fangs dripping venom onto the stone where it bubbled as it dissolved the cistern beneath it.

It reared back and darted forward.

Morgan commando-rolled away. She felt the rush of air against the back of her neck as the snake barely missed her. She rose to her feet again, glancing over to see Jake rummaging through the pack for the vial.

"Now would be good." She ran around the perimeter of the cistern and ducked behind what remained of one of the gigantic pillars.

The serpent curled around, forked tongue flickering as it tasted the air. Then she felt a presence in her mind, pushing into her brain.

Become part of me and you will see eternity. Jussst rest now.

Morgan shook her head, trying to wrestle the voice away but it persisted, echoing through her mind, offering her the world if she would just let it consume her.

But she knew this foe.

He was the persuader. The liar. The whisper that convinced Eve to eat the fruit of forbidden knowledge. He would be the End of Days, consuming all that was good in creation. But he was also seduction and some part of her wanted to let him take her, to end her last breath here beneath the ancient Holy of Holies. She was so tired.

"I've got it," Jake called, breaking the spell. He eased out of the tunnel, holding the vial aloft in his hand. He met Morgan's eyes across the stone chamber.

But the Great Serpent blocked the path between them. Its head whipped around to look at Jake, then it spun and lunged forward towards Morgan.

She darted left but the serpent's coils slammed into the sarcophagus in front of her, smashing what was left of it into tiny pieces. She zigzagged away but there was nowhere left to go.

She was trapped. It would be upon her in a second.

"Throw it!" She held her hands up as the serpent coiled around her lower body.

Its first embrace was firm but not tight, the pressure like being rolled in a blanket. Immovable and yet somehow comforting.

Then she felt a burning sensation on her legs and gasped. It didn't want to crush her, but it was dissolving her somehow, consuming her straight into its flesh.

While its tail end held Morgan tight, the serpent

pursued Jake as he tried to get to her across the room. It was like a stone obstacle course, but he kept coming, darting between pillars, leaping over broken masonry.

Then he tripped.

His eyes widened. The snake's head darted in, fangs bared.

In that moment, Jake threw the vial. He rolled to the floor behind the remains of the sarcophagus as the snake bit down into his flesh.

Morgan reached up and caught the vial in the zenith of its arc. What was it for? Should she drink it? Inject it into the snake somehow? She searched desperately for an answer even as she heard Jake's scream of agony.

Her friend was dying. There was no time left.

The scientist in her understood that the serpent must have some kind of membrane on its skin to dissolve and consume flesh that way. As the burning intensified in her legs, she could only think of one thing to do.

She pulled the top from the vial and poured it between their flesh into the space where its coils consumed her lower body. She wrapped her arms around it and hugged it closer to her, willing the liquid to work.

The snake's head whipped up, its fangs bloody. It let out a high-pitched squeal of pain. It shook its coils, unraveling from Morgan, trying to shake her off.

But she held on.

She pressed her body onto it, keeping the liquid from the vial between them, forcing it onto the serpent's flesh. It was a cool balm to her, softening the flames that burned her lower limbs but the snake thrashed as if it were the fires of Hell itself. She just needed to hold on …

The serpent reared up on its powerful tail and thrashed in the air, shaking its body as it tried to escape the burning. Morgan spun out of its grip and smashed into the stone wall of the cistern, her body broken and bruised.

The serpent screamed, a sound that came from the depths of the pit, a bubbling, drowning screech accompanied by the stench of rotting flesh from the depths of the ocean. Morgan looked up to see a deep wound opening up on its side, like a flesh-eating disease that consumed it even as it continued to grow.

The serpent thrashed and twisted. In its need to escape the pain, it smashed into the great wall of the cistern. It hurled itself against the stone, breaking it apart, and tunneled away, screaming, up towards the Western Wall.

Morgan laid her head down on the cool stone beneath her, eyes fixed on Jake lying prone by the sarcophagus, his body a mass of blood. The pain of bubbling fire burned her legs and she dared not look down at them. But the serpent was wounded and she could only hope that it would die before it laid waste to the city above.

She and Jake could do no more.

* * *

As the sun went dark under the full eclipse, crowds gathered at the Western Wall to pray for deliverance. Men in their shawls and curls, women in modest dresses. Children ran around playing, unaware of the devastation that had been foreseen in ancient times.

The giant stones at the bottom of the Wall suddenly exploded out with the force of the great creature beneath.

Shards of rock splintered away, raining down on those close by. Screams erupted in the plaza and people ran for the streets beyond as the Great Serpent emerged into the square.

It thrashed its gigantic tail, propelling it forward, shaking its head as it tried to escape the agony of the burning. It crushed those in its path, wrapping its coils around any it could catch, trying to subsume their corpses even as it plunged its fangs into more bodies. But the wound ate away at its flesh faster than it could replace it with fresh blood.

The serpent screamed in agony, rising up on its coils to tower above the square, daring these mortals to challenge it.

But this was not the Israel of thousands of years ago.

Israeli soldiers stationed permanently in the square opened fire from all sides. International police on the Temple Mount shot down from on high. A military helicopter darted in overhead, soldiers peppering the serpent with bullets from above.

The Great Serpent felt the sting of the bullets, fighting to repair its wounds, but it weakened as the burning in its flank spread, the hole growing.

It fell to the ground, writhing in agony as it succumbed to the overwhelming force of destruction. Gunfire tore apart what was left until only chunks of flesh remained. Soon only piles of grey-green dust lay in the square, clouds of it blowing away, scattered by the wind.

The military moved in to take control of the scene. A group of soldiers approached the massive hole in the Western Wall, aiming flashlights down into the depths.

"Get the medics," one shouted. "There's people down here."

CHAPTER 29

Oxford, England. A week later.

MORGAN WATCHED AS THE coffin was lowered into the ground of the Catholic graveyard. This would be Ben's last resting place and one he would appreciate because he loved this city. Not that Ben was in there. Morgan looked up at the grey sky into the falling drops of rain. She didn't know what happened after death, but Ben had been a man of faith so she hoped he was with the God he'd served for a lifetime.

Even after death, he had saved her life one more time. The contents of the vial had wounded the serpent enough that the military were able to finish it off. The press was still on fire with speculation about what had happened. Amateur footage of the serpent bursting through the Western Wall shook the international news headlines. Some called it a relic of the dinosaur era that had somehow slept under the Temple Mount. Others called it the Great Serpent from the pit in Revelation heralding the beginning of the End Times.

Whatever they said, it was gone now but Morgan knew the threats weren't over. The news would always be filled with the next crisis. Such was the drama of human life. But perhaps she didn't have to take part in the next chapter.

She used her new walking stick to hobble around the

grave and back to the path. Jake joined her but he didn't try to take her arm and help. Morgan appreciated his respect for her independence. She was getting treatment for the unusual chemical burns that lacerated her legs but pain still lanced through her every day. Jake had deep wounds from the fangs that pierced his flesh that night, but he had recovered quickly. Whatever had happened in New York had given him some kind of healing ability. Morgan wished she could have some of it. She wanted to run again, she needed to move, but her wounds kept her at this slow pace.

Together they walked slowly back through the city to the Museum of Natural History. They entered the Pitt Rivers Museum and descended into the ARKANE labs beneath the city. Morgan remembered the first night she had come here, when Jake was still a stranger, when she knew nothing of ARKANE. Her family were safe and back home now, so she had come full circle. Perhaps that was as it should be.

They walked into one of the labs. Director Marietti stood up from one of the desks and came over to greet them both.

"I'm so sorry, Morgan. I know Ben meant a lot to you."

Morgan nodded. Marietti shook hands with Jake.

"You did a great job stopping the serpent, and I hope you're ready for a new mission." Marietti turned and brought up the details on screen. "A body has been found in New Orleans, covered in occult markings. It's not the first. ARKANE New York have sent agent Naomi Locasto down there. I know you've worked with her before, Jake, when you were in New York, and I think you'll work well with her too, Morgan."

Morgan took a deep breath. She was suddenly sure of what she needed to do. "I'm not going."

Jake spun around to face her. She saw the hurt in his eyes, but no surprise.

"I'm done for now. I need time to think, time with my family."

Marietti nodded. "Of course." He paused. "But we'll need to rescind your security access. I'll have Martin process your exit."

His words were so clinical, so final. Morgan hesitated. She could still stay, still change her mind. She could be part of the next mission with Jake. They could still be a team. She looked up at the screen. It would be a fascinating case.

But not for her.

Marietti put out his hand. "We'll miss you, Morgan. The door is always open for you to return."

Morgan took his hand and shook it, feeling the reassuring strength in his grip. "Goodbye, sir."

* * *

Jake walked out of the door with her, saying nothing as they headed towards the exit, but his mind was in turmoil. He couldn't let her go. As they turned the corner, out of hearing range from the lab, Morgan stopped him.

"I'm so sorry. I just can't keep doing this." She placed a hand on his arm. "I've put my family at risk, and Ben …" A tear ran down her cheek. "I might as well have killed him myself."

"Don't say that." Jake pulled her to him, enfolding her in his arms. "Ben wouldn't have wanted you to blame yourself."

She laid her head against his chest and he stroked her hair, trying to soothe the tears that came freely now.

"Please don't ask me to stay, Jake." She pulled back a little and looked up at him. Her blue eyes glistened with tears and the violet slash burned with intensity. "I need time to think about whether this can work. Whether I can work for ARKANE again."

Jake saw the conflict in her eyes and he understood why she felt so torn. He had no family left to risk, and the years as an agent had made him more independent, separated from those around him. Morgan was the closest he had to a friend, Director Marietti and Martin were his family. ARKANE was his stability. When he thought about a separate life, of giving up being an agent, he found he couldn't even consider another option. This life defined him. But Morgan had other options and other people she loved.

He was not her world.

"I understand," he said quietly. He pulled her close again and kissed her forehead gently. "I'll miss you so much."

Jake knew he would go to America and join Naomi Locasto in New Orleans. He could only hope that Morgan would be here when he returned.

AUTHOR'S NOTE

As with all my books, the plot of *End of Days* is taken from my own experience and research of real places and events, twisted into an original story. For all the images behind the story, check out: www.pinterest.com/jfpenn/end-of-days

Why snakes?

I first handled a python in the Northern Territory of Australia when I was traveling back in 2000. The weight of its body, the smooth cool skin and the fact that I wasn't scared, all surprised me. Then I went into the desert of the Northern Territory and spent some time camping on the red earth, considered by the Aboriginal people to be the blood of the Waugyl, the creation serpent. I started to look into the mythology of snakes and found it fascinating. I actually bought a mulga wood snake at Uluru and I have it here beside me at my writing desk. I consider the snake to be my totem animal, so perhaps it was inevitable that I would eventually write a book with so many in.

I decided on the title, *End of Days*, before I had a plot idea. Then, when I read the verse in Revelation about the ancient serpent and discovered Lilith had been portrayed as a serpent in painting, I knew I could work them into a story that would also satisfy those longing for something apocalyptic.

Appalachian snake handling churches and venom as a hallucinogen

There are some fascinating videos on YouTube from churches that handle snakes, in accordance with the Great Commission of Mark 16:18. I wrote Lilith's scene based on reading about actual experiences of believers.

Some snake venom can be hallucinogenic, but it's likely to kill you first, so don't try this at home! Mithridatism is a real practice of self-administering venom in non-lethal amounts to build up tolerance over time.

Moses and the graven serpent

I have always found the story of Moses and the graven serpent strange. The snake is used as a symbol for evil in the Garden of Eden, and yet in Numbers 21:9, it becomes a bronze idol with healing powers and then in John 3:14, it's used as a metaphor for Jesus. These types of theological mysteries are where I often find story ideas.

When I visited Salisbury Cathedral and found the window above the altar, which is just as described in the story, I knew I had to use it somehow.

International locations

The Temple of Hatshepsut is real but as far as I know, there's no escape tunnel into the Valley of the Kings. Although if you look on Google Maps, it's definitely possible. The Laocoon is in the Vatican Museums and the replica stands in the castle at Rhodes. The Delphi site is as described.

Israel. I first visited Tel Megiddo in the 1990s and after reading James Michener's *The Source*, the area really came alive for me. I revisited in November 2016 and it was amazing to see the layers of history revealed at the dig. You can find all the pictures from that trip here: www.jfpenn.com/israel-pics

We also took some video of the trip, which you can view on YouTube:

- A Walk in the Old City of Jerusalem:
  www.jfpenn.com/old-city-jerusalem
- Behind the scenes of my research trip. Difference locations in Israel:
  www.jfpenn.com/israel-arkane-research

I did take some artistic license with the location. Most of the artifacts from the dig are at in the Rockefeller Museum, Jerusalem and other places away from Megiddo itself.

The Old City of Jerusalem continues to evoke my imagination and when we visited last, it was awesome to go down into one of the cisterns under the Holy Sepulchre, one of the few able to be accessed. The cistern used for the resurrection of the serpent may actually exist, although of course, let's hope that the sarcophagus is still deep in the Mariana Trench …

What's next for the ARKANE series?

While Morgan takes a well-earned rest, I'll be focusing on the United States of ARKANE. Jake heads to New Orleans to work with Naomi Locasto, who also featured in *One Day in New York*. In the last nine books, I've mostly focused on European history, so now I'm turning my gaze further west. Expect more ARKANE adventures to come!

ACKNOWLEDGMENTS

For ONE DAY IN NEW YORK

Thanks, as every, to my great team of professionals: Jen Blood at Adian Editing for the fantastic editing, Derek Murphy at Creativindie for cover design, Wendy Janes at WendyProof.co.uk for proofreading and Jane Dixon Smith at JDSmith-Design.com for the print formatting.

Thanks to my readers and especially to my PennFriends. Your continued support allows me to write these stories, which makes me a happy writer and, hopefully, makes you a happy reader!

For DESTROYER OF WORLDS

Thanks to my editor, Jen Blood, for her help with the book, and my proofreader, Wendy Janes. Thanks to Jane Dixon-Smith for the cover and interior print design.

Thanks to Uma Aiyer for her beta reading and helpful comments about Mumbai. A huge thanks to the Pennfriends, who support my book launches, and thanks to all my readers, for enabling me to tell the stories that burn in my heart.

Jane Dixon-Smith at JDSmith Design for the print interior.

For END OF DAYS

Thanks to my editor, Jen Blood, for her help with the book, and my proofreader, Wendy Janes. Thanks to Jane Dixon-Smith for the cover and interior print design. Thanks as ever to my readers and to the Pennfriends, who encourage me to keep writing these stories.

Thanks for joining Morgan and the ARKANE team!

If you loved the book and have a moment to spare, I would really appreciate a short review where you bought the book. Your help in spreading the word is gratefully appreciated.

You can also get a free copy of the bestselling ARKANE thriller, *Day of the Vikings*, when you sign up to join my Reader's Group at:

WWW.JFPENN.COM/FREEBOOK

More books in the international bestselling ARKANE thriller series. Described by readers as 'Dan Brown meets Lara Croft.'
Available in print, ebook and audio formats at all online stores.

Stone of Fire #1
Crypt of Bone #2
Ark of Blood #3
One Day in Budapest #4
Day of the Vikings #5
Gates of Hell #6
One Day in New York #7
Destroyer of Worlds #8
End of Days #9

The London Psychic Series. Described by readers as 'the love child of Stephen King and PD James.'
Available in ebook, print and audio formats.

Desecration
Delirium
Deviance

A Thousand Fiendish Angels, short stories inspired by Dante's Inferno, on the edge of thriller and the occult.

Risen Gods
American Demon Hunters: Sacrifice

WWW.JFPENN.COM

ABOUT J.F. PENN

J.F.Penn is the New York Times and USA Today bestselling author of the ARKANE thrillers and London Psychic crime series as well as other dark fantasy stories. Her books weave together ancient artifacts, relics of power, international locations and adventure with an edge of the supernatural. Joanna lives in Bath, England and enjoys a nice G&T.

Try a free thriller at: www.JFPenn.com

Connect with Joanna online:
(e) joanna@JFPenn.com
(w) www.JFPenn.com
(t) @thecreativepenn
(f) www.facebook.com/JFPennAuthor
www.pinterest.com/jfpenn/

For writers:

Joanna Penn also writes non-fiction. Available in print, ebook and audiobook formats.

Joanna's site www.TheCreativePenn.com helps people write, publish and market their books through articles, audio, video and online products as well as live workshops. Joanna is available internationally for speaking events aimed at writers, authors and entrepreneurs. Joanna also has a popular podcast for writers on iTunes, The Creative Penn.

Milton Keynes UK
Ingram Content Group UK Ltd.
UKHW051139250324
439991UK00005B/606